John W. Jud

The Geology of Rutland and Parts of Lincoln, Leicester, Northampton, Huntingdon, and Cambridge

Anatiposi

John W. Judd

The Geology of Rutland and Parts of Lincoln, Leicester, Northampton, Huntingdon, and Cambridge

Reprint of the original, first published in 1875.

1st Edition 2024 | ISBN: 978-3-38282-954-4

Anatiposi Verlag is an imprint of Outlook Verlagsgesellschaft mbH.

Verlag (Publisher): Outlook Verlag GmbH, Zeilweg 44, 60439 Frankfurt, Deutschland
Vertretungsberechtigt (Authorized to represent): E. Roepke, Zeilweg 44, 60439 Frankfurt, Deutschland
Druck (Print): Books on Demand GmbH, In de Tarpen 42, 22848 Norderstedt, Deutschland

MEMOIRS OF THE GEOLOGICAL SURVEY.

ENGLAND AND WALES.

THE GEOLOGY OF RUTLAND

AND

PARTS OF LINCOLN, LEICESTER, NORTHAMPTON,
HUNTINGDON, AND CAMBRIDGE,

INCLUDED IN

SHEET 64 OF THE ONE-INCH MAP OF THE GEOLOGICAL SURVEY;

WITH AN

'RODUCTORY ESSAY ON THE CLASSIFICATION AND
CORRELATION OF THE JURASSIC ROCKS OF
THE MIDLAND DISTRICT OF ENGLAND.

BY

JOHN W. JUDD, F.G.S.

PENDIX, WITH TABLES OF FOSSILS, BY R. ETHERIDGE, F.R.S.

PUBLISHED BY ORDER OF THE LORDS COMMISSIONERS OF HER MAJESTY'S TREASURY.

LONDON:
PRINTED FOR HER MAJESTY'S STATIONERY OFFICE.
PUBLISHED BY
LONGMANS & Co., PATERNOSTER ROW;
AND BY
EDWARD STANFORD, CHARING CROSS, S.W.

1875.
[*Price* 12*s.* 6*d.*]

NOTICE.

WHILE the mapping of the district was in progress, the geology of which forms the subject of this Memoir, I had several opportunities of verifying the accuracy and skill with which Mr. Judd. traced the geological boundary lines, and the truly scientific manner in which he formed those deductions, the result of which has been expressed in a new classification of some of the formations comprised in the area. I may add that the circumstances which led to the resignation by Mr. Judd of his post on the Geological Survey have always been matter of deep regret to me, for it is not often that men are to be found who possess that rare combination of knowledge on so many special branches of geological inquiry which characterises the author of this memoir. I also feel that we are deeply indebted to Mr. Judd for having so frankly consented, after he had left the Survey, to make his work complete by the gratuitous preparation of a memoir which he was in nowise bound to write. That this important work has been thoroughly well done all geologists will allow. No one but the man who mapped the ground, who examined the fossils *in situ,* and determined so many of the species, could

32108.   a 2

have done anything like equal justice to the subject, and the generous devotion which Mr. Judd has shown in giving so much valuable time to our work, after he ceased to be a member of the Survey, deserves the most grateful acknowledgment.

ANDREW C. RAMSAY,
Director-General.

13th March 1875.

—————————

To the Director General of the Geological
Survey of the United Kingdom.

Geological Survey Office,
28, Jermyn Street, London, S.W.,
20th February 1875.

Sir,

THE country comprised in Sheet 64, which takes
in the whole of the county of Rutland, was surveyed
by Mr. J. W. Judd, between the years 1867 and 1871.

This Map is of special interest as being the first
published by the Survey upon which the limestone, that
was formerly considered to be a part of the Great Oolite,
has been referred to its true position in the geological
scale as a member of the Inferior Oolite, to which the
distinctive name of Lincolnshire Oolite was assigned by
Mr. Judd, from its great development in that county.

When Mr. Judd left the Survey, on the completion of
his fieldwork connected with the above area, he disin-
terestedly consented to write the Memoir in explanation
of the Map; and the present important work is the
result of his labours.

In it, besides giving a detailed description of the
geological structure of the district, Mr. Judd has discussed at length the more general and purely scientific
questions connected with the subject, and has explained
the grounds upon which the conclusions were founded
that led him to propose an entirely new and altogether
original nomenclature and classification for the Oolitic
rocks of the midland district of England, which have
been since accepted by the Geologists of this and other
countries.

Mr. Judd has been aided by Mr. Etheridge in the preparations of the tables shewing the geographical and stratigraphical distribution of the fossils and in the palæontological portion generally. Several views of oolitic scenery have been contributed by Mr. Rutley from sketches made on the ground.

Mr. Whitaker has also assisted in the bibliographical portion ; and Mr. Holloway has rendered valuable help in constructing and drawing illustrative geological sections, as well as generally in passing the work through the press.

I have the honour to be,

Sir,

Your obedient servant,

HENRY W. BRISTOW,

Director for England and Wales.

To Andrew C. Ramsay, Esq., LL.D., F.R.S.,

&c. &c. &c.

PREFACE.

In obedience to a very general demand for the more rapid completion of the maps illustrating the coal-producing districts of the country, the officers of the Geological Survey of Great Britain, who were employed in tracing northwards the boundaries of the Jurassic Strata, were nearly twenty years ago transferred to the northern counties. ·

Thus the mapping of the Lias and Oolites remained during a considerable interval in abeyance. This period was, however, marked by many important advances made by geologists in their knowledge of the rocks in question, and by the introduction of new principles and methods of classification. The views gradually elaborated by Quenstedt, Fraas, Marcou, Oppel, and others on the continent, were applied by Dr. Wright and other geologists to the rocks of this country, and the necessity for modifications of the classification, adopted in some of the former publications of the Survey, were thereby rendered manifest. In particular, we may mention the conviction arrived at by many geologists, that certain rocks supposed to be of *Great* Oolite age, ought in fact to be classed with the *Inferior* Oolite.

Having been engaged during six or seven years in preparing a geological map and description of that interesting county—so little known to geologists — Lincolnshire, 1 had been gradually led to the adoption of the views referred to above; and in 1867, when it was determined to resume the mapping of the Jurassic rocks, I was requested to join for a time the staff of the Geological Survey, and to devote my attention to the country intermediate between Lincolnshire and the districts already mapped. It soon became clear to me that not only would the doubtful beds have to be classed with the Inferior Oolite, but, that, in consequence of the very local character of many of the formations in the district, a new classification and nomenclature was rendered absolutely necessary in order to adequately represent them.

During several years I was employed in working out the details of this question and in mapping the most critical portion of the district; and in 1870, after the results which I had arrived at had been examined and approved by the responsible officers of the Survey, the new classification was published in the Index, and a little later, in sheet 64 of the Survey map. I then examined the country to the southwards, revising the maps already published and preparing new editions of them.

This task completed, my connexion with the Survey ceased, and my attention was directed to entirely new fields of geological inquiry. On its being pointed out to me, however, that the want of a memoir, explaining the grounds of the classification which I had originated, would be productive of inconvenience, I undertook to write the present work; the form assumed by which has been, to some extent, determined by the peculiar circumstances under which it has been prepared.

Questions of an exclusively scientific nature, such as those involved in the methods of classification adopted, are discussed in the Introductory Essay; while subjects of general and local interest, in connexion with the district more especially described, are treated of, in large and small type respectively, in the second part of the volume. The circumstance that the work has been written in the intervals snatched from many other occupations and studies, may not perhaps be accepted as any apology for imperfections and inequalities in its mode of execution, but it must be pleaded as an excuse for the delay in its completion.

Fortunately, however, geologists have not been compelled to await the appearance of this volume for an illustration and defence of the classification and nomenclature of the Jurassic rocks in the Midland district, now employed by the Survey; for, not only has my friend Mr. SAMUEL SHARP of Dallington entirely adopted these views himself, but he has chivalrously maintained and ably exemplified them in two memoirs read before the Geological Society, a task for which his extensive knowledge of the rocks and fossils of the district eminently fitted him.

During my execution of the survey of the area, I received much valuable assistance, not only from Mr. SHARP, but from many other local geologists, among whom I may especially mention Mr. BEESLEY of Banbury, the REV. MILES J. BERKLEY, formerly of King's Cliffe, Mr. BIGGE of Islip, Mr. BENTLEY of Stamford, and the late Dr. PORTER of Peterborough. While writing the memoir, too, I have had recourse to the kind aid of several palæontologists including DR. LYCETT, the late PROFESSOR PHILLIPS, MR. DAVIDSON, PROFESSOR MORRIS, and PROFESSOR HUXLEY, and especially to my former colleagues on the survey MESSRS. ETHERIDGE and SHARMAN. MR. ETHERIDGE has, moreover, written an appendix to the work.

My labours in preparing the work and carrying it through the press have been lightened in every possible manner by the kind and able assistance of my friend MR. W. H. HOLLOWAY, who is now engaged in carrying on the survey of the country to the northwards. For the beautiful drawings of scenery which have been copied in the lithographic plates, I am indebted to the skilful pencil of MR. FRANK RUTLEY. MR. WHITAKER has contributed very largely to the Appendix of Bibliography, and MR. BRISTOW, the Director of the Survey, has afforded me the benefit of his advice and general supervision.

JOHN W. JUDD.

Brixton,
30th January 1875.

xi

TABLE OF CONTENTS.

21g1INTRODUCTORY ESSAY ON THE CLASSIFICATION OF THE JURASSIC ROCKS OF THE
MIDLAND DISTRICT OF ENGLAND AND THEIR CORRELATION WITH THOSE OF
THE COTTESWOLD HILLS AND THE NORTH-EAST OF YORKSHIRE RESPECTIVELY.
Differences between the sections of the south-west of England and those of Yorkshire, p. 1. Key to their correlation found in the Midland district, p. 2. History of
previous opinion upon the subject, p. 2. Confusion produced by the identification
with one another of the fissile beds ("slates") at different horizons in the Lower
Oolites, p. 5. Table illustrating the changes of the several formations as we pass
northwards from the Cotteswolds to the south of Yorkshire, pp. 7, 8. Variations
in the subdivisions of the Oxford clay, p. 7. Variations in the subdivisions of the
Great Oolite, p. 7. Variations in the subdivisions of the Inferior Oolite, p. 11.
Thinning out of Lower Oolite beds northwards and eastwards, accompanied by
changes in petrological character, p. 13. Northampton Sand, the attenuated and
littoral representatives of the Inferior Oolite and the Lower Zone of the Great
Oolite, p. 13. Description and comparison of the principal sections of the Lower
Oolite strata on either side of the vale of Moreton, pp. 14, 17. Northampton
Sand, of South Midland district, p. 30. Upper and Lower Estuarine Series, p. 31.
Appearance of a new formation (the Lincolnshire Oolite Limestone) between them,
p. 33. Great thickness and importance of this formation. Extent and peculiar
characters. Physical and palæontological evidences of its age, p. 36. Unconformity
between the Great and Inferior Oolite beds of the Midland district, p. 36. Lincolnshire Oolite represents the Zone of *Ammonites Sowerbyi*, p. 38. Formations absent,
p. 40. Lias. Changes as we pass northwards. Penarth or Rhætic, p. 40.
Persistence of two series of "fish and insect beds," p. 41. Appearance of new
series of beds in the Lower Lias. Characters of the zone of *Ammonites semicostatus*,
p. 42. Limits of the Middle Lias, p. 45. The Upper Lias, p. 47. Value of
Palæontological Zones, p. 48. Local character of many of the Jurassic deposits.
Importance of the study of the conditions under which beds were deposited.
Facies, p. 49. Accumulation of beds dependent on amount of subsidence in the
area, p. 50. Zones absent or rudimentary at some points, very finely developed at
others, p. 50 Remarkable examples in the Zones of *Ammonites Sowerbyi* and
A. semicostatus, p. 51. General conclusions, p. 52.

DESCRIPTION OF SHEET 64.

CHAPTER I.

Page

Physical Features, &c. Extent. Configuration of the surface. Rainfall.
Drainage. Relation of Physical features to Geological structure. Soils.
Minerals. Two groups of beds in the area. Jurassic and Post-Tertiary.
Difference of age. Unconformity of two series. Table of strata   -   53

CHAPTER II.

THE LIAS. Extent. Subdivisions.
The Lower Lias. Classification of its beds. Extent   -   -   -   57

CHAPTER III.

The Middle Lias. Subdivisions. Great variation in thickness. The great
escarpments. Inliers. Outliers -   -   -   -   -   -   64

CHAPTER IV.

The Upper Lias. Subdivisions. Area covered by it. Main line of outcrop.
Inliers. Outliers -   -   -   -   -   -   -   -   79

CHAPTER V.

THE LOWER OOLITES. Two great divisions. Great Oolite and Inferior Oolite.
Distinct separation in this district. Unconformity   -   -   -   90
    Northampton Sand, with the Lower Estuarine Series. General characters.
    Outer escarpment. Valleys of the Nene and its tributaries. Inliers.
    Outliers. Iron-ore of the Northampton Sand -   -   -   -   90

ILLUSTRATIONS.

PLATES.

PLATE I. (*facing title page*). SERIES OF COMPARATIVE VERTICAL SECTIONS TO ILLUSTRATE THE VARIATIONS IN THICKNESS AND MINERAL CHARACTERS OF THE SEVERAL MEMBERS OF THE LOWER OOLITES IN THE MIDLAND DISTRICTS OF ENGLAND.—In these vertical sections the maximum thickness of each formation in the particular area is represented. For the Bath district I have followed to a great extent the original memoirs of Lonsdale, while in the three sections in the Cotteswold Hills, namely, those of Stroud, Cheltenham, and Broadway, I have been guided by the descriptive writings of Drs. Lycett, Wright, and other geologists, but have also incorporated results previously published by the Geological Survey. In the remaining ten sections I have been obliged to depend mainly on my own observations made either during my connexion with the survey or before that period, with such aid as could be obtained from wells, borings, &c. The main object of this series of sections has been to show how rapidly the various members of the Lower Oolites thin out or vary in character as they are traced over even limited areas ; the constancy of character in them being actually not greater than those of banks of mud, sand, or shells, at comparatively moderate depths upon the existing sea bottom. The lines drawn between the several sections indicate the approximate equivalences of the different formations in each, as derived from palæontological evidence. In the upper dotted line the distances in miles between the points at which the several sections are obtained is given. The shading in these sections illustrates the nature of the rock, the conventional indications for clay, limestone, sandstone, &c., being employed. The colours indicate the geological positions of the various beds, and correspond with those employed on the Index Sheet and the maps and sections of the Geological Survey of the United Kingdom.

PLATE II. (*facing page 52.*) DIAGRAMMATIC SECTIONS ILLUSTRATING THE THINNING-OUT OF THE LINCOLNSHIRE (INFERIOR) OOLITE.—These sections are not drawn upon a true vertical and horizontal scale, as this would not be practicable in the case of an illustration in a book. Such will, however, be published in forthcoming sheets of horizontal sections of the Geological Survey. The object of the two sections on this plate is to show the manner in which the great masses of limestone of Inferior Oolite age (the Lincolnshire Oolite) in the North Midland district, thins out rapidly southward and eastward, thus giving rise to very different successions of beds according to its presence or absence. A similar section showing the same easterly attenuation of this great calcareous formation has been given by Mr. Sharp in his paper on the district. See Quart. Journ. Geol. Soc., vol. xxix. (1873), Plate X.

In the upper section the attenuation, towards the south, of the Lincolnshire Oolite, as seen near Sutton Basset, Leicestershire, when it is traced to the point where it finally disappears near Warkton in Northamptonshire, is illustrated.

In the lower section a similar dying out of the calcareous strata of the Inferior Oolite as they were traced from near Stamford, south-eastward into the Nene Valley is made apparent.

PLATE III. (*at end of volume*). DIAGRAMMATIC SECTIONS ILLUSTRATING THE POSITION AND RELATIONS OF THE STRATA IN SHEET 64.—The insertion of a small index map in this volume having been found impracticable owing to the rather complicated structure of the district, two horizontal sections have been drawn through the northern and southern portions of the area respectively, which will serve to illustrate the position of the several escarpments, lines of valley, and outliers of the district specially described in the memoir. The manner in which the whole structure of the district is dependent on the general dip of the rocks to the south-eastward, combined with the occurrence of hard beds of limestone, sandstone, or ironstone rock in the midst of thick masses of clays, will be made clearly apparent by an inspection of these sections. Like those of Plate II., and for similar reasons, these sections are purely diagrammatic, and no attempt has been made to conform the vertical to the horizontal scale.

The upper section shows the two great escarpments formed by the Marlstone Rock-bed and the Inferior Oolite respectively, and the general decline of the whole plateau eastward towards the Fenland.

The lower section illustrates the great drift covered area of Lower Oolite rocks in the centre of the area, outliers of which also, having escaped denudation, are seen to the westward, while beds higher in the series are exposed to the eastward along the sides of the river valleys which intersect the district.

In these sections, and also in those on Plate II., the faults and curvatures of the strata have been omitted in order to avoid complicating the appearance of the sections, and thereby defeating the object in view, that of making clearer the general relations of the several formations as described in the text of this volume.

PLATE IV. (*facing page* 53). CASTLE HILL, WEST OF UPPINGHAM, ILLUSTRATING SOME OF THE BOLDER FEATURES TO WHICH THE LIAS AND OOLITES GIVE RISE IN THIS DISTRICT.—In this and the seven succeeding plates, which are lithographed after sketches from the able pencil of my former colleague, Mr. FRANK RUTLEY, F.G.S., some of the most characteristic features of the scenery of the district depending on its geological structure are represented. Plate IV. shows, in the steep escarpment on the left capped by Northampton Sand (and crowned by an old Roman? camp), and in the undulating and well-wooded country in the distance, how much the scenery of the district has gained in boldness and character over that to the southward, in consequence of the greater thickness of the masses of clays between the hard beds which give rise to the formation of the escarpments. The plateau on the left of the landscape is constituted by the Inferior Oolite, that on the right by the Marlstone rock-bed and the overlying beds of the Upper Lias covered with Boulder Clay, and clothed, as is so frequently the case, with ample woods. The view is taken from the north-east.

PLATE V. (*facing page* 77). SLAWSTON HILL, LEICESTERSHIRE. OUTLIER OF MARLSTONE AND UPPER LIAS CAPPED BY NORTHAMPTON SAND. — This is one of the best illustrations to be seen within the district of an outlying mass of strata isolated by denudation. The hill crowned by the windmill is composed of a vestige of the Northampton Sand with the underlying Upper Lias Clay, as will be seen by a reference to the lower section on Plate III. which passes through this hill. The whole rises from a plateau formed by the rock-bed of the Marlstone. The view is taken from the southwards.

PLATE VI. (*facing page* 93). VIEW OF THE GREAT ESCARPMENT OF THE LOWER OOLITES NEAR GRETTON, NORTHAMPTONSHIRE.—This view illustrates the great line of the escarpment northward from Rockingham, the bold spurs, one of which is crowned by the village and church of Gretton, and the deep receding bay-like hollows being alike conspicuous. In the foreground is shown the comparatively steep slopes of the Upper Lias Clay, with the broken ground resulting from the slipping of the overlying strata as a consequence of the outburst of springs. The view is taken from the south-west.

PLATE VII. (*facing page* 106). ROBIN-A-TIPTOES, LEICESTERSHIRE. AN OUT-LIER OF THE NORTHAMPTON SAND.—No hill in the district could be chosen as showing better the characteristic tabular forms assumed by the outliers of harder strata in the district. The view is taken from the southwards, and the gentle dip of the hard beds of Northampton Sand capping the hill, which exhibits traces of old entrenchments at its summit, is well illustrated by it. The steep slopes of the hill are of course constituted by the Upper Lias Clay, the flat ground around it by the Marlstone rock-bed, a quarry in which is shown on the left of the picture, near the farm-house. A deep ravine cut by a small stream, the sides of which are densely wooded, cuts down into and exposes the clays of the Middle Lias.

PLATE VIII. (*facing page* 200). SECTION OF THE UPPER ESTUARINE SERIES AND LINCOLNSHIRE OOLITE AT THE RAILWAY-CUTTING AND BRICKWORKS AT LITTLE BYTHAM.—Travellers to or from the North by the main line of the Great Northern Railway can hardly fail to notice this interesting exposure of the rocks, which for the district is an unusually extensive one. The section is crowned by traces of the beds of Great Oolite Limestone; the strikingly horizontal banded strata are the clays of the Upper Estuarine Series, here extensively dug for brick-making. The rocks exposed in the sides of the railway-cutting belong to the Lincolnshire Limestone, the false-bedding of the highest course of rock here at once arresting the attention of the geologist.

PLATE IX. (*facing page* 211). SECTION OF THE GREAT OOLITE LIMESTONES WITH THE UNDERLYING UPPER ESTUARINE CLAYS SEEN IN THE ESSENDINE CUTTING OF THE GREAT NORTHERN RAILWAY.—In this section the Great Oolite Limestones resting on the variegated clays are seen in a deep railway-cutting. At this place some of the best specimens of the freshwater shells in the Estuarine Clays were collected during the formation of the railway; in the limestones were obtained the bones of the gigantic *Cetiosaurus*. The contrast presented between the jointed limestones above and the laminated clays below is well seen in this drawing. This section, like the last, may be noticed by passengers on the main line of the Great Northern Railway.

PLATE X. (*facing page* 231). VIEW OF THE LOW TABULAR HILLS FORMED BY THE GREAT OOLITE BEDS AT GRIMSTHORPE PARK, LINCOLNSHIRE.—This view taken from the north-west well illustrates the general characters presented in the numerous small valleys cut through the alternating limestone and clay beds of the Great Oolite Series. The broad flat hills are capped by Cornbrash, while the Great Oolite Limestone and the Upper Estuarine Series crop out in the lower parts of the valleys. The flat bed of the valley is formed by the limestones of the Lincolnshire Oolite, and hence the stream is subterranean during the greater part of the year.

PLATE XI. (*facing page* 264). ILLUSTRATING THE TABULAR OUTLINES OF THE HILLS WEST OF UPPINGHAM.—This view, taken from Wardley Hill and looking over Bushy Dales and the neighbouring ravines, illustrates very clearly the flat-topped hills with steep slopes below and the general tabular outlines characterising this district. The hills are capped by the Marlstone rock-bed, and the deep valleys between are cut into the beds of the Lower Lias Clays, the whole being masked and their outlines somewhat softened by the extensive development of the Boulder Clay in the area.

WOODCUTS.

1

INTRODUCTORY ESSAY.

On the Classification of the Jurassic Strata of the
Midland District and their Correlation with
those of the Cotteswold Hills and the North-
east of Yorkshire respectively.

The present memoir is the first issued by the Geological
Survey, in which some important modifications of the Classification and additions to the Nomenclature of the Lower Oolites are
employéd ; these it has been found necessary to adopt in order
to explain the relations of the beds of this age as they are
traced northwards into the Midland district. It has, therefore,
been thought advisable to preface the description of the area, to
which the memoir more especially refers, with some account of
the grouping of the strata employed for the purposes of the
survey, of the terms used to indicate them, and of the reasons
which have led to the adoption of that classification and terminology. In doing this it has necessarily been found impossible to avoid a more technical mode of treating the subject than
is employed in the later and purely descriptive portions of the
memoir.

No fact in connexion with the English Jurassic strata is of *Difference be-*
more striking character and significance than the wonderful *tween Oolites*
differences between the sections displayed in the typical localities *England and*
of the south-west of England, and those of the north-east of *Yorkshire.*
Yorkshire. The more thoroughly and minutely the rocks in
these two districts are studied, the more striking do the dis-
crepancies between the several members of the two series appear ;
these differences being equally marked alike in regard to their
thickness, their petrological character, and the distribution of their
organic remains.

It was by the careful study of the Oolites in the south-west
of England that the accepted classification of the Jurassic
system was first arrived at ; but it was in Yorkshire that this
classification, and the principle on which it was founded, (that
of the identification of strata by their organic remains) were
submitted to a crucial test. Never had a new theory to pass
through a severer ordeal than when the conclusions, arrived
at from the study of the alternations of the limestones, sands,

32108. A

and clays, of the Bath district, were first applied to the eluci-
dation of the massive coal-bearing sandstones and shales of the
Moorlands of the north-east of Yorkshire; and never, certainly,
did a theory come out of such trial more triumphantly, or with
stronger proofs of its general soundness and great capabilities,
than did this.

Since the period of the pioneer labours of Smith and his coad-
jutors Richardson and Townsend, the Oolites of the south-west
of England have been made the object of indefatigable study
by many observers, such as Conybeare, Murchison, Buckland,
De la Beche, Lonsdale, Buckman, Strickland, Lycett, Wright,
Etheridge, Moore, Brodie, Day, Hull, and others; while the
whole district has been mapped and described by the officers of
the Geological Survey. The magnificent sections of the Yorkshire coast, which were first brought into general correlation
with those of the south by the skill of Smith and Phillips, have
also attracted the attention of many subsequent writers, including Williamson, Louis Hunton, Wright, Leckenby, and Oppel,
who have succeeded in explaining some, at least, of the anomalies
which remained after the labours of the two former geologists.

*Key found in
Midland dis-
trict.*
But the intermediate Midland district, where we might
reasonably hope to find a key to many of the unsolved problems,
which still confronted the geologist who should attempt an
exact correlation of the strata of the northern and southern areas,
has unfortunately received far less attention. Smith's county
maps of Northamptonshire and Lincolnshire were, at the time
of his death, left incomplete and unpublished, and comparatively
little has been done by subsequent explorers to supply the great
gap thus left in our knowledge concerning the Jurassic rocks of
England.

*History of pre-
vious opinion.*
The general maps of England, by Smith and Greenough, represented the thick limestone series, which constitutes so conspicuous
a feature in Lincolnshire, as being of *Great Oolite* age, while the
underlying ferruginous sands, which have since proved to be of
such great commercial value, are placed in the *Inferior Oolite;*
and in this view most succeeding writers have concurred. It
must be remembered, however, that at the early date of Professor
Phillips' work on the Geology of Yorkshire—in which beds, in
that county, now regarded as Inferior Oolite, were called Bath or
Great Oolite—but little had been done in working out the faunas
and showing the essential points of distinction between the two
series which together make up the Lower Oolite. A striking
illustration of this may be found in the description of the Oolites
on the north of the Humber by the Rev. W. Vernon Harcourt and
Professor Phillips, published in 1826 (Thompson's Ann. of Phil.,

new series, vol. xi., pp. 435–439). In this paper the strata
forming the most northern development of the Lincolnshire
Oolite limestone are shown to be of *Inferior* Oolite age, and the
identification is supported by a number of fossils which are cited.
It is true that this correlation—undoubtedly the correct one—which
was then maintained both by Smith and Phillips, was to some extent
abandoned, and in subsequent works the identity of the Lincolnshire with the Great Oolite indicated; but as Professor Phillips
pointed out in 1854, this correlation was, in the first instance,
put forward rather as a useful suggestion than as an established
fact.* It must be borne in mind too that there is an unfortunate
confusion, not even yet removed from works on Systematic Geology,
as to the sense in which the term "Bath Oolite" should be
used. The majority of authors employ it as synonymous with
"Great Oolite," but several geologists, including Professor Phillips
and the late Professor Jukes, have constantly used it as alternative
with "Lower Oolite."

The identification of the Lincolnshire Oolite with that of Bath,
which was for a long period so generally accepted among geologists, appeared to receive the strongest support from the fact of
the existence, at the base of either of the great calcareous series,
of the fissile sandy rocks known as the Stonesfield and Collyweston Slates respectively. This striking circumstance appears
to have had great weight with Lonsdale in preparing his manu-
script maps of the Oolites of the Midland districts, which were
constructed for the Geological Society†; and equally does it
appear to have influenced Professor Morris in drawing up that
description of the country about Peterborough and Stamford, the
result of repeated studies, which in conjunction with Captain
Ibbetson, he laid before the British Association in 1847.‡

It is true that the Rev. P. B. Brodie, on submitting a series
of fossils collected by him in the Lincolnshire Oolite near
Grantham, to Dr. Lycett, was confirmed by that palæontologist
in the view which he had been led to adopt, namely, that the
beds which contained them were of *Inferior* rather than of *Great*
Oolite age, but as he proposed to place the beds in question *below*
the Collyweston Slate, Mr. Brodie's views, which were published
in 1850,§ did not attract much attention from those acquainted
with the general succession of beds in the area.

* Quarterly Journal, Geol. Soc., vol. xiv. (1857) p. 85.
† These maps are still preserved in the Library of the Geological Society.
‡ Notice of the Geology of the Neighbourhood of Stamford and Peterborough,
Rep. Brit. Assoc. for 1847, Trans. of Sections, p. 127.
§ Sketch of the Geology of the Neighbourhood of Grantham, Lincolnshire, and
a comparison of the Stonesfield Slate at Collyweston, in Northamptonshire, with

The publication in 1853 of Professor Morris' most valuable paper
" On some Sections in the Oolite District of Lincolnshire " marks
an important era in the history of the geology of the Midland
districts.* The general succession of beds as seen in the cuttings
of the Great Northern Railway was very clearly described, and the
great differences between the fauna of the Lincolnshire Oolite and
that of the Great Oolite distinctly recognised. In spite of this, however, the resemblance of the beds above the limestone in question to
the Forest Marble, and of the beds below it to the Stonesfield Slate,
were considered to be so great, that this supposed stratigraphical
evidence was allowed to outweigh the palæontological, and the great
limestone series was referred, though with much doubt and hesita-
tion, to the Great Oolite. Professor Morris has, however, more
recently (in 1869) taken the opportunity of correcting this point
and of expressing his adhesion to the view that the Lincolnshire
Oolite, as well as the " slate beds " below it, belongs to the Inferior
Oolite.†

The conviction that the Lincolnshire Oolite and the Northampton Sand are really of Inferior and not of Great Oolite age has
gradually gained ground among geologists. It has been maintained by Dr. Lycett ever since the year 1850 on purely palæontological grounds; and in 1858 the Rev. T. W. Norwood, in a
paper read before the British Association, and subsequently at
Professor Phillips' request published in the first volume of the
" Geologist," showed that the fauna of the northern prolongation of
the Lincolnshire Oolite about Hotham and Cave, especially the
Echinodermata, agreed very closely with that of the pea-grit which
forms the base of the Inferior Oolite of Cheltenham, but that it
had but few, if any, resemblances to that of the Great Oolite.
Mr. Sharp of Northampton, and Mr. Beesley of Banbury, were,
by the study of the fossils in their respective areas, independently
led to similar conclusions. While studying the general relations
of the Lincolnshire strata and the characters of their faunas in
the year 1866, the author of the present memoir was induced,
both on stratigraphical and palæontological grounds, to regard
both the great calcareous series in that county, so frequently
referred to, and also the ferruginous beds below it, as undoubted
Inferior Oolite.

that in the Cotteswold Hills. Ann. Mag. Nat. Hist., Ser. 2, vol. vi., p. 256, and
Proc. Cotteswold Nat. Club, vol. i., p. 52.

Remarks on the Stonesfield Slate at Collyweston, near Stamford, and the Great
Oolite, Inferior Oolite, and Lias in the neighbourhood of Grantham. Rep. Brit.
Assoc. for 1850, Trans. of Sections, p. 74.

    * Quart. Journ., Geol. Soc., vol. ix., p. 317.

    † Geological Notes on parts of Northampton and Lincolnshire; Geol. Mag.,
vol. vi., p. 446.

When the officers of the Geological Survey found that the Lower Zone of the Great Oolite (which included the well known Stonesfield Slate) passes in its northern extension into a sandy and ferruginous rock, they were led to regard the whole of that formation—to which they gave the appropriate name of the " Northampton Sand"—as representing the base of the Great Oolite. The subsequent progress of the Survey, however, furnished the strongest grounds, both palæontological and stratigraphical, for the modification of this view, and in the year 1870 the changes found to be necessary were introduced into the maps and index of the Survey.

It is an interesting circumstance, and one by no means devoid of suggestiveness, that a similar confusion to that we have noticed in the case of the Midland district, long prevailed with regard to the correlation of the beds of the Great Oolite series in the south-western area. The difficulty arose in this case in consequence of the erroneous identification of the Stonesfield Slate with the fissile beds of the Forest Marble, which is worked for roofing materials at Fairford, Chavenage, &c. on the skirts of the Cotteswold plateau. In 1832 Lonsdale—by demonstrating that these two sets of beds were, in spite of their resemblances in mineral character, of very different age*—at once made clear the true order of sequence of the Great Oolite strata of the Southern Cotteswolds, concerning which such conflicting opinions had been before maintained. The separation of the Collyweston from the Stonesfield Slate has produced a similar revolution in our views concerning the correlation of the Oolites of the Midland district; it has also been attended with a great simplification of our classification and the removal of many apparent anomalies.

It may be interesting to notice that the occurrence of these so called " slate beds" of the Oolites, which have been the source of such great confusion in the classification of the Jurassic Rocks of England, is in almost every instance a phenomenon of very local character. The presence of such beds depends on the existence, in a rock mass of a finely laminated structure, of a due admixture of calcareous and arenaceous materials; and as the necessary conditions for their formation can scarcely be expected to prevail over any extended district, we are not surprised to find that the peculiar features of such rocks are only found over compara- tively small areas ; the " slate " passing within very short distances either into loose sand on the one hand, or into solid limestone rock on the other. This is the case alike with the Stonesfield, the Collyweston, and other similar "slates."

marginalia Confusion arising from occurrence of "slate beds."

It will be instructive to exhibit in a tabular form the various horizons of these several "slate beds" at present known in the Lower Oolites of this country.

Great Oolite.	⎧ Slates of Fairford, Chavenage, &c. - - - -	Forest Marble.
	⎨ Slates of Stonesfield, Eyeford,	
	⎩ Sevenhampton Common, &c. -	Base of Great Oolite.
Inferior Oolite.	⎧ Slate of Brandsby (Yorkshire) -	Middle part of Inferior Oolite (Zone of Ammonites Humphresianus ?).
	⎨ Slates of Collyweston, Kirby, Dene Park, &c.- - -	Lincolnshire Oolite (Zone of Ammonites Sowerbyi).
	⎩ Slate of Duston - - -	Northampton Sand (Zone of Ammonites Murchisonæ).

The progress of exact observations among the Jurassic Rocks has shown how much more local in character are many of the subdivisions of that system than was formerly supposed. At one time names like Kellaways Rock, Cornbrash, Forest Marble, and Bradford Clay were applied to many deposits upon the continent, which were of about the same age and at the same time happened to resemble in mineral character the English beds to which the names were originally applied. The fallacy of such nomenclature and its mischievous results have been pointed out by many authors, and by none with more force of argument and justice of illustration than by Jules Marcou, in his "Lettres sur les Roches du Jura." The practice of identifying distant strata on the ground of petrological resemblance, which has been almost wholly abandoned in France and Germany, lingers to a somewhat greater extent perhaps in this country; but as the accurate mapping of the several formations proceeds, the unsoundness of the method becomes every day more and more obvious. To be convinced of this it is only necessary to compare the successive editions of the Index Sheet of the Geological Survey. In the earlier ones each formation is represented by a single column, one series of subdivisions answering for all the country then mapped; but as the survey proceeded it was found necessary to adopt distinct systems of classifications for different areas, these being represented in parallel columns. The portions of the Geological series in which we find this change most marked, or in other words the systems which exhibit beds of the most local character, are the Jurassic and Carboniferous. The very slight persistence of many of the well marked Oolite beds, and the manner in which they thin out or entirely change their characters, often within distances of a few miles only, has been admirably illustrated in the descriptions of the strata of the Cotteswold Hills by Drs. Wright, Lycett, and Holl, and Mr. Hull.

In the introductory essay to this memoir we propose to notice the changes which take place in each of the subdivisions of the Jurassic strata of the Cotteswold Hills (where their characters and faunas have been so well illustrated by the labours of many observers) as we follow them northwards through the Midland Counties into Yorkshire. The following table (see next page) illustrates the succession of Lower Oolite strata in the Northern Cotteswolds as illustrated by Mr. Hull, Dr. Wright, and other observers, with their equivalents in the Midland district and South Yorkshire respectively. *Table illustrating changes in Oolites.*

The highest of the Jurassic formations which it is necessary to notice in the present essay is the *Oxford Clay.* The several horizons (each marked by the successive appearance of certain species of *Ammonites* and other fossils, and the simultaneous disappearance of others) which have been distinguished alike in Germany, Switzerland, France, and England, are clearly traceable, as will be shown in the present memoir, in our Midland district. The well known Kellaways Rock of Wiltshire has been found in a more or less rudimentary condition as far north as Tetbury ; in Oxfordshire, according to Professor Phillips, it is entirely wanting, but in Bedfordshire, Northamptonshire, and Lincolnshire irregular sandy beds, often crowded with the characteristic fossils of the zone, make their appearance at the base of the Oxford Clay. In South Yorkshire the whole of the Middle Oolite is greatly reduced in thickness, and is represented by more or less ferruginous sandy beds, evidently deposited in shallow water near land. These beds have been called the Kellaways Rock ; but an examination of their fauna appears to indicate that they represent a littoral condition of the whole of the Middle Oolite series. It is not necessary, for the purpose of this memoir, to describe the remarkably interesting manner in which the various zones of the Middle Oolite series are represented in the North Yorkshire area, the strata in question being entirely cut off from those of the district under consideration by the overlap of the upper Cretaceous series. *Variations in Oxford Clay.*

The *Cornbrash* is one of the most strikingly persistent beds of the Jurassic series. Although of such insignificant thickness, it can be traced through the whole of the Southern and Midland districts of England, everywhere maintaining its well marked mineral and palæontological characteristics. But in North Lincolnshire even this most constant bed begins to undergo a change; its thickness is greatly reduced, it exhibits evidence of more littoral conditions, *Variations in Great Oolite strata.*

TABLE illustrating the VARIATIONS which the BEDS of the LOWER OOLITE undergo in the MIDLAND DISTRICT.

Formations.	Geological Horizons.	Cotteswold Hills.	South and West Oxfordshire.	North and East Oxfordshire and South Northamptonshire.	North Northamptonshire and South Lincolnshire.	South Yorkshire.
Middle Oolite	Oxfordian	Oxford Clay, with Kelloways Rock at its base.	Oxford Clay	Oxford Clay	Oxford Clay, with sandy beds representing Kelloways at its base.	Sandy strata with Oxfordian fauna.
Great Oolite	Cornbrash	Cornbrash	Cornbrash	Cornbrash	Cornbrash	Absent.
	Great Oolite Upper Zone	Forest, Marble, Bradford Clay, and Great Oolite Limestones	Forest Marble, thinning out. Bradford Clay, absent. Great Oolite Limestones	Absent. Great Oolite Limestones	Thin argillaceous beds, "Great Oolite Clays". Great Oolite Limestone	Absent.
	Great Oolite, Lower Zone	Great Oolite Limestones with Stonesfield Slate.	Great Oolite Limestone with Stonesfield Slate.	Upper part of the Northampton Sand.	"Upper Estuarine Series."	Absent.
Transition Series	Fuller's Earth	Upper and Lower Fuller's Earth with the Fuller's Earth Rock	Absent	Absent	Absent	Absent.
	Zone of Ammonites Parkinsoni.	The Ragstones of the Inferior Oolite, including the Trigonia Grits, the Gryphite Grit, the Pholadomya Grit, and the Chemnitzia Grit	Represented by the thin Clypeus Grit	Absent	Absent	Absent.
Inferior Oolite	Zone of Ammonites Humphresianus	The Upper Freestones	Absent	Absent	Absent	Absent.
	Zone of Ammonites Sowerbyi.	The Oolite Marl	Absent	Absent	The Lincolnshire Oolite	Sands and Limestones of Cave, &c.
	Zone of Ammonites Murchisonæ.	The Lower Freestones of the Pea Grit.	Lower portions of the Northampton Sand.	Lower portions of the Northampton Sand.	The Northampton Sand	
Transition Series	Midford Sand	Cephalopoda beds and sands	?	?	Upper Lias Clay	?
Lias	Zone of Ammonites communis.	Upper Lias Clay	Upper Lias Clay	Upper Lias Clay	Upper Lias Clay	Upper Lias Clay.

and it is in places almost wholly made up of beds of small oysters, a feature never presented by it in its normal aspect. Before we reach the Humber, the Cornbrash is found to have altogether thinned out and disappeared. The so-called Cornbrash of the North of Yorkshire is not only not continuous with that of the South and Midland districts of England, but, as shown by Dr. Lycett,[*] presents essential points of difference from that formation in its mineral character and still more striking ones in its fauna. It would be well if a local and distinctive name were applied to the Yorkshire rock, which is perhaps the only representative of the Great Oolite series in the northern area.

The *Forest Marble*, which was evidently a shallow-water deposit, and as Professor Phillips has shown, sometimes even exhibits estuarine characters, everywhere presents great variability in the succession and thickness of its various beds of clay, sand, and shelly limestone. In Oxfordshire the limestones thin out and disappear altogether, and the clays with occasional shelly bands, become so thin and insignificant in North Oxfordshire, South Northamptonshire, and the adjoining counties, that it was found impracticable by the Geological Survey to map them separately, and hence they are in those districts grouped with the Great Oolite. As we go northwards into North Northamptonshire and Lincolnshire these beds of clay again thicken, and become of greater importance, but they do not include the characteristic shelly limestones of the Forest Marble of the south of England. They are mapped in sheet 64, and that to the north of it, under the name of " Great Oolite Clays." It is true that the strata of the Upper Zone of the Great Oolite in the Midland district occasionally contain fissile limestones identical in character with those of the Forest Marble, but this is evidently the result of a local similarity of conditions, and neither palæontological nor stratigraphical evidence can be adduced in favour of considering them as part of that formation. The *Bradford Clay* is a more local and inconstant stratum even than the Forest Marble; important and interesting as are its characters in the Bath district, it loses almost all its importance in the Cotteswolds. The identity of the stratum at Tetbury with that at Bradford has even been doubted by some geologists, and it has been found quite impracticable by the Geological surveyors to map it as a separate formation.

The *Upper Zone of the Great Oolite* is, in its persistency and uniformity of character, only second to the Cornbrash itself.

---

* Supplementary Monograph on the Mollusca from the Stonesfield Slate, Great Oolite, Forest Marble, and Cornbrash, by John Lycett, M.D. Published by Palæontographical Society, 1863, p. 117.

Everywhere exhibiting alternations of white marly limestones and clays, crowded with a highly distinctive fauna, in which the *Myadæ, Ostreidæ,* and *Echinodermata* are especially noticeable by their abundance both of species and individuals, these strata (which are constantly burnt for lime in the districts where they are developed) are well known to all who have studied the geology of the Northern Cotteswolds, Oxfordshire, Northamptonshire, and Lincolnshire. At times, it is true, they exhibit local variations ; passing in some places into shelly and occasionally oolitic free-stones which afford good building stones, and in others into fissile beds which present appearances similar to those of the Forest Marble. When the formation is traced through the country, how-ever, the observer cannot doubt of the continuity of the series of beds. In Mid-Lincolnshire the Upper Zone of the Great Oolite is very greatly reduced in thickness, and its lower calcareous portion finally thins out and disappears altogether, at a point considerably to the south of that at which the Cornbrash is lost.

The *Lower Zone of the Great Oolite,* which, in its frequent oblique lamination, its numerous remains of terrestrial organisms, and the often prevailing arenaceous elements of its composition, suggests, like the Forest Marble above, with which indeed its beds were at one time confounded, the littoral conditions under which it was deposited. The thick shelly freestones of Minchinhampton Common pass northwards into fissile shelly and often sandy lime-stones, which in the Northern Cotteswolds and South Oxfordshire present at their base, in local patches, fissile beds ; these at Eyeford, Sevenhampton Common, and Stonesfield are capable of being split, by the aid of frost, into "slates" used for roofing purposes. It was found by the Geological surveyors that these "slate" yielding beds, as they are traced northwards, lose their calcareous characters and are represented by sands, which occasionally become ferruginous. As we shall hereafter show, certain beds of the Inferior Oolite undergo a precisely similar change of character in the same area ; and the two series of sandy beds representing the attenuated and more littoral conditions of two important limestone formations of the Cotteswolds (namely the Leckhampton and Minchinhampton freestones) thus brought together, being frequently altogether destitute of fossils, the line of demarcation between them can no longer be traced. These sandy strata, which in places are reduced to only a few inches in thickness, have been mapped together under the name of the " Northampton Sand." As we go northwards, however, the sandy representative of the Lower Zone of the Great Oolite is found gradually to change in character and to become mainly argillaceous in its com-position. These beds of clay are evidently of estuarine character presenting alternations of bands with freshwater and marine fossils, and mineral characters identical with those of the Purbeck and the beds which form the top of the Wealden. These strata, which in North Northamptonshire and Lincolnshire present very marked characters, have been mapped by the Survey under the name of the " Upper Estuarine Series ;" they form the base of the Great Oolite. The strata in question were first described by Professor Morris in 1853, from their exposures in the cuttings of the Great Northern Railway, then in course of construction; the beds were at that time however regarded as the equivalents of the Forest Marble. As we pass northwards in the county of Lincoln the Upper Estuarine Series, like the other members of the Great Oolite, becomes gradually reduced in thickness, and by the thinning out of the Upper Zone of the Great Oolite, the two argillaceous series, representing the Forest Marble and the Stonesfield Slate respectively, are brought together; thus the only vestige of the Great Oolite formation below the Cornbrash in North Lincolnshire is a thin series of clays of more or less estuarine character. It is doubtful whether any representative of these argillaceous beds extends to the north of the Humber.

The *Fuller's Earth*, which appears by its fauna to form a transition series between the Great Oolite and Inferior Oolite of the Cotteswolds, is a very variable member of the Jurassic series. Near Bath it is 150 feet thick, at Sapperton Tunnel only 70, and in the northern part of the Cotteswolds it thins out and disappears altogether.

The *Ragstones of the Inferior Oolite*, as shown by Dr. Lycett in his valuable " Handbook to the Cotteswold Hills," undergo many variations in character within that area. As we pass northward and westward into Oxfordshire, however, this portion of the Inferior Oolite no longer presents its well-marked subdivisions, but, as was shown by Mr. Hull, is represented only by the " Clypeus Grit," which, becoming gradually more and more reduced in thickness, finally disappears near Chipping Norton, and to the north of Witney. The Ragstones of the Inferior Oolite are shown by Dr. Wright to represent the Zone of Ammonites Parkinsoni.

Variation in the Inferior Oolite strata.

The *Upper Freestones*, which in places are almost destitute of fossils, have been shown by Dr. Wright to be represented at Cleeve Hill by a series of strata, yielding the characteristic fossils of the Zone of Ammonites Humphresianus. This division is perhaps the least constant of all the beds of the Inferior Oolite of the Cotteswolds ; besides undergoing numerous and rapid changes in mineral character, it thins out and disappears northwards and eastwards before even the Oolite Marl.

The. *Oolite Marl* is a thin, but an interesting and well marked, stratum, which has been regarded by Dr. Wright as representing the upper part of the Zone of Ammonites Murchisonæ, but by Dr. Waagen has been referred to the Zone of Ammonites Sowerbyi. It can only be traced over the middle and northern parts of the Cotteswolds, and even within those areas undergoes very considerable changes in mineral character and thickness.

The *Lower Freestones*, which form so large a portion of the mass of the Inferior Oolites of the Cotteswolds, partake of the general attenuation of the beds of that series towards the north and east. Near their base the Lower Freestones become sandy and sometimes ferruginous, and thus graduate into the Pea Grit below. In their northern extension these sandy and ferruginous characters become still more marked, as may be well seen in the Great Outliers of Ebrington and Bredon Hills.

The *Pea Grit*, with the " roe-stone " in its upper part, and the sandy ferruginous beds at its base, has but a very limited range in the Northern Cotteswolds. North of Stanley Hill it can no longer be recognised as a distinct bed; but it may possibly be represented, together with the freestones above, in the sandy and ferruginous beds which constitute the base of the Inferior Oolite in those northern spurs and outliers of the Cotteswolds, known as Broadway, Campden, Ebrington, and Bredon Hills.

The *Midford Sand* appears to form a transition series between the Upper Lias Clays and the Inferior Oolite. At this horizon in Swabia there is developed a series of most richly fossiliferous beds distributed by the German geologists into two Zones—the Zone of Ammonites Jurensis and the Zone of Ammonites torulosus; and between these is the line which is generally accepted upon the continent as separating the Upper Lias from the Inferior Oolite. In this country, however, the strata at this horizon, though attaining a great thickness in some places, are almost wholly unfossiliferous, except in one or two thin bands; hence a division similar to that adopted by foreign geologists does not appear to be practicable in England. From a thickness of 150 ft. in the Southern Cotteswolds they thin out rapidly in going northward, and cannot be mapped as a separate bed farther in that direction than Chipping Campden; as pointed out however by Dr. Holl, there are some grounds for believing that, in the sandy and ferruginous beds of the extreme northern spurs of the Cotteswold range, the Midford Sand as well as the Pea Grit and the Lower Freestones are represented. The palæontological evidence in favour of this view is not, however, altogether conclusive. *See* the Series of Vertical Sections in Plate I.

It has usually been thought that the sandy and ferruginous beds of the northern spurs and outliers of the Cotteswolds, which represent the Zone of Ammonites Murchisonæ, are entirely lost as we pass northwards and eastwards. Such however is not the case. Crossing the broad Vale of Moreton we pass from the northern promontories of the Great Cotteswold plateau to the hills of North Oxfordshire: in the nearest of these, Brailes Hill, we find the same rocks as in Ebrington Hill, namely oolitic limestone alternating with sandy ferruginous beds, the only difference being the preponderance of the latter at the more easternly locality. The position of these beds in the series is put altogether out of question by the fauna which they yield; and this unmistakeably indicates that they are the representative of the Zone of Ammonites Murchisonæ. *Changes of Inferior Oolite Strata to north and eastward.*

We have already noticed how the beds of limestone, constituting the base of the Great and Inferior Oolite series respectively, pass into strata of an arenaceous character to the northwards and eastwards, while they are at the same time greatly reduced in thickness. We have also seen how the intermediate subdivisions of the Lower Oolite thin out and disappear as we trace them to the northwards. Consequently we have in North Oxfordshire and South Northamptonshire that series of sandy and sometimes ferruginous strata, known as the "Northampton Sand," lying between the Upper Lias Clay and the Upper Zone of the Great Oolite. *The "Northampton Sand."*

As the facts which have been ascertained with regard to the relations of the beds representing the Lower Oolites in the northern part of Oxfordshire, taken in connexion with the changes which the several members of the series undergo as they are traced northwards and eastwards, form the grounds on which the classification of these beds in the Midland district, that has been adopted by the Geological Survey, is based, it will be necessary to explain them in this introductory essay in some detail.

We have described the manner in which the strata representing the Zone of Ammonites Murchisonæ in the Cotteswolds, namely the Pea Grit and Lower Freestones, as we trace them to the northwards, undergo considerable changes in mineral character, becoming sandy and ferruginous, while the highest bed of the Zone, the Oolite Marl, thins out altogether. This change of mineral character of the Inferior Oolite is well displayed at Broadway Hill, and in the great outliers of Bredon Hill and Ebrington Hill, which lie to the north of the Cotteswolds.

Rocks on west side of the Vale of Moreton, vide Sheet 44 of the Geological Survey. In the former of these outliers the Inferior Oolite strata which cap it have been preserved from denudation by the great fault, that has let them down far below their original level. Above the village of Kemerton there are extensive pits in the ferruginous, sandy, oolitic rock, which here forms the base of the Lower Free-stone series. This rock is occasionally banded with iron, and precisely agrees in character with the beds included in the North-ampton Sand at many localities, both in Oxfordshire and North-amptonshire. In places certain of the beds are almost wholly made up of fragments of *Pentacrinus.* Above the sandy and ferruginous beds the white freestones, presenting their usual characters, are quarried.

In an old pit opposite to "Kemerton Castle House" we find the upper beds composed of white freestone, and passing down into a ferruginous rock of the most variable character; some-times consisting of loose brown sand, at others of brown sand indurated by carbonate of lime into a hard rock, and at others again becoming oolitic and shelly, as in the last pit. Certain beds consist of brown sandstone, including hard calcareous ramifying masses, which cause the whole to weather into blocks with very rough surfaces. Some of the stone has a curious vesicular structure, being made up of rounded fragments of white or pink oolitic limestone cemented together by crystallized carbonate of lime, the interstices being filled with brown sand. Occasionally the rock is traversed by bands of hydrated peroxide of iron, and in places these assume that cellular and concentric arrangement, due to weather-ing from the joint planes, which is so commonly presented by both the calcareous and arenaceous varieties of the Northampton Sand.

In the same great outlier of Bredon Hill, we find, above the villages of Conderton and Overbury, a similar series of sections. The higher beds consist of the ordinary white freestones, and pass down gradually into a rock of more or less ferruginous character. In some places the rock is a fine oolite limestone often with large oolitic grains; in others it is very sandy; and it is occasionally seen to be almost wholly made up of fragments and joints of *Pentacrinus,* with plates and spines of other Echinoderms, a few fragments of shells, and waterworn corals and Polyzoa. In this latter variety of the rock, all the constituents exhibit evidence of having been drifted. The ferruginous rock forming the base of the Inferior Oolite in this outlier is often intensely hard and compact, and fossils can only be obtained from the surfaces which have been weathered. The most abundant shell in the sandy and ferruginous rock at the base of the Inferior Oolite at Bredon Hill is *Pecten personatus*, Münst.; Brachiopoda, including *Terebratula perovalis*, Sow.; *T. submaxillata*, Mor.; *Rhynchonella Gingensis?* Waagen, and *Rhynchonella cynocephala*, Rich., are not rare, but almost always occur with their valves separated and much waterworn. With these are found, but in lesser abundance, *Belemnites ellipticus*, Mill.; *Ostrea Sowerbyi*, Mor. and Lyc.; *Hinnites abjectus* Phil. *sp.*, and drifted, waterworn corals.

Crossing the Vale of Evesham, we find in the northern spur of the Cotteswolds which forms Campden and Broadway Hills, and in the outlier of Ebrington Hill, the same alterations in the characters of the strata belonging to the Zone of Ammonites Murchisonæ, well exemplified. At Campden Hill is seen the Oolite Marl, which is here about 6 feet thick, presenting its usual characters of a soft white chalky-looking rock, sometimes highly indurated and crowded with fossils, among which are *Natica Leckhamptonensis*, Lyc.; *Ostrea flabelloides*, Lam.; *Modiola imbricata*, Sow.; *Lima pectiniformis*, Schloth; *Perna quadrata*, Sow.; *Trigonia costata*, Sow.; *Terebratula fimbria*, Sow.; *T. plicata*, Buckm., *Rhynchonella concinna*, Sow., and *R. Lycetti*, Dav.; and beneath this occur representatives of the Lower Freestones and Pea Grit. These are about 45 feet thick, and consist of oolitic limestones of a yellowish colour, which, as we trace them downwards, are seen to become more and more sandy and ferruginous in character; they rest on the representative of the Midford Sand (here reduced to a rudimentary condition). Towards the base of the series occurs a very sandy oolitic rock with ferruginous banding, like that so common in the Northampton Sand. The attenuated beds of the Lower Freestones are also seen at many points on Broadway Hill; and here we find the upper parts everywhere consisting of yellow or brown oolitic limestone, and the base of very variable beds, but usually of a more or less sandy and ferruginous character, passing locally into tolerably pure oolitic or shelly limestone.

In Ebrington Hill the beds of the Inferior Oolite, which constitute an outlying mass, consist mainly of yellow and brown, somewhat silicious and coarsely oolitic limestone rock, and exhibit in places ferruginous banding like that of the Northampton Sand. Some of the beds are composed of a ferruginous shelly rock, in places almost wholly made up of plates of *Pentacrinus*, with abundant specimens of *Pecten personatus*, Goldf.; *Trigonia signata*, Ag.; *Terebratula perovalis*, Sow., &c. In one of the pits we have a very instructive section.   At its southern end are yellow and ferruginous sands, a little to the northward irregular hard beds occur in these sands, and still farther north the whole passes into a calciferous sandstone rock with ironstone banding; in fact there is presented to us in one section examples of the different aspects which the Northampton Sand assumes at various points.   Still further north, however, the rock becomes more and more oolitic in structure, and thus passes into the ordinary yellow oolitic limestone which caps the hill.   All these changes take place within a distance of about 40 yards.   Everywhere on this outlier of Ebrington Hill, the limestones of the Lower Freestones may be seen to assume arenaceous characters, thus graduating in places into calcareous sand-rock, or into sandy calcareous stone with some imperfect cellular ironstone.   Above Ilmington Downs, on the north side of the Hill, we find the ordinary yellow freestones passing down into beds of sand, sometimes containing " pot-lids," and gr aduating into a mass of fissile calcareo-siliceous rock with ferruginous banding.   Similar beds to these are found above Stoke Wood.   In the extensive pits above Little Hilcote occur courses of the fine oolitic rock with ferruginous banding, sometimes interstratified with beds of sand.   At the rabbit-warren above Great Hilcote, though no good faces of rock are exposed, the strata which constitute the lower part of the Inferior Oolite are seen to consist of yellowish-red, calcareo-ferruginous sand, with layers of fissile, iron-banded, calcareo-siliceous stone.   These beds are undistinguishable in character from many portions of the North-ampton Sand, as seen in Oxfordshire and Northamptonshire.

The whole of the strata hitherto described are admitted on all hands to be the northerly prolongation of the Pea Grit and Lower Freestones of the Inferior Oolite and to represent the Zone of Ammonites Murchisonæ.   That this is the case is proved, not only by the fact that their beds can be followed continuously from the typical section of Leckhampton Hill to their develop-ment in the Northern Cotteswolds, but also by the interesting series of fossils characteristic of the horizon which they yield.   Dr. Holl has suggested that these limestones may also include a representative of the Midford Sand, which as a distinct series of beds can only be obscurely and doubtfully recognised in the Northern Cotteswolds.   It is certain that the great mass of ferru-ginous and often sandy limestones, forming the lower part of the Inferior Oolite in this district, contains *Rhynchonella cyno-cephala*, Rich. in its lower beds, as does also the Northampton Sand.   It may, however, be doubted whether the presence of this single species, which is occasionally found above the Midford

Sand in the Cheltenham area, can be considered as sufficient to establish the correlation in question.

Crossing another area occupied by the Lias, that of the Vale of Moreton, we arrive at other outliers of the Oolites capping a number of more or less isolated hills in the north of Oxfordshire, such as Brailes Hill, Mine Hill, Tysoe Hill, Shenlow Hill, Epwell Hill, Long Hill, and the high grounds above Epwell, Sibford, and Whichford. The variable beds of limestones, sands, ironstones, &c., which form these outliers have been classed with the Northampton Sand, and indeed they can be traced from this point northward and eastward almost continuously with that series of more or less ferruginous beds, which in the counties of Oxford Northampton, Rutland, and Lincoln are designated by that term and immediately overlie the Upper Lias Clay. *Rocks on east side of the Vale of Moreton, vide Sheet 45 of the Geological Survey.*

Whether we study the mineral characters presented by these beds, or the series of fossils which they yield, we shall be convinced that the strata capping the hills on the *western* side of the Vale of Moreton are identical with those which form the outliers on the *eastern* side of that valley. No one who examines the sections presented in the two areas and compares the series of fossils obtained from them, can doubt that the beds called *Inferior Oolite Freestone* in North Gloucestershire once extended continuously over what is now the Vale of Moreton into North Oxfordshire, where the portions of the same series now preserved are known as part of the *Northampton Sand*. Thus we are led to the conclusion that a part, at least, of the beds known as " Northampton Sand" represents the Zone of Ammonites Murchisonæ, that is the lowest portion of the Inferior Oolite, and possibly also the Midford Sand, or the strata which constitute a transition series between the Inferior Oolite and Upper Lias.

On the opposite side of the Vale of Moreton to the Ebrington Outliers, at a distance of only six miles, is situated Brailes Hill. Here we find, in the pits opened at the summit of the hill, a series of beds identical with those in Gloucestershire. In the upper part of the principal pit now open (1869) are seen beds of white oolitic freestone, but slightly siliceous, which by weathering assume a somewhat fissile character. Among these upper beds is a white, coarsely oolitic rock, graduating into a regular freestone undistinguishable from that of the Lower Freestones of Gloucestershire ; in its upper part this bed becomes shelly and contains numerous Corals and fragments of Echinoderms. Below is an irregular bed of brown sand and good ironstone, presenting the usual features of the Northampton Sand. Beneath the sand and ironstone, a thickness of about 8 feet of calcareo-siliceous rock is exposed, one bed near the bottom being crowded with shells, among which I recognised the following:—

CEPHALOPODA.

Belemnites giganteus, *Schloth.*
,,   ellipticus, *Mill.* (Abundant.)
,,   Aalensis, *Ziet.*
Ammonites Murchisonæ, *Sow.* (Very large.)
,,   ,,   var. corrugatus, *Sow.*

GASTEROPODA.

Nerinæa sp.

LAMELLIBRANCHIATA DIMYARIA.

Pholadomya spec. nov. (Very large.)
Ceromya Bajociana, *d'Orb.* (Very fine.)
Gresslya peregrina, *Phil.*, sp.
Myacites sp.
Cucullæa oblonga, *Sow.*
Trigonia costata, *Sow.*
Astarte elegans, *Sow.*
,,   minima, *Sow.*

LAMELLIBRANCHIATA MONOMYARIA.

Hinnites abjectus, *Phil.*, sp.
Pecten demissus, *Phil.*
,,   personatus, *Münst.*
,,   articulatus, *Schloth.*

ECHINODERMATA.

Pentacrinus Milleri, *Aust.*

ZOANTHARIA.

Montlivaltia trochoides, *Edw. & Haime.*
Latomeandra Davidsoni, *Edw. & Haime.*
Thamnastræa Defranciana, *Mich.*

PLANTÆ.

Wood.

Less than two miles to the south-east of Brailes Hill, we find another outlier of the Oolite strata, capping the Upper Lias Clay at Mine Hill. In the several old pits on this hill, calcareo-arenaceous beds are seen, passing in places into ferruginous sandstone and ironstone rock. In these pits the following fossils were collected :—

CEPHALOPODA.

Belemnites giganteus, *Schloth.*
      „   ellipticus, *Mill.* (Abundant.)

LAMELLIBRANCHIATA DIMYARIA.

Pholadomya fidicula, *Sow.*
      „   spec. nov. (Very fine.)
Ceromya Bajociana, *d' Orb.* (Very large.)
Gresslya peregrina, *Phil.* sp.
Trigonia signata, *Ag.*
      „   costata, *Sow.*
Cucullæa cucullata, *Goldf.*
      „   oblonga, *Sow.*
Astarte minima, *Sow.*
Macrodon Hirsonensis, *d'Arch.*
Modiola imbricata, *Sow.*

LAMELLIBRANCHIATA MONOMYARIA.

Pecten articulatus, *Schloth.*
      „   personatus, *Münst.*
      „   demissus, *Phil.*

BRACHIOPODA.

Terebratula submaxillata, *Mor.*

ANNULOSA.

Serpula socialis, *Goldf.*
      „   sp.

ECHINODERMATA.

Pentacrinus sp.

ZOANTHARIA.

Montlivaltia sp.

PLANTÆ.

Wood.

The most northernly of the outliers of "Northampton Sand" on the east side of the Vale of Moreton are those of Shenlow

Hill and Tysoe Mill Hill. At the former no section can be seen, but it is evidently capped by ferruginous sand, which in places passes into more or less calcareous flaggy beds.   The hill on which Tysoe Mill stands, however, yields an interesting section in a pit about 20 feet deep; this exhibits the silicious limestones with ironstone bandings, in some places passing into loose calcareous sands, in others into the ordinary iron-ore of the Northampton Sand.   At this place marine fossils appear to be rare in the beds, but fragments of wood and plant-remains are very abundant. The following species were obtained from the pit near Tysoe Mill :—

CEPHALOPODA.

Belemnites giganteus, *Schloth.*

LAMELLIBRANCHIATA DIMYARIA.

Macrodon Hirsonensis, *d'Arch.*
Astarte elegans, *Sow.*
Trigonia compta? *Lyc.*
Lucina Wrightii, *Opp.*

LAMELLIBRANCHIATA MONOMYARIA.

Lima pectiniformis, *Schloth.*
Pecten demissus, *Phil.*

BRACHIOPODA.

Terebratula submaxillata, *Mor.*

In the long spur capped by Northampton Sand, which stretches northwards as far as Compton Winyate, we find many illustrations of the variable character of the beds which lie upon the Upper Lias Clay.   Sometimes, as near White House Warren, white sands with numerous bands of carbonaceous matter occur; in some places these white sands are found passing into hard sand-rock, at others into ferruginous sand, and at others again, as near Broom Hill Farm, into cellular ironstone rock.

At not a few points the sands graduate, within very short distances, into a more or less fissile calcareo-siliceous rock traversed by hard ferruginous bands. The same rapid variations—so characteristic of the Northampton Sand throughout its whole range—from arenaceous to more or less ferruginous and calcareous rocks, is seen in the numerous outliers to the east of this spur, one of which, Epwell Hill, rises to an elevation of 836 feet, and constitutes the highest point in the county of Oxford.

Tracing the same beds to the southwards, we find in the outlier above Whichford and Long Compton, thick beds of white freestone underlaid by sands; beneath these occur beds of the calcareo-siliceous stone with but few well preserved fossils. The succession of beds here is evidently the same as at the other points we have noticed, both on the east and west side of the Vale of Moreton. Near Long Compton a specimen of *Ammonites Garantianus*, d'Orb., was obtained from the Northampton Sand.

Near Hotley Hill Farm, a mile and a half north-west of the village of Hook-Norton (or Hogs-Norton) there are several very interesting sections in the Northampton Sand. In the higher of these is seen a wbitish, oolitic, siliceo-calcareous rock (like that which forms so large a part of the formation to the north of Northampton) with bands of brown hæmatite in many of the beds. In this upper part of the series, which is well exposed in a pit above the farm-house, we find scarcely any marine fossils, but fragments of wood are especially abundant. Lower down the hill, however, and just above the junction of the Northampton Sand with the Upper Lias Clay, we find in another pit the base of the series; this is seen to consist of beds precisely similar in mineral character to those of the upper pit, but which yield large numbers of marine fossils, including many corals. In this section there are bands almost wholly made up of oyster-shells and a bed of stone exhibiting borings of *Lithodomus*.

The following fossils have been collected from this pit by Mr. Richard Gibbs, the former fossil-collector of the Survey, and myself; they clearly show that this part of the Northampton Sand is referable to the Inferior Oolite, and to its lower part, the zone of Ammonites Murchisonæ:—

CEPHALOPODA.

Ammonites Murchisonæ, *Sow.*
           „   „   var. corrugatus, *Sow.*
Belemnites Aalensis, *Ziet.*
     ,,   ellipticus, *Mill.*
Nautilus, spec. nov. (Very large.)

GASTEROPODA.

Pleurotomaria ornata, *Ziet.*
Natica sp.
Nerinæa sp.

LAMELLIBRANCHIATA DIMYARIA.

Pholadomya fidicula, *Sow.*
     „   ovulum, *Ag.*
     „   Zieteni, *Ag.*
     „   Heraulti, *Ag.*
     „.   spec. nov. (Very large.)
Gresslya latirostris, *Ag.*
     „   peregrina, *Phil.,* sp.
Ceromya Bajociana, *d'Orb.*
Cypricardia sp.
Isocardia cordata, *Buckm.*
Trigonia costata, *Sow.*
     „   signata, *Ag.*
     „   pullus, *Sow.*
     „   producta, *Lyc.*
     „   spec.
Cucullæa oblonga, *Sow.*
Lucina Wrightii, *Oppel.*
Modiola Lonsdalei, *Lyc. & Mor.*
     „   Leckenbyi, *Lyc. & Mor.*

LAMELLIBRANCHIATA MONOMYARIA.

Pinna cuneata, *Phil.*
     „   sp.
Lima pectiniformis, *Schoth.*
     „   punctata, *Sow.*
     „   cardiiformis, *Lyc. & Mar.*
Gervillia Hartmanni, *Goldf.*
     „   lata, *Phil.*
Hinnites abjectus, *Phil.,* sp.
Pecten articulatus, *Schoth.*
     „   demissus, *Phil.*
     „   lens, *Sow.*
Ostrea flabelloides, *Lam.* (O. Marshii, *Sow.*)
     „   Sowerbyi, *Lyc. & Mor.*

BRACHIOPODA.

Rhynchonella sp.
Terebratula globata, *Sow.*
     „   submaxillata, *Mor.*
     „   sp.

POLYZOA.

Berenicea (sp.) on Terebratula.

ZOANTHARIA.

Isastræa Richardsoni, *Edw. & Haime.*
Montlivaltia trochoides, *Edw. & Haime.*
Thamnastræa Terquemi, *Edw. & Haime.*
Thecosmilia gregaria, *M' Coy.*

PLANTÆ.

Wood (abundant).

As we pass eastward from the localities particularly described above, we find many opportunities for studying the very variable strata of the Northampton Sand; these consist in some places of white unfossiliferous sands, in others, of red sandstone graduating into ironstone, and, in not a few localities, pass into beds of generally fissile, calcareo-siliceous rock; in this latter condition they are seen at many points about Sibford-Ferris and Sibford-Gower, Great Tew, and Milcomb Hill, and also in the neighbourhood of Hook-Norton and Great Rollwright (or Rollreich). The fossiliferous beds appear to occur towards the base of the Northampton Sand series, but are by no means constantly present; the fossils which they yield are always those of the Zone of Ammonites Murchisonæ of the Inferior Oolite.

At several pits in the vicinity of Sibford and Hook-Norton the following fossils have been collected in the impure siliceous limestones of the Northampton Sand :—

CEPHALOPODA.

Ammonites Murchisonæ, *Sow.*
    ,,   corrugatus, *Sow.*
Belemnites Aalensis, *Ziet.*
    ,,   ellipticus, *Mill.*
Nautilus, spec. nov. (Very large.)

GASTEROPODA.

Cerithium limæforme, *Ròm.*
Natica sp.
Patella cingulata, *Goldf.*

LAMELLIBRANCHIATA DIMYARIA.

Pholadomya fidicula, *Sow.*
Ceromya Bajociana, *d'Orb.*

Gresslya peregrina, *Phil.*, sp.
„   abducta, *Phil.*, sp.
„   latirostris, *Ag.*
Myacites æquatus, *Phil.*, sp.
„   dilatatus, *Phil.*, sp.
„   compressiusculus, *Lyc.*
Arcomya sp.
Goniomya angulifera, *Sow.*
Isocardia cordata, *Buckm.*
Unicardium gibbosum, *Lyc.*
Tancredia axiniformis, *Phil.*, sp.
Cyprina dolabra, *Phil.*
Trigonia signata, *Ag.*
„   v-costata, *Lyc.*
„   costata, *Park.*
„   pullus, *Sow.*
Lucina Wrightii, *Opp.*
Astarte elegans, *Sow.*
Macrodon Hirsonensis, *D'Arch.*
Cucullæa oblonga, *Sow.*
Modiola Sowerbyana, *D'Orb.*

LAMELLIBRANCHIATA MONOMYARIA.

Lima pectiniformis, *Schloth.*
Pinna cuneata, *Phil.*, sp.
Gervillia prælonga, *Lyc.*
Hinnites abjectus, *Phil.*
Pecten personatus, *Munst.*
„   demissus, *Phil.*
„   articulatus, *Schloth.*
„   sp.
Gryphæa sp.
Ostrea acuminata, *Sow.*
„   Marshii, *Sow.* var.

BRACHIOPODA.

Rhynchonella sp.
Terebratula submaxillata, *Mor.*
„   globata, *Sow.*
„   perovalis, *Sow.*

ZOANTHARIA.

Montlivaltia trochoides, *Edw. & Haime.*
Isastræa Richardsoni, *Edw. & Haime.*

As we pass eastwards, the Northampton Sand is found to contain fewer beds of a calcareous character and to be more usually made up of loose white sand and sandrock, graduating in many places into ironstone ; these strata yield numerous plant remains, but contain scarcely a trace of marine fossils. Occasionally, however, as near Milcomb, they are seen passing into a shelly calcareous rock which yields similar series of fossils to those already quoted. About a mile north-west of Deddington, in the parishes of Barford St. John and Barford St. Michael, there are two small outliers which have been preserved, in consequence of the Inferior Oolite having been let down by faults. In these the lower beds of the Inferior Oolite exhibit evidence of a local, but remarkable and highly interesting, recurrence of conditions, very similar to those which must have prevailed during the deposition of the beds of this age in their typical development in the Cotteswold area.

In the small outlier north of the River Swere (Combe Hill) we find about 15 feet of white oolitic limestone, some of the beds being very shelly. The rock, which here shows considerable signs of disturbance, consists of a number of courses, each from 18 inches to 2 feet in thickness, separated by marly partings. Fossils are extremely abundant in these beds, but are generally very difficult of extraction. The following species have been found at this place by Mr. Beesley of Banbury, Mr. Richard Gibbs, and myself:—

Fossils from Combe Hill, near Deddington, Oxfordshire.

CEPHALOPODA.

Ammonites Murchisonæ, *Sow.*
Belemnites ellipticus, *Mill.*
Nautilus spec. nov. (Very large.)

GASTEROPODA.

Natica Leckhamptonensis, *Lyc.*
Patella rugosa, *Sow.*
Pleurotomaria ornata, *Defr.*
    ,, . sp.
Trochus sp.
Cerithium limæforme, *Röm.*
Nerinæa Jonesii, *Lyc.*
Phasianella striata, *Sow.*

Lamellibranchiata Dimyaria.

Arca Pratti, *Lyc. & Mor.*
„ sp.
Myoconcha crassa, *Sow.*
Mytilus lunularis, *Lyc.*
 „ imbricatus, *Sow.*
Modiola aspera, *Sow.*
Macrodon Hirsonensis, *d'Arch.*
Astarte elegans, *Sow.*
Trigonia pullus, *Sow.*
 „ Beesleyana, *Lyc.*
Lucina Wrightii, *Opp.*

Lamellibranchiata Monomyaria.

Lima cardiiformis, *Lyc. & Mor.*
 „ pectiniformis, *Schloth.*
 „ Rodburgensis, *Lyc.* MS.
 „ spec. nov. (Very large.)
 „ sp.
Pecten demissus, *Phil.*
 „ lens, *Sow.*
 „ vimineus, *Sow.*
 „ articulatus, *Schloth.*
 „ annulatus, *Sow.*
 „ personatus, *Münst.*
Hinnites abjectus, *Phil.*, sp.
Perna rugosa var. quadrata, *Mor. & Lyc.*
Gervillia pernoides, *Desl.*
Harpax sp.
Ostrea flabelloides, *Lam.* (O. Marshii, *Sow.*)
 „ „ var.

Brachiopoda.

Terebratula globata, *Sow.*
 „ perovalis, *Sow.*
 „ Phillipsii, *Mor.*
 „ submaxillata, *Mor.*
 „ fimbria, *Sow.*
 „ plicata, *Buckm.*
Rhynchonella sp.

ANNULOSA.

Serpula socialis, *Goldf.* .
,,   convoluta, *Goldf.*
,,   sp.

ECHINODERMATA.

Pentacrinus Milleri, *Aust.*

POLYZOA.

Spiropora (Cricopora) straminea, *Phil.* sp.

ZOANTHARIA.

Thamnastræa Defranciana, *Mich.*
,,   sp.
· Montlivaltia trochoides, *Edw. & Haime.*
,,   Delabechii, *Edw. & Haime.*
Cladophyllia sp.

On the south side of the River Swere, at a place known as Blackingrove, we find a pit opened in beds of stone similar to that on the other side of the river at Combe Hill ; as we go lower in the series, however, the oolitic limestones are seen passing down into beds of a more siliceous and shelly character, and finally into the hard siliceo-calcareous rock, which occurs so commonly in the Northampton Sand. The whole of these beds are crowded with shells which have been collected both by the late Mr. Faulkner, of Deddington, and the officers of the Geological Survey ; thus we have been made acquainted with a very large and interesting fauna from this locality, which enables us to refer the beds without doubt to the base of the Inferior Oolite. The strata representing the Northampton Sand here, as at many other places, contain numerous rounded pebbles of argillaceous limestone ; it is in places banded with brown oxide of iron in its lower part, and rests directly upon the Upper Lias Clay.

The fossils which have been collected at Blackingrove in the sandy limestone of the Northampton Sand are as follows :—

Fossils from Blackingrove, near Deddington, Oxfordshire.

PISCES.

Strophodus magnus, *Ag.*

CEPHALOPODA.

Ammonites Murchisonæ, *Sow.*
,,   ,,   var. corrugatus, *Sow.*

Ammonites Murchisonæ var. sublævis, *Sow.*
      ,,   sp.
Belemnites giganteus, *Schloth.*
    ,,   ellipticus, *Mill.*
Nautilus spec. nov. (Very large.)

GASTEROPODA.

Patella rugosa, *Sow.*
Pleurotomaria sp.
Natica Leckhamptonensis, *Lyc.*
   ,,   cincta, *Phil.*
Turbo sp.
Trochotoma calix, *Phil.*
Chemnitzia sp.
Cerithium sp.
Nerinæa sp.

LAMELLIBRANCHIATA DIMYARIA.

Pholadomya fidicula, *Sow.*
        ,,   spec. nov. (Very large.)
Gresslya peregrina, *Phil.*, sp.
Cardium Buckmani, *Lyc. & Mor.*
     ,,   sp.
Cucullæa cucullata, *Münst.*
Astarte elegans, *Sow.*
Trigonia costata, *Sow.*
    ,,   Beesleyana, *Lyc.*
Mytilus lunularis, *Lyc.*
Modiola imbricata, *Sow.*

LAMELLIBRANCHIATA MONOMYARIA.

Lima pectiniformis, *Schloth.*
   ,,   cardiiformis, *Lyc. & Mor.*
   ,,   rigida, *Sow.*
   ,,   spec. nov. (Very large.)
   ,,   spec. nov.
Avicula sp.
Pteroperna plana, *Lyc. & Mor.*
Perna rugosa, var. quadrata, *Lyc. & Mor.*
Pinna cuneata, *Phil.*
Gervillia sp.
Placunopsis sp.
Hinnites abjectus, *Phil.*, sp.
Pecten lens, *Sow.*

Pecten personatus, *Munst.*
Ostrea flabelloides, *Lam.* (O. Marshii, *Sow.*)
,, sp.

BRACHIOPODA.

Terebratula perovalis, *Sow.*
,, submaxillata, *Mor.*
Rhynchonella sp.

ANNULOSA.

Serpula socialis, *Goldf.*
,, sp.

ECHINODERMATA.

Clypeus Plotii, *Klein.*
,, ,, var. altus, *M'Coy.*
Pygaster semisulcatus, *Phil.*, sp.
Hyboclypus agariciformis, *Forbes.*
Stomechinus germinans, *Phil.* sp.
Pseudodiadema depressa, *Ag.* sp.
Acrosalenia (spines).
Pentacrinus Milleri, *Aust.*

ZOANTHARIA.

Montlivaltia trochoides, *Edw. & Haime.*

Over a considerable area in the neighbourhood of Banbury the Lower Oolites have been almost wholly removed by denudation; but we nevertheless get evidence at a few points, of the occurrence of calcareous and shelly beds in the Northampton Sand series. The fossils which these yield agree for the most part with those of the preceding lists, and prove that the lower portion of the Northampton Sand in this area also belongs to the Zone of Ammonites Murchisonæ or the base of the Inferior Oolite.

Northampton Sand in the South Midland district.   We have seen how the shelly limestones of the Inferior Oolite, as they are traced northwards and eastwards, assume sandy characters and exhibit evidence of having been deposited under more littoral conditions, but that, nevertheless, the series of fossils collected at a number of different points place the *age* of the beds beyond question. It has been shown by the Geological Survey that the Lower Zone of the Great Oolite, which includes the Stonesfield Slate, is found to undergo precisely similar changes when it is followed in the same direction. Thus the two series of sandy beds, representing the attenuated, littoral, and sometimes estuarine conditions of the lower parts of the Great and Inferior Oolite respectively, are brought together. The higher parts of this mass of arenaceous strata are unfortunately almost always unfossiliferous, and it is found impracticable in the Oxfordshire area, except at a few widely-distant points, to separate that portion of them which belongs to the Great Oolite, from that which is included in the Inferior. Indeed, although the sandy beds at the top of the Lias never disappear altogether, they are at some points, as near Towcester, reduced to only a few inches in thickness. It has consequently been found impracticable in this district to draw a line of boundary between the representatives of the Great and Inferior Oolite. Thus it has arisen that under the term "Northampton Sand" are included, in North Oxfordshire and South Northamptonshire, the whole mass of variable sandy strata, (passing at some points into imperfect ironstones, and at others into impure limestones,) which intervene between the Upper Lias Clay and the marly limestones of the Upper Zone of the Great Oolite. At a few points in the south of Northamptonshire we find the Northampton Sand passing locally into a calcareous rock, as at Thorpe Mandeville, Stowe, &c., but in the northern part of the county, especially in the neighbourhood of Northampton, Pitsford, Moulton, Sywell, Brixworth, Lamport, Wold, Draughton, &c., it is frequently represented by thick masses of more or less shelly, oolitic, siliceo-calcareous rock, of the kind so frequently alluded to in the description of the country to the south. At Duston a thin bed of this siliceo-calcareous rock, in the midst of the Northampton Sand series, exhibits such a fissile character that it was formerly largely dug and used for roofing purposes under the name of "the Duston Slate." At a spot one mile and a half north-east of Draughton, calcareous beds occur in the Northampton Sand of sufficient purity to be burned for lime. To the northwards, although the beds of this formation often become very shelly and highly calcareous, they do not, except at a few points, pass into the remarkable fissile oolitic rock so frequently alluded to. The places at which calcareous beds are developed to a considerable extent in the Northampton Sand series are indicated by the sign CALC. upon the maps of the Geological Survey.

We have further seen how remarkably the beds of the Inferior Oolite and the Lower Zone of the Great Oolite become rapidly attenuated as we pass northwards and eastwards, so that the strata representing these formations which, in the Cotteswold Hills, attain a thickness of about 300 feet, are reduced in a distance of 30 to 40 miles to the few inches of irregularly ferruginous sandy rock ; these, in some parts of South Northamptonshire, alone separate the Upper Lias Clay from the white, marly limestones, forming the Upper Zone of the Great Oolite. It is probable that at some points the extremely variable beds, constituting the Northampton Sand, thin out altogether, and that the higher beds of the Great Oolite series lie directly upon the Lias. Over considerable tracts it has been found impracticable by the Geological Surveyors to represent the Northampton Sand at all on the maps, so thin and inconstant are its representatives. The diminution in thickness of the lower beds of the Oolite series is attended with changes not less striking and remarkable in their mineral characters ; the massive marine limestones of the south-western area being replaced by the variable sandy, usually littoral, and sometimes estuarine deposits of the South Midland districts.

While the changes above described take place in the Inferior Oolite and the lower part of the Great Oolite, it is interesting to notice the relative constancy of the characters presented by the formations, which respectively underlie and succeed this variable series of beds, in the district in question. The Upper Zone of the Great Oolite and the Cornbrash are remarkably persistent in character over the whole of the district, and apparently do not undergo any very marked variations in thickness. The Forest Marble, on the other hand, which lies between these two divisions, presents us with a series of changes on a small scale, parallel with those of the oldest beds of the Lower Oolite. The very variable shelly limestones, sands, and clays of the Forest Marble become rapidly reduced in thickness as we pass northwards and eastwards. In North Oxfordshire, as shown by Professor Phillips, they sometimes assume estuarine characters, while still further northwards this formation is of such insignificant thickness and inconstant characters that its outcrop could no longer be represented on the Survey maps. In the North Midland district beds of clay, which, lying as they

Upper and Lower Estuarine Series.

do, between the limestone series of the Cornbrash and the Upper
Zone of the Great Oolite, may be fairly assumed to be the
approximate equivalent of the Forest Marble, assume sufficient
thickness and importance to be represented on the maps; to
these beds the name of " Great Oolite Clays " has been given.

The Midford Sand, which underlies the Inferior Oolite series,
either thins out altogether in the northern spurs and outliers of
the Cotteswolds, or its attenuated representative is lost in the
Northampton Sand.   The thickness of the Upper Lias Clay is
at places in North Oxfordshire reduced to about 30 feet, and
the Middle and Lower Lias are also probably of considerably
less thickness in the South Midland area than in the country to
the north and south of it respectively.

Professor Hull has shown in how remarkable a manner the beds
of the Jurassic series are reduced in thickness as we pass to the
south and east, so that the Inferior Oolite, Upper Lias, and
Middle Lias, which at Leckhampton Hill measure severally
about 300, 200, and 115 feet, are near Burford reduced to 20, 20,
and to 24 feet, and near Ascott to 10, 6, and 10 feet respectively.

In North Northamptonshire the variable beds of the Northampton Sand rapidly increase in thickness, so that in the neighbourhood of Northampton, where their palæontological and general
characters have been perseveringly and successfully studied by
Mr. Sharp, they exhibit their maximum development, and attain a
thickness of more than 70 feet.   Here it is possible to draw a
line of demarcation between the beds of the formation which
represent the Great and the Inferior Oolite respectively.   The
upper strata consist of clays of a more or less sandy character,
which occasionally exhibit such alternations of beds containing
fresh water and marine species of fossils, with old terrestrial
surfaces, &c. as to prove them to be of estuarine origin.   These
beds have been separately mapped by the Geological Surveyors
since the year 1867 under the name of the " Upper Estuarine
Series ;" and, as will be shown in a later chapter of this memoir,
they acquire a considerable development and present very interesting features and relations in the country to the northwards.   The
lower part of the Northampton Sand (to which the name is here
more strictly confined) in the Northampton district, consists in
its upper part of sands with inconstant beds of clay; these beds
are usually unfossiliferous, but occasionally exhibit the same
evidence of the alternation of marine, freshwater, and terrestrial
conditions as the beds above, and they have been accordingly
called the " Lower Estuarine Series." The base of the Northampton Sand is composed of marine beds yielding at a few
points a most interesting fauna, which is unmistakeably that

of the Zone of Ammonites Murchisonæ; unfortunately the great majority of the fossils of these beds are preserved only in the condition of surface casts and internal moulds. Sometimes the whole thickness of the Northampton Sand is made up of white sands with occasional beds of clay; at many points it passes into an oolitic, siliceo-calcareous rock; but in the majority of instances a greater or less portion of its mass, usually towards its lower part, is converted into a solid bluish or greenish ironstone rock of oolitic structure, exactly resembling many parts of the Dogger and Middle Lias ironstones of Yorkshire; this rock, by weathering action set up from its joint planes, assumes a brown colour and a banded or cellular structure of a very peculiar and striking character.

Wherever the junction of the Upper and Lower Estuarine *Appearance of* Series can be examined there are seen to be proofs of an uncon- *a new forma-* formity between them. The bottom bed of the Upper Estuarine *tion, the Lin-* *colnshire* Series, whenever this formation is distinctly developed, is found to *Oolite.* be a band of ironstone nodules, and these always rest on an eroded surface of the Northampton Sand beds beneath. As an example, among many which might be cited, of the appearance presented by the junction of these two series of beds, the sketch on page 34, of a pit near the Race-course at Northampton is given. Here we have, in the lower part of the pit, beds of well stratified white sand with vertical plant markings and sandrock (the latter quarried as a building stone), passing downwards into a dark brown sandstone with a very thin representative of the North-amptonshire ironstone at its base. On the eroded surface of these beds lies the light-blue, and often highly carbonaceous, clays of the Upper Estuarine Series, with the very constant layer of nodules ("ironstone junction-band") at its base. (Fig. 1, p. 34.)

Bearing in mind the existence of an uncomformity between these two series of estuarine beds, we are not surprised to find that, in the country to the north, a thick series of beds (the Lincoln-shire Oolite) comes in like a great wedge between them. Thus in the northern part of the county of Northampton, along the valley of the Nene, the succession of beds is the same as that which we have already pointed out as presented in the neigh-bourhood of Northampton, while along the valley of the Welland and in the country to the westward and northward we have the same series of beds, with the addition of a new forma-

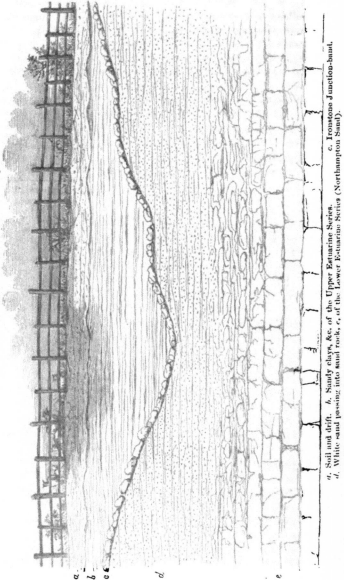

Figure 1. Section exhibited in a pit at the Race-course near Northampton.

a, Soil and drift. *b*, Sandy clays, &c. of the Upper Estuarine Series. *c*, Ironstone Junction-band. *d*, White sand passing into sand rock, *e*, of the Lower Estuarine Series (Northampton Sand).

TABLE illustrating the DIFFERENCE in the SUCCESSION of BEDS within the MIDLAND AREA, caused by the thinning out of the LINCOLNSHIRE LIMESTONE.

Succession of Beds in the Eastern and Southern Parts of the Midland District.	Succession of Beds in the Northern and Western Parts of the Midland District.
1. Cornbrash.	1. Cornbrash.
2. Great Oolite Clays and Limestones.	2. Great Oolite Clays and Limestones.
3. Upper Estuarine Series.	3. Upper Estuarine Series.
	LINCOLNSHIRE OOLITE WITH THE COLLYWESTON SLATE AT ITS BASE.
4. Northampton Sand including the Lower Estuarine Series.	4. Northampton Sand including the Lower Estuarine Series.
5. Upper Lias Clay.	5. Upper Lias Clay.'

tion, to which the Geological Survey has given the name of " the Lincolnshire Oolite Limestone." See Table on page 35.

These facts with regard to the relations of the great series of limestones of Lincolnshire and the adjoining counties were first made out during the survey of the area in 1867, and a nomen-clature and grouping of the beds adopted in accordance with them. They have since been illustrated in great detail in a paper on the Lincolnshire Oolite by my friend Mr. Sharp,* who on these questions has been led by his own studies to adopt in their entirety, the views put forward in the maps and other publications of the Geological Survey.

The two horizontal diagram sections (Plate II.) will serve to illustrate clearly, the manner in which the beds of the Lincoln-shire Limestone make their appearance in the midst of the Lower Oolite series and rapidly acquire preponderating thickness and importance in it.

Palæontological and Physical evidences of age.

That the Lincolnshire Limestone was of *Inferior* rather than *Great* Oolite age has been suspected, as we have already seen, by many authors, and may now be considered as generally adopted by geologists. If any doubts were still entertained on the subject it would only be necessary to point to the overwhelming palæontological evidence on the subject, which has been published by Mr. Sharp in his valuable paper, together with the tables, drawn up by Mr. Etheridge from Mr. Sharp's and the Survey collections, and appended to the present memoir. The not less conclusive physical evidences afforded by the unconformable relation of the beds representing the Lower Zone of the Great Oolite with the limestones below, which were first made manifest during the mapping of the area, are now illustrated and explained in this essay.

Unconformity between Great and Inferior Oolite.

We have seen how the Upper Estuarine Clays, forming the base of the Great Oolite series, usually rest on an eroded surface of the Northampton Sand. The same phenomenon is presented by the junction of the former beds with the Lincolnshire Lime-stone. Further—at some points, as for example the Ketton Quarries, the upper surface of the Lincolnshire Oolite is seen to be not only waterworn and denuded, but to have been bored by *Lithodomi* before the deposition of the beds of the Great Oolite series.

But there exist sections which show in a much more marked and striking manner the interval that must have elapsed between the deposition of the Lincolnshire Limestone and the commence-ment of the Great Oolite period. In openings near the north end of the village of Weekley (Fig. 2), and at Old Head Wood

---

* Quart. Journ. Geol. Soc. vol. xxix. (1873), p. 225.

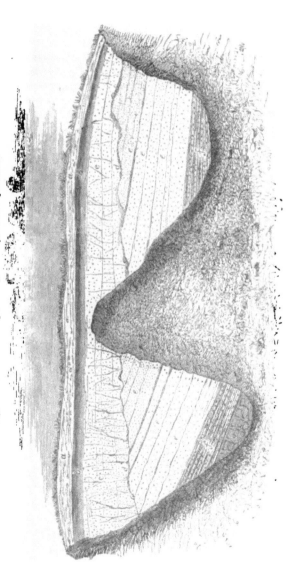

Figure 2. *Section in sandpit west of Weekley, Northamptonshire.*

Upper
Estuarine
Series
(Great
Oolite).
{
a. Soil, 1 to 2 ft.
b. Blue, stratified, carbonaceous, clays becoming lighter coloured
   towards and passing into c, 1 ft. 6 in.
c. White sandy clay with carbonaceous markings, 4 ft.
d. More or less ferruginous bands, in places containing ironstone nodules ("Ferruginous junction-band"), 0 to 3 in.
}

Lower
Estuarine
Series
(Inferior
Oolite).
{
e. Ash-coloured, and white, stratified sands, containing seams
   of light-blue clay (up to 2 inches thick), 6 to 8 ft.
f. White sands with much carbonaceous matter, generally in
   thin seams, 4 to 5 ft.
g. "Red-rock." The Northamptonshire iron-ore with usual
   characters, to bottom of pit.
}

The talus possibly hides a small fault with a downthrow to the East. There is certainly a more considerable fault a little east of this pit.

(Fig. 3), both localities a few miles north-east of Kettering,
we have the most complete evidence that the Inferior Oolite beds

Figure 3. *Section at Old Head Wood, Northamptonshire.*

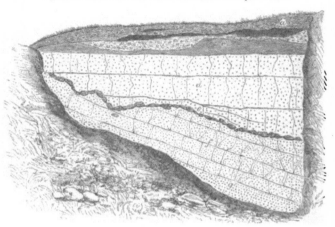

a. Soil, &c.
b. Gravelly drift.
c. Light-blue, estuarine clays.
d. White, marly clays.   } Upper Estuarine Series.
e. Ironstone junction-band.
f. Soft, much-jointed oolite rock. } Lincolnshire Limestone.
g. Harder, oolitic rock.

of the area were disturbed, upheaved, and denuded, and that on
their truncated edges the strata of the Great Oolite were laid
down, with consequently unconformable relations to them. Indeed,
there is every reason to believe that at Weekley a small fault
traverses the Inferior Oolite strata, but does not affect the Great
Oolite beds above; so that this fracture must have been produced
in the interval between the deposition of these two series of beds.
In mapping the small inliers of Inferior Oolite at Brigstock Parks
and between Little-Oakley and Stanion, I met with numerous
evidences of the fact, that the lower series of beds underwent
considerable disturbance and denudation before the deposition
upon it of the younger series of strata.

Age of Lin-
colnshire
Oolite.

We are now met by the problem of the exact age of the
several beds representing the Inferior Oolite in the Midland
district. The fauna of the Northampton Sand, as already pointed

out, is that of the Zone of Ammonites Murchisonæ. Possibly
its lowest beds may in some localities represent the Midford Sand,
but the existence of *Rhynchonella cynocephala*, Rich., and some
other Brachiopods cannot, as we have seen, be regarded as conclusive upon the subject. It is true that specimens of *Ammonites
bifrons*, Brug., have been collected in the lowest stratum of the
Northampton Sand near Northampton; but the bed which yielded
these specimens contains numerous pebbles of argillaceous limestone, and I have found that the chambers of the Ammonites in
question are filled with a similar material, and not with the sandy
ferruginous rock of the matrix; moreover, there is still considerable doubt among palæontologists whether the species in
question has ever been obtained above the Upper Lias Clay. I
cannot, therefore, help regarding these specimens of *Ammonites
bifrons*, Brug., as having been derived, with the associated pebbles,
from the septaria of the latter formation, which, in many districts,
shows signs of having undergone denudation prior to the deposition of the Inferior Oolite upon it. This is especially the case,
as might be anticipated, when no representative of the Midford
Sand is present; and we must, therefore, regard it as still very
doubtful whether any equivalent of the last-mentioned beds
exists in the Midland district.

The researches of several German geologists, especially those *Zone of Am-*
of Dr. Waagen,* have shown that the higher beds of the Zone of *monites*
Sowerbyi.
Ammonites Murchisonæ, which Dr. Oppel regarded as constituting
a district sub-zone, and to which he applied the name of the Zone
of Ammonites Sowerbyi, in some districts acquires a great development and very distinct characters. If this zone be represented
at all in the Cotteswold area, it is probably the insignificant and
inconstant Oolite Marl or Fimbria Bed which, as suggested by
Dr. Waagen himself, must be regarded as its equivalent. But
in the Lincolnshire Limestone we appear to have a magnificent
local development of the beds of this horizon in the Midland
district. That this is really the case is proved, not only by the
marked absence of numerous forms which are, as shown by Dr.
Oppel and Dr. Wright, highly characteristic of the upper portions
of the Inferior Oolite (namely, the zones of Ammonites Parkinsoni
and Ammonites Humphresianus), but by the presence of a number
of very interesting species which have been shown by the German
palæontologists to be especially characteristic of this horizon, such
as the *Ammonites Sowerbyi*, Mill, *Ammonites polyacanthus*, Waagen,

---

* Der Jura in Franken, Schwaben und der Schweiz vergleichen nach seinen
palæontologischen Horizonten, von W. Waagen (Munich, 1864). Ueber die Zone des
Ammonites Sowerbyi, von Dr. W. Waagen (Benecke, Geognostische-palæontologische
Beiträge, Erster Band, p. 507, Munich, 1867).

several peculiar varieties of *Ammonites Murchisonæ*, Sow. (to which distinct names have been applied in Germany), *Belemnites brevispinatus*, Waagen, *Pecten aratus*, Waagen, and some other forms, which may be regarded either as new species or as distinct varieties, characteristic of this horizon.

Formations absent.   We are thus led to see the significance of the unconformity which has been shown to exist in the Midland district between the Great Oolite series and the beds of the Lincolnshire Limestone; for in this area, strata representing the Fuller's Earth and the Ragstones and Upper Freestones of the Inferior Oolite (Zones of Ammonites Parkinsoni and Ammonites Humphresianus) appear to be wholly wanting.

It is true that a considerable number of species pass from the Lincolnshire Oolite to the Great Oolite, but the differences between the faunas of these two series are at least as great as exist between those of the Coralline Crag and of the deposits now taking place in the adjacent sea. The signs of unconformity between the two series of Jurassic deposits, which we have pointed out in this memoir, need not awaken greater surprise among geologists than the proofs of considerable disturbance and denudation which are so frequently found in deposits of Pliocene age, and the unconformity which. must necessarily exist between these rocks and such as are now in course of formation.

Changes in the Lias strata.   When we trace the beds of the Lias northwards, we find them to undergo changes in mineralogical composition and thickness, not less considerable in degree nor less striking in character than those which we have described as occurring in the case of the Lower Oolites. Unfortunately, however, owing to the paucity of sections in the argillaceous strata of the former series and the extent to which they are covered with drift, it is found to be much more difficult, than in the case of the latter, to trace the variations which take place in the beds representing its several zones.

Rhætic beds.   The junction of the Lias and Keuper is almost everywhere concealed by drift; but, wherever an opportunity of observing it occurs, the Rhætic beds are seen. They appear to exhibit, almost everywhere, very similar mineral characters, but to vary very greatly in thickness; and although there are such considerable areas in the Midland district, within the limits of which they have not yet been detected, yet, as no section has been observed in which they are undoubtedly absent, we may for the present conclude that their outcrop is continuous across England. I am familiar with a number of exposures of the Rhætic beds in North,

Mid-, and South Lincolnshire and also in Nottinghamshire; but to the southwards they have only been detected in outliers until we come to Warwickshire.

The two series of " Fish and Insect Beds," at the base of the *"Fish and* Lower and Upper Lias respectively, first detected, and since so *Insect Beds."* admirably illustrated, by the Rev. P. B. Brodie, appear to stretch continuously from the south-east of England quite into Yorkshire; and everywhere these strata yield, in greater or less abundance, their characteristic and remarkably interesting fossils.

The fine-grained argillaceous limestones, constituting the Zone of Ammonites planorbis, with the accompanying Oyster-beds, also appear to be continuous throughout the Midland district, and are present in South Yorkshire. They are worked at many points for burning into hydraulic lime; and, in the sections exposed, the beds, while preserving great constancy in mineralogical character, are seen to present considerable variation in their order of succession and thickness.

The interesting strata of the Zone of Ammonites angulatus are still more variable in character. At Barrow-on-Soar this division of the Lias is represented by only 12 feet of blue clays, with Ammonites and other fossils preserved in pyrites. Northwards it increases greatly in thickness, and beds of stone containing numerous fossils are found alternating with the clays. In Mid-Lincolnshire the beds representing this zone are of great thickness, and at one point have yielded Mr. R. Tate [*] a very interesting series of characteristic fossils. In North Lincolnshire I have traced the beds gradually diminishing in thickness, and in South Yorkshire they are, like all the divisions of the Jurassic series, reduced to comparatively insignificant proportions. Their characters and fossils in this district have been described by the Rev. J. Blake.[†]

As noticed by Professor Phillips, the great series of alternating limestones and clays constituting the " Lima-" or " Bucklandi-beds " of palæontologists are generally very feebly represented in the Midland districts; beds of clay, often of insignificant thickness, with scattered shells of *Gryphæa arcuata,* Lam. (*G. incurva,* Sow.), in this district take the place of the great oyster-banks made up of shells of that species which occur in the South of England. Passing northwards into Lincolnshire we find the normal condition of these beds reappearing and the series gradually increasing in thickness, till in the northern part of the county we observe in the Froddingham Cutting of the Manchester, Sheffield, and Lincoln-

---

[*] Quart. Journ. Geol. Soc., Vol. xxiii. (1867), p. 305.

[†] Quart. Journ. Geol. Soc., Vol. xxviii. (1872), p. 133.

shire Railway one of the finest illustrations of the typical characters presented by the beds on this horizon. Here we see a thickness of probably not less than 600 feet of alternating limestones and shales, yielding in the greatest abundance the characteristic fossils of the Zone of Ammonites Bucklandi. Still farther northwards, in South Yorkshire, these beds thin away, and within a remarkably short distance are reduced to the most insignificant proportions.

Zone of Ammonites semicostatus.

The upper part of the great series just noticed was separated by Dr. Oppel as a sub-zone, under the name of the Zone of Ammonites geometricus, and the study of the Lias of the Midland district demonstrates what good grounds exist for this distinction. The *Ammonites geometricus* of Dr. Oppel is quite distinct from Phillips' species of that name, which is the *Ammonites spinatus* of Bruguiére ; Oppel's species on the other hand appears to be identical with that known in this country as the *Ammonites semicostatus* of Young and Bird, and is so accepted by Dumortier and other palæontologists. In the South of England and at certain points in the South Midland district there are to be found sections in which a *rudiment* of this zone may be traced ; but it is not until we reach the neighbourhood of Grantham that it acquires any important development. In the country about Redmile, Barkston, and Plungar beds of slightly ferruginous stone, which make a distinctly marked escarpment rising above the Lias plains, and have been very constantly mistaken for the Marlstone Rock-bed, clearly belong to the Zone of Ammonites semicostatus, and have yielded a very interesting fauna. The succession of beds here is illustrated in the accompanying diagrammatic section (Fig. 4). The fossils collected from the beds of the Zone of Ammonites semicostatus are recorded in the following list :—

Fossils from the hard ferruginous beds in the Lower Lias (Zone of Ammonites semicostatus) Redmile, &c., Vale of Belvoir, Lincoln-shire.

CEPHALOPODA.

Belemnites acutus, *Mill.*
Ammonites semicostatus, *Y. & B.*
Ammonites, sp.

GASTEROPODA.

Pleurotomaria precatoria, *Desl.*
      "   princeps, *K. & D.*
Terebra sp.
Chemnitzia sp.

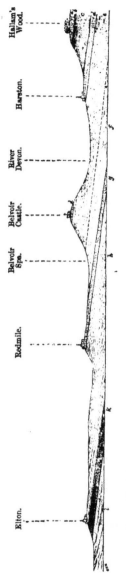

Figure 4. *Diagrammatic Section illustrating the relations of the beds of the Zone of Ammonites semicostatus of the Lower Lias, in North Leicestershire and South Lincolnshire.*

a. Lincolnshire Limestone.
b. Northampton Sand.
c. Upper Lias Clay.
d. Marlstone Rock-bed.
e. Middle Lias Sands and Clays.
f. Lower Lias Clays.
g. Ferruginous rock of the Zone of Ammonites semicostatus.
h. Lower Lias Clays, &c.
k. Rhætic or Penarth beds.
l. Red and green marls with gypsum (Keuper).

Cerithium ligaturalis, *Tate.*
,,   subfistulosa, *Tate.*
Trochus imbricatus, *Sow.*
,,   sp.
,,   sp.
Turbo sp.
Rotella expansa, *Sow.*, sp.

LAMELLIBRANCHIATA DIMYARIA.

Modiola scalprum, *Sow.* (*var.* Morrisi, *Oppel*).
,,   Hillana, *Sow.*
Cardinia gigantea, *Quenst.*, sp.
,,   copides,*de Ryck.*
,,   Listeri, *Sow.*, sp.
,,   hybrida, *Sow.*, sp.
,,   ovalis, *Stutch.*
Pleuromya unioides, *Röm.*, sp.
Unicardium cardioides, *Phil.*
Cardium sp.
Astarte sp.

LAMELLIBRANCHIATA MONOMYARIA.

Gryphæa arcuata, *Lam.*
Pecten textorius, *Schloth.*
,,   æquivalvis, *Sow.* (disparilis, ? *Quenst.*).
,,   liasianus, *Nyst.*
Lima gigantea, *Sow.*
,,   pectinoides, *Sow.*
,,   punctata, *Sow.*

ANNULOSA.

Serpula capitata, *Phil.*

BRACHIOPODA.

Terebratula punctata, ? *Sow.*
Rhynchonella variabilis, *Schloth.*

ZOANTHARIA.

Lepidophyllia Hebridensis, *Dunc.*

I have traced these beds through the county of Lincoln, and found that they acquire great thickness and importance as we follow them northwards, till in the country about Scunthorpe and

Froddingham they attain their fullest development and include beds of ironstone with a maximum thickness of 27 feet. These are of the highest commercial value and bid fair to lead to the transformation of the district of North Lincolnshire into a second Cleveland. The fauna of the Zone of Ammonites semicostatus, as developed in North Lincolnshire, is a remarkably beautiful one, being exceedingly rich in new and interesting forms, as I have seen by the inspection of the splendid collection made from these beds by the Rev. John Edward Cross, F.G.S., of Appleby. It is to be hoped that a description of this very important fauna may at no distant date be given to science.* Tracing them still farther northwards, we find the representatives of the Zone of Ammonites semicostatus thinning away as rapidly as those of the Zone of Ammonites Bucklandi on which they rest; and in South Yorkshire, though still recognisable, they are perfectly rudimentary.

The different horizons of the Lower and Middle Lias, which are *Limits of Middle Lias.* so well characterised, as shown by Quenstedt, Oppel, Wright, and other palæontologists, by particular assemblages of fossils, can be proved to exist in the Midland district of England; but the limits and the extent of the development of these zones can only be very imperfectly made out in an area, which is so greatly obscured by drift as is that referred to, and in which, therefore, the strata are only exposed in widely scattered artificial openings. Thin limestone bands, like the so-called Banbury Marble, which occur in tho midst of the thick series of clay, prove on examination to be of a merely local character, and afford us but little help in tracing the outcrops of the different zones over an extended area.

On one point, however, there exists much difference of opinion among geologists, and concerning which the course adopted by the Geological Survey may require some explanation. I allude to the question of the line of division between the Lower and Middle Lias. Of the six stages into which Quenstedt as early as 1843 divided the Lias, the members α and β have been usually grouped by German geologists as Lower Lias, γ and δ as Middle Lias, and ε and ζ as Upper Lias. On the other hand French geologists have usually carried the base of the Middle Lias much lower down, and made it to include the divisions δ and γ and a great part of β. In England, however, our Marlstone or Middle Lias series has usually been restricted to the Lias δ of Quenstedt. If the question be made one of priority, there can be little doubt that this last would be the method that ought to be adopted. If on the contrary it be made to depend on the existence of breaks in

---

the Liassic series, different answers to the question would probably be returned by geologists working in different districts,
according to the more or less complete development of the series
at their respective localities.   Mr. R. Tate has shown that in
the Cheltenham area, as in Swabia, a tabulation of the species
occurring in the several divisions of the Lias points to the existence
of a break between the Lias γ and β of that district. This would of
course incline us to adopt the classification of the German palæontologists.   But, on the other hand, when we turn to the North-
Midland district, we there find largely developed beds, apparently
intermediate between these two series, and representing probably
the Zone of Ammonites armatus, which is only reckoned as a
sub-Zone by Dr. Oppel.   These beds appear to contain many
fossils both of the Lias β and the Lias γ, and thus to link these
two series together.

It is very possible that no sharp lines of division which might
be adopted for the grouping of the beds of the Liassic series
would be found to continue satisfactory over any very considerable
areas.   This we may regard as a necessary consequence of the
fact that the breaks at any particular spot are in all probability
due to the non-development of certain zones, and that such zones
may in another locality be well represented, thus causing the break
to disappear.   We find many illustrations of this conclusion in
tracing the Liassic beds over any large district.   Even in the
case of the Upper Lias, the *planulate* Ammonites (A. communis, A.
annulatus, &c.), which appear usually to be so eminently characteristic of that division, are found in the Midland counties passing
downwards and becoming associated with a well marked Marlstone fauna.

The restriction of the Middle Lias in England to the stage δ of
Quenstedt has been to a great extent determined by the fact, that
between the periods γ and δ a more or less considerable change
evidently took place in the conditions of deposition of the beds;
and consequently over large areas a marked change in mineral
character is found to occur at this horizon, while no such change
is found between the deposits of the stages β and γ.

The limits between the clays of the Lias β and γ and that of
the sands, sandy shales, and ferruginous limestone of δ can usually
be conveniently represented in a map; while it is almost impossible
to draw a line of boundary in the midst of a series of clays of
almost uniform character like those composing the Lias and γ.
On the other hand there are not wanting good palæontological
grounds for the division of the Lias adopted in this country as
was to some extent shown, even as early as 1836, in the pioneer

work of Louis Hunton. At the top of the stage γ of Quenstedt Ammonites of the group of the *Capricorni* disappear and are replaced in the Lias δ by the remarkable forms of the *Amalthei* group; and this appearance of a considerable number of new forms, with the disappearance of others at the same horizon points to the conclusion that, in some areas at least, the line of division is a defensible one. On these grounds the lines of division of the Lias adopted by the Geological Survey, before the results of more accurate palæontological research were known, have been continued. It has been thought advisable, however, in continuing the mapping of the country to the northwards to separate by a boundary line the distinctly marked, and often economically valuable, "rock-bed" of the Marlstone, from the sands, clays, &c. below, a division not attempted in the earlier maps.

It may here be necessary to point out that a little confusion in terminology has arisen, from the name "Marlstone" being often used in two somewhat different senses in the south of England and in Yorkshire respectively. William Smith applied the name to the whole series of limestones, sands, and clays, between the thick argillaceous formations of the Upper and Lower Lias respectively; but not a few authors by the term indicate only that hard, ferruginous, and often highly fossiliferous, limestone which forms its upper member, and to which the Survey applies the name of the "Marlstone Rock-bed." On the other hand, Professor Phillips has named the Middle Lias of Yorkshire, "the Ironstone and Marlstone Series;" the representative of the "Rock-bed" of the south appearing to be his top ironstone bed, while the term Marlstone is restricted to the sandy clays at the base of the series.

The Upper Lias Clay, like all the other members of the Jurassic series, exhibits great differences in thickness as we trace it northwards through the Midland district. Attaining a thickness of nearly 300 feet in parts of the Cotteswold Hills, it rapidly diminishes as we pass northwards, till in parts of Oxfordshire it is only about 30 feet thick at its outer escarpment, while it is greatly attenuated and almost lost towards the south-east, as has already been pointed out by Mr. Hull. Still going northwards, we find it gradually increasing again in thickness, till in South Lincolnshire it is probably not less than 200 feet; and from this point it again gradually diminishes and seems to disappear altogether in South Yorkshire. Whether this attenuation of the whole formation is due to the disappearance of certain of its members, or whether all of its subdivisions are simultaneously reduced in thickness, it is not in most cases easy to determine;

The Upper Lias.

but from the constant presence at least over very great areas, of
the Fish and Insect Limestones and the Serpentinus beds at its
base, and the clay, characterised by the abundance of Ammonites
belonging to the group of the *Planulati* in its upper part, perhaps
the latter view may be regarded as the more probable.

Value of
Palæontolo-
gical " Zones."   The remarkable variations presented by the strata of the Lower
Oolite and Lias series are suggestive of a number of considerations
of great interest to the geologist, which have important bearings
alike on his theoretical researches and the practical applications
of his science.   In no group of formations do the great principles
which must guide the geologist in his studies find more fitting
illustration than in that which constitutes the Jurassic System;
for not only does it present us with a series of formations,
possessing many features of the highest intrinsic interest but it is
also that which was first systematically studied, and which has been
subsequently made the subject of the greatest amount of patient
and minute research over very considerable areas.

The importance and value of a careful study of the distinctive
faunas of the zones, into which palæontologists have shown the
Jurassic Series to be divisible, can scarcely be exaggerated; but
there are some errors on the subject, which though neither partici-
pated in nor promulgated by those who have been the founders
of this method of classification, constitute a source of danger
in geological reasoning which it may be necessary to point out.
It has been found necessary to use the name of some prominent
species in each fauna (usually an Ammonite) as the index of the
zone.   Unfortunately, some have taken it for granted that
wherever this particular species occurs, the zone which takes
its name from it may at once be assumed to be represented by the
beds containing it.   Some, indeed, have raised objections to
the whole method of classification, on the ground that they have
not realized the expectations founded on this unwarranted definition of a palæontological zone.   By the adoption of zones of life,
palæontologists simply endeavour to indicate the well ascertained
fact that in consequence of the mode of distribution of the forms of
life in a formation, certain horizons in it can be recognised—either
by the restriction of the range of certain groups of species, or by the
peculiar assemblage of these, or by their greater or less relative
abundance between certain vertical limits.   These species are not
uniformly the same over a great area ; many of the highly abundant
and most characteristic forms of one locality, indeed, becoming rare
or entirely disappearing, or being replaced by others at a different

point, while the *general assemblage* of forms, nevertheless, remains the same. Though the *zones* have a real existence, their *limits* are not usually sharply defined; and even when such is the case the cause of the break may usually be traced in the absence of beds representing the intermediate zones. The tendency of continued study over large areas is, by the detection of intermediate zones of life at particular points, to make our knowledge of the whole series more complete, and thus to render the gradation between its subdivisions more imperceptible.

It must be remembered too, that every zone may present several *facies*; the petrological and palæontological features which characterize these being dependent on the conditions under which the strata were deposited at different points. The faunas of deposits belonging to two facies of the *same* zone may differ from one another more widely than those of beds of corresponding facies of *different* zones. Thus, the ragstones of the Inferior and the Coralline Oolite, or the freestones of the Great Oolite and Inferior Oolite respectively, are found to have more species in common than the freestone and ragstone of either series. Consequently, in comparing the faunas of two sets of strata, the conditions of their deposition require to be in all cases most carefully studied and taken into account. *Facies dependent on conditions of deposition.*

As we trace a deposit over a considerable area, too, we must be prepared to find gradual changes taking place in its fauna, from the more or less limited distribution in *space* of each of the species which constitute it.*

Every fauna therefore is the resultant of three sets of causes, namely geological age, condition of sea bottom (such as depth, temperature, nature of sediment, &c.) and geographical position; and the changes which we find to take place in the grouping of species must be resolved into its elements; those which are attributable to each of these three sets of causes being carefully ascertained. Thus the determination of the age of a series of beds from the study of its fauna often becomes a most complicated and difficult problem. The laws of the succession of life forms is as much a fact for the Geologist as are the laws of planetary motion to the Astronomer; both, however, have ever to bear in mind the circumstance of the existence of perturbing causes; and these require

* No palæontologist supposes that such zones of life can be traced beyond the limits of the areas which formed the provinces of marine life of the period; but these were probably not less extensive than those of the present day. A careful study of faunas by many workers, has shown conclusively that the Jurassic strata of England, Northern France, and Western Germany were all deposited within the same life province.

to be as carefully studied and allowed for in the determinations of the one as in the calculations of the other.

In cases, like those which we have been considering, the Lower Oolites, of which many of the deposits are of such a remarkably local and peculiar character, the careful study of the conditions under which each of the beds was deposited becomes a point of the first importance ; in order that we may not refer to difference of age, that which is due to a change of the nature of the sea bottom, or *vice versâ.*

Effects of subsidence on nature of deposits. The *causes* of the phenomena of the rapid variation in the thickness and mineral characters of the sedimentary deposits on a sea-bottom, which are made so strikingly apparent by a careful study of the changes that take place in the several subdivisions, of the Jurassic rocks, were long ago pointed out by Mr. Darwin, and more fully illustrated in his recent works. Except in the case of beds formed under abysmal conditions, such as the chalk, the deposition of a considerable thickness of strata must be dependent on the continued subsidence of the sea-bed on which the accumulations are taking place. As long as deposition and subsidence keep even pace with one another, the formation of beds of uniform character goes on continuously. If the subsidence either diminishes in its rate of progress or altogether ceases, while the deposition of sediment continues as before, the depth of water will begin to decrease, and a change will take place both in the mineral character of the deposits and in the facies of their fauna. When, on the other hand, the deposition of sediment goes on more slowly than the subsidence of sea-bottom, changes of an opposite kind, both in mineral character and in the fauna of the beds, at once manifest the nature of the movement. If, however, elevation of the sea bottom take place, not only does deposition cease, but the rocks last deposited run the greatest risk of being again removed by denundation.

These considerations serve to explain the phenomena so strikingly presented by the English Jurassic rocks, and to which we have specially to allude in the present memoir—namely, the repeated change in the character of the beds both vertically and horizontally, the total absence of certain members of the series at many localities, and the very unequal and capricious manner in which that series is represented in all cases. Only where continued subsidence takes place, accompanied by a tolerably equal deposition of sediment, can a thick mass of strata belonging to any particular zone be found ; and during the prevalence of movements which do not comply with these conditions we shall have, either a gap in the series, the formation of a *rudimentary* deposit, or the production of a more or less complete unconformity ; the latter phenomenon resulting from the disturbance and destruction of the strata already formed, in the interval which elapses before the laying down of the newer sediments.

Of formations belonging to the first of the categories indicated above, we may perhaps point to the Oxford Clay and parts of the Lias Series. In these, very favourable conditions of subsidence combined with an uniform supply of sediment, appear to have given rise to a remarkably even deposition of beds. We therefore find that, within a thickness of some hundreds of feet of evidently very slowly deposited strata of fine clays, the several zones of life are all represented, and the changes take place from one to the other in the most imperceptible manner ; the several species in each of the faunas becoming more and more *rare* and finally extinct one by one, while new forms make their appearance in an equally gradual manner. The extinction and appearance of species takes place in these cases by individuals and not in groups. When especially favourable conditions of subsidence coincide with the existence of an abundant supply of sediment during the period characterised by a particular assemblage of life-forms, the zone may attain abnormally fine representation, both as regards thickness of beds and abundance of fossils. When, by deposition going on faster than subsidence, the sea bottom is raised, the fine sediment of clays passes into sands, and then, as a shallowness of water is attained favourable for the development of numerous shell bearing mollusca, into shelly limestone. When a movement of an opposite character occurs this series of changes takes place in reverse order. The former case is illustrated in the Midland district by the passage of the clays of the Lower Lias, through the sands, &c. of the Middle Lias up to the Marlstone Rock-bed ; the latter case, by the passage of the shelly Cornbrash through the sand representing the Kellaways Rock into the Oxford Clay.

The absence of the representatives of a zone, from the cessation at that particular period of the subsidence, which is necessary to the deposition of beds containing its relics, is illustrated at many points of the Midland district ; as is also the reduction of the representatives of a particular period to a rudimentary condition ; this will be seen by a glance at the series of vertical sections in Plate I.

The abnormal development of beds representing particular *Cases of the* horizons finds admirable exemplification in the cases of the Zone *Abnormal de-* of Ammonites Sowerbyi, and the Zone of Ammonites semicostatus, *velopment of* which have been fully explained in the foregoing pages. *Zones.*

Of cases of the non-representation of certain pe
production in the interval of changes giving rise
formable relation of the succeeding beds, we hav
tration in the case of the junction of the Infer:
Oolites of the district. We find that in the Mic
upper part of the Inferior Oolite period is unrepre
of rock, for there are no strata yielding the faunæ
of Ammonites Humphriesianus and Ammonites Parl
is, however, clear evidence that the period—of whi
are in other areas the relics and monuments—was,
district, marked by considerable subterranean movel
we see the effects in the peculiar relations of
estuarine beds to those which represent the low
Inferior Oolite series.

General con-
clusions.   The phenomena explained in this Introductory I
point to the fact that, during a considerable portion
period, the area now forming the county of Oxfor
far less amount of subsidence than that to the]
South-west of it respectively. The consequences of
of movement are manifested in the disappearance of
of the series, the attenuation of many others, al
characters presented by nearly all of them.

Note to page 45. Since the writing of this Introductory Essay
expressed in the text has been realized through the publication
Society of an interesting paper on the strata of North Lincolni
Rev. J. E. Cross is the author.

The new edition of the late Professor Phillips' Geology of Y
completed by Mr. Etheridge, will also contain many details illust
variations within short distances of some of the Jurassic formatio
local characters of certain of the beds which compose them.

THE GEOLOGY OF RUTLAND, WITH PARTS OF LINCOLN, LEICESTER, NORTHAMPTON, HUNTINGDON, AND CAMBRIDGE.

Figure 5. Village of Somerby, Rutland, situated in one of the deep sinuous valleys of the great escarpment formed by the Marlstone Rock-bed.

CHAPTER I.

PHYSICAL FEATURES, &c.

Sheet 64 of the Ordnance map of England embraces an area of rather more than 800 square miles. Its eastern portion includes a part of the Fenland, while its western belongs to the great table-land of the Midland counties; the intermediate tract forms a segment of the very undulating but, on the whole, gradually rising land which lies between the former and the latter. While parts of the Fen district in this map are only a few feet above the sea level, the height of the general surface in the western part is about 500 feet, and many of the hills attain to more than 700 feet. The highest point included within the sheet appears to be the Ordnance station at Tilton-on-the-Hill which is 755 feet above the level of the sea, but a number of other points as Burrow Hill Camp, Whadborough Hill, Colborough Hill, Robin-a-Tiptoes, Ram Head, Cold Overton, and Neville Holt, attain to scarcely inferior elevations.

Owing to the greatly increased thickness of several members of the Lias and Oolite, the escarpments in this area are considerably higher than in the Oolitic districts immediately to the south-west, namely central and south Northamptonshire and Oxfordshire; indeed the country included in the western part of this sheet and that immediately to the north presents features almost comparable for boldness with those of the Cotteswold Hills. The thickness of the Upper Lias Clay, which reaches 200 feet, the important character locally assumed by the Marlstone Rock-bed, and the appearance of a great mass of limestone of Inferior Oolite age, principally contribute to this result. See Plate IV. p. 53.

From Wilbarston northward the Inferior Oolite forms an unbroken escarpment as far as Harringworth; between this last point and Burley-on-the-Hill the escarpment is cut through by the river Welland with its tributaries the Chater and Gwash; from Burley northward to the limits of the sheet, the escarpment is again continued and indeed runs through the whole of Lincolnshire, where it is known as "the Cliff," being intersected only at two points, namely at Grantham and Lincoln, by the river Witham. To the west of the line of the Inferior Oolite escarpment the Upper and Middle Lias form a plateau gradually rising towards the north-west, and terminating in a number of bold spurs and outliers, capped by the Marlstone Rock-bed, which overlook the plains of Lower Lias. Situated upon this plateau are a number of outliers of Upper Lias, often surmounted by Inferior Oolite, some of them being of great size. East of the Inferior Oolite escarpment the country occupied by the Lower and Middle Oolites forms another plateau gradually sinking towards the east until it reaches the Fenland. This plateau, which is to a great extent covered with Boulder Clay, is intersected by the sinuous valleys of numerous streams, along the sides of which valleys the various Oolitic rocks are admirably exposed. The surface of the Fenland itself is by no means an uniform one; tracts of clay land or gravel, which were once islands, and still bear names pointing to that fact,* rise above the level of the peat, silt and warp, and constitute the sites of most of the towns and villages.

Owing to the position of this area in relation to the great mountain and hill chains and to the sea, the amount of rainfall within it is very small; indeed it is not exceeded in dryness by any other district in England.

The drainage of the district is effected by the Nene (with its tributaries the Barford Brook, Harper's Brook, the Willow Brook and Billing Brook), the Welland (with its tributaries the Eye Brook, the Chater and the Gwash), the Glen and the Witham (which last rises in the northern part of the sheet). All of these flow into the Wash. A small tract in the north-west is drained by the River Eye, which flows by the Wreak, the Soar, and the Trent into the Humber.

An examination of the district by the aid of the geological map will show how completely the contours and scenery have been

---

* Such as Eye, Whittlesey, Ramsey, Thorney, Ely, Estrea, Manea, &c.

determined by the presence of beds of different degrees of hardness, and of varying susceptibility to denuding forces. It will also illustrate in a striking manner how the sites of all the towns and villages, and the general distribution of the population, have been determined by the outcrops of water-bearing beds.

In ancient times the Fen district of this area consisted of almost impassable marshes and meres, which yielded little besides fish and wild fowl. The high table-lands of Boulder Clay also were formerly covered by extensive woods; Rockingham Forest alone occupying the whole of the centre of this sheet. Now, however, the Fens are completely drained, their lakes have disappeared, and a large part of the Fenland is now unrivalled for the wonderful crops which it produces: on the other hand, the forests of the high lands have been almost wholly cleared, and the heavy clay soils on which they grew now constitute, when sufficiently drained, very valuable corn land, continually increasing areas of which are being brought under the plough. The western portion of this sheet, which is occupied by Lias clays usually covered with drift, still remains for the most part as pasture land, and constitutes a portion of the most celebrated hunting district in England.

Within the limits of this map heaths and waste lands have now almost disappeared.

In former times the district was celebrated for the manufacture of iron, and traces of the old workings in the form of slag heaps abound; but, as the wood became less abundant and the method of smelting iron with coal was introduced, this manufacture gradually forsook the district. Of late years iron-ore has begun to be dug rather extensively in the south-western part of the area, and the erection of iron-furnaces commenced. The district has always been celebrated for the beautiful building-stones yielded by its various limestone and the other strata, the several clay beds have been used for brick-making, and occasionally for the production of finer and more ornamental materials. The peat of the Fenland is still extensively dug and used locally for fuel. The occupations of the inhabitants of this district are, however, still mainly agricultural.

The rocks which form the area included in Sheet 64 fall naturally into two groups, which are of widely different age, the Jurassic and the Post-Tertiary.

The Jurassic rocks form regular strata which have all a general, though very slight, dip towards the south-east. In consequence of this dip some of the oldest beds of the series, as the Marlstone Rock-bed, form the highest ground in the western part of the area, while the younger beds of the series, as the Oxford Clay, occupy the low ground of the Fens. But although the *general* dip of these beds is thus seen to be towards the south-east, they are nevertheless sometimes found to be locally inclined in various directions, while occasionally they are even bent and contorted and not unfrequently thrown far from their proper position by great dislocations or " faults."

Between the periods of the deposition of the Jurassic and the Post-Tertiary rocks there is evidence of the lapse of an enormous interval of time, during which the older series of beds was upheaved, bent, faulted and extensively denuded.

In this vast interval the whole of the Cretaceous and Tertiary beds, which are not represented in this area, were deposited. The Post-Tertiary deposits, which are usually of a much more local and inconstant character than the Jurassic strata, lie indifferently on the eroded surfaces of the latter, and are often to a great extent made up of their detritus.

The following table exhibits the several formations which occur within the area included in this sheet, arranged as far as possible in chronological order.

POST-TERTIARY.

POST-GLACIAL.	Marine Alluvium or warp of the Fenland.
	Alluvium of present rivers.
	Alluvium of old fen lakes.
	Peat interstratified with marine silt.
	Marine gravels of the Fenland.
	Estuarine gravels.
	Low-level valley gravels.
	High-level valley gravels.
	Cave deposits.
GLACIAL.	Glacial or Boulder Clay.
	Gravels.
	Sands.
PRE-GLACIAL?	Pebbly gravels and sands.
	Brick-earths.
	River gravels.
	Lacustrine deposits.

JURASSIC.

MIDDLE OOLITES.—Oxford Clay with Kellaways sands and sandstone at its base.

LOWER OOLITES.	Great Oolite.	Cornbrash.
		Great Oolite Clays.
		Great Oolite Limestones (Upper Zone).
		Upper Estuarine Series.
	Inferior Oolite.	Lincolnshire Oolite Limestone with Collyweston Slate.
		Northampton Sand with Lower Estuarine Series.
LIAS.		Upper Lias Clay.
		Marlstone Rock-bed.
		„ Clays, ironstones, sands, &c.
		Lower Lias Clays.
		„ „ Limestones and Shales.

CHAPTER II.
THE LIAS.

In the district we are describing the Lias formation is very fully developed, and attains a thickness of probably not less than 800 feet. Consisting, however, almost entirely of clays it has been very extensively denuded, both before and since the deposition of the glacial series, and its beds are to a great extent concealed by the masses of drift which lie upon them. The Rock-bed of the Marlstone has, however, owing to its superior hardness resisted denudation to a greater extent than the rest of the formation, and everywhere forms a bold escarpment, constituting indeed some of the highest points in the district; other hard beds in the Lias, even when only a few inches in thickness, frequently give rise to perceptible features in the contour of the country.

The great mass of the Lias appears to have been deposited under moderately deep-water conditions, but the two series of finely laminated shales and limestones, which occur at the base of the Upper and Lower Lias respectively, and are crowded with the remains of plants, saurians, fish, crustaceans and insects, exhibit evidence of the alternation of very shallow water, if not of estuarine, conditions. That the deposition of the Lias occupied a period of vast duration there can be no question; although a few species might be cited which are found passing from the bottom to the top of the Lias, and even recurring in the overlying Oolites, yet the great majority of the forms have undergone very striking changes within the period. During the Lias epoch certain genera make their first appearance, and others die out, while the entire range of a few (such as *Cardinia* and *Hippopodium*) is included within its limits; in some groups too, as the Cephalopoda, the species have been almost wholly replaced several times over during the Lias period. Of great and sudden breaks in the succession of life, the Lias exhibits but little evidence; the transition from one fauna to another appears to have been in almost every instance a gradual one, the several species disappearing individually and not in groups.

THE LOWER LIAS.

Nearly the whole thickness of this division, including representatives of most of the palæontological zones into which it has been divided, occur within the limits of Sheet 64. We do not, however, find any sections which exhibit the actual base of the Lias, and its junction with the Rhætic or Penarth beds; as, however, these latter appear in the district immediately to the north, it is possible that, if the necessary sections existed, they would be found just beyond the area included within the north-western corner of the Sheet; the beds directly above them in the series being present there as will be shown in the sequel. The Rhætic beds of the district consist of highly pyritous black shales crowded with *Avicula contorta*, Portl. *Cardium Rhæticum*, Mer., *Axinus cloacinus*, Quenst., &c., alternating with fissile sandy beds. These strata, good sections of which are rarely seen, rest directly upon the red and green gypsiferous marls of the Keuper, so extensively developed in the country to the westward.

Although occupying a considerable area the beds of the Lower Lias rarely appear at the surface, for they are to a great extent covered with drift, while the exposures of the several members of the formation are few and insignificant, being restricted to occasional brickyards, with some railway-cuttings, and temporary field-drains. By far the best illustration of the succession of its beds is afforded by the cuttings on the Syston and Peterboro' Railway between Kirby and Whissendine; unfortunately, however, these were not studied when first opened, and, as they are now turfed up, we are dependent for information as to the beds and fossils on the exposures caused by occasional slips, and the opening of field-drains, holes for telegraph-posts, &c.

a. " Fish and Insect Limestones."* — Traces of these beds are found in the railway-cutting at Kirby, which is just beyond the limits of Sheet 64. They consist of a number of finely laminated and much jointed beds of argillaceous limestone of a blue colour, but weathering nearly white when near the surface, and alternating with thicker beds of laminated shale. They abound with the remains, often very beautifully preserved, of fish, crustaceans, saurians, plants, and sometimes insects, and are very extensively dug (as at Granby and Barrow-on-Soar, in adjoining sheets of the map), for the manufacture of hydraulic cement.

b. Above the last are coarser grained, sometimes shelly, limestones, alternating with shale; the number and thickness of these courses of limestone and shale being very variable. They are very imperfectly seen in a railway-cutting at Sysonby. These beds are characterised by the abundance of varieties of a species of *Ammonite* known by the names of *A. planorbis*, Sow., and *A. Johnstoni*, Sow. Some of these acquire a well marked keel and an approach to lateral furrows, and thus approximate to *Am. Conybeari*, Sow. This appears to be the *Am. laqueus*, Quenst. and the *Am. Kridion* of some authors, but is not the form originally described under the latter name by Zieten. With the Ammonites there also occur *Nautilus striatus*, Sow., the dwarfed and ill defined form of *Gryphæa arcuata*, Lam., known as *Ostrea irregularis*, Münst., *Lima gigantea*, Sow. (which never, however, attains its full dimensions in these beds), *Lima Hermanni*, Ziet., and *Rhynchonella variabilis*, Schloth. These beds are like the last, sometimes worked for lime-burning.

· * These beds, which were first made known by the researches of the Rev. P. B. Brodie, might be appropriately called, from the locality where a section of them was first noticed, the " Strensham Series," to distinguish them from the similar beds at the base of the *Upper Lias* ; these latter might on similar grounds be distinguished as the " Dumbleton Series."

c. At Barrow-on-Soar the preceding beds are overlaid by a thick mass of clay, containing several bands of pyrites, one of which is crowded with many different varieties of *Ammonites angulatus*, Schloth. I have not been able to find any exposures of this part of the series within the limits of this map.

d. The beds of limestone and shale, the former almost made up of *Gryphæa arcuata*, Lam., *Lima gigantea*, Sow. (of great size), and *Ammonites* which make so marked a feature in Dorsetshire, North Lincolnshire, and elsewhere, appear in this district, as well as in most of the Midland counties, to be represented only by blue clays with numerous scattered specimens of *Gryphæa arcuata*, Lam. and *Ammonites* of the group of the *Arietes.* These beds appear to have been reached by a deep well in Stapleford Park.

e. The bed of ferruginous limestone containing *Ammonites semicostatus*, Y. & B., *Cardinia gigantea*, Quenst., *C. Listeri*, Sow., *Gryphæa arcuata*, Lam., and other fossils, which, in the sheet immediately to the north of 64, is so well developed, making a conspicuous feature in the Vale of Belvoir, and exhibiting mineralogical characters, which have caused it to be generally mistaken for the Rock-bed of the Marlstone, appears in this district either to have wholly thinned out, or to have become much diminished in importance. It has not as yet been recognised within the limits of Sheet 64.

f. In Freeby cutting we find beds of the clay with much pyrites (producing selenite by its decomposition) and small light brown septaria. *Belemnites clavatus*, Schloth., and *Plicatula spinosa*, Sow., are abundant.

g. About this horizon is found a series of beds which, although nowhere well exposed in Sheet 64, can be well studied at many points in Lincolnshire and Leicestershire. At Loseby brickyard, which is just beyond the western limits of Sheet 64, there occurs one of the best sections of these beds with which I am acquainted, and which will be hereafter described in detail. The strata appear to consist everywhere of clays, usually very sandy, which alternate with sands, sometimes indurated into an imperfect sandstone or sandrock, like that which occurs at the base of the Oxford Clay of the district, and to be hereafter described.

At some points the beds of indurated sandy stone acquire a much greater thickness and importance than at this place. The fossils of this horizon are numerous, and include abundant specimens of the unsymmetrically developed *Ammonites*, which D'Orbigny placed in the genus *Turrilites*, with some other Cephalopods, *Cardinia hybrida*, Sow., and somewhat more rarely of specimens of a variety of *Hippopodium ponderosum*, Sow. These beds appear to represent the "Zone of Ammonites armatus" of Dr. Oppel, which in the Midland district of England attains to some importance, and appears to constitute a link between the Lias β and the Lias γ of Quenstedt; that is between the Middle and Lower Lias of most German authors. The considerations which have induced English geologists to adopt the limit of the Lias γ and the Lias *b* for the boundary of the Middle and Lower Lias have already been adverted to in the Introductory Essay.

h. In Saxby cutting there are exposed light-blue, laminated, highly pyritous shales with some thin bands of limestone, almost made up of *Pentacrinites* and small bivalve shells. They contain also small septaria, concentric balls of ironstone and pieces of jet. The same beds were exposed in a deep ditch to the south of Thorpe Langton. The most abundant fossils were *Ammonites bipunctatus*, Röm., *Plicatula spinosa*, Sow., *Inoceramus substriatus*, Goldf., *Lima acuticosta*, Goldf., *Spirifer Walcotti*, Sow., *Rhynchonella variabilis*, Schloth., and *Pentacrinus punctiferus*, Quenst.

k. At Dalby and near Staunton Wyville there are found beds with thin bands of shelly limestone, containing *Cardinia attenuata*, Stutch. sp. and *Hippopodium ponderosum*, Sow.

l. In the railway-cuttings by the side of Stapleford Park, as well as in some openings in the Park itself, and about Little Dalby, there occur clays with septaria and some thin bands of indurated argillaceous sand. These beds abound with Ammonites of the groups of the *Armati* and *Capricorni*, including *Ammonites latæcosta*, Sow., *A. brevispina*, Sow., *A. Jamesoni*, Sow., *A. Normanianus*, D'Orb., *A. armatus*, Sow., &c; also *Panopæa elongata?* Röm., *Pholadomya decurata*, Hartm., *Gryphæa obliquata*, Sow., and *Pentacrinus punctiferus*, Quenst.

m. The highest beds of the Lower Lias consist of dark blue clays with much pyrites and many septaria, the latter acquiring a red colour and concentric structure by weathering, and frequently containing thin laminæ of Specular Iron. These beds abound with specimens of *Ammonites capricornis*, Schloth., and also contain, but more rarely, *Pentacrinus robustus*, Wr., and some other fossils. They are exposed in the railway-cutting at Galley Hill, and also at Neville-Holt and Little Bowden brickyards.

The Lower Lias occupies a strip of country stretching along the west of the district included in Sheet 64. This area is divided into two portions by the elevated spur of ground, composed of Middle Lias and higher beds, which form the steep escarpments about Billesdon and Tilton. The northern of these two districts of Lower Lias forms portions of the valleys of the River Eye, and its tributaries, and of the Twyford Brook; the southern constitutes parts of the valleys of the Eye Brook (a tributary of the Welland) and of the Welland itself.

Everywhere these tracts are covered by enormous masses of Boulder Clay and gravels, which not only cap the hills but are of such thickness that the existing valleys rarely cut through them so as to expose the Lias strata below. The sections of the Lower Lias in this area are, therefore, as already intimated, few in number and widely separated.

In the northern of the two areas indicated, the deep brickyards of Melton Mowbray have been thought to reach the Lower Lias clay, as many beautiful specimens of Liassic fossils have at various times been procured from them. As will, however, be shown in this Memoir the strata exposed here belong, without exception, to the drift, and the fossils obtained from them are all *derived*.

The various sections exposed along the Syston and Peterborough branch of the Midland Railway between Sysonby and Whissendine, namely, at Sysonby, Freeby, Stapleford, and Galley Hill cuttings have already been sufficiently noticed (pages 58, 59, and 60).

To the southward the Lower Lias clays with *Gryphæa arcuata*, Lam. (*G. incurva*, Sow.) have been reached in a well in Stapleford Park; and it is probable that the mineral (chalybeate) springs of Burton Lazars and Little Dalby rise from the same strata. At a part of the parish of Great Dalby a series of field-drains exposed beds belonging to the higher part of the Lower Lias. From this place I procured specimens of *Ammonites Jamesoni*, Sow., and *Hippopodium ponderosum*, Sow., *Gryphæa obliqua*, Sow., *Avicula* sp. *Belemnites*, &c. There was formerly a brickyard near this place which is to the south of Garrety Hill.

Near Little Dalby I found in several ditches on the slopes of the hills to the south-east and south-west of the Hall, evidence of the existence of the same set of beds as at Great Dalby. They consisted of somewhat sandy clays, with septaria and ferruginous nodules, which yielded *Ammonites Jamesoni*, Sow., *Gryphæa cymbium*, Lam. (*G. Maccullochii*, Sow.) and joints of *Pentacrinus*. On the other side of the village some ditches by the roadside exposed clays with thin bands of impure limestone, which yielded *Ammonites Maugenesti*, D'Orb., *Belemnites* sp., *Gryphæa obliqua*, Sow., *Plicatula spinosa*, Sow., and *Montlivaltia rugosa*, Wr. sp. Near the park were seen clays with fine specimens of *Ammonites armatus*, Sow., and at the village an excavation for a cistern exhibited 12 feet of dark blue clay belonging to the Lower Lias, but without septaria or fossils.

At the bottom of the new brickyard at the village of Whissendine blue clays forming the upper beds of the Lower Lias appear to have been reached under a considerable thickness of drift. From this locality I obtained good specimens of *Ammonites capricornus*, Schloth.

Along the banks of the River Eye, where it passes through Stapleford Park, there are a number of small exposures of the clays of the Jamesoni beds at the top of the Lower Lias. These have yielded the following interesting series of fossils.

Specimens from openings in the Lower Lias clays of Stapleford Park.

Ammonites latæcosta, *Sow.* abundant.
        ,,   brevispina, *Sow.* rare.
        ,,   capricornus, *Schloth* rare.
        ,,   Jamesoni, *Sow.* var. confusus, *Quenst.* rare.
        ,,   Jamesoni, *Sow.* var. Bronni, *Röm.* rare.
        ,,   Normanianus, *D'Orb.* rare.
        ,,   Jamesoni, *Sow.*
        ,,   polymorphus lineatus, *Quenst.*
Belemnites clavatus, *Schloth.*
      ,,   elegans, *Simps.*
Trochus sp.
Lima Hermanni, *Ziet.*
Lima acuticosta, *Schloth.*
Plicatula spinosa, *Sow.*
     ,,   lævigata ?, *D'Orb.*
Gryphæa cymbium, *Lam.*
Unicardium cardioides, *Phil.* (U. Ianthe, *D'Orb.* ?)
Cypricardia cucullata, *Goldf.* sp.
Serpula sp.
Pentacrinus punctiferus, *Quenst.*

The above, with some small openings along the sides of the Twyford and Marefield brooks, exhibiting some of the harder calcareous bands with *Pentacrinites* and fragmentary shells, are the only exposures of the Lower Lias strata in the northern area, which I was able to find during my survey of it.

At Loseby brickyard, which is a little beyond the western limits of Sheet 64, we have an interesting section of a series of strata, which, though present, are nowhere so well exposed within the area. They consist of beds of blue clay with soft septaria of a whitish colour, and some bands of ironstone balls. These clays alternate with grey sandy beds, which are sometimes indurated into a sand-rock or easily decomposing sandstone, like that of Kellaways age to be here-after described. The section is as follows :—

(1.) Beds of clay, with a few septaria and ironstone balls -   6 feet.
(2.) Band of large septaria - - - - 6 inches.
(3.) Clay - - - - - - - 3 feet.
(4.) Sandy beds indurated into stone - - - 6 inches to 1 ft.
(5.) Clay with septaria and ironstone balls - - dug to 12 feet.

The fauna of these beds is a very interesting one, namely,--

Vertebræ of .Saurians, &c.
Ammonites Loscombi, *Sow.*, sometimes very large, the specimens covered
              with attached oysters, serpulæ, &c.
    "   armatus, *Sow.*, abundant.
    "   (Turrilites) Coynarti, *D'Orb.*
          These always exhibit, but in very various degrees, the
          curious unsymmetrical character which led D'Orbigny
          to place this and similar forms in the genus *Turrilites.*
Nautilus truncatus, *Sow.*, very large.
Belemnites acutus, *Mill.*
Gryphæa cymbium, *Lam.* (G. Maccullochi, *Sow.*)
      "   obliqua, *Sow.*
Modiola scalprum, *Sow.*
Hippopodium ponderosum, *Sow.*, large rugose variety.
Avicula sp.
Lima Hermanni, *Ziet.*
Panopæa elongata, *Röm.*
Pholadomya ambigua, *Sow.*, var.?
Cardinia sp.
Pentacrinus sp.

Near Billesdon Coplow a boring for coal, which was made nearly 30 years
ago, is said to have been carried to the depth of more than 600 feet. It commenced at some distance below the bottom of the Marlstone Rock-bed, and it is
evident from the descriptions of those who watched the work that it did not
pass through the Lower Lias Clays and reach the Keuper.

The southern of the two districts occupied by the Lower Lias is almost
equally obscured by the thick overlying masses of drift. With the exception
of a few somewhat doubtful openings along the courses of the Eye Brook and
the Medbourn Brook, the only places at which the beds were seen during the
survey of the area, were the brickyards of Neville-Holt, Medbourn, Little
Bowden and Staunton-Wyvile (the last of these, however, being a little to the
west of the limits of Sheet 64), some deep ditches which were opened along
the side of the road running southwards from Thorpe-Langton, and in a road-
section and railway-cutting south of Market Harborough.

At Neville-Holt the brickyard at the foot of the hill is seen to be opened in
the beds immediately underlying the Middle Lias ferruginous rocks and clays,
which, as will be pointed out in the sequel, are here only developed to a very
limited extent. The Clays seen in the brickyard are dark-blue and pyritous,
with a few septaria and concentric ferruginous nodules : they yield *Ammonites,
capricornus,* Schloth, *Ammonites fimbriatus,* Sow., and *Nucula variabilis,* Quenst.,
and evidently belong to the top of the Lower Lias.

The brickyard at Medbourn is probably opened in the same beds, but the
clays were very imperfectly exposed during the time of the survey of the district, and I was unable to obtain any fossils from them.

At Little Bowden brickyard the same beds are beautifully exposed, being
dug under thick masses of drift; the fossils obtained here which are numerous
and well preserved are given below. The rock is a deep-blue, highly micaceous
and ferruginous clay.

         Ammonites capricornus, Schloth.
         Belemnites clavatus, Mill.
         Crenatula ventricosa, Sow.
         Modiola scalprum, Sow.
              "   *Hillana,* Sow.
         Trochus imbricatus, Sow.
         Pentacrinus basaltiformis, Mill.

At Hallaton brickyard (to be noticed hereafter) it is possible that the same
beds are reached at the bottom of the clay-pit.

Staunton Wyvile pit (which is now in part filled up) exposes the hard shelly
limestone bands crowded with *Cardinia attenuata,* Stutch, sp., and *C. hybrida,*
Sow., sp., and many other shells, including *Hippopodum ponderosum,* Sow.,
and the Ammonites of the Zone of *Ammonites Jamesoni* usually found associated

with these species; also *Belemnites clavatus*, Schloth, *Gryphœa obliqua*, Sow., *Littorina imbricata*, Sow., sp., *Pentacrinus*, &c.

These bands of limestone, although so insignificant in thickness, yet, occurring as they do in the midst of a great mass of clays, are sufficient to produce by their greater relative hardness and power of resisting denudation, a well marked feature wherever the country is sufficiently free from drift. This may be seen at several points in the southern area of the Lower Lias in this sheet; thus the ridge on which the village of Thorpe Langton is built owes its existence to the presence of these limestone bands of the Zone of *Ammonites Jamesoni*. A deep ditch south of the village afforded me an admirable exposure of these beds in the year 1867, and yielded *Ammonites bipunctatus*, Röm., *Belemnites elongatus*, Mill, *Plicatula spinosa*, Sow., *Pecten sublævis*, Phil., *Modiola*, sp., *Ostrea*, and *Pentacrinites* (very abundant).

South of Market Harborough, and in the immediate vicinity of Little Bowden brickyard, the same beds as are seen in the pit, are exposed in a roadcutting, and also by the side of the Northampton and Leicester Branch of the London and North-Western Railway.

The greater part of the valleys occupied by the drift covered Lower Lias of this area remain in the condition of pasture lands, and form the eastern extremity of the great hunting and stock-rearing district of Leicestershire.

CHAPTER III.

THE MARLSTONE OR MIDDLE LIAS.

This division, which in the northern part of the area embraced in Sheet 64 is more than 150 feet thick, but is reduced to less than half that amount in the southern part, consists of two principal members. The upper is a mass of ferruginous limestone known as the " Rock-bed," the lower a series of sandy and micaceous clays and ironstones with some beds of sand. The latter strata it is not always easy to separate from the Lower Lias Clays, and we have represented their boundary on the map by a broken line. The succession of beds in the Marlstone is as follows, beginning at the base.

a. Soft, yellowish brown, sandy and micaceous ironstone, crowded with casts of shells and alternating with light blue clays. These ferruginous bands vary very greatly in number and thickness, and are sometimes nodular. They are especially characterised by the abundance of several small varieties of *Ammonites margaritatus*, De Montf., and of *Cardium truncatum*, Sow. They are exposed in the Melton and Oakham Canal between Edmondthorpe and Whissendine station, in the hill east of Whissendine station, at Blaston, Loddington, and Deepdale.

b. Beds of blue, highly micaceous, clay, with large septaria crowded with fossils. There are at present only two brickyards in these beds within the area, namely, at Ouston, and between Whissendine and Pickwell. The most abundant species in these beds are *Ammonites margaritatus*, De Mont. (the large typical form), *Belemnites elongatus*, Mill., *Helicina expansa*, Sow., sp., *Avicula inæquivalvis*, Sow., *Mytilus hippocampus*, Y. & B., *Modiola scalprum*, Sow., (very abundant), *Cardium truncatum*, Sow., *Pleuromya unioides*, Röm., and *Pentacrinus subangularis*, Mill.

c. Beds of blue clay with septaria, the latter not unfrequently containing Specular Iron, and weathering to a red colour. They contain many of the fossils recorded from the preceding beds, but less abundantly. They are exposed in Belton, Hallaton, and Cranhoe brickyards.

d. Light blue clays, with bands of ironstone balls of concentric structure, and usually very unfossiliferous. These beds are exposed in some brickyards about Oakham, at Langham, and at Market-Harborough. At some places they contain beds of green and brown sand, as near Horninghold.

e. The " Rock-bed." This is a mass of limestone, more or less ferruginous, and occasionally passing into a good ironstone. When unweathered it is a hard crystalline rock of a blue or green colour, but as usually seen, it is brown and moderately soft. It is usually crowded with fossils, its mass being often made up of fragments of crinoids, spines of echinoderms, serpulæ, and fragments of shells, while certain beds in it (locally known to quarrymen as "jacks") consist of an agglomeration of shells of *Rhynchonella tetrahedra*, Sow., and *Terebratula punctata*, Sow., usually filled with finely crystallized calcspar. *Belemnites* (of the species *B. paxillosus*, Schloth, and *B. elongatus*, Mill., are extremely abundant in the Marlstone Rock-bed, and serve to distinguish it from the Northampton Sand, which often resembles it in mineralogical characters, but in which *Belemnites* are exceedingly rare. *Ammonites* are not abundant in the Rock-bed in this district, but at some points, as Edmondthorpe, Loddington and Horninghold, *Ammonites communis*, Sow., and *A. annulatus*, Sow., occur in considerable numbers; *A. spinatus*, Brug. and some varieties of *A. margaritatus*, De Mont. are also found in it, but much more rarely, in this district. Large specimens, of *Pecten æquivalvis*, Sow., with the highly-characteristic *P. dentatus*, Sow., also *P. sublævis*, Phil., *Hinnites abjectus*, Phil., sp., and *Avicula inæquivalvis*, Sow., are among the most abundant forms in the Rock-bed. Certain beds, especially in its lower part, contain flattened nodules or concretions of argillaceous limestone, similar to those which occur in the bottom beds of the Northampton Sand.

The Marlstone Rock-bed is very variable both in thickness and mineralogical character; it is finely developed in the neighbourhoods of Tilton-on-the-Hill and Somerby, near the former of which places it is seen to measure 18 feet 6 inches in thickness; towards the east and south, however, it attenuates very rapidly, being only 8 or 9 feet thick about Oakham, 2¼ feet at Allexton, 2 feet at Godeby and at Horninghold, and less than 1 foot between Keythorpe and Hallaton. Besides being greatly diminished in thickness the Rock-bed sometimes loses its calcareous character and becomes sandy, in these cases often resembling the other hard beds which occur lower in the Marlstone series. When the junction of the Upper Lias clay and the Marlstone Rock-bed is seen, the latter often presents the appearance of having suffered erosion before the deposition of the former. Insignificant, however, as the Rock-bed often becomes, I have obtained no certain evidence of its actual disappearance within the limits of this sheet, but in places, its presence being doubtful, it is indicated by broken lines only. Taking into account all the characters presented by the Marlstone Rock-bed, and remembering the evidence of shallow water conditions which the beds immediately lying upon it exhibit, it seems probable that an interval occurred between the deposition of the Marlstone and the Upper Lias; but when we remember the fact of the passage of certain species from one to the other, especially of the *Planulate* Ammonites, it is clear that this interval was not one of long duration.

The Rock-bed is nowhere in this area dug as an ironstone, as it certainly was in former times, and as it still is at Adderbury, King's Sutton, and Fawler in Oxfordshire. Wherever it attains a fair thickness, however, it is extensively quarried for building

purposes, for which it is well adapted; near Tilton-on-the-Hill it
is burnt into tolerably good lime.

Where the Rock-bed forms the substratum, as in the Vale of
Catmos, and on the spurs at Somerby and Tilton, the land which
is of a red colour* and highly productive, is almost everywhere
under the plough, forming a marked contrast with the districts
occupied by the clays above and below it, which almost always
remain as pasture.

In tracing the outcrop of the Middle Lias beds through the
area included in Sheet 64, no circumstance is more striking than
the remarkable variations of the beds which compose it both in
thickness and mineral character.

The line of outcrop of the Middle Lias formation is greatly
interfered with in this district by the great east and west fault,
which passes by Billesdon and Lodington and throws down the
strata on the north to the extent of several hundred feet. In
consequence of this fault the Marlstone strata appear far to the
west of their normal line, forming the great spur at Pickwell,
Somerby, and Burrow-on-the-Hill, and that of Tilton-on-the-Hill
and Billesdon. It is at this part of its course through the district
that the Marlstone Rock-bed attains its greatest thickness, and,
lying between two thick series of clays, it has formed a series of
magnificent escarpments overlooking the plains of Lower Lias.
These escarpments are diversified by deep ramifying valleys which,
surrounded by the cliff-like masses of the Rock-bed, give rise to
very picturesque scenery. See Woodcut, Fig. 5, page 53.

The great mass which, rising gradually from south-east to north-west,
culminates in Burrow or Borough Hill (crowned by a fine Roman camp) is the
most northerly of the two great spurs referred to. The strata of the Rock-
bed are exposed in a number of pits about the villages of Somerby, Pickwell, and Burrow-on-the-Hill, the stone being used for building and road-
metal.

At the west end of the village of Pickwell the Rock-bed is dug to the depth
of about 16 feet, and is seen resting on the clays below. The rock, as seen
here, is a fine, blue, crystalline limestone, and at about 6 feet from the top a bed
is seen almost wholly made up of specimens of *Terebratula punctata*, Sow., and
Rhynchonella tetrahedra, Sow. The other portions of the rock at this place
contain but few shells. Scattered through some of the beds of the rock are a
number of rounded and flattened nodules of light-coloured, compact, argillaceous
limestone, probably slightly phosphatic.

In the neighbourhood of Somerby there are some very extensive quarries
in the Rock-bed, from which fine building-stone is extracted. It is not
customary at this place to quarry the rock below the depth of about 10 or 12 feet,
only the upper weathered beds, which are of a rich brown colour and so soft
as to be easily worked, being used for building. The hard, unweathered, blue
limestone beneath is seldom dug, except for road-mending.

Between Ouston and Somerby, but nearer the latter village, there are a
number of good exposures of the Rock-bed. Here, as at many similar points,
there is evidence, along the sides of valleys cut back into the escarpment, of a

* The county of Rutland (red land) probably acquires its name from the preva-
lent colour of its soil. The greater part of the county is occupied by the Lincolnshire Oolite Limestone, the Northampton Sand, and the Marlstone Rock-bed, with
the clay slopes below them, which are coloured by their down-wash.

number of landslips having taken place, the thick, jointed strata of limestone sliding easily over the blue clays below.

The sandy and micaceous clays, sometimes passing into ferruginous sands and sandrock, which immediately underlie the Rock-bed, are seldom well exposed on this spur, and have, at the few points where they are seen in the deep roadside cuttings leading down the steep escarpments, yielded no fossils. There is only one place at which the deeper-seated, blue, micaceous clays, which yield such a beautiful fauna, are exposed, namely, the brickyard between Somerby and Ouston.

At this place we have the following section :—

   (1.) Soil.
   (2.) Light-coloured clay only partially exposed.
   (3.) Band of ironstone - - - - 6 inches.
   (4.) Blue, highly-micaceous, and pyritous clay - 3 to 4 feet.
   (5.) Blue, sandy, calcareous and highly-micaceous rock
       crowded, in places, with fossils - - 2 feet.
   (6.) Clay similar to (4), but with bands of septaria - 21 feet to
                                 bottom of the pit.

This pit has afforded a very interesting series of beautifully preserved fossils, which are enumerated in the following list :—

Fossils from the Middle Lias Clays of Ouston Brickyard.

Ammonites margaritatus, *De Montf.*, typical form, very abundant ; many
   of the specimens attaining a great size.
Ammonites Normanianus, *D'Orb.*
Belemnites elongatus, *Mill.*
Belemnites sp.
Helicina expansa, *Sow.*, sp.
Ostrea sp.
Pecten æquivalvis, *Phil.*
——— sublævis, *Phil.*
Avicula inæquivalvis, *Sow.*
Mytilus hippocampus, *Y. & B.*
——— scalprum, *Sow.* Very variable in form ; very abundant.
Cardium truncatum, *Sow.*
Pleuromya unioides, *Röm.* sp.
Pholadomya decorata, *Hartm.*
——— ambigua, *Sow.*, var. ?
Serpula sp.
Pentacrinus sp.

The southern of the two great spurs of the Marlstone rises into the high escarp-ments of Halstead, Tilton-on-the-Hill, Billesdon Coplow, and Billesdon ; and at its western extremity stretches beyond the limits of Sheet 64. As in the northern spur, the beds are well seen on the sides of the steep escarpments, and in the numerous pits opened for economic purposes.

Between Ouston and Tilton-on-the-Hill the escarpment gradually rises, and the base of the Rock-bed can be easily traced, the junction of the limestone and clay being marked, as usual, by the outflow of numerous fine springs. About Halstead and Tilton-on-the-Hill there are a number of exposures of the Rock-bed in small pits and roadside cuttings ; the beds, however, dip away gradually to the south and west, and then become covered by glacial clays and gravels. The Rock-bed is, however, well exposed in a small pit about three-quarters of a mile south-west of the village of Tilton near the head of a small stream. The steep escarpments and deep sinuous valleys of this southern spur are an exact counterpart of those of the northern one, and give rise to equally striking and pleasing scenery.

In the valley about half a mile west of Wildbore's Lodge there are several pits (situated in the lordship of Tilton-on-the Hill) at the foot of the hill called Robin-a-Tiptoes, which together furnish one of the best sections of the Rock-bed in the district. Some of the stone was here formerly dug for lime-burning, and is said to have produced a fairly good material for dressing the land; its use for this purpose is now altogether abandoned throughout this district. The following is the section exposed at this place:—

(1.) Light blue clay of the Upper Lias, with fragments of *Ammonites communis*, Sow., passing down into - - - - 1 to 2 feet seen.

(2.) Laminated,ferruginous, sandy and marly clay, forming a gradation from the Upper Lias Clay to the Middle Lias Rock-bed - 2 feet.

(3.) Hard, blue or greenish, ferruginous limestone, where weathered passing into a soft brown rubbly stone, which owes its peculiar characters probably to the removal by solution of the calcareous matter - - - 4 feet.

(4.) Bed almost made up of fragments of crinoids, serpulæ, and shells - - - 1 foot.

(5.) Beds similar to (3) - - - - 3 feet.

(6.) "First jack" almost wholly made up of shells of *Terebratula punctata*, Sow., and *Rhynchonella tetrahedra*, Sow., the interiors of which are filled with beautifully crystallized carbonate of lime - - - 6 inches.

(7.) "Building-stone," consisting of two beds of "hards" and two of "softs" - - together 6 feet.

(8.) "Second jack," similar to (6), but much thicker. This bed contains some flattened nodules or concretions, and has a parting of clay in its midst - - - 2 feet 6 inches.

(9.) Two beds of "building-stone," one "soft" and one "hard." These lower beds where dug at some depth become very hard and blue-hearted. They contain the flattened nodules or concretions - - - together 1 ft. 6 in.

Total thickness of the Marlstone Rock-bed, 18 ft. 6 in.

Probably this is nearly the maximum thickness attained by the Rock-bed in the district. The fossils which were found in the rock at this place were as follows:—

Fossils from the Marlstone Rock-bed at Robin-a-Tiptoes.

Ammonites spinatus, *Brug.* Rare.
Belemnites paxillosus, *Schloth.*} Abundant and often of large size
———— elongatus, *Mill.*} found scattered throughout the rock.
Cerithium sp.
Ostrea, small sp.
Placunopsis (attached to, and assuming the markings of a Rhynchonella).
Pecten dentatus, *Sow.* Abundant; a species very characteristic of the Marlstone Rock-bed in this district.
Pecten liasianus, *Nyst.*
———— æquivalvis, *Sow.* Very large.
Hinnites abjectus, *Phil.*, sp. Not rare.
Lima pectinoides, *Sow.*
Terebratula punctata, *Sow.*} In prodigious abundance, and exhibit-
Rhynchonella tetrahedra, *Sow.*} ing great variation in form.
Rhynchonella acuta, var. bidens, *Phil.* Very rare.
Serpula quinque-sulcatus, *Goldf.*
Pentacrinus lævis, *Mill.*
Other crinoids.
Wood. Rather abundant.

It is a remarkable fact that in this district *Rhynchonella acuta*, and all its varieties are excessively rare, while *Rhynchonella tetrahedra* is so prodigiously abundant. This is one of the numerous examples found in the Jurassic rocks illustrating the remarkably local distribution of certain forms among the Brachiopoda.

The Marlstone beds are also seen again on the north side of the fault, in the sides of the small valley to the south-east of Wildbore's Lodge.

At the east end of the village of Billesdon two brickyards, one on either side of the great coach-road from Uppingham to Leicester, furnish us with a valuable section of the strata immediately below the Rock-bed, and although the locality is just beyond the limits of Sheet 64 it will be advisable, on account of the rarity of such sections, to notice it here.

The higher beds are shown in the pit on the north side of the road; although no section of the Rock-bed is seen at this point, there can be no doubt, from the occurrence of springs, the form of the ground, etc. that this bed is in place at less than 10 feet above the top of the following section.

(1.) Laminated, light-blue clay, banded and stained by peroxide
    of iron;—some scattered ironstone balls   -   - about 10 ft.
(2.) Band of brown, cellular ironstone -   -   -   - 6 to 12 in.
(3.) Clay like (1) but darker in colour and containing scattered
    ironstone balls -   -   -   -   - 5 ft.
(4.) Band of ironstone similar to (2)   -   -   - 6 to 12 in.
(5.) Beds of dark-blue clay to bottom of section   -   - 6 to 8 ft.

The upper part of the series appears to be very destitute of fossils, with the exception of a few fragments of Belemnites. Towards its base, however, the clay (5) yields, large flat septaria, some of which decompose by exposure to the air, and assume a reddish brown colour, rapidly falling to pieces. These septaria yield numerous organic remains. The blue clays at the base are sometimes very micaceous, and the septaria contain in their fissures Specular iron, Zinc-blende and Pyrites. The pit on the south side of the road exhibits a section of about 15 feet of dark-blue clay with flat septaria containing fossils. From these two pits we learn that the succession of the Middle Lias beds here is as follows :—

(1.) Rock-bed.
(2.) Light-blue clays with bands of sandy ironstone (few
    fossils) -   -   -   -   -   - about 30 feet.
(3.) Dark-blue clay with Septaria (numerous fossils)   - 15 feet seen.

Fossils from the Billesdon brickyard.   (*Clays below the Marlstone Rock-bed.*)

Belemnites paxillosus, *Schloth.*
Ammonites margaritatus, *De Montf.*   Abundant; large, normal forms, and
                               numerous varieties.
Plicatula spinosa, *Sow.*
Lima pectinoides, *Sow.*
Pecten sublævis, *Phil.*
Modiola scalprum, *Sow.*
Goniomya sp.

As we proceed northwards, southwards and eastwards, from the two great spurs just noticed, which exhibit the Middle Lias strata in their condition of maximum development, the various members. of the formation become greatly diminished in thickness while they lose some of the well marked characters which distinguish them in the district described.

Between Pickwell and Whissendine the Rock-bed, though it still forms a well marked escarpment, is almost wholly concealed by the enormous masses of drift which cover the country. At the foot of this escarpment, however, and about midway between the two villages mentioned, at the place called Rocart on the map, a brickyard gives us an interesting section of the blue micaceous clays (Zone of *Ammonites margaritatus*) which occur at some distance below the Rock-bed. This section is as follows :—

(a.) Boulder clay, of the usual character, crowded with fragments of chalk
    and flint with a few boulders of Oolitic and other rocks. The boulders
    often exhibiting fine glacial polishing and striation. The glacial
    beds rest on an eroded surface of,—
(b.) Beds of dark-blue clay, with numerous layers of septaria, containing
    many fossils. *Cardium truncatum*, Sow., is especially abundant here,
    some of the septaria being almost wholly made up of specimens of
    that shell.

The following fossils were collected at this place :—

Fossils from the Old Whissendine brickyard at Rocart.

Ammonites margaritatus, *De Montf.* Normal form; specimens very numerous, often of large size and great beauty.
Belemnites paxillosus?, *Schloth.* Very large.
Pecten sublævis, *Phil.*
Cardium truncatum, *Sow.*
Lima pectinoides, *Sow.*
Modiola scalprum, *Sow.* Very abundant and large specimens.
Myacites (Pleuromya) unioides, *Röm.*, sp.
Terebratula punctata, *Sow.*
Rhynchonella tetrahedra, *Sow.*
Serpula sp.

In the valley south of Whissendine the Rock-bed is exposed in a number of field-drains, &c. but there are no good sections. The same rock is seen in the road-cutting at the west end of that village, and also in several small openings between it and Ashwell.

Stretching from Ashwell southwards to Oakham and Egleton we have a broad valley, the bottom of which is formed by the Marlstone Rock-bed and the sides by hills of Upper Lias, capped on the eastern side by the Lower Oolites. This is the celebrated and fertile vale of Catmos, which is traversed by a branch of the Midland Railway running between Luffenham and Melton Mowbray. Along the bottom of this valley we find many exposures of the Middle Lias formation; stone-pits and railway-cuttings furnish many opportunities for studying the Rock-bed, while the small brooks which traverse the valley cut through the platform formed by that hard stratum into the clays, &c. which lie below it.

Near Ashwell station a railway-cutting affords an excellent section of the Rock-bed. At Langham a pit which furnishes an excellent section occurs, exhibiting a representative of the Upper Lias, beneath which the Rock-bed, 9 feet thick, is seen to be underlaid by 14 feet of shaley clay without fossils, followed by a thin ferruginous band of 18 inches, also in turn underlaid by clay.

About Oakham and Barleythorpe we find a number of pits in the Rock-bed, which is dug for building-stone and also as road-metal. The calcareo-ferruginous rock is here evidently greatly reduced in thickness and probably never exceeds 6 or 8 feet. In several brickyards about the town we find tolerably good sections of the beds of clay, &c. immediately underlying the Rock-bed.

A brickyard a little north of Oakham on the road to Ashwell furnishes the following section :—

(1.) Marlstone Rock-bed at top of the pit, full of the usual fossils   -   -   -   -   - thickness not seen.
(2.) Soft, brown, sandy bed   -   -   -   - 1 foot.
(3.) Hard, shaley, micaceous clay (without fossils?) a layer of ferruginous nodules near the top, and others scattered through the mass; towards the base the clay abounds in flat nodules of iron pyrites   - about 10 feet.
(4.) Sandy, blue rock (wortbless)   -   -   - 1 ft. 6 in.
(5.) Light-blue clay, sometimes good enough for tile-making, at others full of ferruginous nodules, &c., and worthless   -   -   -   - to bottom of pit.

South of Oakham, on the road to Uppingham, another brickyard exhibits the Rock-bed and the clays lying below it, as follows :—

(1.) Marlstone Rock-bed at the top of the pit containing the usual fossils; it also exhibits numerous very hard, round and flattened concretions of ferrugino-argillaceous limestone   -   -   - thickness not seen.
(2.) Clay without fossils, containing large quantities of iron pyrites   -   -   -   - about 9 ft.
(3.) Two beds of thin and very variable, soft, sandy, ferruginous rock   -   -   -   -   - only a few inches thick.

The road from Oakham to Uppingham and the railway from the former town to Manton cross several small valleys, cut through the Rock-bed into the clays below, and there are several exposures of these beds, both there and in the brook running through the village of Egleton; these however present no features of special interest.

Northward from Ashwell the Rock-bed of the Marlstone forms a fine escarpment about the villages of Teigh, Edmondthorpe, and Wymondham. The Northampton Sand and the Marlstone Rock-bed form successive plateaux with very gradual inclinations to the south-east, while the steep slopes below on the north-west are constituted by the clays of the Upper and Middle Lias respectively.

Near Edmondthorpe the Marlstone Rock-bed is well exposed along the sides of the Oakham and Melton Mowbray Canal, and a little to the north-west of the village there is a stone-pit, which has yielded numerous fossils, including :—

> Ammonites communis, *Sow.* } not rare.
>   „   annulatus, *Sow.* }
>   „   spinatus, *Brug.* Rare.
> Belemnites paxillosus, *Schloth.*
>   „   clavatus ?, *Schloth.*
> Terebratula punctata, *Sow.*
>   „   numismalis ? *Lam.*
> Rhynchonella tetrahedra, *Sow.*

About Wymondham there are numerous openings in the Rock-bed, the positions of which are indicated on the map. As, however, they offer no characters of any novelty it is not necessary to do more in this place than to notice their existence.

Along the banks of the old canal between Edmondthorpe and Whissendine Station we find traces of the soft, brown, sandy strata, which form the real base of the Marlstone or Middle Lias series; at this place, however, the beds are not conveniently exposed for study. On the hill east of Whissendine Station there are traces of some old stone-pits, which appear to have been opened in these beds, and a ditch on the side of the hill still exposes them *in situ.* They consist of soft, earthy, light-brown ironstone full of shells; *Cardium truncatum, Sow.,* being specially abundant. These strata appear to be in every respect similar to those seen at Neville-Holt, Blaston, and other points; though composed of such soft materials they yet make a recognizable escarpment, which can often be traced for considerable distances.

North of Wymondham, though the Rock-bed escarpment still remains to guide us, there are no exposures of the stratum, and in consequence the remainder of its outcrop in Sheet 64 has been represented by broken lines.

South of the great Billesdon and Lodington fault, the Middle Lias beds appear again about the village of Lodington, where however their outcrop is much concealed by drift. At the north-western end of the village there were formerly a number of pits in the Rock-bed, but these are now all closed; within the park and on the north side of the village a pit exhibits a fair section of the same stratum, and its junction with the Upper Lias Shales. At this place the Marlstone Rock-bed yields the usual fossils, *Ammonites communis, Sow.* being by no means rare.

Between Lodington and Belton the outcrop of the Rock-bed can generally be traced by the form of the ground, though there is but one exposure of it on the hill sides. At the latter village a brickyard, now abandoned, was opened in the beds below the Rock-bed, and on the same horizon as the brickyards at Billesdon. Although the Belton brickyard is now closed, heaps of the septaria obtained from the clay pit may still be seen; these are changed by exposure, to a dark red colour, and are so decomposed that they fall to pieces with a slight blow from the hammer. From these septaria I collected the following fossils :

> Ammonites margaritatus, *De Montf.* Several varieties and of all sizes.
> Pleurotomaria Quenstedti, *Goldf.*
> Myacites or Panopœa (fine specimen).
> Leda complanata, *Phil.*

Cardium truncatum, *Sow.* (in masses).
Pecten demissus, *Phil.*
　　,,　　æquivalvis, *Sow.*
Lima pectinoides, *Sow.*
　　,,　　sp.
Plicatula spinosa, *Sow.*
Avicula inæquivalvis, *Sow.*
Rhynchonella tetrahedra, *Sow.* (one specimen).

The deep, winding, branching, and picturesque little valleys which lie on either side of the spur, capped by Inferior Oolite, overlooking Wardley, reveal on either side, in their steep and scarped slopes, many indications of the presence and some good sections of the Marlstone Rock-bed. The valley to the north-west, known as Bushy Dales, exhibits the junction of the Marlstone with the overlying Upper Lias; in the south-eastern or Deepdale we can trace below the Rock-bed, in the sides of the stream, the blue clays, sandy beds, impure ferruginous bands, and courses of argillaceous nodules of the lower part of the Marlstone.

Along the south bank of the Eye Brook there are but few exposures of the Middle Lias. At Allexton is a pit passing through the base of the Upper Lias into the Rock-bed, the details of which section will be given hereafter. Near the great coach road at the village of East Norton there are several small and unimportant exposures of the Marlstone, but about the village of Tugby it can generally be traced only by the form of the ground.

At Godeby the Marlstone Rock-bed can be seen in some ditches on the spurs above the village. The remarkable manner in which the stratum is here reduced to only a foot or two in thickness, while it has at the same time almost wholly lost its calcareous character and its hardness, is very striking; especially when we remember that the locality is only about four miles distant from that of Robin-a-Tiptoes, where, as we have seen, the rock attains its maximum dimensions. But insignificant as the rock has become, it has still been able to resist denuding forces to a much greater extent than the clays above and below it, and consequently forms a well marked and very conspicuous escarpment. At Cross Barrow Hill between Gloostone and Cranhoe, the Rock-bed is still very thin but harder and more calcareous than at Godeby; it is here dug, under seven or eight feet of boulder clay, for road metal, the shallow pits being filled up again as soon as the stone is taken out. At this place a considerable number of fossils, of the usual species found in the rock, were collected. Above the village of Cranhoe the Rock-bed is exposed at a few points of the steep escarpment.

Along the whole of their outcrop from Deepdale to beyond Cranhoe the lower beds of the Middle Lias series are almost wholly unknown, owing to the prevalence of drift at the lower levels at which they are developed. But at Cranhoe brickyard we have an interesting exposure of these beds, consisting of light-blue, stratified clays, with layers of concentric balls of ironstone which fall to pieces on exposure to the air. These nodules contain numerous but imperfectly preserved fossils, and it is evident that the beds which contain them are near the junction of the Middle and Lower Lias; the species collected here were as follows :—

Fossils from Cranhoe brickyard (base of the Middle Lias series).
Belemnites sp.
Ammonites Henleyi, *Sow.*
　　,,　　sp. indet.
Pecten liasianus, *Nyst.*, sp.
　　,,　　æquivalvis, *Phil.*
Avicula inæquivalvis, *Sow.*
Lima pectinoides, *Sow.*
Cardium truncatum, *Sow.*
Leda complanata, *Phil.*
Cucullæa sp.
Crenatula ventricosa (?), *Sow.*
Pentacrinus sp.

Some of the nodules here contain Specular Iron.

The same beds are seen in the Cranhoe brickyard; they appear also in the western slope of Cross Barrow Hill and on an adjoining eminence, where they were exposed in field drains.

The series of narrow and sinuous valleys cut by the Hallaton Brook and its numerous tributaries exhibit the escarpment formed by the Rock-bed running round the flanks of the hills which bound them; but there are few good exposures of the Middle Lias beds.

Near the bridle-road leading from Keythorpe to Hallaton, and at the point where it crosses the brook, some old pits exhibit the following section:—

Upper Lias.—(1.) Laminated shales with traces of the "fish and insect beds" at the top - - 5 to 6 feet.

Middle Lias.—(2.) Marlstone Rock-bed with usual characters containing numerous Belemnites, Ammonites annulatus, Terebratula punctata, &c. As is often the case with this rock. it here contains numerous rounded pebbles or concretions - - - 1 ft. seen.

(3.) Light-blue clays passing down into.

(4.) Clays with bands and layers of nodules of ferruginous and micaceous rock.

The irregular mode of recurrence of the diminutive representative of the Marlstone Rock-bed is illustrated in the following sketch of a section seen at this point (Fig. 6).

Figure 6. Section exhibited in a pit between Keythorp and Hallaton (Leicestershire.)

a. Soil, &c.

Upper Lias { b. Nodular limestones of the Fish and Insect limestones.
{ c. Clays.

Middle Lias { d. Marlstone Rock-bed.
{ e. Clays, &c.

Along the sides of the valley near this spot there are numerous traces of old pits which have been opened in the Rock-bed, and the same formation is again seen near the entrance to the village of Hallaton.

74 GEOLOGY OF RUTLAND, &C.

At Hallaton brickyard we find nodular ferruginous beds alternating with blue, micaceous, sandy clays, which yield the following fossils:—

Ammonites margaritatus, *De Montf.*.varieties.
Avicula inæquivalvis, *Sow.*
    „   sp.
Pecten liasianus, *Nyst.*
    „   sp.
Cardium truncatum, *Sow.*

Below these beds dark-blue clays, with many fossils, were formerly dug.

Near Hallaton Ferns the Marlstone Rock-bed, with the overlying Upper Lias shales, were exposed in a series of field drains along the side of the brook. *See* page 83.

Just above Horninghold, on the road to Hallaton, the Rock-bed is seen as a thin band of brown, micaceous, sandy stone, full of casts of fossils including—

Ammonites annulatus, *Sow.*
Rhynchonella tetrahedra, *Sow.*

Below are light-blue clays, in places full of thin ferruginous bands. Traces of the same sandy and ferruginous beds are seen in the banks of several brooks in the neighbourhood, and were also exposed in some field-drains about the village.

By the side of the brook at Blaston St. Michael's, and near the road leading to Stockerston, we find the beds representing the bottom of the Middle Lias series. These consist of a soft, ferruginous and micaceous sandstone full of casts of fossils, including—

Cardium truncatum, *Sow.*
Avicula novemcostæ, *Brown.*
Nucula sp., &c.

Near to the same village we find traces of sandy, ferruginous beds similar to those representing the Marlstone Rock-bed at Neville-Holt, and underlaid as at that place by light-blue clays containing ironstone balls.

Near Medbourn the lowest calcareous and nodular beds of the Upper Lias (the " Serpentinus Beds," &c.) are of a ferruginous character, and, but for the highly characteristic fossils which they yield, might be mistaken for the Marlstone Rock-bed. The latter is represented in a very attenuated form by a bed of ferruginous sandy rock with few fossils; it is underlaid by clays more or less sandy, with bands of concentric, ferruginous nodules.

At the foot of the Hill on which the Neville-Holt ironworks were opened we find, in a cutting made for the railway incline, the " Serpentinus-Beds " and the " Fish and Insect Beds " of the Upper Lias underlaid by the Middle Lias series, which is here constituted as follows :—

(1.) Irregular beds of micaceous and ferruginous, sandy rock full of casts of shells. These form two or three beds of stone, which are in places more or less calcareous. They do not, however, present the characteristic features of the Rock-bed, but are always of a more or less nodular character. They contain *Belemnites*, usually grouped together in considerable numbers in certain parts of the rock, and also a few rounded pebbles or concretions like those of the Rock-bed. The species of fossils found in these bands were as follows :—

Pecten liasianus, *Nyst.* (large, 5 inches in diameter).
Avicula novemcostæ, *Brown* (A. æquivalvis, *Sow.* var.).
Cardium truncatum, *Sow.*
Leda complanata, *Phil.*

(2.) Light-coloured clays containing bands of ironstone nodules. These are of considerable thickness.

(3.) The lowest beds seen at this point are exposed in the brickyard below, and consist of blue, micaceous clay, containing flattened nodules of clay-ironstone with a few fossils :—

Belemnites (fragments).
Ammonites capricornus, *Schloth.*
Leda complanata, *Phil.*
Cardium truncatum, *Sow.*
Ostrea sp.
Wood.

It may be considered by some as open to question whether, at this and some other points, the Marlstone Rock-bed has not been wholly removed by denudation before the deposition of the Upper Lias Clay. The more probable opinion, and that which has been adopted by the Survey, is that the Marlstone Rock-bed is represented in a greatly attenuated and rudimentary condition by the nodular bands which occur at the top of the Middle Lias Series. Indeed, at some points there occurs a transition from the irregular and inconstant nodular bands to a well defined rock-bed presenting the characteristic features, both lithological and palæontological, of the highest member of the Middle Lias.

Near Ashley, on the road to Wilbarston, the Rock-bed of the Marlstone is clearly exposed, and is seen to consist of several beds of stone, sometimes of a decidedly calcareous character, and containing the peculiar flattened nodules. These beds are interstratified with clays ; they are underlaid by a thick series of shales and covered by the beds containing the "Fish and Insect Limestones " of the Upper Lias. At several other points near the same village the beds at the junction of the Middle and Upper Lias are more or less distinctly seen, and the Rock-bed is of sufficient importance to-give rise to a very distinct feature in the contour of the country. The same rock, with precisely similar characters, is seen about the village of Ashley, especially in a cutting beside the road leading to Stoke Albany. Between East Carlton and Ashley beds of sandy, brown clay were exposed in field drains ; these yielded a specimen of *Ammonites margaritatus*, De Montf.

About the village of Sutton Basset beds of light brown, sandy stone occur, which must probably be regarded as the representative of the Marlstone Rock-bed, though they have yielded but few of its characteristic fossils.

The lower beds of the above section were seen in a well, the higher beds in the pits of the brickyard.

In another brickyard, lying to the north of the last, we find the following section :—

(1.) Soil and Boulder Clay   -   -   -   -   - 3 feet.
(2.) Upper Lias Clay   -   -   -   -   -   - 2 feet.
(3.) Rock-bed of the Marlstone (as in last pit)   -   -   - 4 feet.
(4.) Brown Clay, containing nodules of ironstone   -   - 3 feet.
(5.) " Skerry," a thin band of ferruginous, micaceous rock,
        crowded with fossils   -   -   -   -   - 6 inches.
(6.) Laminated, light-blue clay containing much mica, weathering
        brown near the joint planes   -   -   -   - 8 feet.
(7.) A thin band similar to (5).

In another pit to the north of this the bed (7) is found to be underlaid by about 7 or 8 feet of clay, and this in turn by a continuous bed of stone.

At Little Bowden brickyard, which is probably not much below the level of these pits, we find the micaceous clays of the Capricornus-beds forming the top of the Lower Lias series. These have been already noticed. It is clear from the sections about Market Harborough that the whole Middle Lias is there very thin and its several beds of a somewhat inconstant character.

Southwards from Harborough, the outcrop of the Middle Lias beds is almost wholly obscured by drift, until we come to the Oxendon Magna tunnel on the Northampton and Market Harborough Branch of the London and North-Western Railway. In this tunnel and the cuttings near it the Marlstone Rock-bed, with its characteristic fossils, was exposed. It is remarkable, considering the insignificant character of its beds, how bold an escarpment is formed by the Middle Lias in the country immediately to the west, namely, the ridge on which stands the villages of East Farndon, Clipston, Sibbertoft, &c.

Behind Dingley Lodge is a pit showing the "Serpentinus-beds," and a trace of the " Fish and Insect Limestones " of the Upper Lias, lying upon the Rock-bed of the Marlstone, which is here distinctly calcareous and contains the usual fossils.

About Market Harborough and Great and Little Bowden the Middle Lias is seen in a very attenuated condition, as already noticed, and is exposed to observation in some very interesting sections. In the brickyard opposite to the railway station, under the lower beds of the Upper Lias (which are here, as at many points in the Midland district, sandy and ferruginous, and might easily, if regard were not paid to the fossils, be mistaken for the Middle Lias), we find the following beds, underlying those noticed on page 87.

(10.) Rock-bed (?) consisting of a laminated, ferruginous sandstone, containing much mica; with

      Ammonites margaritatus, *De Montf.* (several varieties).
      Belemnites paxillosus, *Schloth.*
      Cardium truncatum, *Sow.*
      Lima sp.
      Avicula novemcostæ, *Brown.*

(11.) Brown clay - - - - - - 2 to 3 feet.

(12.) " Skerry " or " Kale," with nodules, containing—
      Cardium truncatum, *Sow.*
      Lima sp.
      Avicula cygnipes, *Phil.*

(13.) Brown Clay - - - - - - 2 ft. 6 in.
(14.) Blue Clay - - - - - - 7 to 9 ft.
(15.) " Skerry " (brown sandy stone) - - - - 1 ft. 6 in.
(16.) Brown Clay - - - - - - 2 to 3 feet.
(17.) Rock in which an abundance of water was obtained, and
      which prevented further sinking - - dug to the depth of 2 feet.

Inliers.—South of the Vale of Catmos, two long narrow inliers of the Middle Lias strata are exposed, in consequence of the rivers Chater and Gwash having cut their valleys down through the Boulder Clay and Upper Lias, which form the high plateau in that part of the district. In these inliers the Marlstone Rock-bed is found cropping out, like a ledge near the sides of the valleys, or sometimes forming tolerably level floors at their bottoms. Where the Rock-bed is cut through, the underlying clays, sands, &c. of the Middle Lias are occasionally exposed in the river banks.

Along the valley of the Gwash at the village of Braunston, and from that village eastwards towards Brook and westwards towards Knossington, as also along the valley of the small tributary which the stream receives from the north, the Middle Lias beds are exposed at a number of points. The Rock-bed has been dug south of Flitteris Park, and a large pit opposite to Brook Hall shows the formation with its usual characters and fossils. The outcrop of the hard calcareous rock makes a very distinct feature in this valley, and below it, in artificial openings at the village of Braunston and in the river banks at some other points, I saw traces of the underlying beds of the Middle Lias series presenting their usual characters.

The River Chater, at Laund Abbey and in the valley westward and eastward for a total length of about four miles, has similarly denuded away the Boulder-Clay and Upper Lias covering, and exposed the beds of the Middle Lias below. On both sides of the stream below Laund Abbey we have a tolerably good section exposed of the calcareous and somewhat shelly Rock-bed, which is here of moderate thickness, and of the light-coloured clays with ironstone balls and the ferruginous, sandy beds which underlie it. Near Coles' Lodge there is a pit in the Marlstone Rock-bed; the stone is here full of the usual fossils, and contains bands ("jacks") almost wholly made up of specimens of *Rhynchonella tetrahedra*, Sow., and *Terebratula punctata*, Sow., all filled with calcspar. In the deep lateral valleys west of Withcote Lodge, and between Coles' Lodge and Swinthley Lodge, other pits in the same bed have been opened; also to the eastward, on the opposite side of the valley to Leighfield Lodge, where a tolerably good section of the Rock-bed was at one time exposed. Near the sources of the River Chater and at the foot of Whadborough Hill and Robin-a-Tiptoes, temporary openings yielded other good sections of the Rockbed which is found to thicken rapidly towards the west.

Outliers.—The outliers of the Middle Lias in the district are small and of comparatively little importance. They constitute two

BILLING & CHELTENHAM SOUTH

LAWTON HILL. LEICESTERSHIRE.

From the original drawing... in the... of the late John by C. STANFIELD. ....

hills in the south-west corner of Sheet 64, one of which is crowned by Slawston Windmill, while the other was formerly the site of the Staunton Wyvile Mill. In both cases the upper portions of the hill are formed of beds higher in the geological series than the Middle Lias; in the former case of the Upper Lias Clay with a very thin capping of the Northampton Sand, in the latter of the lower beds only of the Upper Lias. In each case the hard beds at the top of the Middle Lias Series give rise to a very marked feature in the contours of these hills, namely a flat ledge and steep declivity intervening between the gradual slopes formed by the Upper and Lower Lias Clays respectively. (Plate V.)

The Hallaton Brook separates the outlier of Slawston Hill from the main mass of the Middle Lias. Near Medbourne Mill the thin beds of Marlstone Rock-bed were exposed in some road-cuttings; above them were well seen the " Serpentinus-beds " and the " Fish and Insect beds " of the Upper Lias; below them, ferruginous, sandy, micaceous shales with layers of concentric nodules of ironstone. The Marlstone Rock-bed is here constituted by several layers of soft, brown, sandy, micaceous, and ferruginous rock, each layer being about one foot thick, interstratified with light-blue, micaceous clays; the stone bands contain *Avicula novemcostæ*, Brown, and *Leda complanata*, Phil. sp. Owing to the small quantity of calcareous material in it, the Rock-bed here does not present its usual characters, but more nearly resembles some of the bands usually found lower down in the Middle Lias Series. In the road east of Slawston Mill a number of ditch-cuttings show the succession of beds to be as follows:—

    (1.) Clays.
    (2.) Ferruginous beds with *Ammonites serpentinus*, Rein.
    (3.) Clays with nodules of the Fish and Insect limestone.
    (4.) Brown, sandy, ferruginous beds with but very little calcareous
        matter. Casts of shells.
        Cardium truncatum, Sow.
        Leda complanata, Phil., sp.
        (This is here a very inconspicuous bed and does not at all
          resemble the Rock-bed in its normal aspect.)
    (5.) Whitish clays with nodules of ironstone.

On the south side of the same hill we have a good exposure of the beds forming the Middle Lias and the base of the Upper Lias. The surface of some of the fields here is literally strewn with fragments of *Ammonites serpentinus*, Rein., *Ammonites falcifer*, Sow., *Ammonites bifrons*, Brug., and Belemnites. We have at this place the following succession of beds:—

    (1.) Ferruginous, sandy beds with *Ammonites serpentinus*, Rein., &c.
    (2.) Paper-shales with limestone nodules.
        (" Fish and Insect beds ")
    (3.) Marlstone Rock-bed, here very inconspicuous and scarcely trace-
        able.
    (4.) Clays with bands of soft, yellow and brown, sandy ironstone full of
        small shells, *Cardium truncatum*, Sow., *Pecten æquivalvis*, Phil.,
        &c.
    (5.) Clays with ironstone balls.
    (6.) Clays (imperfectly seen).
    (7.) Hard, ferruginous and somewhat calcareous bed, perhaps the
        lowest of the Middle Lias series.

The Middle Lias at this spot may be from 60 to 70 feet in thickness.

At the north-west end of Slawston Mill outlier the Rock-bed of the Marlstone presents its usual characters, and consists of a hard calcareous rock containing *Avicula novemcostæ*, Brown, *Rhynchonella tetrahedra*, Sow., and *Terebratula punctata*, Sow. Large masses of carbonate of lime, crystallized in the forms known as " Dog-tooth Spar " and " Nail-head Spar," are seen in the rock at this place. A series of road-cuttings also exhibited the beds at the base of the Upper Lias, which are here ferruginous, together with the series of light coloured, very ferruginous, sandy shales, containing ironstone nodules of concentric structure and some sandy bands, which here underlie the Rock-bed of the Marlstone. These beds are similar to those exposed in the Cranhoe brick-yard on the opposite side of the valley.

In the hill on which Staunton Mill formerly stood, thin beds of brown, sandy ironstone cap the long ridge and are at the northern and highest part of the hill covered by a small patch of the Upper Lias Clay. The brown, sandy rock is shown by its fossils to be an attenuated form of the upper rock of the Middle Lias; it is underlaid by a series of ferruginous, sandy shales, now very imperfectly exposed, but which were formerly dug for brickmaking in a pit on the eastern side of the hill.

CHAPTER IV.

THE UPPER LIAS.

This division occupies a large area in Sheet 64; it is usually, however, concealed by Drift, except on the steep slopes of the escarpments formed by the Inferior Oolite. Throughout the district its thickness is about 200 feet, and it consists almost entirely of clays. Its principal members are as follows:—

a. "*Paper-Shales with Fish and Insect Limestones.*"*—These consist of finely laminated, blue shales, with bands of flat nodules composed of argillaceous limestone of a blue colour, but weathering white; these beds under the influence of frost become extremely fissile. The surfaces exposed by the bedding planes, both in the shales and limestones, are often completely covered with scales and other portions of fish with fragments of crustaceans and insects. Complete specimens appear to be very rare, but a very fine example of a fish is said to have been found at Edmondthorpe in making the Oakham and Melton Canal. Besides the fossils we have already mentioned there occur in these beds plant remains and wood converted into jet, a few Ammonites of the same species as in the "Serpentinus-beds" above, but always of small size, numerous minute univalves and some small bivalves as *Inoceramus dubius*, Sow., *Pecten sp.*, *Ostrea sp.*, &c. Slight exposures of these beds have been found at many points and they appear to be everywhere present in the area, though varying greatly in thickness, and in the number of bands of limestone which they contain; they may be best studied in pits at Allexton, Barley-thorpe, between Keythorpe and Hallaton, and beside the canal at Edmonthorpe. As is well known, these beds extend southwards into Gloucestershire and Somersetshire, where they have been described by the Rev. P. B. Brodie and Mr. C. Moore. At Allexton these limestones are dug and sent to Tugby, where they are burnt and make a hydraulic lime said to be equal to that of Barrow-on-Soar.

b. "*Serpentinus-Beds.*" These beds are always found lying immediately above the former; they consist of clays with layers of nodules of limestone of much coarser texture than those of the "Fish and Insect Beds." These beds are crowded with *Ammonites*, mostly belonging to the group of the *Falciferi*, and often of large size, such as *A. serpentinus*, Rein.; *A. falcifer*, Sow.; *A. Lythensis*, Y. & B.; *A. elegans*, Sow.; *A. concavus*, Sow.; and *A. radians*, Rein., with some Belemnites and other shells. So abundant are these Ammonites that when the land has been recently drained it is strewn with their fragments, and it is almost always

---

* These beds, as I have before suggested, might conveniently be named the "Dumbleton Series" from the locality at which they were first studied by the Rev. P. B. Brodie.

possible by their means to detect the outcrop of the beds containing them, even in ordinary ploughed fields. Occasionally, as at Market Harborough and near Hallaton Ferns, the Serpentinus limestones become ferruginous, when they are liable to be mistaken for part of the Marlstone Rock-bed, from which, however, they are readily distinguished by their fossils.

c. " *Communis-Beds*." At a little distance above the " Serpentinus-beds " there are found beds crowded with small specimens of Ammonites usually of the group of the *Planulati* (*A. communis*, Sow., *A. annulatus*, Sow., &c.), *Belemnites irregularis*, Schloth.; *Astarte sp.* and other shells also occur. These beds were well seen in the foundations of the blast furnaces at Neville-Holt, in a railway-cutting between Oakham and Ashwell, in that near Manton station, in a pond in Tugby Park, and in the Tugby brickyard, as well as in numerous field-drains, &c.

d. The middle portion of the Upper Lias Clay, to the thickness probably of about 100 feet, consists of dark-blue clays charged with large quantities of pyrites and jet, often in large masses; when exposed to the atmosphere these clays become light-coloured and exhibit much selenite with numerous bands and concentric balls of hydrated peroxide of iron formed by the decomposition of nodules of iron pyrites. Fossils are usually very rare in these beds which are exposed in the brickyards at Moor Hill Lodge, Great Easton, and that at Oakham on the road to Knossington, also in the railway tunnels at Manton and Morcott.

e. " *Leda ovum Beds*."—The highest beds of the Upper Lias consist of clays with numerous layers of septaria, everywhere distinguished by the abundance of specimens of *Leda ovum*, Sow., sp. The prevailing Ammonite is *A. bifrons*, Brug., which occurs in great numbers; the *Planulate* Ammonites are also numerous, and attain to a much larger size than in the " Communis-beds " below; they are represented by *A. communis*, Sow., *A. annulatus*, Sow., *A. crassus*, Phil., *A. fibulatus*, Sow., *A. Holandrei*, D'Orb. &c.; species of the group of the *Falciferi* are comparatively rare, but *Am. heterophyllus*, Sow., is tolerably abundant. *Belemnites*, *Myacites donaciforme*, Phil., *Arca truncata*, Sow., *Discina reflexa*, Sow., also abound in these beds. I have seen them well exposed at Thornhaugh, Manton, Stamford, and Stanion Mill; they are dug for brick-making at Rockingham, Gretton, Helpstone, Pilton, and Seaton Station.

The clays of the Upper Lias occupy the wide undulating plains, which lie between the two escarpments formed by the Inferior Oolite and the Marlstone Rock-bed respectively. Composed of beds which are easily denuded and are almost always covered with drift, the exposures of this formation are few in number, and not often of such a character as to enable us to study its relations to other strata or the succession of its own beds; in these respects it resembles the Lower Lias Clays.

The great mass of the Upper Lias in this area, which stretches from the north of Wymondham to south of Braybrook, and attains its greatest breadth between Tilton-on-the-Hill and Barrowden,

ected by many winding valleys, which cut down deeply to expose the Middle Lias strata, sometimes forming the midst of the Upper Lias. On the other hand, the portions of the Upper Lias are capped by the beds of the Oolite, which form outliers, often of great size, scattered district of the Upper Lias. The valleys which breach the escarpment of the Inferior Oolite, namely those of the Nash, Chater, and Welland, and their numerous tribu- cut down to the level of the Upper Lias, but the bottoms of these valleys being masked by superficial detritus, its beds are seldom exposed in them.

A few small outliers of Upper Lias rising above the plateaux of the Marlstone Rock-bed also exist, as those of Great Bowden, Slawston, Staunton Mill, and Barleythorpe, and some of these are capped by beds of Inferior Oolite.

The Upper Lias also forms a series of inliers in the midst of the Lower Oolite plateaux. Some of these form the bottoms of the valleys of the rivers which cut through these strata, which, as we shall show, thin out rapidly to the eastward, so that the Upper Lias is reached at comparatively small depths. This is the case in the parts of the valleys of the Glen, the Wansford Brook, and the Welland. In other cases, as at Stanion, Corby, and Help-stone brickyard, the Upper Lias is brought up by faults and exposed as inliers along the lines of certain small valleys.

Along the line of the Barford Brook, by Desborough, Rushton, Newton and Geddington, the Upper Lias Clays can be easily traced at the base of the escarpments of Northampton Sand, which form the sides of the valley. But along this line there are no valuable and instructive sections.

Near Braybrook there are some small exposures of the Upper Lias, principally in ditch-cuttings.

The Oxenden Magna tunnel, on the London and North-Western Railway, leading from Market Harborough to Blisworth, and situated on the edge of Sheet 64, passed through the Upper Lias Clay, which is here thickly covered with Boulder Clay and other drift. In the heaps of clay brought out from this cutting numerous Upper Lias fossils may be collected, including,—

    Ammonites serpentinus, *Rein.*
      ,,   falcifer, *Sow.*
      ,,   communis, *Sow.*
      ,,   Holandrei, *D'Orb.*
      &c.   &c.

Behind Dingley Lodge a pit shows the Serpentinus beds with traces of the fish and insect limestones which lie at the base of the Upper Lias series. These are seen to repose on the thin representative of the Marlstone Rock-bed, which contains the usual fossils.

From Stoke Albany northwards, the Upper Lias forms the slope of the steep escarpment of the Inferior Oolite and also the plains which stretch along its foot; sections are however very scarce.

At Sutton Basset Mill the Upper Lias Clay was reached in sinking a well. Just above Ashley, on the road to Stoke Albany, the lowest beds of the Upper Lias, containing *Ammonites serpentinus*, Rein., are seen. Between East Carlton and Ashley a number of field-drains exposed some of the middle beds of the Upper Lias, consisting of stiff, blue clays which yielded,—

    Ammonites communis, *Sow.* Very abundant.
      ,,   bifrons, *Brug.*
    Belemnites, sp.
    Fossil wood.

At Rockingham brickyard (half way between Rockingham and Cottingham) the highest beds of the Upper Lias are exposed. The blue clays, which are dug for brick-making, contain much pyrites and the fossils are badly preserved. They include the following :—

> Ammonites bifrons, *Brug.*
> „   sp.
> Belemnites compressus, *Voltz.*
> Ostrea sp.
> Pecten sp.
> Inoceramus dubius, *Sow.*
> Leda ovum, *Sow.*, sp.
> Astarte sp.
> Rhynchonella sp.

Between Rockingham and Harringworth the straight and steep slope, formed by the Upper Lias lying under the great plateau of Inferior Oolite, is very striking. In the sides of the numerous roads leading up this slope the Upper Lias Clay can be frequently examined, but there are few deep sections. It is also sometimes exposed along this escarpment in ditches and field-drains.

At Great Easton there is a brickyard in the Upper Lias Clay. In one part of the pit a layer of ironstone nodules is seen in the midst of the clays. *Ammonites, Belemnites,* and wood in the form of jet are found in this pit.

At the iron-works at Neville-Holt we have a number of interesting sections illustrating the Upper Lias Series. The upper portions, consisting at the top of dark-blue, pyritous clays, and lower down of lighter-coloured clays with ferruginous banding, are imperfectly seen. Towards the lower part, the excavations for the foundations of the blast-furnaces showed clays crowded with small specimens of *Ammonites communis,* Sow., and its varieties. The fossils obtained here were :—

> Ammonites annulatus, *Sow.*
> „   communis, *Sow.*
> „   Holandrei, *D'Orb.*
> „   crassus, *Phil.*
> „   bifrons, *Brug.*
> Belemnites compressus, *Voltz.*
> Nucula sp.
> Astarte sp.
> Posidonomya Bronnii, *Voltz.*
> &c.   &c.

Below these, in a cutting for the railway incline, we find the Serpentinus beds consisting of clays with argillaceous limestone nodules, containing *Ammonites serpentinus,* Rein., *Am. elegans,* Sow., &c. &c. Under these again occur the finely laminated clays (paper-shales) containing the flattened nodules of light coloured argillaceous limestone, with remains of fish, insects, and crustaceans. The "fish and insect beds" rest directly upon the thin representatives of the Middle Lias. (See page 74.)

At the bottom of the valley, on the road from Neville-Holt to Blaston, a number of field drains exhibited, at the time the district was being surveyed, admirable sections of the paper-shales and fish and insect limestones of the base of the Upper Lias, with their usual characters and fossils. Above them the Serpentinus beds were well seen, crowded, as usual, with specimens of Cephalopods, including—

> Belemnites compressus, *Voltz.*
> Ammonites serpentinus, *Rein.*
> „   falcifer, *Sow.*
> „   bifrons, *Brug.*
> „   radians, *Rein.*
> „   heterophyllus, *Sow.*
> „   communis, *Sow.*
> „   crassus, *Phil.*

Just above the village of Blaston St. Giles, on the road to Medbourn, a pit opened for obtaining clay to puddle a pond, exposed the Serpentinus beds, the paper-shales and the fish and insect beds at the base of the Upper Lias Series. A little above this was another pit in the ordinary Upper Lias Clays.

On the left bank of the stream at Hallaton Ferns the junction of the Upper and Middle Lias was well seen in a number of field-drains. The succession of beds here is as follows :—

Upper Lias.
1. Dark-blue clays.
2. Ferruginous beds with *Ammonites serpentinus*, Rein. (abundant), and *Am. bifrons*, Brug.
3. Paper-shales, with fish and insect limestones (usual fossils).

Middle Lias.
4. Sandy, ferruginous band with casts of shells. (Marlstone Rock-bed ?)
5. Light-coloured clays with ironstone balls.

Near the bridle road from Keythorpe to Hallaton, at the point where it crosses the brook, some old pits show the base of the Upper Lias, consisting of 5 or 6 feet of laminated shales, with traces of the nodular limestones, with fish and insect remains; these rest upon the Middle Lias beds which have been already described at this place. (See page 73.)

Opposite to Moor Hill Lodge there is an extensive brickyard in the Upper Lias Clays. In this and a pond above we have a section of at least 50 or 60 feet of the series. The highest beds seen consist of laminated, light-coloured clays, with irregular, brown, ferruginous bands in the lines of stratification. The lower part consists of blue clays with few septaria, but with much pyrites, both in nodules and disseminated through the mass, and, in consequence, the weathered beds exhibit much Selenite, often in very large and beautiful crystals. Fragments of *Belemnites* occur in this pit, and *Ammonites* are also found, but I saw none sufficiently well preserved for identification. The clays exposed in this pit probably belong to the middle portion of the Upper Lias, which is generally very unfossiliferous.

In Keythorpe Park a pond, dug in the lower part of the Lias Clays, exhibited the richly fossiliferous bands crowded with small *Ammonites*, &c., which characterise that part of the series. I collected here—

Ammonites communis, *Sow.* (Very abundant.)
      „ annulatus, *Sow.* (Very abundant.)
      „ Holandrei, *D'Orb.*
      „ radians, *Rein.* (Abundant.)
      „ bifrons, *Brug.*
Belemnites compressus, *Voltz.*
Leda ovum, *Sow.*, sp.
Inoceramus dubius, *Sow.*
    &c.   &c.

The brickyard opened on the opposite side of the road to Tugby Hall exhibits the same beds, consisting of finely laminated, blue clays with a few septaria. These clays when dug show a few small crystals of Selenite. The beds are crowded with small fossils of the same species with those found at the last noticed locality.

At several points about the village of East Norton, and also at Finchley Bridge, roadside cuttings and field-drains have exposed the fish and insect beds with the usual fossils. Small bivalves, such as *Inoceramus dubius*, Sow.; and *Pectens* with dwarfed *Ammonites* occur in some of the bands of flattened limestone nodules.

An interesting pit at Allexton exhibits the following section of the lower beds of the Upper Lias.

1. Soil - - - - - - - - 1 ft.
2. Blue, laminated clay - - - - - 6 ft.
3. Irregular, stony band ("kale") full of *Ammonites serpentinus*, Rein., *Belemnites*, and other fossils - - 1 to 2 ft.
4. Laminated clay - - - - - - 6 in.
5. First, irregular bed of hard, argillaceous limestone - - 6 in.
6. Laminated clay - - - - - - 1 ft.
7. Second, irregular bed of hard, argillaceous limestone - 6 in.
8. Laminated clay - - - - - - 1 ft.
9. Third, or Best bed of limestone - - - - 3 to 6 in.
10. Laminated clay - - - - - - 4½ in.
11. "Kale" - - - - - - - 6 in.
12. Marlstone Rock-bed full of the usual fossils; 4 courses of stone - - - . - - together 2½ ft.

In the clays large masses of wood, converted into jet, are found. These, after being soaked in oil to prevent cracking, are used by the workmen and others for whetting razors.

The three layers of limestone contain the usual fragments of fish, insects, and crustaceans with the following shells :

Belemnites sp.
Ammonites serpentinus, *Rein.*
  „   elegans, *Sow.*
  „   annulatus, *Sow.*
  „   sp.
Small univalves.
Astrea, (small species).
Inoceramus dubius, *Sow.*
Astarte sp.
Lima sp.
Pteroperna sp.
Other small bivalves.
Fragments of wood.

The limestone, which is hard and fissile, and of a blue colour weathering white, occurring sometimes in continuous bands and at other times in nodules, is carried to Tugby where it is burnt for lime. It is said to produce a hydraulic lime fully equal in quality to the celebrated " Barrow lime," which is made from the fish and insect limestones of the *Lower Lias* series.

It is worthy of notice that the Serpentinus bed, which in many places is ferruginous and has often, when attention has not been given to the fossils, been mistaken for the Marlstone Rock-bed, is at Allexton, either not at all, or only very slightly coloured with oxide of iron.

At Deepdale traces of the fish and insect limestones of the Upper Lias are seen lying on the Marlstone. At several points about Lodington there are small exposures in the road-cuttings of the same beds. On the road between Tilton-on-the-Hill and Burrow-on-the-Hill, but near the former place, there is good evidence of the existence of the fish and insect limestones immediately above the Rock-bed of the Marlstone. The same beds are seen at the top of a pit in the Marlstone at Pickwell.

At Uppingham there is a brickyard opened in the highest beds of the Upper Lias clays, and here their junction with the Northampton Sand is well seen. The same portion of the Upper Lias series is again exposed at the brick-yard and in some roadside cuttings at Seaton. Here I collected—

Ammonites communis, *Sow.*
  „   Holandrei, *D'Orb.*
  „   bifrons, *Brug.*
  „   serpentinus, *Rein.*
Belemnites compressus, *Volts.*
Leda ovum, *Sow*, sp.,
  &c.   &c.

The tunnel at Morcott, on the Rugby and Stamford Branch of the London and North-Western Railway, passed through the Upper Lias clays, and from the spoil heaps about the air-shafts many of the characteristic *Ammonites* and other shells may be collected.

In the railway-cuttings about Luffenham the Upper Lias clays are exhibited at several points, and between that village and Pilton a brickyard has recently been opened in the beds of the same formation.

At Manton, on the Leicester and Stamford branch of the Midland Railway, the Upper Lias Clays were dug in the shafts, cuttings, and tunnel, and the clays are now used for brickmaking. The tunnel passed through the clays at about 100 feet below their junction with the Northampton Sand. The clays here abound with masses of iron-pyrites. *Ammonites bifrons*, Brug, is abundant here, and *Am. elegans*, Sow., rare.

At Manton Station a ditch-cutting exposes the " Communis-beds," lying towards the lower part of the Upper Lias. They consist of blue clays with small white septaria, the whole crowded with fossils, among which are the following species,—

Ammonites communis, *Sow.* Very abundant.
  „   annulatus, *Sow.*   „
  „   Holandrei, *D'Orb.*

Ammonites serpentinus, *Rein.*   Rare.
Belemnites compressus, *Voltz.*
,, sp.
Leda ovum, *Sow.*, sp.
&c.   &c.

South of Oakham on the road to Brook a small roadside cutting exposes the Fish and Insect limestones and clays, lying on the Marlstone Rock-bed and covered by the Serpentinus beds, here consisting of a single layer of nodules.

At Langham brickyard (see description, page 70), the Serpentinus beds are present, and some bands of septaria below them seem to represent the Fish and Insect beds, but the characteristic fossil remains of the latter were not found at this place.

The railway-cuttings between Oakham and Ashwell pass through the Upper Lias clays, and a slip in one of these exhibited, at the time the district was being surveyed, the beds crowded with small specimens of *Ammonites communis*, Sow., &c.

The long valleys which run up into the great plateau formed by the Lower Oolites, are often cut down to the Upper Lias, which is, however, seldom exhibited in sections. Along the valley of the Gwash near Empingham, at Wild's Ford, where the Lias is thrown up by a fault, near Tickencote Lodge and at Ingthorpe the clays of the Upper Lias are seen. In the tributary of the Gwash which runs through Exton Park, the Upper Lias clays were well exposed in making the reservoirs and ornamental water near the new Hall.

From Burley-on-the-Hill northwards the Upper Lias clays form the slopes of a steep escarpment. They are exhibited at a number of points about Burley, below Cottesmore and around Barrow and Market Overton, but do not in this neighbourhood exhibit any features of special interest, nor are they exposed in any deep sections.

The banks of the Oakham and Melton Canal, between Teigh and Edmond-thorpe, exhibit a number of good exposures of the bottom beds of the Upper Lias resting on the Marlstone Rock-bed.

A little south of Edmonthorpe there is a very fine section in the Fish and Insect beds. Here the limestones are very poorly developed, but the paper-shales themselves, which are of considerable thickness, are crowded with fragments of fish, insects, and crustaceans. At this place a very perfect specimen of a fish is said to have been found during the cutting of the Canal.

North of Wymondham and in the neighbourhood of the village, the Upper Lias is completely covered and concealed by drift.

Inliers.—In the valleys of the Welland and Chater, the Upper Lias clays, which, through the easterly dip, were lost at Barrowden and Luffenham, reappear in consequence of the great faults which run near Duddington and Ketton. The Upper Lias clays here form the steep slopes below the Lower Oolites, but seldom afford good sections. Their junction with the beds above is, however, almost always marked by the outburst of numerous springs.

At Collyweston Parks there are the remains of a number of reservoirs or fish-ponds which have been dug in the clays and filled by such springs. At the Collyweston Quarries some of the deeper wells have been sunk into the Upper Lias clay to a considerable depth. At Stamford the Lias clay forms the bed of the river; in a deep excavation made at the gas-works I found *Ammonites bifrons*, Brug., *Belemnites compressus*, Voltz., *Leda ovum*, Sow., &c. &c.

The same beds are met with in many wells in the southern part of the town of Stamford, where the great Stamford and Helpstone fault has thrown the Upper Lias clay to a much higher level. The Upper Lias clay is dug at Lumby's Terra Cotta Works. A boring here is said to have passed through 140 feet of Upper Lias, and to have been carried to a depth of 500 feet. Unfortunately, however, I was unable to obtain any reliable information as to the nature and thicknesses of the several beds passed through. This boring was undertaken in an attempt to find coal. The ornamental water of Burleigh Park rests on the Upper Lias clay, some small exposures of which may be seen in the neighbourhood. Its junction with the overlying Inferior Oolite beds can be traced by means of numerous springs in the Park.

The great Stamford and Helpstone Fault also brings up the Lias clay so that it is exposed along the valley of the Wansford Brook. The best exposure within the inlier thus formed, is at Thornhaugh, where a deep drain and well showed thick beds of blue clay, the highest beds of the Upper Lias, containing much selenite and many fossils. Among the latter were :—

Ammonites bifrons, *Brug.* Very abundant.
Belemnites compressus, *Voltz.*
Leda ovum, *Sow.*, sp.
Arca, sp.
Myacites donaciformis, *Phil.*
&c.   &c.

Near this place a well was sunk for upwards of 70 feet in the blue clay without reaching the bottom.

Along the valley of the Nene the Upper Lias clay forms the bed of the river, but it is very seldom that it is exposed, owing to the thick strata of gravel and alluvium by which it is covered. Deep wells, however, reach it, and I was able to detect it at a number of small openings between Wansford and Fotheringhay, at Cotterstock, Oundle (where it was reached in a deep excavation by the side of the railway), and at Wadenhoe near the Mill.

At Helpstone brickyard we have a very interesting exposure of the Upper Lias Clay in a small inlier, which has been produced in consequence of the removal by denudation of the upper part of a small anticlinal, into which the beds are here bent. The beds consist of blue, pyritous clays with much selenite, and are the highest of the series; they yield,—

Ammonites bifrons, *Brug.* Abundant.
„   serpentinus, *Rein.* Rare.
Belemnites compressus, *Voltz.*
Nucula ovum, *Sow.*, sp.

Along the line of Harper's Brook faults bring in the Upper Lias clays as small inliers at Pipwell Abbey, Little Oakley, and Stanion. Although the position and relations of the Upper Lias clays can be readily traced in these inliers, there are no good sections in any of them, except the last mentioned. At Stanion Mill some excavations gave a good exposure of the dark-blue, pyritous clays of the Upper Lias, yielding abundantly *Ammonites bifrons*, Brug., and *Leda ovum*, Sow., sp.

The two small branches of the Willow Brook also expose, through the action, of a fault, two inliers of Upper Lias, and in roadside cuttings, field-drains, and wells, tolerably good sections of these have been obtained.

Lastly, in a small brook at Brigstock Parks where the beds are much faulted, an inlier of Upper Lias clay of very small size is exposed.

Outliers. — At the hill south-west of Cranhoe, which was formerly the site of the Staunton-Wyvill Windmill, we find the thin and imperfect representative of the Marlstone Rock-bed, capped by a mass of Upper Lias Clays. These are seen near the foundations of the old mill, and in the ploughed fields numerous fragments of the small specimens of *Ammonites communis*, Sow., may be picked up.

In the outlier which forms Slawston Hill, and which is just capped by a vestige of the Northampton Sand, the highest beds of the Upper Lias are seen on the slopes of the hill.

On the south side of the hill, where field-draining had lately been going on, I found the surface of the ground literally covered with fragments of *Ammonites serpentinus*, Rein., *Ammonites bifrons*, Brug., *Am. falcifer*, Sow., and *Belemnites compressus*, Voltz., also occur. Below, fragments of "the fish and insect limestone" abound. For the succession of beds here see the section given on page 77. Near the same place I found some beautiful exposures of the "Fish and Insect Limestones," with the usual lithological characters and organic remains. They are interstratified with the ordinary paper-shales, and, as usual, are immediately covered by beds crowded with *Ammonites serpentinus*, Rein. In the neighbourhood the "Serpentinus-Beds" are markedly ferruginous, and, unless due attention is paid to the fossils, they may be easily confounded with the Marlstone Rock-bed. On the east of Slawston Hill by the road leading to Medbourn we have the following section :—

(1.) Clay.
(2.) Ferruginous bands. Serpentinus beds with usual characters, but no fossils were found here.
(3.) Fish and Insect Limestones and Shales.
(4.) Marlstone Rock-bed (imperfectly seen).

At the north-west of Slawston Hill on the road to Cranhoe the ferruginous, rocky bands occur crowded with *Ammonites serpentinus*, Rein, and its allies, and resting on the shales containing the "fish and insect limestone nodules." Field-drains in the neighbourhood afforded some beautiful exposures of the same beds, and a considerable number of fossils.

At Great Bowden and Market Harborough there are two small outliers of Upper Lias. The only important sections here are in the Market Harborough brickyard, opposite to the railway station, and in the adjoining railway-cutting. Here we have the following section,—

1. Soil - - - - - - -	1 ft.
2. Boulder Clay - - - - - -	2 to 3 ft.
3. Upper Lias Clay with *Ammonites communis*, Sow., and *Belemnites compressus*, Voltz. It consists of laminated, blue clay weathering to a yellow colour - 1 to 4 ft. seen in the pit.	

┌ 4. Hard, brown, ferruginous band of impure ironstone - 9 in.
│ 5. Softer and more sandy bed completely full of,—

"Serpentinus beds."

Ammonites serpentinus, *Rein.*
     ,,   bifrons, *Brug.*
     ,,   communis, *Sow.*
     ,,   Holandrei, *D'Orb.*
Belemnites compressus, *Voltz.*, and other shells - 9 in.

└ 6. Hard, very ferruginous bed - - - - - 3 to 6 in.
  7. Light-blue, laminated clays - - - - 3 to 4 ft.
  8. A thin vein of sandstone (very inconstant) - - about 1 ft.
  9. Light-blue, laminated clays - - - - 5 ft.
10. Marlstone Rock-bed.

For remainder of this section, see p. 76.

At the Market Harborough brickyard, the "Fish and Insect *limestones*" were not detected. In the cutting just north of Market Harborough station the Serpentinus beds are again well exposed, and are seen to be crowded with the usual fossils.

At Barleythorpe, near Oakham, there is a vestige of the Upper Lias Clay which has escaped denudation, and is seen lying on the top of the Marlstone Rock-bed. The section at a stone-pit here is as follows :—

(1.) Soil.
(2.) Blue clay - - - - - - 3 feet.
(3.) Bed of white, very fissile, limestone with many compressed shells, and some obscure markings, which may be the remains of fish (and insects ?) - 9 inches.
(4.) Very finely laminated, whitish, shaley beds, with masses of jet and many hard, flattened septaria, which give forth a foetid odour under the hammer - - - - - 3 feet.
(5.) Dark-blue, laminated, ochraceous shales with jet - 2 feet.
(6.) Marlstone Rock-bed, with the usual rounded concretions and fossils.

The limits of this small outlier are somewhat uncertain, and it may be stated generally that the boundary between the Upper and Middle Lias is a very difficult one to trace, and over a large part of the area it has in consequence been represented on the map by a broken line.

In concluding the description of the Lias strata in this area, it may be convenient to exhibit its subdivisions in a tabular form, and to show their correlation, as nearly as this can be made out, with the several palæontological zones, as defined by geologists in England, France, and Germany respectively. These latter are based on the study of more complete sections, yielding finer series of fossils, than can be obtained in the drift-covered areas of the English Midland counties. It must be remembered, however, that the correlation suggested is approximative only; that in every fresh district examined, new groups of beds appear, more or less completely filling up the gaps, which their absence had caused in earlier studied series; and that, as these breaks constitute the limits of divisions necessarily adopted by geologists, in their classification of the strata of a district, the boundaries between the several groups of strata become continually less sharply defined, as the formations are traced over more extended areas.

The following table exhibits the several series of Liassic beds described in this Memoir; their position in the palæontological scale being shown by reference both to the divisions first suggested by Quenstedt in his " Flötzgebirge Würtemburgs " in 1843, and also to the more modern classification by Ammonite Zones, adopted by later authors, such as Oppel, Hébert, and Wright.

TABLE to illustrate the CORRELATION of the various BEDS of the LIAS in the DISTRICT.

English Classification.	Continental Classification.	Divisions of Quenstedt.	Ammonite Zones.	Strata exhibited in the District described in the Memoir.
Upper Lias	Upper Lias	Lias ζ	Zone of Am. jurensis	Northampton Sand ((lower part?). e. "Leda-ovum Beds." Clays with numerous bands of septaria (many fossils).
		Lias ε	Zone of Am. communis	d. Highly pyritous clays, with much jet in places (few fossils). c. "Communis Beds." Laminated blue clays with bands containing numerous small fossils. b. "Serpentinus Beds." Clays with nodules of limestone, sometimes ferruginous (Ammonites abundant). a. "Paper shales with Fish and Insect Limestones." ("Dumbleton series.")
Middle Lias	Middle Lias	Lias δ	Zone of Am. spinatus / Zone of Am. margaritatus	e. "The Rock-bed of the Marlstone." Ferruginous sandy limestone with many fossils. d. Light-blue clays, with bands of ironstone balls, and occasional beds of sand. c. Blue clay, with septaria weathering to a red colour (fossils abundant). b. Blue, highly micaceous clays, with large septaria (fossils very abundant). a. Soft, yellowish brown, sandy and micaceous ironstone (many casts of fossils).
		Lias γ	Zone of Am. capricornus / Zone of Am. ibex (?)	m. Dark-blue clays, with much pyrites and many septaria (fossils abundant). l. Clays with septaria, and some thin bands of indurated argillaceous sand (fossils). k. Clays with bands of shelly limestone, sometimes crowded with fossils. h. Light-blue, laminated, pyritous shale, with thin beds of limestone almost made up of shells.
Lower Lias	Lower Lias	Lias β	Zone of Am. armatus / Zone of Am. oxynotus	g. Sandy clays with sands occasionally indurated into stone (many fossils). f. Beds of blue clay with much pyrites and small light brown septaria.
			(Zone of Am. obtusus.)	(The beds at this horizon are very obscure in the district, if they exist they are nowhere well exposed.)
		Lias α	Zone of Am. semicostatus (A. geometricus of Oppel) / Zone of Am. Bucklandi / Zone of Am. angulatus / Zone of Am. planorbis	e. Beds of ferruginous limestone alternating with clay (many fossils). d. Beds of blue clay, with numerous Gryphæa scattered through them with other shells. c. Beds of dark-blue, pyritous clays, containing Ammonites mineralised by pyrites. b. Coarse grained, sometimes shelly, limestone, alternating with shales (numerous fossils). a. "Fish and Insect Limestones." ("Strensham series,") alternating with laminated shales (numerous fossils).
Keuper?	Infralias? (in part).		Penarth (Rhætic), or Zone of Avicula contorta	Thin representative of the White Lias. Sandy, calcareous, somewhat fissile beds. Black, highly pyritous shales, with bone bands (many fossils).

CHAPTER V.
THE LOWER OOLITES.

THE strata of this age present, in the district under consideration, a somewhat novel and peculiar type. The relation of the several groups into which they are classified, with the formations of the same age either of the Yorkshire series or that of the Cotteswold Hills, are by no means obvious. As great diversity of opinion has existed on these questions of classification and correlation, and as it is necessary to go into some details concerning districts outside the limits of this sheet, in order to explain the grounds on which the grouping of strata, adopted in the maps of the Geological Survey, has been arrived at, it has been considered advisable to devote to the discussion of these more purely theoretical questions the introductory essay which is prefixed to this memoir.

The strata of the Lower Oolites in the area embraced within Sheet 64 fall naturally into two very distinct groups, the lower of which is equivalent to the older part of the Inferior Oolite, while the upper appears to represent the whole of the Great Oolite. The lower of these series appears to have been to a certain extent disturbed and denuded, before the deposition of the latter which lies unconformably upon it. The evidence on this subject has been fully considered in the introductory portion of this memoir.

The Inferior Oolite formation consists of two members, the lower of which is mainly arenaceous and is known as the "Northampton Sand," while the upper is almost purely calcareous and is distinguished by the name of the "Lincolnshire Oolite Limestone." These two divisions, however, frequently pass into one another by insensible gradations; and occasionally, at their junction, beds of fissile sandy limestone occur, which constitute the "Collyweston Slate." Like other similar "slates" these are very local in their mode of occurrence. The Great Oolite strata are divisible into four groups (the highest of which is the well characterised Cornbrash), which have been separately mapped in Sheet 64. A series of clays apparently representing the Forest Marble of the south of England underlies the Cornbrash and reposes on the white, shelly, argillaceous limestones of the Great Oolite, which are scarcely ever oolitic in structure. The last-mentioned strata in turn rest on a variable set of beds, some of which contain shells of marine, others of freshwater species, while thin bands of lignite and vertical plant remains indicate the former presence of old land surfaces. These beds, which we have called the "Upper Estuarine Series," appear to represent the "Stonesfield Slate" or Lower Zone of the Great Oolite of the South of England.

THE NORTHAMPTON SAND WITH THE LOWER ESTUARINE SERIES.

These beds constitute the base of the Inferior Oolite in this district, and are often seen lying upon an eroded surface of the Upper Lias Clay. In their mineralogical composition they are extremely variable, but almost everywhere arenaceous characters prevail in them. Sometimes they are almost wholly made up of beds of white, or but slightly ferruginous, sands, with occasional thin seams of clay; but usually more or less of their lower portion is converted into a rich ironstone rock. This ironstone, when not altered by the percolation of atmospheric water, is a hard, compact rock of a blue or green colour, composed of carbonate and silicate of iron, and usually made up, as is shown when sections of it are examined under the microscope, of rounded grains with an oolitic structure. In this form, however, the ironstone is seen only when it is dug in deep wells, under a considerable thickness of clays. As it more commonly occurs near the surface, it presents very different characters, consisting of a brown, by no means compact, rock usually with a very remarkable " cellular " structure. This structure is due to the chemical action set up in the mass by the atmospheric waters, which, penetrating from the joint and bedding planes, have caused the concentration of hydrated peroxide of iron along surfaces having a general parallelism with those planes. The hard bands are often concentrically arranged. Frequently the change by weathering from blue and green carbonate and silicate to brown hæmatite has only partially taken place, and the centres of the blocks consist of the former while their outer portions are constituted by the latter, displaying the usual hard bands. The brown ore, when examined microscopically, is often seen to retain the same oolitic structure which is found in the unweathered rock.

In places, the rock of the Northampton Sand contains a considerable proportion of calcareous matter, and it is then extensively used as a building material and even for lime-burning; beds of this character, however, are not so frequently seen in this district as in that to the south-west. Examples occur at Desbro' and near Uppingham.

The thickness of the Northampton Sand is very variable; in the area to which this memoir specially refers, it probably never exceeds 40 feet, while it is frequently reduced to very insignificant proportions, and sometimes, as about Luffenham, almost entirely disappears.

The Northampton Sand is usually very barren of fossils ; at certain points, however, very fossiliferous bands have been found which have yielded a very rich fauna. In the lower ironstone beds the fossils are all marine. Cephalopods are far less rare than in the overlying limestone, the various varieties of *Ammonites Murchisonæ*, Sow., *Belemnites giganteus*, Schloth, and a gigantic *Nautilus* being the prevailing forms. Among the other very abundant fossils we may mention *Astarte elegans*, Sow., *Lucina Wrightii*, Opp., *Ceromya Bajociana*, D'Orb., *Pholadomya fidicula*, Sow., *Isocardia cordata*, Buckm., and *Pecten personatus*, Goldf., with the Echinoderms *Galeropygus agariciformis*, Forbes sp., and *Pygaster semisulcatus*, Phil. sp.[*] The study of this fauna enables us to refer these marine beds at the base of the Northampton Sand, without doubt, to the lower part of the Inferior Oolite. In

---

[*] Very beautiful series of the interesting fossils of the Northampton Sand have been collected at Duston, near Northampton, and at other points by Mr. Samuel Sharp, F.S.A., F.G.S., &c. Vide *Quart. Journ. Geol. Soc.*, vol. XXVI, p. 382.

the lowest part of the Northampton Sand *Rhychonella cynocephala*, Rich., and some closely allied forms occur; and in a band full of pebbles or concretions (like those of the Marlstone Rock-bed) which is frequently seen quite at its base, specimens of *Ammonites bifrons*, Brug., have been found at several localities; but a number of circumstances seem to point to the conclusion that this Ammonite was derived from the Upper Lias Clays below. As yet we have no *conclusive* evidence that any part of the North-ampton Sand represents the "Midford Sand" of the south of England and Yorkshire.

The upper part of the Northampton Sand contains beds of white sand with plant remains, sometimes vertical, also thin seams of lignite and miniature "underclays"; very occasionally thin seams containing *Cyrena* occur in this part of the series. These highest beds of the Northampton Sand, which are well exposed about Helpstone, Ufford, Edith Weston, &c., were, like those above the Lincolnshire Oolite which we shall presently describe, evidently deposited under Estuarine conditions; we have therefore called them the "Lower Estuarine Series."

When we study the equivalents of the Northampton Sand in the eastern Moorlands of Yorkshire, we find the upper or estuarine portion attaining to a great thickness and simulating in its general characters the strata of the coal-measures. These beds are known as the "Lower Sandstone, Shale and Coal of Yorkshire." The lower or marine portion of the series, however, retains in York-shire its more moderate dimensions; the representative of the "Midford Sand" or "Upper Lias" sands being more distinctly developed. The marine beds at the base of the Inferior Oolite in Yorkshire are called the "Dogger," and at Rosedale yield an ironstone, almost identical in character with that of the Northamp-ton Sand.

Southward and eastward, owing to the thinning out of the Lincolnshire Oolite Limestone, the Upper and Lower Estuarine series are brought into contact, the former graduating in Oxford-shire into the Stonesfield Slate, and the latter into the Lower Freestones of the Inferior Oolite.

The ironstone rock of the Northampton Sand often yields from 30 to 50 per cent. of metallic iron; but its highly siliceous charac-ter causes it to be of more value when used in admixture with other ores than when smelted alone. This ore is now (1869) very extensively worked at many places in Northamptonshire; the only points within the limit of Sheet 64 are about Desborough and Rushton; some years ago this ore was raised at Neville-Holt and the erection of blast-furnaces commenced, but these works are now abandoned.

The ferruginous or calcareous rock of the lower part of the Northampton Sand is locally largely used for building purposes, but it does not usually possess much durability. The white sands in the upper part of the series are extensively dug at many points for making mortar; certain of the beds of clay in the same part of the series are used for brick-making, as at Cottingham and Deene; while at Stamford-Baron one such bed is used for the manufacture of terra-cotta.

The beds of the Northampton Sand constitute a rather light soil, and where, as is usually the case, they are ferruginous this is of a red colour. This soil is a very rich one, especially adapted for the growth of spring-crops.

Outer Escarpment of the Northampton Sand.

The ironstones and superimposed sands and clays of the Lower Estuarine Series, capping the Upper Lias Clay, forms a bold escarpment, which in the southern half of the area included within Sheet 64, has a general direction from south-west to north-east, namely, from Desborough to the valley of the Welland; but in the northern half of the area the bearing of this escarpment changes to due north, which direction it maintains through the whole of Lincolnshire and South Yorkshire. Thus we have within the area the commencement of the remarkable feature known as "the Cliff" of Lincolnshire, a bold escarpment facing the west and running in an almost straight line for about 90 miles. Along the top of this escarpment for a great part of its length runs the celebrated Roman road known as the "Ermine Street." The escarpment of the "Lincolnshire Cliff" is breached by valleys at two points only, namely, those forming the site of the towns of Grantham and Lincoln; the same river, the Witham, which rises in the oolitic plateau first cutting its way westward through a gap in the escarpment at Grantham into the Liassic Valley, and then back again through the still more striking gorge in which the city of Lincoln is built, away to the Wash. The Upper Lias continually diminishing in thickness as we go northwards, the "Cliff" of Lincolnshire gradually decreases in height, until in South Yorkshire, though still recognisable, it becomes quite inconspicuous. (Plate VI.)

As the Upper Lias Clay is, in the district under consideration, about 200 feet thick, the escarpment of the Northampton Sand makes a well marked feature, and in that portion of the area where the River Welland runs at its foot, namely between Rockingham and Harringworth, it presents very bold characters.

At the extreme southern part of the area a branch of the River Ise, a tributary of the Nene, cuts out the long valley in which are situated the villages of Desborough, Rushton, Newton, and Geddington.

At Geddington the ironstone forming the base of the Northampton Sand is seen in some small openings, and was well exposed at the time of the survey in the foundation of some houses. Copious springs arise at the line of its junction with the Upper Lias, and over one of these the beautiful Eleanor Cross, which forms such a striking ornament to this village, is erected. At several other points in the neighbourhood of Geddington, the sands and clays forming the Lower Estuarine series can be traced.

At Rushton Station on the Midland Railway, the light-coloured, carbonaceous clays and sands of the Lower Estuarine series attain a considerable development, and are seen covered by the Lincolnshire Oolite Limestone. The section at this place is as follows :—

1. Rubbly, slightly oolitic rock (Lincolnshire Oolite Limestone).
2. Pale-brown, sandy limestone, 1 ft. (Representative of the Collyweston Slate).
3. Brown sand, becoming nearly white below, 2 ft. 6 in. } (Lower Estuarine
4. Brown, ferruginous sand, 1 ft.   }   Series.

32108.   G

5. Light-bluish, sandy clay, with carbonaceous markings and ferruginous nodules, 9 in. ⎫
6. Similar clay of much darker colour, 2 ft. ⎬ (Lower Estuarine Series—cont.)
7. Light-coloured, indurated, argillaceous sands, passing into sandy clay, with carbonaceous markings, 4 to 5 ft. seen. ⎭

The deep valley at Rushton cuts quite down into the Upper Lias, and many good exposures of the ironstones of the Northampton Sand are seen along its sides. To the south of Rushton the very deep Glendon cutting on the Midland Railway exposes a fine section of the ironstone beds, covered by the Lower Estuarine sands and clays. Here the ironstone is largely worked by the Glendon Iron Company, but these sections are just beyond the limits of Sheet 64, and have been described by Mr. Sharp.*

At Desborough the ironstones and overlying sands and clays are well exposed in a deep railway-cutting near the station, where they are covered by Boulder Clay, and also in the numerous large pits at which the iron-ore is very extensively dug for the purpose of being sent away by rail into Staffordshire, Derbyshire, and Yorkshire. Near this place we have an interesting example of the development of calcareous beds in the midst of the Northampton Sand, perhaps the best within the limits of the area now under description. These calcareous beds form a band of hard, blue, ferruginous and very shelly limestone in the midst of the ironstone beds; this ferrugino-calcareous rock is dug for road-metal. In the country to the southwards, however, the Northampton Sand often locally assumes calcareous characters, and passes, sometimes throughout the greater part of its thickness, into an impure limestone of oolitic structure. Such limestones in the Northampton Sand are very extensively developed to the north of the town of Northampton, and as shown by Mr. Sharp, include at one point a bed of fissile rock, once quarried for roofing purposes, and known as the Duston Slate. These limestones of the Northampton Sand usually contain much siliceous matter; they are quarried for building purposes, and in one place, namely, near Draughton, were formerly even burnt for lime. At several points within the limits of Sheet 64 calcareous bands occur, and their position is indicated upon the map by the sign CALC. The development of thick-bedded, oolitic limestones in the midst of the Northampton Sand appears, however, to be confined to the area to the south, and we find such beds both in the northern and the southern portions of the county of Northampton.

The iron-ore which is dug about Desborough forms the upper 6 feet of the ironstone beds of the Northampton Sand, the lower portions not being found rich enough to pay for working. The upper 12 inches consist almost wholly of the hard, dark-brown fragments of the septa, forming the characteristic cellular structure, which by the removal through meteoric causes of their sandy admixture are separated from impurities and constitute an ore of greater richness than the rest of the deposit; this is known to the workmen as "curley."

Between Desborough and Stoke Albany the Northampton Sand stretches westwards in two spurs, which are, however, obscured by thick masses of Boulder Clay; hence we find along these spurs but few sections, and the boundaries of the hard beds which cap them are very obscure.

The ironstones and overlying clays and sands of the Lower Estuarine Series can be traced at many points in the vicinity of Stoke Albany, Wilbarston, and East Carlton, but they present no good sections or features of special interest. Here, as at almost all points of their outcrop, we find evidence, in heaps of old slags, of the extensive working of these beds in former times. At Cottingham we have a series of interesting sections illustrating the junction of the Lincolnshire Oolite and the Northampton Sand. In a great pit in the Inferior Oolite we see a section of about 20 feet of that rock, which in its lower part contains numerous plant remains (*Polypodites Lindleyi*, Göpp. sp.), Wood, &c., and in other pits we find the series continued in descending order.

1. Calcareous sands.
2. White clay.
3. Ironstone rock (very thin).

---

* The Oolites of Northamptonshire, Part II.—*Quart. Journ. Geol. Soc.* vol. xxix. pp. 231-232.

Pit in the Lower Oolites, below Cottingham Church.

(1.) Light brown, sandy beds at the bottom of the
    Lincolnshire Oolite (representative of the
    Collyweston Slate) - - - - 2 to 3 feet.
(2.) Dark bluish-black marl full of plant remains - 4 inches.
(3.) Marl of lighter bluish-black colour with plant
    remains running through it (" plant-bed ")- 3 feet.
(4.) Whitish and drab, laminated sands - - 2 feet 6 inches.
(5.) Dark-blue clay - - - - 3 feet.
(6.) White sand - - - - - 2 feet.
(7.) Ironstone - - - - - 6 feet to 8 feet.
(8.) Hard, red rock with greenish centres (rock used
    for building)- - - - 20 feet seen.

In a pit still lower down we find—
(1.) Whitish sands and clays - - - 6 to 8 feet.
(2.) Light-blue marl with plants - - - 1 foot.
(3.) Light-coloured sands and clays, becoming
    ferruginous at their base - - - 8 feet.
Ironstone beds and red rock below.

At Cottingham brickyard the beds of the Lower Estuarine Series are dug for brickmaking. The sections exposed show that at this place the Northampton Sand, which is so variable a formation, both in thickness and mineral characters, has acquired considerable importance, both of its members being well represented. The Lower Estuarine sands and clays attain a thickness of at least 20 feet, the beds exhibiting great variations within very short distances; the ferruginous rock is probably nearly 30 feet thick in places, its higher portions, as is usual in this immediate neighbourhood, affording the richest iron-ore.

The Northampton Sand is seen at a number of points along the small valleys which traverse Rockingham Park, and also in the deep cuttings in the sides of the great road passing through Kettering and Uppingham, above the village of Rockingham.

At a new farm beside Long Mantle Wood a deep well exhibited an interesting section in 1867.
(1.) Boulder Clay - - - - -
(2.) Whitish and light-blue sands and sandy clays,
    (Lower Estuarine series) - - - 12 feet.
(3.) Hard, blue, green, or grey, ferruginous, sandy
    and pseudo-oolitic rock. Not dug to bottom,
    for at 10 feet down in it a powerful spring
    was found.

It may be necessary here to call attention to the fact that whenever the ironstone of the Northampton Sand is, dug under a considerable covering of Boulder or other clays, which have prevented atmospheric action upon it, its normal character of a dark brown cellular rock is never exhibited, but, on the contrary, it is always compact or oolitic in structure, and blue, grey, or green in colour.

Between Rockingham and Gretton numerous exposures of the ironstone beds occur in the frequently slipped masses along the steep escarpment. At a few points the beds of white sand or of whitish, sandy clay, with numerous plant remains, which overlie that rock, are also seen. At Gretton the Lower Estuarine beds were well exposed in an artificial opening; and, between that village and Harringworth, we have many exposures of the ironstone beds, while we can everywhere trace their junction with the Upper Lias by means of the numerous springs.

Following the Northampton Sand eastward into the valley of the Welland, it is found to diminish rapidly in thickness. At the bridge between Barrowden and Wakerley, it is seen lying upon the Upper Lias, and is apparently, at this place, not more than two or three feet thick. In the same diminished form the Northampton Sand was seen in the foundations of a house at the village of Wakerley, but as we go eastwards all trace of it is lost, and the Lincolnshire Oolite appears to rest directly upon the Upper Lias Clay.

Along the spur which runs out to Morcot, the ironstone beds can be traced, but are of no great thickness; near this village they are overlaid by beds of white sand, dug for building purposes. On the opposite side of the valley to Morcot, we find the usual white and light-blue clays overlying the ferruginous sands. As we pass into the valley of the Chater, the Northampton Sand is again found to become rapidly attenuated, and its beds almost or quite disappear to the eastward, in the same manner as they do in the valley of the Welland.

At Luffenham Railway Station the Northampton Sand was found, in an excavation, to be very thin; within a space of ten feet we pass from the Lincolnshire Limestone into the Upper Lias Clay, the white sands, clays, and ironstone rock being present, but reduced to insignificant proportions. In the South Luffenham railway-cutting the ferruginous rock of the Northampton Sand is seen, but is not more than three or four feet in thickness. The white sands are seen underlying the representative of the Collyweston Slate in North Luffenham churchyard when new graves are opened there.

At Edith Weston the white sands forming the higher part of the Northampton Sand are well seen, and have frequently been dug for mortar at several different points within the lordship. Between the last named village and Martinsthorpe, the Inferior Oolite beds stretch westward in a long spur, along the sides of which the Northampton Sand can be seen at several points. The exact boundaries of the strata on this spur are greatly obscured, however, by the thick masses of Boulder Clay and Gravel which cover it. The causes which have brought about the variation of the outcrop of the beds from their normal direction in this place are easily discovered in the series of faults, which traverse the Martinsthorpe spur and the neighbouring outliers of Wing and Pilton, Lyndon, Hambleton, Normanton, and Whitwell; these faults will be further alluded to hereafter.

A great breach is effected in the escarpment by the river Gwash. The ferruginous beds of the Northampton Sand are exposed in the steep river-banks at the village of Empingham, but the series does not appear to attain to any great thickness at this place. The tributary brooks which flow by the villages of Greetham and Exton have cut deep, gorge-like valleys quite through the Inferior Oolite limestones and sands, down to the Upper Lias Clay. At Horne Mill the beds of light-blue clay of the Lower Estuarine Series are seen lying upon the ironstone beds of the Northampton Sand. At Exton a number of interesting sections in the Inferior Oolite were exposed during the works about the New Hall; one of these behind the new memorial chapel was as follows:—

		ft.	in.
(1.) Soil - - - - - -		2	0
(2.) Light-blue, laminated, sandy clay, with ferruginous stains in the bedding planes, and traces of plant remains - - - - - -		1	4
(3.) Fawn-coloured and ferruginous sands, finely laminated, with one or two argillaceous bands, each overlaid by a lamina of hard brown hydrated peroxide of iron - - - - -		2	6
(4.) Light-coloured, finely stratified, sandy clay, occasionally passing into sand and then becoming very ferruginous - - - - -		3	0
(5.) Ordinary cellular ironstone-rock - - -		2	0 seen.

Farther back behind the Hall the beds are again dug, and this pit showed that the highest stratum in the foregoing section is covered by 2 feet of light brown sand, and this again by beds of hard sandy fissile stone, the base of the Lincolnshire Oolite, and the representative of the Collyweston Slate. A well in the kitchen of the Hall showed the thickness of the ferruginous rock here to be 11 feet, the Upper Lias Clay being reached at its base. The generalised section at Exton is therefore as follows:—

		ft.	in.
(1.) Representative of the Collyweston Slate	-		
(2.) Lower Estuarine sands and clays	-	9	0
(3.) Ironstone rock of the Northampton Sand	-	11	0
(4.) Upper Lias Clay - - - -	-	top only seen.	

As illustrating, however, the great variations in thickness and mineral character to which the strata of the Northampton Sand are liable, we may notice a section seen in the small lateral valley, north of the boat-houses in Exton Park.

This section is described in detail, as it presents some features which have a very important bearing with reference to the mode of formation of the deposit. It is as follows :—

(1.) Oolitic limestone, with hard, flaggy, siliceous beds at the base; the latter is the equivalent of the Collyweston Slate.

(2.) Bed of light-blue, tenaceous clay about 1 foot thick.

(3.) Beds of light-coloured sand, with ferruginous stains in the lines of bedding and interstratified with thin seams of clay and laminæ of hard, dark brown ironstone, about 2 feet thick.

(4.) Beds of ironstone of the usual cellular structure, characteristic of the Northamptonshire iron-ore. These attain a considerable thickness.

(5.) Upper Lias Clay.

The stratum (3.) presents some interesting characters. The interbedded laminæ of ironstone, which are dense and brittle, and in every respect similar to the harder portion of the iron-ore below, vary in thickness from $\frac{1}{4}$ to $\frac{1}{6}$ of an inch. On careful examination it is seen that each of these laminæ rests on a seam of clay, and is covered by a layer of sand of greater or less thickness. Similar sections are seen in other pits in the immediate neighbourhood ; but this, though a very curious and suggestive, is by no means a common aspect of the Northampton Sand. It finds a curious parallel in parts of the Bagshot Sand series of the Lower Tertiaries.

Between Oak Inn Farm and Greetham Mill, the junction of the Northampton Sand and the Upper Lias is well seen. There is here exposed a good section of the ferruginous sands, very copious springs flowing out at their base. As a general rule, however, along these narrow valleys the sands and clays are altogether concealed by the masses of the Lincolnshire limestone which have almost everywhere slipped over them.

At Whitwell we find the flaggy beds at the base of the Lincolnshire limestone underlaid by white sands. At this place a small east and west fault, approximately parallel to that which traverses the Hambleton outlier, brings down the beds of the Northampton Sand to the south, giving rise to a small outlier. In a deep road-cutting near Whitwell we have an admirable exposure of the succession of beds at this place, though their exact thicknesses cannot be measured. The series is as follows :—

(1.) Oolitic limestone (Lincolnshire Oolite).

(2.) White siliceous limestone with mammillated surfaces (equivalent of Collyweston Slate).

(3.) White and fawn coloured sands } Lower Estuarine Series.
(4.) Light blue clays.

(5.) Ironstone beds of the Northampton Sand.

(6.) Upper Lias Clay.

At Burley Park the Northampton Sand beds form a very steep escarpment above the Upper Lias Clay, the numerous landslips having given rise to a very sinuous boundary line between the two formations. This line can be easily traced by the numerous springs, which flow out along the junctions of the pervious with the impervious beds ; several of these are utilized for the supply of the reservoirs in the park. There are many small openings in the Northampton Sand, which present the usual characters ; at one or two points thin beds of whitish clay are seen intercalated in the ironstone series. From Burley northwards, to the extreme limit in this direction of the area under description, the Lincolnshire Oolite does not reach the edge of the escarpment, the sands forming a tract about a mile wide at the top of the ridge on which stand the villages of Cottesmore and Market Overton. The junction of the limestone and sands of the Inferior Oolite in this part of the district is often greatly obscured by drift; the boundary between the latter and the subjacent Upper Lias Clay is, however, very distinct and easily traceable until we get to Wymondham, where the great Boulder Clay sheet overlaps the edge of the escarpment on to the Lias plateau below. Below Cottesmore, at Barrow, and under Market Overton, numerous small sections of the ironstone rock and of the overlying Estuarine sands and clays can be seen, but they afford only a repetition of the characters so fully described at many points to the south. The escarpment along this line, from Burley-on-the-hill to Market Overton, is nearly as bold and striking in appearance as that between Rockingham and Harringworth.

Valley of the Nene and its tributaries.—Along the Nene Valley we find the Lower Oolites, which are here comparatively thin, cut through completely, so that the beds of the streams are in the Upper Lias Clay. In this part of the district the Northampton Sand, which is itself often very thin, constitutes the only representative of the Inferior Oolite ; the Lincolnshire Oolite, as already explained having quite thinned out and disappeared, so that the structure of this part of the country is precisely similar to that of the district south of Kettering where the Lincolnshire Oolite has disappeared in the same manner, and the estuarine beds at the base of the Great Oolite, rest directly upon those of the Inferior. As we go northward along the course of the Nene and its tributary the Willow Brook, we find the Lincolnshire Oolite coming in as a wedge between the two Estuarine series, the beds of which, westward and northward, gradually assume great thickness and importance.

Immediately to the south of the area included in the sheet under description, we have, in the Aldwinkle and Tichmarsh railway-cuttings, interesting illustrations of the non-ferruginous characters presented locally by the Northampton Sand. Here we see the Great Oolite limestones resting on the clays of the Upper Estuarine Series, these last reposing on an eroded surface of the Northampton Sand, which is here constituted by beds of white sand and sandy clay yielding in some bands freshwater fossils and plant remains, and in others marine shells ; the marine characters prevail altogether at the base of the series, where there is a band of ironstone usually only about six inches thick. As showing the extreme liability to variation in mineral characters in the beds of this series, we may mention that in a road-drain, only a short distance from the railway-cuttings, the Northampton Sand was seen with its normal characters and having thick beds of ferruginous rock in its lower part.

The section of the Tichmarsh cutting presents some features of special interest. The Northampton Sand is here composed principally of white sands which abound in carbonaceous matter, occurring either in minute fragments between the laminæ, in larger masses scattered irregularly through the beds, or forming thin seams of lignite. As at Ufford, and many other points, the lower beds of sand become gradually more and more ferruginous, and thus pass almost insensibly into a bed of ironstone, which forms the base of the formation and presents all the usual characters of the Northamptonshire iron-ore, but is never more than one foot in thickness. The sudden variations in character of the Northampton Sand are strikingly exemplified in this case, for in several places in the immediate neighbourhood of this section, as at Thrapstone and Wadenhoe, the beds of ironstone acquire a considerable development.

But the most noteworthy circumstance in connexion with the section at Aldwinkle, is the presence of beds containing well-preserved organic remains. In the lower part of the cutting is seen a bed of sand, cemented by calcareous matter and about one foot thick, which is crowded with shells. These fossils are tolerably well preserved, the substance of the shell usually remains, sometimes even, when first exposed, retaining the nacreous lustre. The Conchifera and Brachiopoda have their valves united, and neither they nor the univalves exhibit any trace of erosion ; these circumstances of course negative the idea that they might be drifted shells, and indicate that they lived at or near the spot where they are now found. That the fauna of this bed is a truly marine one, will be at once demonstrated by the following list of genera :—

Ostrea.	Arca.	Pholadomya.
Gervillia.	Lucina.	Trigonia.
Modiola.	Astarte.	Euspira.
Perna.	Tancredia.	Terebratula.
Cardium.	Neæra.	

A thin seam in the sand, occurring at some distance above the bed just described, appears to be crowded with shells of *Cyrena*, but these are in a very crushed and imperfect condition.

At Wadenhoe, just above the level of the river, we have sections illustrating the extremely attenuated condition of the Lower Oolites. It is only in very good sections that the exact limits between the Upper and Lower Estuarine series can be traced, both being often greatly reduced in thickness ; wherever a clear section, however, can be traced, the ironstone junction band is more or less distinctly exposed, and the Upper or Great Oolite beds are found to repose on an eroded surface of the Lower or Inferior Oolite beds.

The succession of beds seen at Wadenhoe is as follows :—

(1.) Cornbrash
(2.) Great Oolite clay } Traceable in slopes above the pit.
(3.) Great Oolite limestone
(4.) *a.* White clays - - - - 1 foot.
    b. Yellow, sandy clay - - - - 1 foot.
    c. Dark, laminated, sandy clay - - 1 foot 6 inches.
    d. White clays, with vertical plant markings - 9 inches.
    e. Dark, carbonaceous clays - - - 6 inches.
    f. White clays, with vertical carbonaceous
        markings and ferruginous stains - - 2 feet.
(5.) Ironstone beds, to bottom of pit - - 8 feet.

A little below the level of this pit the Upper Lias Clay was dug. Possibly we may regard *a, b, c,* and *d* as belonging to the Upper, and *e* and *f* to the Lower Estuarine series.

Below Pilton and Stoke Doyle the Northampton Sands can be clearly traced, but we get no good sections till we arrive at Oundle Wood, situated in a small lateral valley west of the town of Oundle. The ironstone beds at this place have been extensively quarried in ancient times. There are several large mounds in this wood, some composed of masses of ore as brought from the pit, and others of the same broken into small fragments, together with heaps of calcined ore and of slag. From the remains of pottery and coins found at this place it would appear that these workings were carried on by the Romans. In a pit, opposite the boat-house on the lake, the ironstone rock, which here contains *Terebratula submaxillata*, Mor., and other shells, is covered by a considerable thickness of freshwater sands and clays. At several points along this valley, the ferruginous deposits of the springs probably indicate the presence of the ironstone beds, sections of which are however very seldom seen along this and the neighbouring valleys.

At Southwick the Northampton Sand is seen, and has been worked in ancient times ; this is manifest from the large quantities of slag found there. The ironstone is here overlaid by ferruginous sand with some seams of clay, the whole being covered by beds of gravel composed of fragments of Oolite. The ironstone beds at this point contain a few fossils, such as *Terebratula, Rhynchonella,* and *Avicula.* The beds are much disturbed here by landslips. Along the sides of this valley the Lincolnshire Oolite can be traced, like the thin end of a wedge, coming in between the Upper and Lower Estuarine beds.

At Wood Newton brickyard we find the beds of the two estuarine series, here separated only by the greatly attenuated rock of the Lincolnshire limestone, very well exposed. Both the clays above and those below the limestone are dug for brickmaking. By the aid of a well we are able to construct the following section :—

(1.) Clay (Upper Estuarine) - - - 3 to 4 feet.
(2.) Ironstone junction band - - - 0 to 1 foot.
(3.) Limestone (Lincolnshire Oolite) - - 15 inches.
(4.) *a.* White sand and clay
    b. Brown sand - - } - - - 16 to 18 feet.
    c. Ironstone beds -
(5.) Upper Lias Clay. - - - - at bottom.

At the foundations for the new bridge at Wood Newton, the ironstone bed and the overlying sands and clays were well exposed, the whole resting on the Upper Lias Clay. In the Wood Newton parish-pit and in the sides of the brook between Wood Newton and Apethorpe, the white sands under the oolitic

limestone are exposed. At the Apethorpe "town-pit" beds of light-blue clay
and marl appear in the same position. Upon the side of the hill, on the right
bank of the Willow Brook, and opposite to the village of Kings Cliffe, a pit
shows the limestone with hard, quartzose, laminated beds exhibiting mammillated surfaces at its base, and resting on the white sands with carbonaceous
markings and plant remains.

At Yarwell, on the west bank of the Nene, the Northampton Sand is evidently
thin ; it is composed principally of white sand, and its junction with the limestone
above and the clays below was seen. On the opposite side of the river, at
New Close Cover, the Lower Estuarine beds are dug in a small pit, affording the
following section :—

    (1.) Soil.
    (2.) Brownish-yellow sand -   -   -   3 inches to 1 foot.
    (3.) Black band, entirely made up of car-
        bonaceous matter showing vegetable
        fibres-   -   -   -   -   3 inches.
    (4.) Clayey sand of a grey colour with some
        plant remains   -   -   -   4 inches.
    (5.) White sand.

North of Stibbington the ferruginous sands can be traced at the fish-ponds,
and the white sands have been found underlying the oolitic limestone in the
great pits south of Wansford. The same beds are seen underlying the Lincolnshire Oolite in the cutting between Wansford station and the Wansford or
Sibson tunnel, and here, as will be afterwards shown, we have a complete
series of the Great and Inferior Oolite beds exposed.

At Water Newton brickyard the sands and clays of the Lower Estuarine
series are dug under the beds of oolitic limestone which are here only of
insignificant thickness. Along the small tributary valleys in which are
situated Southorpe, Thornhaugh, Wittering, &c., the sands and ironstones of
the lower part of the Inferior Oolite can be traced, but they appear to be
generally very thin and afford no good sections. Along the valley of the Nene
eastward, the beds in question are almost always concealed by the thick deposits
of valley-gravel. At Milton Park and at Peterborough, wells have been sunk,
which passed from the Upper Estuarine clays directly into white sands of the
Lower Estuarine, the Lincolnshire Oolite having entirely thinned out.

Inliers. The great plateau formed by the Lower Oolite beds is
frequently cut through by the numerous streams which intersect
it, so as to expose in the sides of narrow valleys all the strata
down to the Upper Lias Clay. This exposure of the lowest beds
of the Inferior Oolite is frequently aided by the numerous faults
which intersect the district, and throw the beds in question to
much higher levels than those which we might anticipate they
would occupy, from their general dip.

In the inlier at Pipwell, which is cut down to the Upper Lias
Clay in its western part, through an upthrow of the beds, we find
a number of exposures of the Northampton Sand. Near Pipwell
Upper Lodge the ironstone beds are dug in a small pit ; and half-
a-mile westward traces of an old reservoir are seen in the valley,
at a point where abundant springs issue at the junction of the
ironstone with the Upper Lias Clay. The Northampton Sand is
also well exposed in the deep gorges near the junction of the
two small streams above Pipwell Abbey.

At the inlier at Corby and Weldon there are many exposures
of the Northampton Sand, the succession of the beds exhibited at
a number of different points in road-cuttings, &c. being :—

    (1.) Lincolnshire Oolite Limestone, becoming sandy at its base
        and sometimes exhibiting traces of fissile stone (Colly-
        weston Slate).

(2.) Very variable beds of sand and clay with numerous plant remains. (Lower Estuarine Series.)
(3.) Ironstone beds, with usual characters.
(4.) Upper Lias Clay.

The Northampton Sand here exhibits the usual very great variation in thickness and mineral characters. Between Corby and Little Weldon the same succession of beds is seen at several points; near the latter place they suddenly disappear, the lime-stone being let down against them by a fault.

The manner in which a rock of the impure shelly and oolitic limestone of the Northampton Sand passes, often within very short distances, into beds of white sand or ironstone is very strikingly exemplified in this neighbourhood. In many places the limestones are themselves very ferruginous and exhibit the peculiar banding with thin seams of brown hæmatite, developed along lines parallel to those of bedding and jointing, which is so striking a feature in the Northampton Sand. Precisely similar phenomena are exhibited in Yorkshire in the country south and west of Malton, where the great estuarine series of the Lower Oolites, which form the north-east moorlands of Yorkshire are greatly reduced in thickness, while in their midst there are developed a number of, sometimes locally important but always extremely inconstant beds of more or less sandy oolitic and shelly limestone, precisely agreeing in character with those of the Northampton Sand. The presence of these inconstant calcareous rocks appears to be very characteristic of series of strata, exhibiting other evidences of the alternations of freshwater and marine conditions at the period of their deposition.

The small valley at Brigstock Parks exhibits the Inferior Oolite limestones and sands considerably disturbed, and as already explained, unconformably overlaid by the series of Great Oolite beds. Between Sudborough Lodge and the Brigstock Park Lodges we find a pit opened in the summit of a small anticlinal in the ironstone beds of the Northampton Sand.

About Little Oakley and Stanion the valley, cut through the Boulder Clay and Great Oolite beds by Harper's Brook, exposes the Inferior Oolite strata along its sides similarly faulted and rolled, and unconformably overlaid by the Great Oolite series. The ironstone beds at the base of the Northampton Sand have frequently been dug in the wells and cisterns at the village of Stanion; while about Little Oakley there are numerous exposures of the white sands and clays of the upper part of the series, and the ferruginous rock of its lower part; they offer, however, no special features of interest at this place, and will be noticed in connexion with the beds of the Lincolnshire Limestone in this inlier. At Brigstock Mill, an interesting section in the brickyard and wells, to be here-after fully described, exhibits the whole of the Lower Oolite series from the Upper Estuarine series down to the Upper Lias, this place being near the line of the easterly disappearance of the Lincolnshire limestone by attenuation. The succession of the Northampton Sand beds at this place is given on page 191.

A long narrow inlier of the Northampton Sand is seen in the upper part of the valley of the Willow Brook, near Dene, Bulwick, and Blatherwycke, but there are seldom good exposures of the strata. At Dene brickyard we have the following section :—

(1.) Marly limestone - - - - 1 to 2 feet.
(2.) Whitish, calcareous sands - - - 1 foot 6 inches.
(3.) Hard, blue-hearted, sub-crystalline limestone - 1 foot 6 inches.
(4.) Brownish, calcareous sand, becoming indurated
    into stone at its base - - - 2 feet.

(5.) Hard and compact, coralline limestone, full of
     Nerinæa, with partings of clay -   -   3 feet.
(6.) Irregular bed of siliceous concretions with
     mammillated surfaces below. This bed is
     intensely hard; between its laminæ are
     contained numerous plant remains; it
     appears to be the representative of the Colly-
     weston Slate -   -   -   -   1 foot.
(7.) Irregularly stratified and false-bedded, varie-
     gated sand - -   -   -   -   6 to 8 feet.
(8.) Black, carbonaceous, sandy clays, with nodules
     of pyrites, and many fragments of wood con·
     verted into the same mineral -   -   6 feet.
(9.) Bed of hard sandstone of a dark-grey colour
     ("kale" of the workmen) - -   -   1 foot.
(10.) Clay, similar to (8) but lighter coloured and
     more sandy - -   -   -   -   3 feet.
(11.) Sandy ironstone (dug in a well) -   -   3 to 4 feet.
(12.) Upper Lias Clay.

1 regard all the beds from (7) to (11) inclusive as belonging to the Northampton Sand.

This section is of great interest as presenting another type of the Northampton Sand, namely that in which a great part of the formation is represented by
beds of dark-coloured clay. These beds have in some instances been mistaken
for the Upper Lias, and have, indeed, been sometimes mapped as such. A
close inspection, however, soon convinces the observer that the resemblance is
a very superficial one, and is confined almost entirely to colour. The clays in
question are totally wanting in the tenaceous character of the Upper Lias,
and indeed they are composed quite as largely of arenaceous as of argillaceous
materials; their dark colour appears to be due to the large quantity of organic
(vegetable) matter which they contain.

At Blatherwycke Park similar beds to those at Dene brickyard have been
penetrated in several wells.

About 30 years ago a well at the top of the hill sunk to the depth of 60
feet (?) appears to have reached, at the level of the ornamental water in the park,
a spring, the water of which is said to have been strongly impregnated with
sulphuretted-hydrogen, and to have acted as a powerful purgative. Another
well sunk into the rock of the Northampton Sand was the means of obtaining
a very copious supply of water.

In the valley known as "Hollow Bottom," the freshwater sandy clays of the
Lower Estuarine Series are exposed in the brook to the south of Bulwick
Woods. Higher up the brook the ironstone beds can be traced, and the very
numerous fragments of slag seen on the ploughed fields indicate that the
smelting of the ore was carried on at this spot at some former period.

The various beds of the Northampton Sand were also traced, though
somewhat obscurely, at the bottom of the little valley at Tryon's Lodge, where
they form a very small inlier in the midst of the great spread of Lincolnshire
limestone.

The clays of the "Lower Estuarine Series" can in like manner be traced in
the valley in which Fineshade Abbey is situated.

In consequence of the great north and south fault of Ketton and Duddington, the Northampton Sand and Upper Lias clays again make their appearance
in the valley of the Welland, at a distance of two miles from the points at
which they have disappeared (Wakerley and Barrowden) owing to their south-
westerly dip.

Traces of the Northampton Sand are seen at Duddington, below the old
pits which are said to have been worked for "slates."

At Collyweston a number of wells have been sunk through the thick limestone beds of the Lincolnshire Oolite, and the underlying slates and sands, into
the "red-rock" or ironstone of the Northampton Sand. The considerable
supplies of water required in the working of the slate-pits are said to be
obtained from the ironstone rock itself; it being found unnecessary to sink
down into the clays of the Upper Lias.

The beds of the Northampton Sand can also be traced on the opposite side
of the Welland Valley at Ketton, but there offer no features of special interest.

Along the sides of the Welland Valley to the westward, the beds of the Northampton sand are much obscured by masses of river-gravel, composed of oolitic detritus. They are seen again, however, at Wild's Ford opposite Tickencote Lodge, and at Ingthorpe.

The springs at Wothorpe, which are collected in a reservoir for the supply of the town of Stamford, take their rise at the junction of the Northampton Sand and the Upper Lias Clay. A good section of the former beds is exposed in a deep road-cutting near this place. Along this part of the Welland Valley many landslips have taken place owing to the numerous springs which arise at the junction of the ironstone rock and the clays, and the facility with which the former, being undermined by this agency, slide over the latter.

At the village of Easton the ironstones of the Northampton Sand are well exposed. The whole formation here is seen to have a thickness of about 20 feet. The striking "cellular" appearance presented by the ironstone rock is well exemplified at this point, and the connexion of this peculiar structure with the original jointing of the rock is here very manifest. This subject will be more fully treated of in the next chapter. The junction of the Northampton Sand with the Upper Lias Clay forming the channel of the River Welland is seen at this point. Very copious springs of water, which supply the village, are given off at the base of the ironstones.

At Stamford, owing to the great east and west fault, the Northampton Sand which on the north side of the valley is at the level of the river, is on the south side exposed high up on the hill beside Burleigh Park. The whole of the beds exhibit signs of considerable disturbance. The ironstone and overlying sandy clays were exhibited at a number of points about the Midland and London and North-Western Railway Station at Stamford. At one point, where a small cross fault has thrown the sandy clays and ironstones of the Northampton Sand against the limestones of the Lincolnshire Oolite, a railway-cutting affords us a very interesting section (Fig. 7.)

Figure 7. Section exposed in a railway-cutting at the Stamford Station of the Midland and London and North-Western Railways.

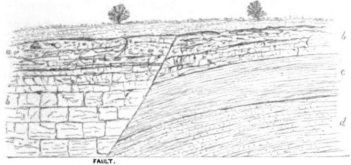

FAULT.

    a. Rubble Oolite.
    b. Oolite Limestone (Lincolnshire Oolite).
    c. Light-blue and white clays (Lower Estuarine Series).
    d. Ferruginous sands and ironstone (Northampton Sand).

Higher up the hill Lumby's Terra Cotta Works expose an interesting section, which is as follows :—

    (1.) Rubbly Oolite (in patches).
    (2.) Brown sand (irregular in thickness).
    (3.) "Terra-cotta clay," sandy and of a light blue colour, very irregular in thickness, 1 to 4 feet.
    (4.) Ironstone rock, 8 to 13 feet.
    (5.) Upper Lias Clay.

The clay bed (3) has been analysed by Mr. Lumby (formerly a student in the Royal School of Mines). It is of a pale colour, and composed of almost pure silicate of alumina with a little free sand in very fine grains ; sandy lumps also occur in the mass, which are ground up with the clay in the mill. This admixture of the clay with fine sand is said to greatly improve its quality. Mixed with a very small quantity of the white clay from Poole, Dorsetshire, these clays of the Lower Estuarine Series make an excellent terra-cotta.

Some years ago, in a futile attempt to find coal at this point, a boring was put down by the late Marquis of Exeter to the depth, it is said, of 500 feet. Unfortunately, however, no accurate record was kept of the beds passed through. From the information which I received, however, I infer that the Lias formation was not penetrated, no red rocks having been reached; if the information which I received can be relied upon, the Upper Lias Clay would appear to be about 140 feet in thickness at this place.

. Both the estuarine clays and sands, and the marine ironstones of the Northampton Sand are exposed at a number of points about Burleigh Park ; and since the mapping of the area has been completed the quarrying of the latter as an iron-ore has been commenced by the Marquis of Exeter. (See Mr. Sharp's Paper in the Quart. Journ. of the Geol. Soc., vol. xxix. p. 273.)

The light-coloured sands with ironstones at their base are seen at Wittering and many other points along the sides of the valleys of Southorpe and Thornhaugh, the beds being thrown far above their normal position by the great Stamford and Helpstone fault.

At Ufford the white sands of the Lower Estuarine Series are found to be highly micaceous, and to contain many thin layers of lignite and fragments of wood. One of the pits at this point affords a very interesting section (Fig. 8).

Figure 8. Section of the Northampton Sand seen in a pit east of Ufford, Northamptonshire.

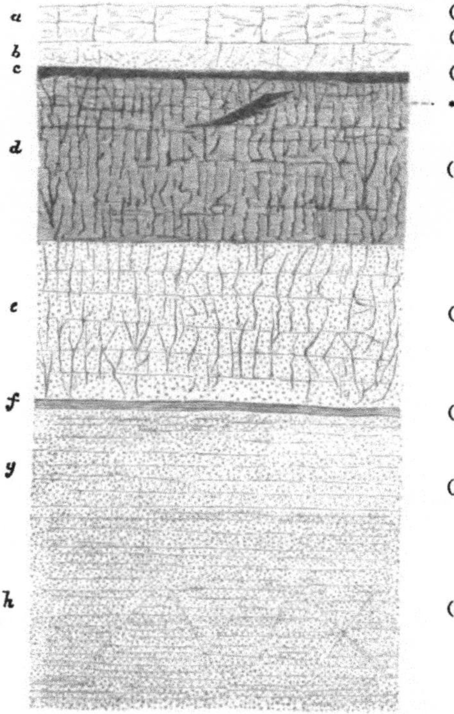

(a.) Oolitic limestone.

(b.) Yellow, sandy limestone, with marine shells.

(c.) Bed of lignite, 3 inches thick.

* Fragment of fossil wood.

(d.) Pale-purplish, micaceous clays, with vertical, carbonaceous remains of plants, 3 ft.

(e.) White and fawn-coloured sands, with vertical plant remains, 3 ft.

(f.) Thin seams of lignite, together, 4 inches thick.

(g.) Bed of very fine white sand, 1 ft. 6 in.

(h.) Yellow sands, becoming more and more ferruginous downwards, dug to 4 ft.

(b) is similar to and corresponds with (a) of the section, Figure 9, on page 105.

The vertical carbonaceous markings which occur in the beds (d) and (e), appear to indicate that plants actually grew upon the spot, and were embedded as they stood, by the quiet deposition of fine sediment around them. The beds called "root-beds" by Professor Morris,* which occur in another, but very similar, formation, greatly resemble (d). The clay of (d) is very fine grained, and the surfaces of its laminæ are covered with scales of mica : in it the carbonaceous matter is always preserved, while in the sands below (e) it is more frequently removed, and the sides of the empty tubes stained with oxide of iron.

In descending through the lower beds of sand (h) we find them more and more impregnated with oxide of iron, which exists as a coating around the individual grains ; when this coating is removed by the action of acid a white sand remains similar in every respect to that forming the bed (g). From the statements of workmen it appears that this ferruginous character still increases in going deeper, and that the bed which rests directly on the Lias Clay is a thin band of the ordinary ferruginous rock of the Northampton Sand.

The section at Ufford lies about one mile to the west of that at Helpstone, to be hereafter noticed, and on passing still farther towards the west and south we find the thickness of the ferruginous rock to continually increase, until, at no great distance, it is seen to constitute nearly the whole mass of the Northampton Sand.

At the Helpstone brickyard the Northampton Sand, with the beds above and below it, is bent into a sharp anticlinal fold ; the great disturbance of the strata at this point being connected with the fault so often referred to.

About a mile to the south-east and near Helpstone Heath Farm, where the beds are also disturbed but in a much less violent manner than in the last-mentioned section, we have a very instructive exposure of the Northampton Sand formation.

In this section one of the most interesting aspects of the Northampton Sand is well exhibited. It is represented below :—

Figure 9. Pit in the Northampton Sand between Ufford and Marholm (Northamptonshire.)

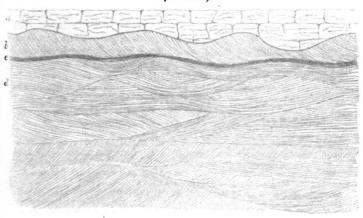

(a.) Siliceous limestone (" pendle ") with mammillated surfaces below.
(b.) Obliquely-laminated, fawn-coloured sand, 1 ft.
(c.) Purplish finely laminated clay, 3 in.
(d.) Finely-laminated, fawn-coloured sands, with much oblique lamination, 5 ft. exposed.

* Quart. Journ. Geol. Soc., vol. ix., p. 330.

The bed (a.) forms the base of the oolitic limestone series, the beds of which, as we pass downwards, are found to become more and more siliceous in character, and to be not unfrequently interstratified with beds of sand. This stratum is a very persistent one over a large area; it is a hard, usually blue, calcareous sandstone, well characterised by the mammillations of its under surface; when finely laminated and capable of being rendered fissile by exposure to frost it constitutes the well-known "Collyweston Slate." This rock is crowded with marine fossils.

The sands below this bed are remarkable for the great amount of oblique lamination which they present. The surfaces of the laminæ of sand are covered with fragments of carbonaceous matter, which appear in the section as fine black lines beautifully marking the bedding. Besides these minute particles in the planes of bedding, larger patches of carbonaceous matter occur, scattered through the mass, which are probably the vestiges of fragments of wood. Some of the beds of sand are crowded with shells, either whole or in fragments, but these are so much decomposed as to be incapable of removal; in some of the layers there occur undoubted specimens of marine shells as *Pinna cuneata*, *Ostrea acuminata* and *Trigonia costata* var. *pullus* Sow., in others, numerous *Cyrenæ*.

The base of the sands is not seen in this pit, but in another in the vicinity, where the beds are inclined, the white sands are found resting directly on the Upper Lias Clay, without the intervention of any ferruginous rock. The total thickness of the Northampton Sand at this place is rather more than twenty feet.

In the extreme north of the area included within Sheet 64 two small inliers of the Northampton Sand occur at Castle Bytham and Little Bytham, owing to the streams having cut their valleys through the Lincolnshire Oolite into the beds below. At neither of these localities, however, is there any clear section of the strata.

Outliers. In the western part of the district which we are now describing numerous outliers of Northampton Sand occur, usually capping the hills or plateaux of the Lias Clay. Many of these outliers are of very considerable area, one of them, that on which the town of Uppingham is built, occupying a very considerable proportion of the southern half of the county of Rutland. Not a few of these patches of Northampton Sand owe their preservation to the action of faults, which have thrown the beds into a position far below their normal level. Capping as they do the long ridges between the deep and sinuous valleys cut by numerous streams in the underlying Upper Lias Clay, these outliers of the Northampton Sand are usually of very irregular form. They give rise to the remarkably flat topped hills which are so characterestic of this district. (See Plate VII.)

The most southernly of the outliers in the district is that upon which the villages of Dingley and Brampton are situated. Here the Northampton Sand is mostly covered with boulder clay; and the limits of the former are difficult to trace, owing to the great extent to which the ironstone rock has in many cases slipped over the subjacent Upper Lias Clay.

South of Dingley a pit exhibits the beds of the Northampton Sand dipping N. at an angle of 2°. Above them are seen calcareous beds of slaty structure with a few traces of fossils (representative of the Collyweston Slate?) In the ironsand itself were found fragments of *Belemnites* (rare) and *Terebratula submaxillata*, Mor. Some other small exposures of the beds on this outlier occur, but they present no features of interest.

North of the Welland at Neville-Holt another considerable outlier of Northampton Sand is preserved, and is in this instance capped by the fissile beds representing the Collyweston Slate and the overlying oolitic limestones. Large ironstone workings have been commenced on the south side of this outlier. A trial hole is said to have proved a thickness of 15 feet of ironstone ;

RUIN. A. TIPTRES LEE. HAMPSHIRE. AN OUTLIER OF THE NORTHAMPTON SAND

some of the lower beds, however, appear to have been too poor in iron to be sent away for smelting and were used for building purposes.

The total thickness of the Northampton Sand formation in the Neville-Holt outlier appears to be about 20 feet. A boring to the depth of 100 feet was put down in the Upper Lias Clay at Neville-Holt in the hope of finding coal! The preservation of the considerable tract of Inferior Oolite at Neville-Holt is evidently due to the fault which bounds the outlier on its northern side and has produced a considerable subsidence of the beds.

To the west and east, respectively, of the considerable outlier just described, there occur two small and somewhat obscurely exposed patches of the beds of the Northampton Sand. The first of these caps the hill on which Slawston Mill is built and gives rise to its peculiar and striking form (see Plate V.), the other caps a less conspicuous hill lying east of the celebrated Neville-Holt Spa.

Above Hallaton-Ferns there occurs a small patch of the Ironstone-rock the peculiar position of which can only be accounted for by regarding it as brought to a much lower level by faults, and thus preserved when the surrounding masses of the formation were removed by denudation. The beds, which are well exposed in a pit, show considerable signs of disturbance and are capped by a mass of Boulder Clay (Fig. 10).

Figure 10. *Sketch of section in pit above Hallaton Ferns, showing a small outlying patch of the Northampton Sand capped by Boulder Clay.*

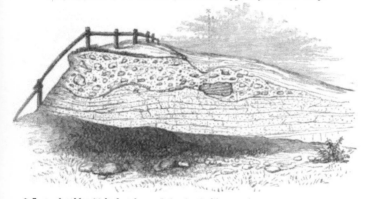

* Large boulder 18 inches long of the hard siliceous limestone (Pendle) of the Inferior (Lincolnshire) Oolite.

On the north side of the Welland Valley, between Gretton and Uppingham, three conspicuous hills, known as Bee Hill, Priestley Hill, and the Burrows, owe their preservation and striking form to the patches of the hard beds of the Northampton Sand which cap them. The last mentioned of the three is crowned with a small mass of the Lincolnshire Oolite limestone; and in all of them the strata are more or less obscured by superincumbent drift. At Bee Hill the rock capping the hill is nowhere well exposed; while at Priestley Hill the Northampton Sands are almost free from the covering of drift, but are not displayed in any artificial openings. At the hill known as the Burrows, however, the strata are much more clearly displayed. In one pit we find beds of Northampton iron-ore of the usual character, alternating with white, sandy clays; the whole being covered by five or six feet of drift clay, full of boulders. Strong springs arise at the base of the Northampton Sand. In a second pit (near Lyddington Lodge) a similar alternation of ironstone beds with white, sandy clays is also seen. The drift covering at this point is composed of very coarse gravel.

As already stated, the little market-town of Uppingham is situated upon an outlier of considerable size, which is, however, by the numerous streams intersecting it, divided into numerous long spurs. At several points on this outlier, as south of Uppingham, near Lyddington and at Glaston, hard beds of a calcareous nature, approaching in character those which are seen at Desborough and which make so conspicuous a feature in the country to the southwards, are seen at the base of the Northampton Sand series. At Uppingham these calcareous beds are about two feet thick.

The lowest beds at Uppingham, as at many other points in the area, appear to be considerably less ferruginous than those above them, and are extensively quarried for building purposes. A large quarry near the town gave the following section.

1. " Bearing," (ironstone rock with the usual characters) - - 8 ft.
2. Hard building-stone, of a blue colour - - - - 8 ft.
3. Mass of concretions or pebbles embedded in a blue ironstone
    matrix (very similar to the beds which occur at the base of the
    Marlstone Rock-bed) - . - - - - 6 in.
4. Upper Lias Clay

As illustrating the great variations in thickness within short distances of the strata which compose the Northampton Sand, I may cite, for comparison with the last, the following section obtained in a well at the town of Uppingham.

1. Sand and Clay - - - - - - 12 ft.
2. Good ironstone rock - - - - - - 5 to 6 ft.
3. " Rock," building stone - - - - - 3 ft.
4. Clay (Upper Lias) - - - - - dug to 4 ft.

A stone-pit just outside Uppingham on the road to Stockerston illustrates very admirably the gradual passage from the unweathered blue rock at the base, up to the perfectly weathered, deep brown, " cellular " ironstone above, and the transition upwards of this ironstone into loose sands (Fig. 11).

Figure 11. Stone pit near Uppingham, on the road to Stockerston.

Soil.

Clay.

Fine white sand

(with thin bands of clay)

gradually passing into

brown sand,

sand rock,

cellular ironstone,

and finally into

hard, ferruginous rock.

Clay (Upper Lias.)

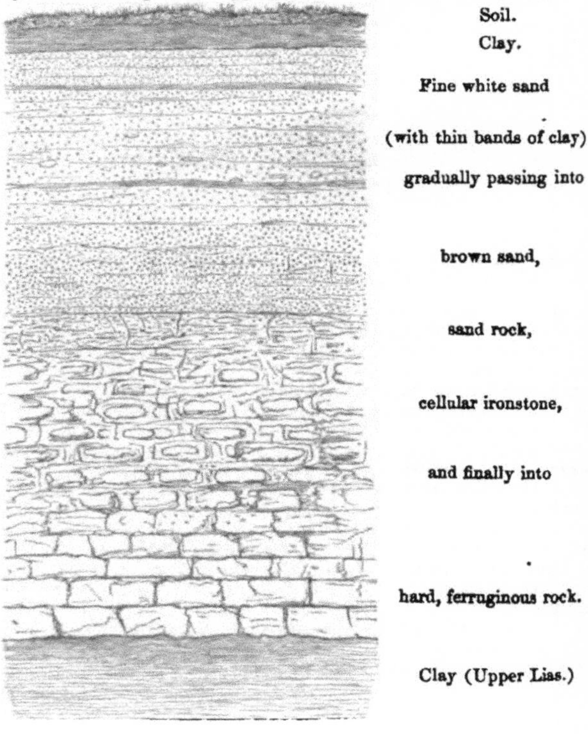

This section is about 20 feet deep. At its base is seen the Upper Lias Clay, and at its summit the light-blue, sandy clays of the Lower Estuarine Series. The beds of Northampton Sand in the Uppingham outlier seldom yield many fossils.   At one of the pits above Lyddington I obtained, however, Ammonites Murchisonæ, *Sow.* var. subradiatus, *Sow.* Pleurotomaria, sp. (cast.)

Another pit, near the same village, exhibited at the base a hard, blue, calcareous rock, which is a water-bearing bed.   Above this the beds are "bluehearted," each block, into which the mass is divided by the joints and bedding planes, showing an irregular central mass of blue rock, surrounded by a varying thickness of brown ferruginous material.   As we pass upwards in the section, the size of the central, unweathered nuclei diminishes, while that of the surrounding weathered crusts is found to increase, till at last the former entirely disappear.   A large portion of the ironstone in this pit is not traversed by the hard cakes of brown oxide of iron which form such a striking feature in most of the beds of the Northamptonshire iron-ore.   The rock here exhibits the interesting oolitic structure which will be hereafter described, but instead of the usual banded appearance displays sections of an uniform yellowish brown tint, where it has been subjected to weathering operations.

At Seaton, a pit behind the church exposes beds of white sands and sandy clays with many carbonaceous markings, and the outcrop of the ironstones below can be traced at many points in the immediate vicinity.

At Bisbrook, the line of junction of the Northampton Sand and the Upper Lias is indicated by numerous springs.   The lowest beds of the former series were at one time dug at this place for lining ovens, a purpose for which they are said to be admirably adapted.

At Glaston there occurs, at the base of the Northampton Sand, a very hard, somewhat calcareous band, which is crowded with a shell which closely resembles, if it is not actually identical with, the *Rhynchonella cynocephala,* Rich.

At Wardley, Ayston, Morcott, Stoke Dry, King's Hill Lodge, and many other points upon the skirts of the great Uppingham outlier, there occur exposures of the ironstone beds of the Northampton Sand.   None of these sections, however, present us with features of any novelty.

The villages of Ridlington and Preston are situated upon a long narrow outlier of the Northampton Sand, which is separated by a deep and narrow valley from that last described.   The hard rock of the ironstone gives rise to well marked steep escarpments, but the highest portions of the outlier are capped and obscured by drift deposits.   A number of small sections are afforded at different points, and there is evidence in the abundant furnace cinders that the ironstones in this neighbourhood were formerly smelted.

Immediately to the westward of the last, two smaller outliers of the Northampton Sand occur, on the larger of which stands the farm-house, called on the map Ridlington Lodge.   These outliers afford several exposures of the ironstone beds, which do not however present any features of interest.   Another small outlier lies to the north of the village of Preston.

Still further to the west a number of outliers of the Northampton Sand evidently owe their preservation to the great Billesdon and Loddington fault. These cap the prominent hills known as Whadborough Hill, Robin-a-Tiptoes, see Plate VII., Barrow Hill, and the nameless eminences rising above the village of Loddington and at Laund Wood.   All of these afford more or less complete sections of the ironstone rock, but in the three last mentioned the strata are to a certain extent obscured by deposits of drift gravel and clay.

At Whadborough Hill hard calcareous beds occur near the base of the Northampton Sand, and contain *Terebratula submaxillata,* Mor. and some other shells.   Beds of a somewhat similar character can also be traced upon Robina-Tiptoes.   From its elevation and striking form it might be anticipated that the neighbouring hill called Colborough Hill would also be found capped by the hard ironstone beds; but a careful examination of the summit failed to detect any such rock *in situ,* so that we must infer that the Inferior Oolite has been wholly removed from this eminence by denudation.

Small pits in the ironstone beds have been opened in the outliers of Laund Wood, Loddington and Barrow Hill, the position of which is indicated upon the map.   At the last mentioned locality the rocks show considerable signs of disturbance, owing to landslips.

At Lyndon a small outlier of Northampton Sand, capped by the beds of the Lincolnshire Oolite, occurs between the spurs which run out from the main escarpment to Wing and Martinsthorpe. The preservation of this outlying patch of Inferior Oolite rocks has evidently been brought about and its form determined by the somewhat complicated series of faults which is found in this area.

By the same series of faults the beds which form the outliers of Hambleton, Normanton and Whitwell have been powerfully affected.

In Normanton Park there were several sections of the Northampton Sand at the time the survey was made; one of these exposed a thickness of 8 feet of ironstone rock capped by the light-coloured sandy clays of the Lower Estuarine Series.

The outlier at Hambleton is crossed by an East and West fault, which appears to have a throw of about 20 feet. Through its agency the beds of the Northampton Sand have for a considerable distance been brought to the same level as the Lincolnshire Oolite Limestone. At the time of the survey a number of field drains afforded great facilities for determining the exact position of this line of fracture. The ironstones and overlying sandy clays, which were well exposed at a number of points, exhibit the usual features which we have already described as characteristic of this formation.

South of Whitwell a small fault has let down the Northampton Sand, which is in consequence found capping the hills of Upper Lias Clay. No clear sections are however presented at this point.

The last of these outliers of the Northampton Sand which we have to notice is a singularly isolated one of very insignificant proportions. It is found capping the conspicuous eminence known as Ranksborough Hill, situated about five miles to the north-west of Oakham. The beds of Northampton Sand are here quite destitute of any covering of drift, and there can be no doubt that the "red-rock" is here *in situ*, although but such a small portion of it has escaped destruction by denudation. It is probable that the preservation of this minute vestige of the formation, so far from the general line of its outcrop, may have been in part due to its subsidence through faults; but in the district which surrounds it, composed of Lias Clays deeply buried under drift, the field-geologist is destitute of the necessary data for determining the presence and position of such dislocations of the strata. There are some indications which would point to the conclusion that, beneath the thick masses of drift clay and gravel crowning the very elevated ridge upon which the village of Cold-Overton stands, beds of the ironstone rock may occur. But while the existence of such an outlier of the Northampton Sand is, at best, very doubtful, its limits are altogether unknown, and therefore no attempt has been made to indicate it upon the map.

The Iron-Ore of the Northampton Sand.

Frequent allusion has already been made to this important mineral production of the district now being described. The history of the working of these iron-ores in the Inferior Oolite of the Midland district has been a somewhat remarkable one. There is evidence that, at least as early as the period as that of the occupation of the country by the Romans, the beds of brown hydrated oxides of iron were known and extensively worked. We have already noticed that in a wood near Oundle heaps of broken ore, of the same calcined, and very large quantities of slag occur, associated with which have been found Roman coins and pottery. We have historical evidence that in mediæval times, the district of Rockingham forest vied with that of the Weald of Sussex and Kent as a great iron producing district. The Norman Castle of Rockingham is said to have been built for the protection of the iron-furnaces in Rockingham Forest. In both of these areas the presence of beds of tolerably rich iron-ore, in a district abounding with timber, led to the erection of numerous furnaces of the small kind then in use, and the extensive production of iron.

Throughout nearly the whole of the district described in this memoir enormous masses of slag, which are, of course, especially conspicuous where the land has been newly cleared for cultivation, testify to the extent to which the manufacture of iron was carried on in the area in ancient times. The slags are of a very dark, almost black, colour and extremely heavy; they bear witness to the want of skill of the ancient smelters and it is evident that only a comparatively small proportion of the iron contained in the ores was extracted from them by the imperfect methods then in use.

The causes of the decline of the iron manufacture in this district were the same as those which operated so powerfully in the case of the Wealden district of the south of England. In the first place, the enactment of rigorous laws to prevent the reckless destruction of timber-trees by the charcoal-burner operated powerfully, by restricting the supplies of fuel. In the second place, the discovery of the possibility of smelting iron-ores by means of coal and coke caused the transference of the industry to the coalbearing districts, in which the ore and mineral fuel are found in close association with one another.

For about two centuries the iron manufacture was thus wholly banished from the district, and scarcely a tradition of its former importance remained. With the introduction of railways into this country, and the consequent very suddenly increased demand for iron, new deposits containing iron-ores began to be sought for, in order to supplement the supplies yielded by the coalfields. At first this new demand appeared to be fully met by the opening out of the extensive Liassic and Oolitic ironstone beds of the Cleveland district, which have the great advantage of being in close proximity to the Durham coalfield. Still increasing demands for iron-ores of this class led to the re-opening of iron-mines in the Northampton Sand, and although the competition of the Cleveland and North Lincolnshire district, both more favourably situated in relation to the fuel producing areas, must have tended powerfully to retard the development of the industry in the midland district, yet the following table, kindly supplied to me by Mr. Robert Hunt, F.R.S., Keeper of the Mining Records, will show with what rapidity the working of the iron-ores of the Northampton Sand formation has been extended.

*

Annual produce and value of the iron-ores raised in Northamptonshire from the year 1860 *to* 1872 :—

			Tons.	£
1860	-	-	95,664	23,416
1861	-	-	113,139	28,535
1862	-	-	116,718	31,940
1863	-	-	126,587	41,644
1864	-	-	335,787	84,761
1865	-	-	364,349	96,137

			Tons.	£
1866	-	-	476,981	118,940
1867	-	.	416,765	104,191
1868	-	-	449,116	112,279
1869	-	-	540,259	135,065
1870	-	-	887,020	177,404*
1871	-	-	914,435	182,887*
1872	-	-	1,174,211	234,842*
1873	-	-	1,412,256	282,451*

The circumstances under which the working of the iron-ore of
the Northampton Sand was resumed in modern times are noticed
by Dr. Percy in the following terms :—

" The introduction of the Northamptonshire ore is only of
recent date. Not long previous to the International Exhibition
of 1851, Colonel (now General) Arbuthnot called upon me in
Birmingham, where I then resided, and requested my opinion on
a specimen of the ore which he left with me. I found it to contain a sensible quantity of sesquioxide of iron and a very large
amount of siliceous sand. I made no quantitative examination
of it; and, certainly, the specimen in question did not prepossess
me in its favour. However, I referred the Colonel to my friend,
Mr. S. H. Blackwell of Dudley, who visited the locality of the
ore in order to examine it *in situ*. He obtained samples much
richer in iron than that which was placed in my hands. He
prosecuted inquiries on the subject with his usual energy, and
the result has been the discovery of an extensive deposit of
ore, which has since been smelted in large quantities in South
Staffordshire, Derbyshire, and South Wales."†

At a few points blast-furnaces have been erected for the smelting of these iron-ores at the locality in which they are raised.
The only place within the area of Sheet 64, at which any attempt
has been made to manufacture the iron upon the spot, is at
Neville-Holt; the works at this place have not, however, been
completed. But by far the larger portion of the ironstone of the
Northampton Sand is sent away to the coal-bearing districts; the
highly siliceous ore of the oolites being found better adapted for
smelting in admixture with the calcareo-argillaceous ores of the
coal-measures than alone, or with the simple admixture of a
limestone flux.

Besides the ore of the Northampton Sand, the ironstone contained in the Great Oolite Clays, the "junction-band" of the
Upper Estuarine series and the Marlstone Rock-bed, were also
worked in ancient times. An attempt to revive the working of
the first-mentioned of these deposits near Peterborough resulted
in failure. Of late years proposals have been made to open mines
in the Marlstone Rock-bed, which farther south, in Oxfordshire,
(Adderbury and King's Sutton) yields a valuable ore.

---

* The values in each of these years are estimated at four shillings per ton.
† Percy's Metallurgy, Iron and Steel (1864), p. 225.

CHAPTER VI.

ORIGIN OF THE NORTHAMPTON SAND.

The formation described in the last chapter presents the geologist with many features of great interest. The remarkable concentration of iron in the thick beds which compose it, is accompanied by many striking peculiarities of physical and microscopical structure. As in the district under description many of these interesting features are very admirably illustrated, the occasion was taken during the survey of the area to study the chemical and microscopic peculiarities of the rocks composing the several beds of the formation, in connexion with their position and relations as observed in the field. The results of these observations, with a discussion of their bearing upon the various theories which have been put forward in explanation of the origin of these remarkable rocks, are contained in the present chapter.*

Every geological formation may be studied under two different aspects ;—either it may be regarded in its relations as one member of a series, and the record, more or less imperfect, of a period of the earth's history ; or it may be viewed as the product of the various forces, mechanical, chemical, and vital, which have operated in its original accumulation or its subsequent metamorphoses. In the *former* case we are called upon to investigate with the field geologist the mutual relations of great rock masses, their order of superposition, their conformity or unconformity, and the nature and amount of their disturbances ; in the *latter* we are led to study with the mineralogist and microscopist the various details of their intimate and minute structure. In the *former* case the most important aids to our inquiries will be found in the remains of organised bodies contained in the beds, and hence as our principal guide we must look to the naturalist; in the *latter* the greatest assistance to our investigation will be afforded by the crystallised minerals enclosed in the rock, and therefore, for direction in our inquiries, our chief dependence must be placed in the chemist. Hitherto the labours of geologists have been chiefly devoted to the former class of researches, but the latter offers subjects of at least equal interest and importance.

Every rock is more or less "*metamorphic.*" Ever since its deposition it has undergone and it still is undergoing a constant series of internal changes, the result of the action of various causes, as heat, pressure, solution, the play of many chemical affinities, and of crystallographic and other molecular forces,—causes insigni-

---

* These observations were originally laid before the Geological Society of London in the year 1869; but, it being found that, by the rules of the Geological Survey, an account of the various sections referred to could not be published at that time, the paper was withdrawn in order that it might make tis appearance in the present Memoir.

ficant perhaps in themselves, but capable under the factor *time* of producing the most wonderful transformations. The geologist is called upon to unravel the complicated results, to pronounce what portion of the phenomena presented by a rock is due to the forces by which it was originally formed, and what must be referred to subsequent change; to discriminate the successive stages of the latter and to detect their various causes; in short, to trace the history of a rock from its deposition to the present moment.

The object of this chapter is to examine the Northampton Sand from the *second* of the points of view which we have indicated. We propose to describe the various characters—petrological, lithological, microscopical, and chemical—of the formation in question, and to attempt to base on a discussion of these, definite conclusions with regard to the following points. *Firstly*, the conditions under which the rocks composing it were originally deposited, and, *secondly*, the changes which they have since undergone.

I.—GENERAL FEATURES OF THE NORTHAMPTON SAND.

These have been somewhat fully illustrated by the local descriptions of the preceding chapter. Especial attention may be directed to the accounts given of the sections at Aldwinkle railway-cutting (p. 98), Ufford (p. 104), that near Helpstone Heath Farm (p. 105), one at Exton Park (p. 97), and that at Dene brickyard (p. 102).

In the following remarks, the most interesting features of the deposits of this formation, and especially such as appear to throw light upon its mode of origin, are briefly noticed.

In some localities, as at Helpstone, Ufford, Aldwinkle, Kingsthorpe, &c., the deposit is mainly or wholly composed of beds of white sand, siliceous, calcareous, or micaceous, usually exhibiting much oblique lamination, often more or less indurated, and sometimes interstratified with beds of clay. Both the sands and clays usually contain much carbonaceous matter, either in particles lying between the laminæ, in vertical stem-like markings, or forming thin beds of lignite, each of which usually rests on a seam of " underclay."

The mass of the beds is usually very destitute of fossils; but thin seams occur crowded with shells, in some cases of marine in others of brackish-water species, the animals of which evidently lived and died upon the spot. When followed, either vertically or horizontally, these beds of sand are frequently found to graduate into the ordinary Northamptonshire iron-ore.

At Exton there occur in the midst of the white sands thin, hard, and brittle laminæ of dark-brown hydrated peroxide of iron, each of them being underlaid by a thin seam of clay.

Not unfrequently we find, as at Dene and near Burton Latimer, the formation in great part composed of beds of carbonaceous sandy clay, which from their dark colour have sometimes been mistaken for, and even mapped as, Upper Lias.

By far the most frequently occurring type of the Northampton Sand, however, is that in which the *upper* portion of the formation is composed of sands and clays similar to those which we have been describing, and the *lower* portion by strata of greater or less aggregate thickness of the well-known ironstone.

Everyone is acquainted with the great amount of change, both physical and chemical, which many rocks undergo in consequence of the passage through them of atmospheric water. Thus the Cornbrash when dug under the Oxford Clay is an extremely hard, dark-blue limestone, in which the planes of bedding are scarcely visible, and joints, though present, so little open that the rock scarcely admits of the passage of water through it, and it can consequently only be quarried by blasting; but when the same rock is dug at the surface its whole thickness is made up of a loose rubbly brown limestone, the appearance of which in sections ·has been, not inaptly, compared to that of a rough stone wall; each of the separate fragments into which the bed is disintegrated is often more or less thickly coated with a stalagmitic deposit.

Similarly, if we enter almost any quarry in an oolitic district we shall find striking illustrations of the same kind of change. The upper part of such a quarry will be found to be made up of " rubble" or disintegrated rock; below this the blocks of stone will be seen to be solid, but soft, and throughout of a white or brown colour. Lower still they will be found to have hard nuclei of a blue colour, or in the language of quarrymen will be " blue-hearted "; the lower we go, the larger shall we find these blue centres to become, till at last the blocks will be seen to be through-out of a blue colour. If the same limestone be quarried under beds of clay it will probably be found to be entirely of the same blue colour.*

We have been thus particular in adducing these instances, because no geologist will hesitate for one moment in ascribing the changes described to the weathering action of atmospheric water, which, finding access to the rock by the planes of bedding and jointing, traverses its substance, and acts chemically on its materials, especially the compounds of iron.

Now, changes precisely similar in kind, though much greater in degree (on account of the very large proportion of iron which it contains), have in the case of the Northamptonshire iron-ore resulted in some of the most marked and characteristic features presented by that rock. As, however, the very obvious cause to which we have referred has, in the case of the rock in question, been neglected or ignored by some authors on the subject, in favour of others, purely hypothetical, it may be necessary to describe in some detail the facts, which are, I believe, sufficient to place the subject altogether out of the region of controversy.

When quarried at the surface, the Northamptonshire iron-ore is seen to be composed to some considerable depth of the hydrated

---

* See some interesting remarks on this subject and on the necessity of a knowledge of it to those who seek for building-stone, by Prof. Morris. Quart. Journ. Geol. Soc., vol. ix., p. 329, note.

peroxide of iron only; we shall see hereafter that it is only the
superficial portion of the bed which is used as an ore, and hence
most of the quarries and pits present only this variety of the ironstone rock. But if the beds be followed vertically to some depth,
or horizontally some distance into the side of a hill, remarkable
changes in the nature of the rock will be found to occur. When
quarried at some depth from the surface each block will be found,
when broken, to contain a nucleus of compact, impure carbonate
of iron of a bluish or greenish-gray colour, and, as we go farther
from the surface, these nuclei will be found to gradually increase
in size till, in the end, the whole mass of each block is found to be
composed of the carbonated mineral. While the upper peroxidized
beds are easily traversed by water, the solid carbonated beds
below, on account of the closeness of their joints, are much less
pervious, and become "water-bearing." These facts are perfectly familiar to the well-sinkers of the district, who find that
to obtain water it is always necessary to pass quite through the
"kale" (the soft weathered beds), but that copious springs will
be found in the "rock" (the solid unweathered beds), without
going down to the "blue bind" (the Upper Lias Clay) ; but that
nevertheless, to prevent a failure of water in times of great
drought, it is always safer to penetrate to the latter.
    When the Northamptonshire iron-ore is met with at the bottom
of very deep wells, it is, throughout its whole thickness, composed
of the hard, compact, gray carbonate, and this is also the case
when it is dug beneath beds of Boulder Clay.
    In connexion with this gray, carbonated condition of the rock,
there are two circumstances of great interest and importance
which require remark :—firstly, that the fossils in it retain their
shelly substance, though the carbonate of lime is frequently
replaced by carbonate of iron, and are not, as in the weathered
rock, merely double casts ; and secondly, that there occur in the
beds of lignite, vertical plant remains and fragments of carbonaceous matter.
    In the gray, carbonated centres of blocks dug at some depth
in the weathered Northamptonshire iron-ore of some localities,
as at Holt, fossils similarly retaining their shells are found ; in
these also the casts of vertical plant remains are very frequently
seen. In the upper beds such changes have taken place, owing to
the redistribution of the oxide of iron, that it would be in vain
to expect to be able to detect such traces in them.
    The Northamptonshire iron-ore is generally almost destitute
of fossils throughout the greater part of its mass ; occasional
beds however occur which are crowded with marine shells, preserved as we have already seen as double casts. These shells
present every appearance of having lived in the places where
they are found, and not of having been drifted ; they belong
principally to the orders *Lamellibranchiata* and *Brachiopoda*,
but a few *Gasteropoda* also occur, as in the overlying limestone.
Cephalopoda are extremely rare, though specimens of *Ammonites,*
Belemnites, and *Nautilus* have been found. Occasionally seams

are found in the ironstone which appear to be crowded with shells of *Cyrena*.

Near Stamford the Northamptonshire iron-ore is overlaid by a thin bed of clay, with fine grains of white sand disseminated through it, but without any other foreign admixture. In other localities, as Holt and Desbro', lenticular beds of a similar material occur in the midst of the ironstone itself.

The most striking feature of the Northampton Sand may be summarized as follows: —

(1.) The formation is usually composed of sand, sometimes purely siliceous but at other times micaceous, carbonaceous, calcareous, argillaceous, or ferruginous.

(2.) In this formation there occur rapid alternations of evenly stratified beds, with some exhibiting much oblique lamination, and others indicating the existence of terrestrial surfaces.

(3.) The organic contents of the formation suggest the proximity of land at the time of its deposition, and also indicate remarkably rapid transitions from marine to brackish water and terrestrial conditions.

(4.) In this formation ferruginous beds are usually present, but not unfrequently altogether absent.

(5.) These ironstones vary greatly in thickness, occasionally constituting the whole of the formation, frequently forming the greater part of it, not seldom being reduced to very small proportions, and sometimes being wholly wanting.

(6.) The ironstone when present always constitutes the *lowest* portion of the formation and lies immediately upon the Lias Clay.

(7.) The ironstone, when unweathered, consists of a hard, solid, compact or oolitic rock of a bluish or greenish-gray colour, composed principally of carbonate of iron.

II.—LITHOLOGICAL CHARACTERS OF THE NORTHAMPTON SAND.

The prevailing mineral characters of the clays and sands of this formation have been sufficiently illustrated in the descriptions of the typical sections before referred to; the ferruginous beds, however, present some remarkable and highly interesting features of rock structure, which it will be desirable to examine in some little detail.

The unweathered beds of ironstone consist of a mineral, composed mainly of carbonate of iron (but containing disseminated through it grains of quartz and siliceous oolitic concretions) which is coloured, usually of a bluish or greenish tint, by minute quantities of other ferrous compounds. The rock usually exhibits only slight traces of the planes of bedding, and although it is traversed by joints, yet these, as we have already seen, are so little open that the stratum is almost constantly water-bearing, and cannot be quarried without blasting. Of banding or concretionary structure, with the exception of the minute oolitic features to be hereafter described, this rock does not exhibit the slightest trace. The different beds vary greatly in hardness, the oolitic rock being much softer than the compact or granular.

But when we turn our attention to the *weathered* beds of iron-stone, which are composed of hydrated peroxide of iron with disseminated grains of quartz and minute quantities of a few foreign materials, we find a remarkable contrast in many features with the rock just described. Occasionally, as near Lyddington in Rutland, beds of considerable thickness of the weathered iron-stone are made up of an almost homogeneous rock, of yellowish brown colour, friable texture, and oolitic structure; this is how-ever exceptional, and the rock in question usually presents a very marked and characteristic heterogeneous structure. In these cases its mass is seen to be made up of two very different materials ; that which forms the larger portion of the rock is of a yellowish-brown colour and soft earthy texture; the other portion is of a dark-brown colour, compact, hard, and brittle; the latter contains a considerably larger proportion of iron than the former. The relative distribution of these two materials in the rock is also a feature of very great importance. The hard, brown mineral always occurs in thin plates of from one-third to one-tenth of an inch in thickness ; these plates form complete prismatic cells, each of which encloses a mass of the light-coloured, earthy mineral, and is itself often surrounded by another layer of the same mineral, never more than one inch thick and usually much less. The form of these cells, though presenting much irregularity, usually approximates to a nearly rectangular prism, the relative dimensions of which are subject to the greatest variations; occasional cells of other irregular polyhedral figures also occur, but these are certainly exceptional. The absolute dimensions of these cells also vary between wide limits in different beds, but are tolerably uniform in the same beds, the length of one of the sides may be a few lines only, or it may amount to several feet. Sometimes these cells formed by the dark-brown mineral, are arranged in a concentric manner, the intervals between them being filled with the light-coloured variety; this structure prevails in certain localities, and a very beautiful example of it may be seen in a section at Easton; the examples of it are however, on the whole, much less frequent than those of the non-concentric cellular structure. The centres of the cells in both the varieties may be occupied, as already explained, by larger or smaller nuclei of the gray carbonated mineral. The *inner* surface of the hard laminar material, forming the walls of the cells, is always sharply and clearly defined from the mass of the enclosed softer mineral, and in fact an empty space of greater or less extent usually exists between them ; in this latter case the hard and brittle walls of the cells being unsustained are often fractured by the pressure of the surrounding materials. The *outer* surface of the laminæ, on the other hand, almost always graduates to a greater or less extent into the investing, light-coloured material. Frequently also, there is a marked gradation of density in the laminar material itself, and in such cases the denser portion is always found to be that nearest the interior of the cell.*

The form of the internal and well defined surfaces of the laminæ is extremely irregular, constantly tending towards mammillated and botryoidal characters, not unfrequently being extended into long finger-like projections, and sometimes being further complicated by a secondary series of more or less regular sculpture-like markings. This inner surface, though usually detached from the enclosed mass of the soft mineral, is nevertheless frequently coated with an extremely thin layer of the latter, and thus presents a bright yellow colour.

That portion of the bed of ironstone lying nearest to the surface has, in addition to chemical disintegration, usually undergone a certain amount of mechanical denudation, by which means a portion of the soft earthy material is carried away, and the hard laminæ being broken by mutual pressure, the result is a confused mass of irregular fragments of the hard mineral, intermingled with a larger or smaller proportion of the soft mineral. Thus a mass is formed, which of course contains a larger per-centage of iron than the undenuded rock, and it is this portion of the bed which, to the depth of about six feet, is usually dug as an iron-ore. Doubtless, if some ready mechanical means could be contrived for separating the hard layers from the earthy portion of the rock, its value as a source of iron would be greatly increased.

III.—MICROSCOPICAL CHARACTERS OF THE NORTHAMPTON SAND.

The ordinary sands and clays of this formation do not present any microscopical features of particular interest. The former consist principally of more or less rounded and waterworn fragments of white quartz, the size of which is usually very uniform in the same bed, but varies very considerably in different ones, from a general diameter of from $\frac{1}{100}$ to $\frac{1}{400}$ of an inch. In some of the beds, as already observed, each of these grains is invested with a coating, of greater or less thickness, of the hydrated peroxide of iron. The calcareous sands contain, in addition to the rounded quartz grains, fragments, usually angular, of carbonate of lime, which by their minute structure are seen to be comminuted particles of shells. Of minute organisms either siliceous, as diatomaceæ, or calcareous, as foraminifera, I have not been able to detect any trace in this formation. The carbonaceous fragments, which are so abundant in some of the beds, do not, owing to the imperfect state of their preservation, present any well defined histological structure under the microscope. In the

* The peculiar distribution of the materials composing the Northamptonshire iron-ore is very admirably illustrated in one of the beautiful plates which form part of Mr. Maw's interesting paper "On the distribution of Iron in Variegated Strata." Quart. Journ. Geol. Soc. vol. xxiv. (1868), Pl. xv. Fig. 37.

lower part of the limestones, however, which immediately overlie the Northampton Sand, the plant-remains are better preserved, and in many of the small fragments there found, the characteristic venation of ferns can be easily distinguished; occasionally, too, larger specimens are preserved in the same beds, and in these the disposition of the *sori* can often be observed, thus affording the botanist safer materials for the construction and comparison of species than is usually the case with fossil plants. Well preserved masses of wood, both exogenous and endogenous, also frequently occur in these beds, though these do not, of course, afford sufficiently distinctive features for specific or even generic determination. Some specimens of the upright plants in the clays and sands, which were better preserved than is usually the case, appear to indicate that these belong to the order of the *Equisetaceæ*; the habits of the fossil plants must certainly have been similar to that of some recent members of that order. If this identification should prove to be correct, the fact would be one of considerable interest, from the abundance of plants of the same order in certain Yorkshire beds, which will probably prove to be of the same age as the Northampton Sand.

When we study microscopically the *ironstone* beds many features of very great interest present themselves, which have most important bearings on the problems of the mode of deposition of the rock, and the causes of the changes which it has since undergone.

I may first state that the most careful examination fails in detecting any difference in structure between the gray masses in the midst of the weathered blocks and the mass of the rock when dug at a great depth and unweathered. So strikingly is this the case that, on one occasion, having a large number of fragments of rock illustrating the two conditions mentioned, from which I was preparing sections for microscopical examination, I found myself quite unable, they having become accidentally mixed, to separate the two series; consequently the whole had to be thrown away, and fresh specimens procured.

Notwithstanding their great differences in *lithological* and *chemical* characters, the different varieties of the Northampton-shire iron-ore,—namely, the gray carbonate, the light coloured earthy peroxide, and the hard, dark coloured laminæ,—the *microscopical* features presented by them all are essentially the same. In all, a slight examination is sufficient to show that there is a considerable amount of variation in the intimate structure of the rock from different localities, and of the different beds in the same locality; in some cases the whole mass is seen to be made up of oolitic grains, varying in diameter from $\frac{1}{50}$ to $\frac{1}{100}$ of an inch; in others the structure of the rock is seen to be throughout compact or granular; and in other cases again, and these are by far the most frequent, we find a compact matrix, with oolitic grains disseminated through it in greater or less abundance. In nearly all cases there occur, scattered throughout the mass, rounded or sub-angular grains of quartz.

When fragments, not pulverized, of the Northamptonshire iron-ore are digested in hydrochloric acid, a white mass is left nearly equalling *in bulk* the material acted upon. This insoluble residue under the microscope is seen to be made up of several constituents. The principal of these are rounded or sub-angular grains of pure white quartz, varying in diameter from $\frac{1}{100}$ to $\frac{1}{500}$ of an inch, and rounded, siliceous, oolitic concretions of a pale-green colour, from $\frac{1}{50}$ to $\frac{1}{100}$ of an inch in diameter. Besides these, we frequently find in some specimens a number of scales of mica, and in others black fragments, which disappear on the ignition of the mass, and are thereby recognised as carbonaceous matter. The quantity of the latter substance is in some samples very considerable. Some of these facts concerning this insoluble portion of the Northamptonshire ore have already been noticed by Dr. Percy.*

Owing to the very different degrees of hardness of the various constituents of the Northamptonshire iron-ore, there is considerable difficulty in preparing good sections for microscopic examination. After many trials of different methods, I have found that the best plan for studying the internal structure of the rock is to prepare a number of polished surfaces, and to etch these to a greater or less extent with hydrochloric acid, by which means, of course, the siliceous materials of the rock are seen standing out in relief. In sections thus prepared we observe that the quartz grains are scattered irregularly through the mass of ferruginous matter in which the oolitic concretions are embedded. The latter, when seen in section, present very different appearances. Sometimes we find only a single outer coat of siliceous matter enclosing several more or less decomposed grains of quartz; in other cases the whole mass of the concretion is made up of concentric siliceous coats; and between these two extremes we may observe every intermediate variety. The intervals between the siliceous coats are filled either with carbonate or with hydrated-peroxide of iron. The siliceous coats do not appear in any case to be so compact or continuous, as to prevent the acid from penetrating and extracting the soluble material enclosed between them.

In the hard laminæ of the weathered rock the oolitic concretions can usually only be seen by making polished sections, but in the light-coloured, earthy material they are usually visible, even to the naked eye, and are in such a state of decomposition that the several coats composing them may be successively broken and removed with the point of a needle. The thin layer of a bright yellow tint, which often adheres to the inner surfaces of the dark brown laminæ, is easily seen, when viewed with a low power, to be formed as follows:—The oolitic grains of the interior soft mass have adhered to the investing, dark-coloured mineral, and, owing to the friability of the former, the unattached portions of these grains have been broken away, leaving fragments of one or more of the coats still attached to the laminæ.

* Metallurgy, Iron and Steel, pp. 225–6.

IV.—CHEMICAL CHARACTERS OF THE NORTHAMPTON SAND.

There have been already published a considerable number of very accurate and detailed analyses of the Northamptonshire iron-ore.

In Dr. Percy's work on the " Metallurgy of Iron and Steel,"[*] there are given no less than eight such analyses made by Messrs. Spiller, Riley, and Dick, and these have especial value, as furnishing us with the exact composition of the portions of the ore which are respectively soluble and insoluble in hydrochloric acid.

To Mr. Maw we are indebted for the publication of two very complete analyses by Mr. David Forbes, and of some more partial ones by Dr. Voelcker.[†]

" ANALYSIS, by Mr. JOHN SPILLER, of Northamptonshire Iron-ore from Wellingborough.

				a.	b.
Sesquioxide of iron	-	-	-	52·20	51·93
Protoxide of iron	-	-	-	trace.	—
Protoxide of manganese	-	-	-	0·51	—
Alumina	-	-	-	7·13	—
Lime	-	-	-	7·13	7·39
Magnesia	-	-	-	0·57	0·54
Potash	-	-	-	—	—
Silica	-	-	-	1·60	1·77
Carbonic acid	-	-	-	4·92	—
Phosphoric acid	-	-	-	1·26	—
Sulphuric acid	-	-	-	—	—
Bisulphide of iron	-	-	-	0·03	—
Water { hygroscopic	-	-	-	—	—
{ combined	-	-	-	11·37	11·28
Organic matter	-	-	-	—	—
Ignited insoluble residue	-	-	-	13·55	13·59
				100·27	

Ignited insoluble residue.

Silica	-	-	-	11·56	—
Alumiua	-	-	-	0·26 ⎫	—
Sesquioxide of iron	-	-	-	0·66 ⎬	—
Lime	-	-	-	0·33	—
Magnesia	-	-	-	0·11	—
Potash	-	-	-	—	—
				12·92	
Iron, total amount	-	-	-	37·00	

" This ore consists essentially of earthy hydrated sesquioxide of iron. It is oolitic in structure and ochre-brown in colour. The insoluble residue consisted almost entirely of siliceous oolitic concretions, but on dissolving these in potash a small amount of residue was left, containing quartzose sand, scales of mica, and minute spherical particles of magnetic oxide of iron. A trace of copper was detected in a solution of 660 grains of the ore."

---

* Pp. 208, 209, 225, and 226.
† Quart. Journ. Geol. Soc., vol. xxiv., pp. 395–397.

"ANALYSIS, by Mr. EDWARD RILEY, of Northamptonshire Iron-ore from Wellingborough.

Sesquioxide of iron	34·41
Protoxide of iron	trace.
Protoxide of manganese	0·27
Alumina	6·19
Lime	25·68
Magnesia	0·85
Potash	—
Silica	0·89
Carbonic acid	18·45
Phosphoric acid	1·47
Sulphuric acid	0·07
Bisulphide of iron	0·30
Water { hygroscopic	—
{ combined	6·97
Organic matter	—
Ignited insoluble residue	5·82
	101·37

Ignited insoluble residue.

Silica	5·80
Alumina	
Sesquioxide of iron }	0·21
Lime	0·04
Magnesia	0·02
Potash	—
	6·07
Iron, total amount	24·09

"This was similar to the last, but ochre-yellow in colour. The insoluble residue for the most part consisted of siliceous oolitic concretions, and contained also quartzose sand, mica, and small black particles of magnetic oxide of iron."

"ANALYSIS, by Mr. EDWARD RILEY, of Northamptonshire Iron-ore from Wellingborough.

	a.	b.
Sesquioxide of iron	50·31	50·48
Protoxide of iron	trace.	—
Protoxide of manganese	0·51	0·45
Alumina	7·25	
Lime	11·76	11·87
Magnesia	0·62	0·60
Potash	—	—
Silica	0·22	0·35
Carbonic acid	7·98	7·80
Phosphoric acid	1·28	—
Sulphuric acid	—	—
Bisulphide of iron	0·17	—
Water { hygroscopic	—	—
{ combined	11·00	11·07
Organic matter	—	—
Ignited insoluble residue	9·33	9·34
	100·43	

Ignited insoluble residue.

Silica	-	-	-	-	8·58	8·54
Alumina	-	-	-	-	0·27	0·35
Sesquioxide of iron	-	-	-	0·22	0·26
Lime	-	-	-	-	0·16	0·11
Magnesia	-	-	-	-	trace.	—
Potash	-	-	-	-	0·11*	—

$$9·34$$

Iron, total amount   -   35·37

"This was in all respects similar to the last. A minute trace of a malleable metal, apparently lead, was detected in the ore. Nearly the whole of the silica, it will be perceived, existed in the ¡form of oolitic concretions. The insoluble residue contained quartzose sand, mica, and small particles of magnetic oxide of iron."

"ANALYSIS, by Mr. ALLAN B. DICK, of Northamptonshire Iron-ore from Hardingstone.

Sesquioxide of iron	-	-	-	-	74·12
Protoxide of iron	-	-	-	-	—
Protoxide of manganese	-	-	-	-	0·57
Alumina	-	-	-	-	1·55
Lime	-	-	-	-	0·76
Magnesia	-	-	-	-	0·18
Potash	-	-	-	-	—
Silica	-	-	-	-	0·43
Carbonic acid	-	-	-	-	0·57
Phosphoric acid	-	-	-	-	3·17
Sulphuric acid	-	-	-	-	trace.
Bisulphide of iron	-	-	-	-	0·06
Water { hygroscopic	-	-	-	-	—
{ combined	-	-	-	-	11·89
Organic matter	-	-	-	-	trace.
Ignited insoluble residue	-	-	-	-	7·15

$$100·45$$

Ignited insoluble residue.

Silica	-	-	-	-	5·60
Alumina	-	-	-	-	1·36
Sesquioxide of iron	-	-	-	0·20
Lime	-	-	-	-	—
Magnesia	-	-	-	-	trace.
Potash	-	-	-	-	- undetermined.

$$7·16$$

Iron, total amount   -   -   52·05

"ANALYSIS of Northamptonshire Iron-ore from the East End Iron Works, Wellingborough.

Sesquioxide of iron	-	-	-	-	76·00
Protoxide of iron	-	-	-	-	trace.
Protoxide of manganese	-	-	-	-	0·40
Alumina	-	-	-	-	2·30
Lime	-	-	-	-	0·41 }†
Magnesia	-	-	-	-	0·11 }
Potash	-	-	-	-	—
Silica	-	-	-	-	—
Carbonic acid	-	-	-	-	—

Carried forward   -   -   79·22

* With traces of soda.   † Estimated as carbonates.

Analysis of Northamptonshire Iron-ore—*continued*.

Brought forward	79·22
Phosphoric acid	1·03
Sulphuric acid	—
Bisulphide of iron	—
Water { hygroscopic	1·80
{ combined	12·40
Organic matter	—
Ignited insoluble residue	5·33
	99·78

Insoluble residue consisted almost wholly of silica with a trace of mica.

Iron, total amount - 53·20

" This ore was ochre-brown in colour. The sample analysed was an average of three specimens. No appreciable amount of sulphur was found in the ore."

" ANALYSIS of Northamptonshire Iron-ore from the Heyford Iron Works, near Weedon.

Sesquioxide of iron	56·20
Protoxide of iron	trace.
Protoxide of manganese	0·20
Alumina	2·43
Lime	0·49 } *
Magnesia	0·17 }
Potash	—
Silica	—
Carbonic acid	—
Phosphoric acid	0·84
Sulphuric acid	—
Bisulphide of iron	—
Water { hygroscopic	1·16
{ combined	9·74
Organic matter	—
Ignited insoluble residue	29·07
	100·30

The insoluble residue consisted of silica with a little mica.

Iron, total amount - 39·34

"This ore was similar in appearance to the preceding. The sample analysed was an average of two specimens. No appreciable amount of sulphur was found in the ore."

" ANALYSIS, by Mr. ALLAN B. DICK, of the inner and outer portions respectively of a lump of Northamptonshire Iron-ore.

	Inner portion.	Outer portion.
Sesquioxide of iron	—	38·04
Protoxide of iron	33·29	10·54
Protoxide of manganese	1·11	0·69
Alumina	4·62	12·35
Lime	0·50	trace.
Magnesia	7·96	4·13
Potash	—	—
Silica	1·99	1·96
Carbonic acid	24·79	0·16
Phosphoric acid	0·22	0·26
Sulphuric acid	trace.	trace.
Bisulphide of iron	0·13	0·13
Water { hygroscopic	—	—
{ combined	0·54	6·92
Organic matter	0·08	0·19
Ignited insoluble residue	24·09	24·61
	99·32	99·98

* Estimated as carbonates.

Ignited insoluble residue.

Silica	-	-	-	17·50	21·28
Alumina	-	-	-	3·27	2·67
Sesquioxide of iron	-	-	-	3·31	—
Lime	-	-	-	trace.	trace.
Magnesia	-	-	-	0·81	0·22
Potash	-	-	-	0·20	0·38
				25·09	24·55
Iron, total amount		-		28·28	34·83

" The inner portion, it will be observed, consists for the most part of carbonate or protoxide of iron, and the outer portion of hydrated sesquioxide, the latter having been clearly derived from the former by atmospheric action. No metal precipitable by sulphuretted hydrogen was detected in a solution of 880 grains of the inner portion of the ore. On the contrary, extremely minute traces of copper and lead were detected in a solution of 744 grains of the outer portion of the ore, so that these metals appear to have been communicated to the ore by water from without."

" ANALYSIS, by Mr. DAVID FORBES, F.R.S., &c., of unweathered portions of the Northamptonshire Iron-ore from the upper part of a section exposed at Blisworth, Northamptonshire.

Specific gravity, 3·58.

Protoxide of iron	-	49·58	= 79·9 carbonate of iron.
Sesquioxide of iron	-	5·67	
Bisulphide of iron	-	0·96	= iron, 0·45; sulphur, 0·51
Protoxide of manganese		0·16	
Alumina	-	1·56	
Lime -	-	3·24	= 5·8 carbonate of lime.
Magnesia	-	0·46	= 1·0 carbonate of magnesia.
Carbonic acid	-	34·64	
Phosphoric acid	-	0·44	
Silica -	-	2·16	
Organic matter	-	trace.	
Water of combination		1·56	
		100·43	

" ANALYSIS, by Mr. DAVID FORBES, F.R.S., &c., of unweathered portions of the Northamptonshire Iron-ore from the lower part of the same section.

Protoxide of iron -	-	-	-	-	40·93
Sesquioxide of iron	-	-	-	-	6·14
Protoxide of manganese	-	-	-	-	0·16
Alumina -	-	-	-	-	8·08
Lime	-	-	-	-	3·47
Magnesia -	-	-	-	-	2·21
Potash	-	-	-	-	0·19
Soda	-	-	-	-	0·27
Sulphur -	-	-	-	-	trace.
Carbonic acid	-	-	-	-	22·32
Phosphoric acid	-	-	-	-	1·99
Silica	-	-	-	-	9·04
Water	-	-	-	-	4·92
					99·72

" The specific gravity at 60° Fahrenheit was found to be 3·401 ; and an examination by the microscope showed it to consist almost entirely of two mineral constituents, the one crystalline and colourless, being chiefly carbonate of iron, and the other of a green colour, probably silicate of alumina and iron. Whether the green colour is due to it or to the presence of phosphate of iron is not decided, but it appears probable that a green silicate does exist in the mineral."

" It may be roughly estimated to consist of—
  80 per cent. of carbonate of iron.
  7 per cent. of carbonates of lime and magnesia.
  11½ per cent. of silicates of iron and alumina with phosphoric acid, and 1½ per cent. of water."

" ANALYSIS, by Dr. VOELCKER, F.R.S., of a friable portion of the
    Northamptonshire Iron-ore, near Blisworth.

Protoxide of iron	-	-	-	-	0·875
Sesquioxide of iron		-	-	-	21·280
Phosphoric acid	-	-	-	-	1·030
Sulphuric acid	-	-	-	-	0·219
Silica, lime, alumina, magnesia, &c. not separately					
determined	-	-	-	-	76·596
Carbonic acid	-	-	-	-	none."

" ANALYSIS of hard ferruginous cakes and layers, Northamptonshire Iron-ore
    deposit near Blisworth.

Protoxide of iron	-	-	-	-	1·352
Sesquioxide of iron		-	-	-	76·538
Phosphoric acid	-	-	-	-	0·020
Carbonic acid	-	-	-	-	0·014
Silica, alumina, lime, water, &c., not separately					
determined	-	-	-	-	22·076."

From a comparison of the various analyses it appears that the
gray carbonated mineral in the Northamptonshire iron-ore consists of from 60 to 80 per cent. of carbonate of iron, with from
10 to 25 per cent. of insoluble matter, principally sand and oolitic
siliceous concretions; besides these, and existing in smaller proportions, we find the carbonates of the alkaline earths and alkalies,.
water, carbonaceous matter, sulphur, and phosphorus. These
last two substances are, unfortunately for the value of the rock
as an iron-ore, always present, and frequently in considerable
quantity.

Carbonate of iron is a salt which when crystallized is trans-·
lucent and perfectly colourless, and in its amorphous forms is of
a pure white colour; hence we are at once led to inquire what is
the nature of the colouring matter in the rock which we are
studying. The colours, as we have already seen, are various
shades of dull blue and green; the colouring matter, it is probable, bears only a very small proportion to the mass of the rock,
the blue colour being certainly not more intense than in many
limestones which weather almost perfectly white, and which when
analysed are found to contain only a very small per-centage of
iron. M. Ebelman has shown[*] that the cause of the blue colour
in many oolitic limestones is the existence of a small quantity of
sulphide of iron diffused through the mass, and I feel little doubt
that the blue colour exhibited by some varieties of the unweathered Northamptonshire ore is to be attributed to the same
cause. With regard to the green colour of other varieties there
is probably still less difficulty in deciding on its true origin; the
various protosalts of iron which, with the exception of the carbonate, are almost all of a pale green tint, at once suggest themselves, and especially the silicate and the phosphate. It is the
latter of these salts I am myself inclined to suggest as giving rise to
the colour in question, from the fact that in my various estimations
I have always found sulphur to be in excess in the blue varieties,

* Bull. Soc. Géol. de France, 2me Sér. Tom. IX., p. 221.

and phosphorus in the green ones. This view receives some support from the analyses of Mr. Forbes, which show the following results:—

Green variety.—Sulphur - *trace.* Phosphorus - 1·12
Blue   „   „   - 0·51   „   - 0·25

The skeletons of the oolitic concretions in the Northampton-shire ore, which are insoluble in hydrochloric acid but are readily dissolved by a solution of potash, appear to be composed of more or less acid silicates of the alkaline earths, iron, and the alkalies. It would also seem that there is contained in the rock some basic silicates, as a small quantity of silicic acid is always found in the *filtrate* after digestion in hydrochloric acid. The grains of sand consist of almost pure silica. Besides the quartz grains and the siliceous concretions, the insoluble residue contains scales of mica, carbonaceous particles, both of which are occasionally present in considerable quantities, and, according to Dr. Percy, grains of magnetic oxide of iron.

In both the weathered varieties of the rock, the insoluble residue appears to be identical with that which we have just been describing. The composition of the soluble portion is, however, very different, consisting mainly of hydrated peroxide instead of carbonate of iron; alumina, lime, and magnesia are also present, but in much smaller quantities than in the unweathered rock. The relative proportions of the ingredients of the two varieties of the weathered rock are strikingly different; in the light-coloured earthy mineral the insoluble siliceous matter is in excess, and the proportion of metallic iron seldom exceeds 20 per cent.; in the hard and dark-coloured mineral forming the intersecting laminæ, on the other hand, the per-centage of iron frequently rises to between 50 and 60, while that of the siliceous matter is proportionately small. An interesting inquiry here presents itself as to what are the relative próportions of these two varieties of mineral in the mass of the ironstone rock. This is of course subject to great variation, but by taking average examples and following the method used in similar inquiries by Mr. Sorby, namely, drawing to scale a map of a section and from this cutting out the portions representing the two varieties and weighing them separately on a delicate balance, I obtained the following result:—In 100 parts of the rock there were 23 of the dark-brown material and 77 of the light-coloured.

It will be observed that the brown rock would be formed from the gray by the *subtraction* from the latter of carbonic acid and a quantity of the alkaline earths and alkalies, and the *addition* to it of oxygen, to peroxidize the iron, and water.

V.—ON THE CONDITIONS UNDER WHICH THE NORTHAMP-TON SAND WAS DEPOSITED.

With reference to this portion of the subject a paper was read at the meeting of the British Association in 1868.* Mr. Jecks,

---

* Colliery Guardian, vol. xvi. p. 197, and Rep. Brit. Assoc. for 1868. Trans. of Sections, p. 69.

the author of that paper, suggested that the formation was deposited by large rivers which carried sand, mud, and a solution of iron into the sea, and that, by oscillations of the land, truly marine conditions were alternated with the estuarine.

With that part of the theory which refers the Northampton Sand to the delta deposits of one or more great rivers, I am perfectly ready to agree, believing that few geologists who have examined the irregular manner in which these strata are accumulated, their rapid variations in character both vertically and horizontally, the oblique lamination of some of the beds, indicating the action of currents constantly varying in force and direction, the alternation of brackish water with marine conditions, the abundance of the remains of plants, and the evidences of actual land surfaces, in the intercalated beds of lignite and the vertical vegetable remains, will be disposed to doubt that we have here unequivocal evidence of the existence of estuarine conditions.

When we consider the constant changes which take place in a large delta ;—how, on the one hand, by the throwing up of sand bars, tracts before covered by the sea are converted into lagoons of brackish water, or on the other hand, in consequence of the breaching of these bars by tidal action, the lagoons are put in free communication with the sea, and again by means of the silting up of lagoons land surfaces are formed capable of supporting a rank growth of vegetation,—it will not, I think, be difficult to account for the deposition of the sands and clays constituting the Northampton Sand, without finding it necessary to have recourse to the hypothesis of oscillations of level ; at the same time I am of course far from denying that such a cause may have operated to a certain extent.

From the fact of the beds of the Northampton Sand having a constant tendency to thin out towards the south-east, as Mr. Hull has well shown,* it may be conjectured that the river or rivers which deposited them flowed from the north-west, and this is perhaps confirmed by the fact that the materials of which the beds are composed are such as might be furnished by the degradation of the carboniferous and other palæozoic rocks. It is of course probable that in the Northampton Sand a formation only averaging from 20 to 30 feet thick, we have only a very slight vestige preserved of the large amount of material brought down and deposited during the period.

Towards the close of the period, we find evidences of a gradual passage into the marine conditions, under which the superincumbent limestones were deposited, these latter consisting almost entirely of dead-shell banks and coral reefs. Above the limestones we have indications of the return, probably after the lapse of a very considerable period, to estuarine conditions, in the beds so well exposed in the cuttings of the Great Northern Railway.

---

* Quart. Journ. Geol. Soc., vol. xvi. p. 63.

near Essendine, and so fully and clearly described by Professor John Morris.*

VI.—Mode of Formation of the Northamptonshire Iron-Ore.

That portion of the theory of Mr. Jecks which deals with the question of the origin of the iron in the rocks of this formation is, like all the hypotheses which refer iron-ores to direct deposition, beset with grave, I believe I may even say, insuperable difficulties. The condition in which iron usually exists in solution in nature is as ferrous carbonate, which is soluble to a very considerable extent in water containing an excess of the acid. Thus in chalybeate springs a very considerable per-centage of iron is maintained in solution; but when these springs flow into a running stream the iron, as is well known, is almost instantly deposited as hydrated peroxide ; this is due to two causes, first, the large exposure of the water to the atmosphere in the ever varying surface oi the stream by which carbonic acid is given off, and oxygen from the air absorbed, and second, the action of living plants in the stream, which absorb carbonic acid and give off oxygen ; by these means the very unstable ferrous 'carbonate is rapidly decomposed, and the iron in the form of brown oxide deposited on the plants and stones in the bed or on the sides of the stream. I have on several occasions analysed the waters of small brooks in coal measure districts, and have invariably found that, although many springs which were strongly chalybeate flowed into these streams, and their beds were in consequence coated with thick deposits of peroxide, yet the quantity of iron *in solution* in their waters was almost inappreciable. I do not believe therefore that the water of any great river, or of the sea can ever contain more than the minutest trace of iron in solution. Now in the Northamptonshire iron-ore we are dealing with a rock, not merely coloured by iron, but one which is a true ironstone, containing from 30 to 50 per cent. of the metal; a rock which we cannot possibly conceive of as being deposited in an open sea or river.

It may at first sight appear that in the Swedish lake ores, and in the bog ores we have examples of the *direct* deposition of iron-ores, which contradict the foregoing statements. This is however not the case, as the former class of ores are never deposited in running waters, but only in shallow stagnant pools, among the roots of plants ; while the accumulation of both kinds appears to be due to the agency of organic beings.

We have already seen that the condition in which the iron originally exists in the ironstone is as ferrous carbonate. For the reasons I have already detailed, it is impossible to believe that such an unstable salt could have been slowly accumulated to the thickness of many yards in the sea or an open estuary without undergoing decomposition.

The abundance of molluscan remains in some of the beds of ironstone, indicating as we have seen that the animals lived and died upon the spot, precludes the idea that the medium in which the beds were deposited could have been a strong solution of iron.

The fact that many of the shells in the unweathered rock are more or less completely converted into carbonate of iron is, as Mr. Sorby has shown in the case of the Cleveland ore, a strong proof of the metamorphic character of the rock.

The existence of thin lenticular beds of white clay in the midst of the ironstone in some localities, as Desbro' and Neville-Holt, is a very significant fact. If the strata were deposited in water containing a large amount of iron in solution, the effect of a temporary change from sandy to clayey characters in the suspended matter, would be that we should have an argillaceous ironstone intercalated among the arenaceous ones, and certainly not that we should have a bed of perfectly white clay in the midst of a mass of ferruginous strata. On the other hand by the hypothesis that the iron was introduced after the other materials of the rock were deposited and partly consolidated, this phenomenon is readily accounted for by the pervious character of the sands and the imperviousness of the clay bands.

Again the theory of direct deposition affords no explanation of the origin of the singular oolitic concretions, so characteristic of the Northamptonshire iron-ore.

The foregoing considerations are, I believe, sufficient to lead us to the conclusion that the hypothesis of the direct deposition of the Northamptonshire iron-ore is altogether untenable. Mr. Sorby has shown* that the microscopic and chemical features of the Cleveland iron-ore are such as to lead us to the conclusion that it is an ordinary limestone altered by the percolation through it of water containing carbonate of iron in solution. The various facts which we have adduced in the present chapter all appear to point towards the hypothesis that the iron-ore of Northamptonshire is a similarly altered condition of the ordinary white Northampton Sand,† and that this alteration has often take place in a very local and capricious manner.

We have already described how in the iron-ore, when unweathered, we find many of the characters of the non-ferruginous sands, the abundance of plant remains (many of them vertical), the beds of lignite, the general absence of fossils through the mass, the thin zones crowded with mollusca, sometimes of marine and at others of brackish-water species, and the similarity of a part of the insoluble basis of the ironstone with the materials which compose the white sands of the formation.

The peculiarities of the section at Exton which I have referred to are also readily explained by this hypothesis, when we remember

---

* Proc. Geol. and Polytec. Soc. W. Riding of Yorkshire for 1856.
† It might be argued that the white sands are a bleached condition of the ferruginous beds ; but that the former have not undergone a *double* process of metamorphism is at once demonstrated by the state of preservation of their fossil shells, which not unfrequently retain even their nacreous lustre.

that each of the thin laminæ of ironstone rests upon a band of clay; the fact too that the Northamptonshire iron-ore, whatever its thickness, always rests directly upon the Lias Clay is also in the same way easily accounted for.

It must be remembered that the action of the water contained in the substance of rocks at great depths in the earth is very different from, and much more intense than, that of the same agent on the surface. Under the combined influences of heat and pressure, water has been shown to possess solvent powers of which, under ordinary conditions, it exhibits scarcely the faintest trace. All geologists are now agreed that water, probably often in large quantities, is contained in the substance of rocks deeply seated in the earth; such water is probably the source of supply for most hot and mineral springs, which in many if not in all cases, appear to be connected with faults or other disturbances of the rocks whence they arise; these disturbances appear to have been the means by which the passages have been opened through which the waters reach the surface. I need scarcely refer to the part that these subterranean waters are supposed to play in producing the phenomena of volcanoes and earthquakes, by a large school of geological theorists.

It would be easy to show, were it necessary, from the immense amount of denudation which has taken place in the district, that the beds of iron-ore now exposed to our observation must have been long buried at great depths in the earth; during this period, one of almost inconceivable duration, water containing carbonate of iron would appear to have constantly penetrated the porous sandy rock and thus gradually effected its metamorphosis into an iron-ore. The action of this water would be twofold:—in the first place it would deposit around the grains of sand and in all the interstices of the rock, the dissolved carbonate of iron, and in the second place, acting under the favourable conditions of great pressure and high temperature, it would dissolve a portion of the silica and other ingredients of the rock. Of the matter thus dissolved, one portion appears to have been redeposited in new combinations and, with the ·carbonate of iron, to have formed the oolitic concretions, while the remainder was probably carried away in solution.

That the theory which we have been describing is free from difficulties we are far from affirming, but we nevertheless believe that the difficulties which it may present are rather *negative*, the result of our ignorance of chemical forces and processes, than *positive* and opposed to laws which have been already well established. It must be remembered how little has yet been done in explaining the nature of the operations by which metallic compounds, diffused through great masses of rock, are concentrated and collected into beds and veins. The difficulty of such investigations probably arises from the minuteness of the causes themselves, which nevertheless, by their constant action through periods of time of almost inconceivable duration, have produced results so stupendous in themselves and so beneficial to mankind. The experimentalist, too, is constantly hampered by the circumstance that, limited as is his control over the conditions of heat, pressure, and the other physical forces, yet his command of the all-essential requisite, time, is restricted within still more narrow bounds.

VII.—CAUSES OF THE REDISTRIBUTION OF THE IRON IN THE NORTHAMPTONSHIRE ORE.

We have already pointed out the principal circumstances concerning the relative distribution of the carbonated iron-ore and, that in the condition of the hydrated peroxide, which lead us to the conclusion that the latter is simply the weathered condition of the former. As, however, a theory quite at variance with this has been advanced in a very interesting paper published by Mr. Maw,* it will be necessary to examine some of the phenomena in a little more detail, and to enter on the inquiry of their bearing on the two hypotheses. The author of the memoir just referred to, supposes that originally the whole of the ironstone beds of the Northampton Sand consisted of a nearly uniform mixture of the carbonate and peroxide, and that by two processes of " *segregation*," similar in kind but opposite in their modes of action, the particles of carbonate moved towards a number of nuclei, and thus formed detached nodules in the midst of the mass, while the particles of oxide moving in an opposite direction were accumulated into those hard cakes, which by "mutual pressure" tended to assume that cellular arrangement so characteristic of the rock.

In considering this theory several serious difficulties meet us at the very outset.

First. How, on such an hypothesis, is the strikingly rectangularly prismatic form of the cells to be accounted for? This structure is most admirably illustrated in one of the beautiful plates accompanying Mr. Maw's paper. "Mutual pressure" would tend to the production of cells of irregular polyhedral forms, which would present in section the figures of irregular polygons, and certainly not prisms with nearly rectangular sections. That this cellular structure is in some way connected with the jointing and bedding of the rock will, we believe, be manifest to any geologist who is in the habit of studying sections of the rock; this view is strikingly confirmed by the fact that in some places, as at Easton, the direction of one set of the sides of the cells is found to exactly coincide with that of the "master-joints" of the superincumbent limestones.

Second. We might fairly, on the hypothesis of Mr. Maw, expect to find in the central nodules of carbonate of iron some trace of a concentric arrangement. But although I have had constant opportunities of examining large numbers of these and have frequently prepared polished sections of them, yet I have never been able to detect even the slightest trace of any such structure.

---

* On the Disposition of Iron in Variegated Strata. Quart. Journ. Geol. Soc. vol. xxiv., pp. 395–398.

That the whole of the Northamptonshire ore once existed in the form of the gray carbonated mineral, and that the two varieties of the brown peroxidized mineral are only altered conditions of the original rock is, I believe, at once suggested by a study of the general features of the formation, and strongly confirmed by an examination of its lithological, microscopic, and chemical characters. The cause of this alteration was none other than the percolation of atmospheric water through the substance of the rock, to which it had gained admission by the planes of bedding and jointing. The *competence* of this cause to produce the effects which we have assigned to it will scarcely be doubted by those who have witnessed the great depth of some of the " gossans," which cover mineral veins, and which are admitted on all hands to have been formed from the latter by weathering.

The distilled water which falls upon the earth in the form of rain is, of course, free from solid matter in solution. During its formation and fall through the atmosphere it dissolves a portion of its ingredients, namely oxygen and nitrogen (the former being the more soluble of the two) with traces of carbonic acid and ammonia. In the districts composed of the Northampton Sand and the overlying oolite limestones, the rain which falls is almost entirely and very rapidly absorbed; indeed the capacity of absorption in these rocks appears to be practically unlimited, for not only do many of the streams flowing over boulder clay instantly disappear under ground by means of swallow holes, when they reach the junction of the clay and limestone or sand, but it is a constant practice in the district when draining the clays to carry the pipes not into a stream, but to an excavation in the rock, and these artificial swallow-holes are found never to fail in their object, even during the heaviest rainfalls. The Upper Lias Clay or the unweathered "rock-bed" of the Northampton Sand is, as we have already seen, the great water-bearing bed of the district, and everywhere along the lines of junction, at the surface, or wherever a well is sunk, very copious springs are poured out.

Let us now inquire what is the chemical character of the water of these springs. In the first place we may notice that it is never chalybeate; the few springs of this character in the district have seldom any connexion with the Northampton Sand, but on the other hand appear to be connected with the lines of fault. The water of these springs, however, is very hard, and their hardness is in a great measure of that kind know to chemists as *temporary* hardness; in other words, the water contains a large amount of mineral matter, principally the carbonates of the alkaline earths which are kept in solution by the presence of an excess of carbonic acid. A very simple calculation would be sufficient to show the enormous quantity of material which must every year be removed from the substance of these rocks by the agency of springs. Now the substances which are dissolved in the waters of these springs are carbonic acid, carbonates of the alkaline earths and alkalies, with minute quantities of alumina, silica, and iron, and these are precisely the materials which, if abstracted from the grey carbonated mineral of the Northamptonshire ore, would bring it to the peroxidized condition of the same rock, allowance being made for the addition of oxygen and water which enters into it from the atmosphere.

The action of the atmospheric water entering the rock by means of the bedding and joint planes would have been as follows :—Carbonate of iron is as we have seen rapidly decomposed in the presence of free oxygen, hydrated peroxide of iron being formed and carbonic acid set free, the last being of course at once dissolved by the water. The carbonated water is now in a condition to act on the soluble portions of the iron-ore, which we have seen to consist of a small proportion of the alkalies and a much larger proportion of the carbonates of the alkaline earths, these it rapidly dissolves as well as minute quantities of alumina and silica, while traces of the iron may escape re-precipitation, and thus the hard waters of the springs be formed. Proofs of the constant passage of water through the rock of the Northamptonshire ore are seen in the numerous surfaces covered with stalagmitic deposits and the empty double casts of shells from which the materials of the shell substance have evidently been dissolved.

But, besides the removal of the carbonic acid and certain soluble materials from the rock, it has undergone another most remarkable change, by the redistribution of the iron within it, and the production thereby of the cellular structure. The accumulation of oxide of iron, in laminæ roughly parallel with the bedding and jointing of the rock, is by no means peculiar to the Northamptonshire ore, though perhaps in it carried to a greater extent in it than in any other formation; similar phenomena are exhibited by many rocks containing more or less iron, when they become weathered, as the Marlstone Rock-bed, parts of the Great Oolite, and the Cornbrash. From the study of a large number of these cases, we are led to the conclusion that in all of them the penetration of atmospheric water is the cause, concerning the *modus operandi* of which we venture to make the following suggestion :—

We have already seen that the light-coloured mineral contains a much smaller, and the dark-coloured a much larger, per-centage of iron than the normal condition of the carbonate, in which the iron is evenly distributed throughout; and a moment's consideration is sufficient to convince us that the transfer of the iron through the substance of the rock could only have taken place when the former was in a state of solution. Now, as the water containing oxygen penetrates into the substance of the rock from a joint or bedding plane, its first effect would be to part with its oxygen and to take up a quantity of carbonic acid ; but carbonate of iron being very soluble in water containing carbonic acid, the liquid contained in the inner portion of the rock would soon become strongly chalybeate ; this liquid, passing outwards by diffusion, would meet fresh water entering containing free oxygen, and at the place where the two liquids came into contact we should instantly have a precipitation of hydrated peroxide of iron. This deposition of insoluble material would of course be liable to take place in planes roughly parallel to those from which the water acted, and when once such a barrier as this was commenced in the midst of the rock, to however slight a degree, it would constantly tend to increase, by retarding alike the outward passage of the chalybeate water and the inward passage of the oxygenated water. Thus, along the planes first marked out in the rock in the manner we have described, a fresh precipitation of the oxide of iron would continually take place, and these portions of the rock would become dense, compact, hard, and dark-coloured, while the remaining portions would by the removal of material be rendered light, earthy, soft, and pale-coloured. It is evident that if this operation were repeated a number of times, as it certainly might be, we should have produced a concentric structure similar to that which sometimes occurs in the Northamptonshire ore. Again, it is well known that the hydrated oxide when precipitated from a solution of iron tends to assume mamillated, botryoidal, and other peculiar forms, and thus the similar characters, which we have seen to be so frequently presented by the surfaces of the hard laminæ in the rock, are readily accounted for. The dark-brown, glazed surfaces of the casts of the fossils in the weathered ironstone rock may be similarly accounted for, when we consider the tendency which there will be for water to accumulate in the spaces left empty by the solution and removal of the substance of the shells.

VIII.—CONCLUSIONS.

I will now give a brief recapitulation of the conclusions of the present chapter, in the form of a sketch of what I conceive to have been the history of the formation of the Northampton Sand.

We find, in what is now the Midland district of England, and at a period separated by a long interval of time from that of the last deposit in the area, the Upper Lias Clay, that a number of considerable rivers, flowing through the palæozoic district lying to the north-west, formed a great delta. Within the area of this delta the usual alternations of marine, brackish-water, and terrestrial conditions occurred, and more or less irregular accumulations of sand or mud, in strata of small horizontal extent, took place. Subsequently, and probably in consequence of the gradual depression of the area, the conditions were changed, and in an open sea of no great depth, by the abundant growth of coral reefs and the accumulation of dead-shell banks during enormous periods of time, the materials of the great deposits of the Lincolnshire Oolite limestone were formed. On a re-elevation of the area the former estuarine conditions were also reproduced and similar deposits, but of an argillaceous rather than an arenaceous character, were formed. Confining our attention to the earlier of these two estuarine series, that of the Northampton Sand, we must imagine the beds as being carried down to great depths in the earth by the deposition upon them of the superincumbent strata.

But at the same time another most important cause has come into operation, namely, the passage through some portions of the rock of subterranean water containing carbonate of iron in solution. By this agent carbonate of iron was deposited in the substance of the rock, while portions of the siliceous and other materials were dissolved; and these, entering into new combinations, were in part re-deposited in the mass of the rock in the form of oolitic grains, and in part, probably, carried away in solution During the existence of the beds under a great pressure of overlying rocks, they would likewise become consolidated and jointed. These metamorphic processes would probably take place with extreme slowness, and may possibly still be going on, where the rock remains deep seated in the earth; by their means portions, greater or less, of the sandy strata, but always those resting immediately on the impervious Upper Lias Clay, would be gradually converted into solid and jointed rock beds, composed principally of carbonate of iron. The next stage in the course of alteration in these rocks would commence when, by the action of denudation, portions of them were brought again near to the surface, so as to be traversed by the atmospheric waters, entering them as rain and passing away from them as springs. The action of this water is, as we have seen, to remove the carbonic acid and soluble salts, to change the protoxide of iron into hydrated peroxide, and to redistribute it in such a manner as to produce the remarkable cellular structure of the rock, and also the mammillated, botryoidal, and sculptured surfaces. Finally, by mechanical, as distinguished from chemical, sub-aerial denudation, the beds of Northamptonshire iron-ore nearest the surface are disintegrated and broken up, and the softer and less ferruginous portions to some extent carried away in suspension, and thus deposits, composed of the harder and denser materials, formed, constituting the bed usually worked as an iron-ore.

If the arguments and deductions brought forward in this chapter be accepted, it will be seen that the formation and metamorphoses of this rock are alike principally due to one agent, *water*, acting under various conditions. The rain which falls upon the surface of the land may be disposed of in one of four ways. *First.* It may be returned, almost as soon as it falls, to the atmosphere by evaporation, without producing any effect on the rocks. *Second.* It may produce direct mechanical erosion by flowing over the surface and collecting into watercourses. *Third.* It may penetrate into the rocks by their joints and fissures, and after effecting within them chemical disintegration, thereby rendering them more susceptible of mechanical degradation, reappear as springs to swell the mechanical action of the portion before mentioned. *Fourth.* It may penetrate the substance of the more deeply seated rock-beds and, aided by heat and pressure, effect various metamorphoses within them, probably also giving rise to the phenomena of mineral and hot springs, earthquakes, and volcanoes.

It may fairly be objected that, in the foregoing remarks, we have not succeeded in giving a complete explanation of all the

circumstances connected with the origin of the remarkable and
very interesting rock of the Northamptonshire ore. On the other
hand, as an important part of every inductive inquiry consists in
the examination of all possible hypotheses and the rejection of
those which are proved to be untenable, thus narrowing the range
of speculation within certain determined limits, we venture to hope
that the foregoing observations will prove to be a contribution
towards the solution of a problem of great difficulty and obscurity.
The questions of the original source of the iron, the mode of its
accumulation in subterranean water, of the nature and mode of
action of the molecular forces which produce mammillation and
other allied phenomena, and which certainly follow laws, it may be
more complex, but not less definite than those of crystallization,—
these are subjects which have scarcely yet been attacked by
geologists, but concerning which, in spite of their difficulty and
obscurity, the secrets will assuredly one day be wrung from nature,
by combining patient observation with persevering experiment.

CHAPTER VII.

LINCOLNSHIRE OOLITE LIMESTONE, WITH THE COLLYWESTON SLATE.

This series of limestones was formerly considered as the equivalent of the Bath Oolite, but is now, on conclusive stratigraphical and palæontological evidence, referred to the Inferior Oolite. For the grounds on which these strata have been removed from the Great Oolite to the Inferior Oolite series, and the reasons for the nomenclature which I have proposed for the several members of the Lower Oolites in the Midland district, I must refer to the Introductory Essay to this Memoir (see pp. 1–40). Although the formation extends northwards into Yorkshire, and southwards into North-Northamptonshire, yet it attains its greatest thickness and prominence in the county from which it takes its name. Its horizontal extent is, however, by no means commensurate with its great thickness and importance, for it is found to thin away rapidly southwards, eastwards, and northwards; it should probably be considered as the eastern portion of a great lenticular mass of marine limestones intercalated between the Upper and Lower Estuarine Series.

The beds of the Lincolnshire Oolite display very various characters in different localities. Two aspects which it assumes, however, may be specially characterised.

The first of these we have called the "coralline facies" and it is characterised by beds of slightly argillaceous limestone, of compact, sub-crystalline, or but slightly oolitic texture, abounding with corals, which are usually converted into masses of finely crystallized carbonate of lime. The shells, which by their great abundance specially characterise this facies, often occur in the form of casts only, and consist of several species of *Nerinæa, Natica Leckhamptonensis,* Lyc., *Pholadomya fidicula,* Sow., and *P. Heraulti,* Ag., *Ceromya Bajociana,* d'Orb., *Pinna cuneata,* Phil., *Mytilus Sowerbyanus,* d'Orb., several species of *Lima,* and *Terebratula submaxillata,* Mor. The patches of limestone rock constituted in this manner afford ample evidence of having once been coral reefs; * near Castle Bytham a pit is opened in a rock seen to be almost wholly made up of corals.

The other variety of the Lincolnshire Oolite, which we have called the "shelly facies," consists almost wholly of small shells or fragments of shells, sometimes waterworn and at other times encrusted with carbonate of lime. The shells belong to the genera *Cerithium, Trochus, Monodonta, Turbo, Nerinæa, Astarte, Lima, Ostrea, Pecten, Trigonia, Terebratula Rhynchonella,* &c.; and spines and plates of Echinoderms, joints of Pentacrinites, and teeth of fishes also occur abundantly in these strata, which exhibit much false bedding. The Gasteropods are usually waterworn, and the specimens of

---

* Similar coral reefs in other portions of the oolitic series have been described by Dr. WRIGHT in an interesting memoir published in he Proceedings of the Cotteswold Club.

Conchifera and Brachiopoda usually consist of single valves often broken and eroded. These beds it is clear were originally dead-shell banks, accumulated under the influence of constantly varying currents.

The rocks of the two facies of the Lincolnshire Oolite do not maintain any constant relations with one another; at some places, as Barnack and Weldon, beds of the shelly facies occur almost at the base of the series, while at others, as about Geddington and Stamford, the strata with the coralline facies occupy that position. Sometimes, as at Ketton and Wansford, we find beds in the Lincolnshire Oolite entirely made up of fine oolitic grains, and these constitute some of the most valuable freestones. Very rarely the grains of which the rock is composed are very coarse, and it becomes a pisolite. At some points, as near Little Bytham, the rock assumes a very singular character, being filled with irregular masses, each surrounded by a thin pellicle of carbonate of lime, which when broken across are seen to be made up of the usual oolitic grains. Sometimes, especially at the top of the series, the beds of the Lincolnshire Oolite assume variegated tints, red and purple being the predominant colours.

A striking feature in all the beds of the Lincolnshire Oolite is the almost total absence of shells of the Cephalopoda, and in this respect, as in many others, it resembles the freestone beds both of the Great and the Inferior Oolites of the south-west of England; all of these beds, indeed, were evidently deposited under very similar conditions.

It is evident that the great mass of the Lincolnshire Oolite was deposited under moderately deep-water conditions, but in its lower part we find, in certain beds which indicate a gradual transition between it and the estuarine series below, decided evidence of the prevalence of littoral conditions. These lower beds of the limestone, which are usually more or less arenaceous and alternate with beds of sand, frequently, as about Cottingham, Morcott, and Wansford, contain large quantities of wood with the remains of ferns and other plants; *Polypodites Lindleyi*, Göpp (*Pecopteris polypodioides*, Lindl. & Hutt.), and other species, which are found also in the Lower Sandstone, Shale, and Coal of Yorkshire, characterise these beds. Sometimes the sands which alternate with the lower beds of sandy limestone are full of calcareous concretions, the associated limestones exhibiting broad mammillated surfaces which give rise to the masses known to quarrymen as "potlids"; occasionally, as at Dene, the sands pass into a very hard siliceous rock full of plant-remains.

The lowest of these beds of sandy limestone frequently becomes so fissile, when exposed to the action of frost, as to split under the hammer into thin flags fit for roofing purposes. These constitute the well-known Collyweston Slate. The surfaces of the Collyweston Slates exhibit ripple-markings, worm-tracks, and burrows, and numerous plant-remains, all indicating the close proximity of the shore; they yield numerous shells, among which may be specially mentioned *Gervillia acuta*, Sow., *Pinna cuneata*, Phil., *Trigonia compta*, Lyc., *Lucina Wrightii*, Opp., *Myacites Scarburgensis*, Phil., sp., and *Pterocera Bentleyi*, Mor. and Lyc.; these beds, however, do not afford that abundance of interesting remains of insects, crustaceans, fish, reptiles, and mammals which have made the

Stonesfield Slate so famous. The remarkably local character of such slate beds in the Jurassic series has been already pointed out in the Introductory Essay prefixed to this Memoir (see pp. 5, 6).

At Stamford the Lincolnshire Oolite is about 80 feet thick, and northwards it increases and acquires proportions probably exceeding those of the Inferior Oolite of the Cotteswold Hills. In the southern part of this sheet, at Geddington, it is only 12½ feet thick, and it thins out entirely a few miles further south near Harrington and Maidwell. As we go eastward we also find it rapidly thinning out, and at Water Newton Brickyard, Wansford Tunnel, Wood Newton, and near Cross Way Hands Lodge, and Stone-pit Field Lodge it is seen as a bed only a few feet in thickness separating the Upper and Lower Estuarine Series; these a little further to the east being found in actual contact.

The Lincolnshire Oolite of the district described in this Memoir affords valuable building materials, both ragstones and freestones, which are extensively dug at many places, as Ketton, Clipsham, Casterton, Stamford, Weldon, Wansford, &c. The freestones are of greatest value when they are quarried under the clays of the Upper Estuarine Series ; that of Ketton which, however, is only three feet thick, is especially famous for its strength and durability.

In mediæval times the well-known " Barnack-rag " was very extensively worked and was carried by water to all parts of Lincolnshire and the fen country for the erection of many noble Gothic structures.* The limestones of the Lincolnshire Oolite are extensively used for the manufacture of lime both for agricultural and building purposes.

The Collyweston Slates were formerly dug at many places within this sheet for roofing purposes, as at Kirby, Duddington, Medbourn, &c. The demand for such materials has of late years, however, greatly declined, owing to the competition of the Welsh slate, and they are now only raised at Collyweston, and to a very small extent near Dene.

The Lincolnshire Oolite forms a light and not very productive soil, which is apt to be very treacherous in dry seasons ; it is usually of a red colour, owing to the comparative indestructibility of the thin band of ironstone which lies upon it, and which we shall presently describe.

In consulting the map described in this Memoir it must be constantly remembered that the rocks indicated upon it are not in all cases exposed at the surface. This is especially the case with the Lincolnshire Oolite Limestone. The deposits of boulder clay, sometimes attaining a thickness of over 200 feet, over large areas wholly conceal the subjacent rocks. In these cases, in order to preserve uniformity with the other portions of the Geological

---

* The working of this stone appears to have been almost entirely abandoned before the beginning of the fifteenth century. At the village of Barnack a statue of evident Roman workmanship has been found carved out of the easily recognised " rag "; in the beautiful parish-church the Saxon, Norman, Early English, and Decorated portions are built of the same material, but in the fine mortuary chapel, which is of Perpendicular age, stone from another locality has been employed.

K

Survey Map of England, the probable outcrops of the strata have been indicated by means of dotted lines. It can scarcely be doubted, however, that, as in the portions of the area where the Jurassic beds are fully exposed through the removal of the overlying boulder clay by denudation, the surface of the Lincolnshire Oolite strata is diversified by outliers of the Great and Middle Oolite beds, and by inliers of the several members of the Lias; while curvatures and faultings of the strata have doubtless introduced complications among them, the details of which we are totally destitute of the means of ascertaining. Hence, in those portions of the map where the lines are dotted, it must be remembered that it has been impossible to do more than to strike a balance of probabilities as to the nature of the rocks underlying the superficial deposits, after a careful examination of all the evidence which could be procured.

The main line of outcrop of the strata of the Lincolnshire Oolite Limestone constitutes a band, with a varying breadth of between three and four miles, crossing the area included within Sheet 64 from north to south. In its southern half, or between the valley of the Barford Brook and that of the Welland, the strike of this great band of calcareous strata is almost exactly S.W. and N.E.; but to the northwards of the last-mentioned valley the strata are affected by a series of powerful disturbances, to be more fully described hereafter, and their strike becomes nearly due N. and S. In its southern part this band of Inferior Oolite Limestones is almost entirely concealed by the thick masses of boulder-clay, which are only cut through in some of the deeper valleys intersecting the district; in its northern portion, however, the outcrop of the Lincolnshire Oolite Limestone within Sheet 64 is much more fully exposed, the boulder clay constituting only a number of outlying patches. The difference in the appearance of the tracts to the north and south of the Welland respectively, in the former of which the Lincolnshire Oolite Limestone immediately underlies the surface soil, while in the latter it is thickly covered by boulder clay, is very striking. In the first case we have very light soils of a bright red colour (due to the remarkable persistence of the ferruginous masses of the "Ironstone junction band" which everywhere lies on the top of the Lincolnshire Limestone), while in the second we find cold stiff clay lands, which until very recently were almost everywhere covered by thick forests. The Ordnance Map of this district is unfortunately very old, and the country south of the Welland is represented as it was before the extensive clearances of the forest land of recent years had taken place. This has often rendered the tracing of the outcrops of the various beds a very difficult task.

Besides the exposures along the main line of outcrop stretching from south to north in Sheet 64, the beds of the Lincolnshire Limestone are displayed at many points to the eastward and the westward of that band. In the former case their appearance at the surface is due to the removal by denudation of the overlying rocks along the lines of river valleys, those of the Nene, Gwash and Glen, and their various tributaries. In the latter case, patches of the Inferior Oolite Limestone survive as outliers of various dimensions capping some of the higher hills of the district, their preservation in these cases having been in many cases aided through the strata being let down by faults, as an inspection of the map will show.

In the south-eastern part of the area, namely in the valley of the Nene about Oundle, the Lincolnshire Oolite Limestone is found to have thinned out and wholly disappeared. Thus the Upper Estuarine Series of the Great Oolite, in that neighbourhood, comes to rest directly upon the Lower Estuarine series and the ferruginous beds (Northampton Sand) of the Inferior Oolite without the intervention of the calcareous rocks of the latter formation. Northward, in the valley of the Nene about Stibbington, Castor, and Water Newton, this easterly attenuation and disappearance of the Lincolnshire Oolite can be well studied. Southwards, beyond the limits of Sheet 64 (in 52 N.W.), the same great calcareous formation is again seen thinning out and disappearing.

The details which we have already given in the Introductory Essay of this Memoir concerning the Lincolnshire Oolite Limestone, in its range from North Northamptonshire to South Yorkshire, enable us to conceive of this interesting formation as originally a great lenticular mass of calcareous rocks, the western half of which has been wholly removed by denudation. Of the remaining half of the great irregular "lens" the thickest portion can be traced in Mid- and South- Lincolnshire ; and as we pass northwards, southwards, and eastwards from this district, the strata are found continually diminishing in thickness, and finally disappearing altogether.

The palæontological evidence in favour of regarding the Lincolnshire Oolite as a, locally, very finely developed representative of the Zone of Ammonites Sowerbyi, which in other parts of England is only present in a rudimentary condition, has also been discussed in the introductory portion of this Memoir.

The conclusion, therefore, to which we are led by the study of the Lincolnshire Limestone is as follows:—During a portion of the Jurassic period, well marked within the ancient life-province now constituting Britain, Northern France, and Western Germany, by the abundance of certain characteristic species (those of the Zone of Ammonites Sowerbyi), local depression took place within an area having a diameter of something like 90 miles, the amount of depression being greatest within its centre. As a consequence of this local depression there was slowly accumulated, by the growth of coral reefs, and the action of marine currents sweeping small shells and their fragments along the sea-bottom, a mass of calcareous strata, presenting many variations in its local characters, and constituting the formation to which we have applied the name of the "Lincolnshire Oolite Limestone."

There is evidence that the accumulation of this mass of calcareous strata was followed by upheaval, accompanied by some local disturbances and even faulting of the rocks (see Introductory Essay, pp. 33–38). It is also clear that, both previous to the formation of this series of calcareous strata and subsequently to its upheaval and partial denudation, estuarine characters prevailed within the area of its deposition, and also far beyond those limits.

In order to make more clear the fact of the thinning out of the limestone strata of the Lincolnshire Oolite and the peculiar relations of the Great Oolite Series and the Northampton Sands which result from it, we have given in Plate II. two sections in which the phenomena alluded to are illustrated. A clear perception of the relations of the Lincolnshire Oolite to the other strata of the district is absolutely necessary to anyone who would understand the physical structure of the district included within Sheet 64 of the Geological Survey. As supplying additional illustrations of the same subject I may direct attention to Mr. Sharp's admirable paper on the Lincolnshire Oolite Limestone, forming the second part of his Memoir on "The Oolites of Northamptonshire," (see *Quarterly Journal of the Geological Society*, vol. xxix. p. 225). The line of section between Rockingham and Oundle given on Plate X. accompanying that Memoir, together with the numerous details concerning many very interesting sections, cannot fail in their object of placing the true relation of Lincolnshire Oolite to the beds, respectively below and above it, altogether beyond controversy.

In describing the rocks of the Lincolnshire Oolite series, as developed within Sheet 64, it will be most convenient to deal, in the first place, with the sections of its strata which are displayed along that band forming its main line of outcrop, which we have already noticed as stretching throughout the district from Geddington and Rushton on the south to Thistleton and South Witham on the north. We shall then proceed to notice the more or less isolated exposures of the same rocks revealed to us by the denudation of the overlying strata, to the eastward of the main line of outcrop; and, finally, we shall describe the several outlying patches, usually occurring at high levels to the west of the same line.

Main line of Outcrop of the Lincolnshire Oolite.—As already noticed the Lincolnshire Oolite Limestone constitutes a band, having a breadth of from three to four miles, which between Rushton and Duddington has a general strike from S.W. to N.E., but from Duddington northward strikes nearly from S. to N. This sudden and marked change in the direction of the line of outcrop of the strata is due, as we have seen, to the influence of great disturbances and faulting of the strata along the line now occupied by the valleys of the Welland, Chater, Gwash, and Nene. In the southern part of this great band of calcareous rocks the boundaries of the several members of the Jurassic series is unfortunately rendered very obscure, by the prevalence and great thickness of the overlying drift deposits.

The description of the extreme southern limits of the Lincolnshire Oolite, as seen in the more or less isolated patches of Old (or Wold), Maidwell and Harrington, and at Glendon and Weekley (see quarter-sheet 52, N.E.) does not come within the province of the present Memoir. Some details on the subject will, however, be found in the Introductory Essay prefixed to this Memoir (pp. 36–38), and in Mr. Sharp's paper referred to above (pp. 229–234).

The Strata of this horizon are first encountered, in entering the area of sheet 64 from the south, in the vicinity of the villages of

Geddington, Newton, and Rushton.   The principal sections in this neighbourhood are as follows:—

Limekiln at north-west angle of Weekley Hall Wood.

At this place there are very extensive stone-quarries.

(1.) Soil - - - - - - - 9 inches.
(2.) Rubble Oolite - - - - - - 2 ft.
(Inferior Oolite.)
(3.) Hard, compact and sub-crystalline limestone, in places con- ⎫
taining scattered oolitic grains, with strong joints but ⎪
without clay partings, containing many specimens of ⎬ 4 ft.
Nerinæa, but comparatively few other fossils; among ⎪
the latter are, Natica Leckhamptonensis, *Lyc.*, Lucina ⎪
Bellona, *d'Orb.*, and Corals. This stone is underlain by ⎭
(4.) Well-stratified, calcareous sands of yellowish, brownish,
and greenish tints, containing small lenticular masses of
very sandy clay - - - - - - 4 ft.

These are probably the uppermost beds of the Lower Estuarine Series.
This bed is underlain, at the bottom of the pit, by darker brown ferruginous sands.
The sands at this place are dug for building purposes.

Large pit immediately south of the former, the stone dug for road-metal.

(1.) Soil.
(2.) Boulder Clay of the usual character, consisting of light-blue
clay, containing many boulders, principally of chalk and
flint, grooved and striated - - - - 0 to 6 ft.
(3.) Inferior Oolite, as in the last pit, but very hard and blue-
hearted (from being dug under the Boulder Clay); the bed
is divided into very large blocks by joint-planes, which
are often very much open and filled with Boulder Clay.

This rock consists of three courses, not separated by clayey partings:—

	ft.	in.	
The 1st course	2	0	⎫
„ 2nd „	1	6	⎬ 7 ft.
„ 3rd „	3	6	⎭

Underneath the beds of stone is a hard, sandy layer 3 inches thick, beneath which is seen yellow sand, as in the last pit.

In the limestone in this pit the following fossils occur:—

Belemnites, sp.?
Natica Leckhamptonensis, *Lyc.* (very abundant and sometimes very
large).
Nerinæa cingenda, *Bronn,* and other species.
Ostrea flabelloides, *Lam.* (O. Marshii, *Sow.*) var. (rare).
Modiola, sp.?
Mytilus Sowerbianus, *d'Orb.*
Pinna cuneata, *Bean.* (not rare).
Lima cardiiformis, *Lyc. and Mor.*
„ bellula, *Lyc. and Mor.*
„ sp.? (Rodborough Hill Species).
„ sp.? (the very large form).
Ceromya Bajociana, *d'Orb.*
Tancredia, sp.?
Pygaster semisulcatus, *Phil.*

At the limekiln opposite Geddington Grange we find Lincolnshire Oolite, similar to that at Glendon, of which the bottom is not seen.

South-west of Newton and on the opposite side of the valley are found traces of old iron workings, with abundance of black slag of the usual character.

In a stone-pit on the road from Geddington to Grafton-under-Wood, immediately above Geddington, there occurs an exposure of the Lincolnshire Oolite, presenting its coralline facies precisely similar to that seen at Glendon, and displayed in a face about 6 feet in height.

In the irregular surface of the rubble which covers this rock, traces of the " ferruginous junction-band " and the " carbonaceous clays and sands of the " Upper Estuarine series " are seen.

Pholadomya fidicula, *Sow.*, occurs in the limestone here.

At the limekiln immediately south-east of the last (Mr. Bell's pit), the following section occurs :—

(1.) Soil - - - - - - - - 1 ft.
(2.) Pale bluish-white clay, with carbonaceous markings - 2 to 3 feet.
(3.) Indurated, variegated, sandy clay (bright yellow, pale blue, ash-coloured, pink, crimson, and greenish), occasionally traversed by ironstone laminæ - - - - 1 ft.
(4.) Irregular ferruginous band - - - - 2 in.
(5.) Ash-coloured sands with irregular clay seams - - 5 in.
(6.) Fine white clay with carbonaceous markings - - 3 to 6 in.
(7.) Band of ironstone nodules (ferruginous junction-band) - 6 in.
 (The foregoing beds belong to the Upper Estuarine Series of the Great Oolite).

(8.) Inferior (Lincolnshire) Oolite, consisting of—

a. Rubbly limestone - - - 3 ft.		
b. *Course of hard, somewhat oolitic, limestone - - - - - 1 ft.		
c. Course of compact limestone - - 2 ft.		
d. „ „ „ - - 2 ft. 6 in.		
e. Three courses† of hard limestone, blue-hearted, 1 ft. each - - - 3 ft.	}12 ft. 6 in.	
f. Course of very sandy limestone, micaceous, hardens with drying, finely laminated, and containing many carbonaceous markings (equivalent of the Collyweston Slate) - - - 1 ft.		

(9.) Yellow sand, top of the " Lower Estuarine Series."

N.B.—In a well at a cottage near, the " red-rock " (Northamptonshire Iron-Ore) was reached.

Above and behind the church at Geddington there is an old pit opened in the Lincolnshire Oolite Limestone. Another old stone-pit occurs at the angle of Newton Lane and the Avenue ; and here we find a compact, marly limestone crowded with specimens of *Nerinæa* (the Coralline facies of the Lincolnshire Oolite). Near Geddington Grange there are two large stone-pits in the same marly limestone rock containing an abundance of *Nerinæas,* and along the sides of Newton Lane, and on the road leading from Geddington to Rushton there are several large pits in the same beds.

Near Rushton there occur the following sections :—

In a pit at the north-east corner of Rushton Park, is seen a rock 9 to 10 feet thick (coralline facies) with the usual characters, the lower courses becoming more and more sandy in character ; the lowest bed but one contains plant remains, and the lowest bed of all consists of hard slabs of sandy limestone, having a tendency to split into slates (equivalent of Collyweston Slates). This bed rests on sands and clays of the " Lower Estuarine Series " (Northampton Sand).

In the valley crossing the road, one mile north of Rushton Hall the stream has cut through the Boulder Clay and exposes the Inferior Oolite Limestone, which here presents, for the first time in going northwards, the " shelly facies " of the Lincolnshire Oolite.

Passing northwards from Rushton we again find, at the limekiln half a mile north-east of the village, the beds of the Lincolnshire Oolite Limestone consisting of about 12 feet of rock lying in regular courses ; the stone here is somewhat intermediate in character between that at Glendon ("coralline facies ") and that at Pipwell ("shelly facies ").

---

* In this bed occur numerous specimens of *Pholadomya Heraultii,* Ag., and *Pinna cuneata,* Bean, in their natural positions. The courses of stone are separated by somewhat sandy partings.

† The uppermost of these three courses is almost entirely made up of *Nerinæa;* they become sandier as we pass downwards.

The following fossils were seen here :—

> Pholadomya fidicula, *Sow.*
> Natica Leckhamptonensis, *Lyc.*
> Pinna cuneata, *Bean.*
> Ceromya Bajociana, *d'Orb.*

Northwards from Geddington we find a large stone-pit with a lime-kiln beside the road leading to Little Oakley. The following is the section presented in this pit :—

(1.) Beds of white, compact, slightly oolitic stone - - 6 to 8 ft.
(2.) Beds of hard, white, sub-crystalline limestone crowded with *Nerinæas*, and containing great masses of coral converted into finely crystallized Calcspar (Nail-head and Dog's tooth spar) - - - - 1 ft. 9 in.
(3.) Beds of coarse sandy limestone - - - - 2 ft.
Coarse, sandy, flaggy bed, covered with vermicular and other markings, very inconstant (equivalent of Collyweston Slate) - - - - - - 0 to 3 in.
Brown Sand.

The fossils obtained in this pit were as follows :—

> Natica Leckhamptonensis, *Lyc.*, large and abundant.
> Alaria Phillipsii, *d'Orb.*
> Actæonina glabra, *Phil.*
> Nerinæa, sp.? very abundant.
> Chemnitzia Scarburgensis, *Lyc. and Mor.*
> Pinna cuneata, *Bean.*
> Gervillia acuta, *Sow.*
> Pecten paradoxus, *Münst.*
> Hinnites abjectus, *Phil.*
> Modiola Sowerbyana, *d'Orb.*
> Cardium cognatum, *Phil.*

Large masses of *Isastræa* and other corals, sometimes perforated by Lithodomi, also occur in this pit.

Crossing the high ground between the Barford Brook and Harper's Brook, where the Jurassic strata are entirely concealed by the overlying Boulder Clay, which here attains a thickness of probably not less than 200 feet, we reach a series of fresh exposures of the beds of the Lincolnshire Oolite Limestone, in the vicinity of the villages of Pipwell and Little Oakley.

At Pipwell Upper Lodge, and on the opposite side of the road to the farm-buildings, traces of the outcrop of the Lincolnshire Oolite above the Northampton Sand, there exposed, were detected.

Near Pipwell Abbey there are several large grass-grown quarries which were evidently opened in the beds of the Lincolnshire Limestone. One of these quarries had been used recently, and under the beds of the Upper Estuarine Series, capped by Boulder Clay, I found the shelly freestone presenting its usual characters. The same stone is seen near the mansion of Pipwell Abbey and in the bed of the stream which flows near it; the rock here yields the usual fossils.

The following is the detailed section of the beds seen in the pit referred to in the foregoing paragraph.

Old pit at Pipwell Abbey.

(1.) Boulder Clay - - - - - perhaps 15 or 16 ft
Upper Estuarine Series, the upper part not seen.
(2.) Band of ash-coloured and drab clays - - 2 in.
(3.) Coarse, brown sand becoming more ferruginous at its base - - - - - - 1 ft. 8 in.
(4.) Stiff, bluish-white clay with carbonaceous markings 10 in.
(5.) Brown sand - - - - - - 10 in.
(6.) Variegated clay,—blue, yellow, brown, drab, and greenish - - - - - - 2 ft.
(7.) Irregular band of Ironstone (ferruginous junction-band) - - - - - - 2 in
Lincolnshire Oolite Limestone.
(8.) Decomposed oolitic rock - - - - 1 ft. 6 in.
(9.) Five courses of oolitic limestone seen - together 8 ft.

The woodcut (Fig. 12) represents the face of rock exhibited in a larg
stone-pit still open in the valley, one-third of a mile east of Pipwell Abbey.
This section is exposed on the south side of the quarry, the direction of its
face being nearly due east and west, its length 30 feet and its height 21 feet.

Fig. 12. Stone-pit in shelly beds of the Lincolnshire Oolite Limestone near Pipwell Abbey.

The beds of the Lincolnshire Oolite in this locality present, as is shown in the drawing, the usual false-bedding so characteristic of the shelly facies of the formation.

On the opposite side of the pit to that of which the sketch is taken, in holes and pockets of the rubbly oolite, are seen the light-blue and variegated clays of the Upper Estuarine ¡Series ; and similar indications of the ferruginous " junction-band " exist, the whole being covered with rubble and soil.

The section seen here is as follows :—

(1.) Thin, rubbly, evenly-bedded, shelly oolitic limestone	-	1 ft.
(2.) Harder false-bedded limestone of the same kind	-	2 ft.
(3.) Course of do., evenly bedded oolitic limestone -	-	1 ft.
(4.) „ „ false bedded „	-	2 ft.
(5.) Three irregular courses of „	-	2 ft. 6 in.
(6.) Very coarse false-bedded irregular course	-	1 ft.
(7.) „ „ „	-	1 ft.
(8.) Bed of hard shelly ragstone „ -	-	1 ft. 6 in.
(9.) Softer oolitic bed - - -	-	1 ft.
(10.) „ „ - - - -	-	1 ft.
(11.) „ „ - - - -	-	1 ft. 6 in.
(12.) Hard ragstone bed - - -	-	8 in.
(13.) Two soft freestone beds, each 1 ft. 3 ins. -	-	2 ft. 6 in.
(14.) Two hard „ „ „ -	-	2 ft. 6 in.

(15.) White Clay (top of the Lower Estuarine Series).

N.B.—Possibly sandy beds occur at the base of the series.

The beds in the neighbourhood of Pipwell and Oakley exhibit signs of considerable disturbance, and besides being traversed by the faults shown upon the map, are evidently bent into long folds.

Lower down the Harper's Brook the Lincolnshire Oolite Limestone is well exhibited again ; but the whole of the strata here are affected by a very complicated series of faults, as will be seen by an inspection of the map.

Very extensive quarries, known as Lord Cardigan's pits, are seen in the east side of the village of Stanion. The rock here exposed is a hard, shelly oolite, and is found to rest, not on the usual white clays, but on " kale " (ferruginous sandstone of the Northampton Sand).

To the west of the same village another quarry, known as the "town pit," presents the following section :—

(1.) Boulder Clay - - - - -	3 to 4 feet.
(2.) Oolite rubble, much mingled with clay and containing fine crystallizations of Calcspar · -	2 feet.
(3.) Beds of hard, crystalline, marly oolite used for road-metal - - - -	dug to the depth of 4 feet.

Under the beds of stone about 3 feet of brown sand occurs, at the bottom of which springs arise, indicating probably the presence of the compact ironstone rock of the Northampton Sand.

Between Stanion and Brigstock the Lincolnshire Oolite Limestone is exposed, and its relation to the beds above and below it are well illustrated in a section, which will be described in detail in a later chapter.

At Brigstock Mill there is a stone-pit in the same formation, here presented as a soft, shelly limestone with much false-bedding, many of its beds exhibiting a reddish colour. Fossils are tolerably abundant in this pit, and consist for the most part of small shells, both univalves and bivalves, usually more or less encrusted with a deposit of carbonate of lime.

Between the Harper and Willow brooks the Jurassic strata are again wholly concealed by the thick masses of Boulder Clay. On the outer escarpment, however, at Stoke Albany, Wilbarston, Cottingham, and Rockingham, the beds of the Lincolnshire Oolite are exposed by denudation below the great superficial accumulations. They are also equally well seen along the sides of the valleys formed by the Willow Brook and its tributaries, as about Corby, Weldon, Dene, Bulwick, Blatherwycke, &c.

The beds of the Inferior Oolite Limestone appear on the escarpment between Stoke-Albany and Wilbarston from beneath the mantle of Boulder Clay which overlaps the escarpment to the southwards. The strata here seem to be much disturbed and dip in various directions. The beds are seen similarly in the two pits at the south end of the village of Wilbarston, in one place having a dip of no less than 10°. In the stone pits on the north side of the village of Wilbarston the limestone beds of the Inferior Oolite are again seen to be much disturbed; in one of the pits they dip E. at an angle of 15°, and in another, the beds are in one place horizontal while at a short distance they are inclined to the S.E. at an angle of 20°. It is possible, however, that this appearance of local disturbance in the rocks is due to the fact of their exposure on a steep escarpment, above a great thickness of Upper Lias Clay, &c., and are to be referred to partial landslips rather than to subterranean movements.

On the left-hand side of the road leading from Cottingham to East Carlton, there is a large pit in the limestone of the Lincolnshire Oolite. Under 4 feet of rubble we find about 20 feet of compact and oolitic limestone, lying in distinct beds with clay partings. The upper beds are soft and white and highly oolitic; the middle beds of the section harder, cream-coloured, and slightly oolitic; and the lower beds hard, crystalline, and blue-hearted.

In a pit below the church at Cottingham the strata of the Northampton Sand and Lower Estuarine Series are seen lying below those of the Lincolnshire Oolite.

From the Lincolnshire Oolite limestone of this neighbourhood I obtained,—

> Polypodites Lindleyi, *Göpp.* (Pecopteris polypodioides, *Lindl. & Hutt.*) (abundant in the lower beds, exhibiting the fructification).
> Ceromya Bajociana, *d'Orb.*
> Pecteu aratus, *Waagen.*
> And other fossils.

In Rockingham Park several stone pits have been opened in the Lincolnshire Oolite. One of these exhibits about 5 feet of soft, somewhat fissile and very oolitic limestone with a faint pinkish tint. A larger stone-pit in the same park exhibits the following section :—

(1.) Soil - - - - - - -	9 inches.
(2.) Oolite, similar to that of last pit - -	5 feet.
(3.) Softer, more marly, and compact oolite - - -	5 feet.
(4.) Hard, compact, marly oolite with *Nerinæa*, &c. to bottom of the pit - - - - -	4 feet seen.

In the extensive stone pits at Snatchill Lodge, between Great Oakley and Corby, we find the following sections at different points :—

(1.) Boulder Clay, bluish, greenish, and brown. Mostly of mottled colours, with boulders of all dimensions, those of Oolitic and Cretaceous rocks predominating - - - - -	6 to 8 feet.
(2.) Oolite rubble, often contorted - -	0 to 3 feet.
(3.) Bed of hard, marly limestone of a drab colour (used for road-metal) - - - - -	1 foot.
(4.) Whitish, calcareous sand - - - -	1 ft. 6 in. to 2 feet.
(5.) Shelly limestone - - - - -	1 foot.
(6.) Soft, very oolitic, somewhat shelly limestone (used as building stone) - - - -	6 feet 6 inches.
(7.) Clay parting.	
(8.) Two courses of hard, blue-hearted, sub-crystalline limestone, used for road-metal, each course being about 1 foot thick - - - -	2 ft.
(9.) Blue clay, dug in making a drain - - -	3 feet seen.

A second section obtained in the pits opposite to Snatchill Lodge was as follows:—

(1.) Boulder Clay, of the usual characters, in places - -	6 ft. thick.
(2.) Bed of rubbly oolite - - - - -	2 ft.
(3.) Hard, compact, sub-crystalline limestone with a few scattered oolitic grains, containing Nerinæa, &c.	9 in.
(4.) Softer, sandier limestone - - - -	1 ft. 6 in.
(5.) Hard and coarsely oolitic limestone - -	6 ft.
(6.) Softer, sandier limestone, with fewer oolitic grains	2 ft.
(7.) Coarse, sandy, flaggy limestone - - -	9 in.
(8.) Blue Clay.	

It is evident that the beds exposed in these pits are those which constitute the base of the Lincolnshire Oolite Series.

The beds of the Lincolnshire Oolite can be traced at several points in the neighbourhood of the village of Corby. At the "Mill-pit," between Corby and Weldon, we have the following section :—

(1.) Boulder Clay - - - - - - 1 to 3 feet.
(2.) Oolite rubble - - - - - - 2 to 3 feet.
(3.) Marly Oolites, becoming slaty at the bottom - - 6 to 8 feet.
(Dug for road metal.)

In the great pits to the west of Great Weldon we find the section given below :—

(1.) Boulder Clay, with boulders chiefly of Oolite, but with
some of Chalk and Lias - - - - 8 feet.
(2.) Soft, shelly, oolitic freestone ; this bed is but little used
for building purposes - - - - . 4 ft. 6 in.
(3.) Hard, shelly ragstone - - - - - 2 to 3 feet.
(This bed is known as the " Weldon-rag.")
(4.) Beds of shelly freestone, harder than the top bed.
These form four courses, each from 2 to 3 feet in
thickness, the stone being known as the "Weldon
Freestone" - - - - - - 10 feet.

At about 8 feet below the bottom of this pit another bed of hard "rag" occurs in the midst of the shelly freestones.

Fine joints dividing the stone into large blocks traverse the stone in this pit and render its quarrying easy.

The extensive " hills and holes," by which name the abandoned and grass-grown quarries in this part of England are always known, testify to the enormous quantities of Lincolnshire Limestone which in former times have been raised in the neighbourhood of Weldon for building purposes.

At Great Weldon the shelly oolite of the Lincolnshire Oolite is seen *in situ* in the bed of the stream which flows through the village. A little to the east of the village a small road-side pit offers particularly favourable conditions for the collection of the small shells, corals, fragments of echinoderms, &c. of which the rock is almost wholly made up. These facilities are due to the soft, crumbling, and weathered state of the stone, which here (as in the analogous case at Wakerley to be referred to in the sequel) enables the small organisms to be removed with the point of a knife, or by simply crushing the stone. In this pit at Weldon, the following species rewarded the patient search of Mr. Richard Gibbs, the former fossil collector to the Survey.

Fossils from the Shelly Oolite of Weldon.

Actæonina glabra, *Phil.*
Natica cincta, *Phil.*
Nerinæa cingenda, *Bronn.*
———— Eudesii, *Lyc.* and *Mor.*
———— pseudo-cylindrica, *Lyc.*
———— Stricklandi? *Lyc.* and *Mor.*
———— Voltzii, *Deslong.*
————, sp.
Monodonta lævigata, *Sow.*
Phasianella Pontonis, *Lyc.*
Myoconcha striatula, *Sow.*
———— crassa, *Sow.*
Mytilus lunularis, *Lyc.*
Cardium, sp.
Corbicella Bathonica, *Lyc.* and *Mor.*
Trigonia costata, var. pullus, *Sow.*
Ostrea flabelloides, *Lam.* (O. Marshii, *Sow.*), var.
————, sp.
Terebratula submaxillata, *Mor.*
Rhynchonella spinosa, *Sow.*, var. Crossi, *Walker.*
Pseudodiadema depressa, *Ag.*
Thecosmilia gregaria, *M'Coy.*

At the angle of the road leading down from Great Weldon to Little Weldon the junction of the shelly oolites with the light-blue clays, with plant-remains, belonging to the Lower Estuarine series, is exposed.

It appears that at Weldon, as at Barnack, the base of Lincolnshire Oolite series is formed by the shelly, and not by the compact and marly variety of the limestone.

We have already seen that at several points the lowest beds of the Lincolnshire Oolite Limestone present fissile characters, and thus show a tendency to pass into those "slate-beds" which to the northwards constitute, under the name of the Collyweston Slate, so important a member of the formation. The most southerly points at which such slate beds have been worked for the purpose of obtaining roofing materials, are at Kirby, and near Dene Lodge.

The extensive slate-pits at Kirby are now almost wholly abandoned, and but few opportunities are afforded for studying the succession of beds here.

On the right-hand side of the road leading from Rockingham there is a small pit in the marly or compact limestone, the beds being separated by clay partings. In the upper part of the pit the beds become softer and more oolitic. The total thickness of rock exposed here is from 12 to 14 feet.

On the opposite side of the road are the "slate-pits," now no longer worked. In the upper part of these pits the same beds of marly oolite as were noticed in the pit last described are seen. These appear to have been underlaid by sand, at the bottom of which the slates occurred. Thus the relations of the slate beds at Kirby would appear to have been very similar to those of the equivalent strata in some of the pits at Easton and Collyweston. The slates appear to rest upon clay, and the pits are now full of water.

The best section I could obtain here was the following :—

(1.) Drift or Boulder Clay - - - - - 3 feet.
(2.) Rubble oolite - - - - - 4 feet.
(3.) Thin-bedded oolite (weathered) - - - 4 feet.
(4.) Harder, thick-bedded limestone - - - 5 feet.
(5.) Sands, cream-coloured, and somewhat compacted - 4 feet to bottom.

In another part of the pits the sands are seen to a depth of 5 feet, and are underlaid by 4 or 5 feet of hard limestone with clay partings. Under the last seem to have come other beds of sand, then 2 or 3 feet of slate rock, and finally clay.

The Kirby slate-pits, which belong to Lord Winchelsea, are now abandoned, owing to several causes. The principal of these are as follows :—firstly, the diminished demand for such materials as the "slates" of the Oolite series, now that the increased means of communication afforded by railways offers such facilities for procuring the lighter and more convenient Welsh slates; secondly, the exhaustion of the old pits; and, thirdly, the expense of opening new ones to the required depth.

Near Dene Lodge, upon the border of Long Mantle Wood, there is a small pit, at which, during the time when the survey of the district was made, small quantities of "slate" were being raised and dressed in the same manner as is still practised at Collyweston.

On the main escarpment in the neighbourhood we are now describing, the outcrop of the Lincolnshire Oolite is concealed by the overlap of the Boulder Clay between Rockingham and Gretton; but between the last-mentioned village and Harringworth the beds of this formation again appear. In a pit on the right-hand side of the road from Gretton to Harringworth, we find 2 feet of rubbly oolite resting on 6 feet of cream-coloured sand, full of intensely hard siliceous concretionary masses with irregular rounded forms. The sands at the base show a tendency to become ferruginous. A pit on the opposite side of the road exhibits a somewhat similar section.

The Lincolnshire Oolite is well exposed in a number of pits in the vicinity of Harringworth. Above the cross-roads towards Dene there are several large quarries by the road-side, in which we find hard, somewhat shelly Oolite, covered by much limestone rubble. The rock has here a pinkish tint.

At the brickyard and several other points near Dene, the lowest bed of the Lincolnshire Oolite (representative of the Collyweston Slate) is an intensely hard and very highly siliceous material, presenting mammillated surfaces, and containing plant remains. It is so hard and compact as almost to resemble a quartzite.

A large stone-pit at the angle of the road leading from Harringworth to Dene yields the following section :—

(1.) Soil - - - - - - - - 1 ft.
(2.) Rubble oolite - - - - - - 2 ft.
(3.) White, calcareous sand - - - - - 1 ft. 9 in.
(4.) Thin-bedded, soft, very oolitic limestone - - - 2 ft.
(5.) Brown, calcareous sand in places indurated into stone - 2 ft.
(6.) Bed of hard, compact rock, used for road-metal - - 1 ft. 6 in.
(7.) Several courses of hard, pinkish, shelly oolite, used for
        building purposes - - - - - 5 ft.

Similar beds are exposed at Hollow Bottom and at several other points between Harringworth and Dene.

The interesting section showing the relations of the Lincolnshire Oolite to the beds below have already been noticed (see p. 101).

The beds of the Lincolnshire Oolite Limestone can be traced under the strata of the Great Oolite series at Bulwick and Blatherwycke. At Laxton there are quarries in the same rock ; and at this place also a well was sunk to the depth of 40 feet in the Oolitic Limestone, water being obtained in the sands and clays below.

Over all the area already described the Lincolnshire Oolite is much obscured by Boulder Clay ; but we have now to notice the fine series of sections exposed along the sides of the Welland and Chater, which, in the central part of the area under description, cut completely across the line of outcrop of the formation.

In the neighbourhood of Wakerley there are numerous quarries in the Lincolnshire Oolite Limestone, from some of which stone is still procured, while others are abandoned. Several such pits are seen between the " Great Wood " and the " Spinney." At the northern corner of the former plantation there is a large and deep quarry, exhibiting an admirable example of the " shelly facies " of the Lincolnshire Oolite. Many of the beds are entirely made up of drifted shells, usually of small size, the valves of the Brachiopods and Conchifera almost always having their valves disunited, and the Gasteropods exhibiting equal signs of drifting in their broken spires and other marks of attrition. Many of the shells are coated with a deposit of carbonate of lime, and the beds exhibit much false-bedding. Owing to the softness of the rock here, as in the analogous cases of Great Weldon (already referred to) and of Ponton, where Professor Morris procured so interesting a series of fossils from the shelly beds of the Lincolnshire Oolite, this pit at Wakerley offers peculiar facilities to the collector of fossils. The following species were obtained here by the officers of the Geological Survey.

Fossils from Stone-pit near Wakerley.

Nerinæa cingenda, *Bronn.*
———— Cotteswoldiæ, *Lyc.*
———— Voltzi, *Deslong.*
Vermicularia nodus, *Phil.*
————, sp.
Trigonia tenuicosta, *Lyc.*
———— denticulata, *Lyc.*
———— hæmisphærica, *Lyc.*
———— costata, *Sow.*, var. pullus, *Sow.*
Opis gibbosus, *Lyc.*
Macrodon Hirsonensis, *d'Arch.*
Cardium Buckmani, *Lyc. and Mor.*
Cucullæa cucullata, *Goldf.*
Astarte, sp.
Arca rugosa, *Lyc. and Mor.*
—— Prattii, *Lyc. and Mor.*
—— æmula, *Phil.*
—— cancellata, *Sow.*

Ostrea, sp.
Pecten paradoxus, *Münst.*
—— lens, *Sow.*
Pteroperna plana, *Mor. and Lyc.*
Lima cardiiformis, *Sow.*
—— gibbosa, *Sow.*
—— duplicata, *Sow.*
—— ovalis, *Sow.*
—— pectiniformis, *Schloth.*
—— Pontonis, *Lyc.*
—— punctata, *Sow.*
—— rudis, *Sow.*
Gervillia acuta.
Hinnites abjectus, *Phil.*
——, velatus, *Phil.*
Terebratula submaxillata, *Mor.*
Cricopora Spiropora (straminea), *Phil.*
Cidaris Bouchardii, *Wright.*
Pseudodiadema depressa, *Ag.*, sp.
————, sp.
Pygaster semisulcatus, *Phil.*
Microsolena excelsa, *Edw. and Haime.*
Thamnastræa Defranciana, *Edw. and Haime.*
Thecosmilia gregaria, *M'Coy.*   .

In the neighbourhood of Wakerley the relations of the Lincolnshire Oolite both to the beds above and below it can be studied. The white clays at the base of the Upper Estuarine series, which repose directly upon the Great Limestone series, are here dug for commercial purposes; and in a pit above the great escarpment the sands are seen at the base of the limestones. At this latter point we find very hard mammillated beds which certainly represent the Collyweston Slate, and contain—

Macrodon Hirsonensis, *d'Arch.*
Trigonia (casts).
Cardium (casts), &c.
Much wood and other plant remains.

Between Barrowden and Tixover the beds of the Lincolnshire Oolite appear to come down to the level of the river Welland, which, in this part of its course, crosses the outcrop of these strata. The lowest beds of the limestone series here appear to be hard and cream-coloured; they are of a somewhat sandy nature and alternate with beds of sand. These undoubtedly represent the Collyweston Slate, which is so well developed a little farther to the east.

Near Morcott there are a number of quarries in the Lincolnshire Oolite, one of which shows the following succession of beds:—

(1.) White, oolitic limestone with some shells and echinoderms, and a few plant remains.
(2.) Calcareous sands.
(3.) Hard, blue, siliceous limestone, with few shells but many plant remains, the latter sometimes well preserved (ferns, &c.)
(4.) Fine, white sands.

The rock of bed (1) is used for lime-burning; of (3) for road-metal; and of (4) for mortar.

In the large pit near Morcott Mill beds of calcareous sand alternate with courses of compact, marly limestone. At the base are hard beds of a blue colour exhibiting a tendency to fissile characters. The strata about Morcott exhibit signs of considerable disturbance.

Between Tixover and Ketton the beds of the Lincolnshire Oolite can be traced at many points, but no good sections of them are afforded.

At Duddington there are a number of old pits near the river which still bear the name of "the Slate-pits;" according to tradition slates similar to those of Collyweston were once dug here, and their abandonment was due to their being drowned by the waters of the Welland.

At Ketton the very extensive quarries offer to the geologists many beautiful illustrations of the upper beds of the Inferior Oolite Limestone of the district and of the superposed Upper Estuarine Series. The compact and durable character of the oolitic limestone of Ketton, as in the similar cases of the Casterton, Clipsham, and Ancaster quarries, is doubtless due in great part, as was pointed out by Professor Morris, to the fact of the rock being quarried under a considerable thickness of clays which form the base of the Great Oolite series in this district.

The following is the section exhibited by the quarries at Ketton:—
(1.) Upper Estuarine Clays (Great Oolite). In their lighter coloured bands these clays are crowded with *Cyrena* and other shells; and in the dark coloured beds they contain large fragments of wood and much carbonaceous matter -
(2.) "Junction-bed" full of ironstone nodules. This is of a snuff-brown colour and earthy texture, and is full of white decomposed fragments of a fibrous structure, apparently the remains of shells and bones?   -   -   -
(3.) "The Crash bed"   -   -   -   -   -   - 3 feet.
(4.) "Grits" or "top-rag" harder than the "bottom-rag"   - 3 feet.
(5.) "Bottom-rag"   -   -   -   -   -   - 3 feet.
(6.) "Freestone"   -   -   -   -   -   - 3 feet.

The "Crash-bed" (3) is a coarse oolite full of fragments of shells, which lie on its planes of bedding. When first dug this rock is very soft, but by exposure it acquires extreme hardness. It is of a purplish red colour, but varies greatly in the depth of the tints which it exhibits. It is only used locally for rough purposes, such as field walls, &c. A very interesting circumstance in connexion with the "Crash-bed" is that its upper surface often exhibits the vertical burrows of *Lithodomi*, indicating the long pause which ensued between the deposition, and probably partial denudation of the Lincolnshire Oolite, and the formation of the Estuarine strata which lie immediately above it. This break in the succession of the Jurassic strata in the Midland district is at other points even more strongly marked by actual unconformity between the Inferior and Great Oolite Series (see Introductory Essay, pp. 33–38).

The "grits" and "rag-beds" (4) and (5) are hard limestones of oolitic structure, but not entirely made up of oolite grains. The stone fractures along incipient crystalline or cleavage planes, often exhibiting surfaces with brilliant lustre. As the rock is too hard to be easily dressed it is only used for local purposes.

The following species of fossils were collected at the Ketton quarries:—
Pileopsis, sp.
Nerinæa pseudo-cylindrica, *Lyc.*
Chemnitzia, sp.
Cyprina nuciformis, *Lyc.*
Trigonia costata, *Sow.*   Var pullas, *Sow.*
Lucina Wrightii, *Oppel.*
————, sp.
Unicardium, sp.
Pholadomya fidicula, *Sow.*
Perna quadrata, *Sow.* var.
Terebratula submaxillata, *Mor.*
Isastræa Richardsoni, *Edw. and Haime.*

The celebrated Ketton freestone is a beautiful, oolitic limestone of good colour, combining great freedom of working with remarkable powers of resisting crushing force and wonderful durability. It is almost wholly made up of very uniform oolitic grains, exhibits scarcely any trace of bedding planes, and can be placed indifferently in any position in buildings without exhibiting any tendency to weathering.

The Ketton freestone is highly valued by architects, and its employment is frequently specified by them in cases where great strength is required in any particular construction. The slight thickness of the bed, however, (only 3 feet) and the large quantities of "bearing" which require to be removed in order to obtain it, renders it expensive and prevents its more general use. Hence for general purposes the oolite of Ketton cannot compete with the cheaper materials of Bath, Portland, and Ancaster. The number of men employed in the Ketton quarries is about one hundred.

In the cutting of the Syston and Peterborough Railway near Ketton (Geeston) a good section was exposed, which was examined when first opened and thus described by Captain Ibbetson and Professor Morris:—

"Geeston (Railway Cutting).*

	ft.
Rubbly oolite in shivers - - - - - -	3
Compact marly limestone, *Nerinæa* and Ferns - -	2½
Marly rock, very fossiliferous, *Nerinæa*, *Modiola plicata*, Ferns, and *Isocardia concentrica*, *Pinna*, *Arca* - -	2
Sandy rock, with *Lima*, &c. - - - - - -	2
Crystalline ragstone, with *Nerinæa* and patches of plants -	3
Compact, crystalline, oolitic ragstone - - -	8
Concretionary bed - - - - - -	2½
Slate beds - - - - - - -	3
Greenish clay - - - - - -	2
Ferruginous sand of inferior oolite at bottom."	

On the opposite side of the river to Ketton, in the vicinity of the villages of Collyweston and Easton, the lowest beds of the Lincolnshire Oolite have long been extensively worked for the purpose of obtaining the once famous Collyweston slate. Excepting for ecclesiastical and other Gothic buildings (in which the peculiar colour of the material is greatly admired and much affected by some architects) and for strictly local purposes, there is now, however, but little demand for the Collyweston slate. A considerable number of pits are still worked in the district, but over a large area the "slate-beds" have been wholly exhausted. On a future page we shall give a short account of the methods pursued in quarrying and dressing the "slates" of Collyweston, once a most important industry in this particular district, and which was also extensively pursued at Kirby and some other points in the area which we are describing.

As illustrating the general succession of the rocks among which the slates are obtained, we may give the following section from a deep pit at Easton:—

(1.) Beds of oolitic limestone, varying greatly in hardness, &c.
Some of these beds are of sandy texture - - 12 feet.

(2.) Beds of sand, with hard, siliceous, concretionary masses lying in the planes of stratification. These sands are sometimes indurated and present rounded and mammillated surfaces - - - - - - 4 feet.

(3.) Bed of hard and partially oolitic limestone - - 2 ft. 6 in.

(4.) Bed of more or less indurated sand, with smaller concretionary masses than those of (2) - - - 1 ft. 6 in.

(5.) Hard, blue-hearted, siliceous limestone - - 2 feet.

(6.) Finely laminated, calcareous sandstone beds, which weather into "slates" - - - - - - 2 feet.

(7.) Hard, flaggy, siliceous beds with mammillated surfaces ("pot-lids," &c.), "bastard-rock" of the workmen - 6 inches.

(8.) Sands - - - - - - - 6 feet.

(9.) Ironstone beds of the Northampton Sand.

The "slate-beds" (6) contained fine specimens of *Lucina Wrightii*, Oppel, and other shells.

In an adjoining pit the section is altogether similar in every respect, except that the "slate-bed" is nearly 3 feet thick.

The sands which underlie the "slate-bed" at Easton and Collyweston is said to be 6 feet thick. Underneath them lies the "Red-rock" (Northampton Sand), but this bed is never bottomed here, as abundance of water is obtained in it. Indeed during wet seasons the springs rise so rapidly that it is often found impossible to get out the slates.

In another pit, at a short distance from that in which the section was taken, the upper bed of sand (2) is between 5 and 6 feet thick and is dug for building and foundry purposes, for which it is found to be well adapted.

---

* Brit. Ass. Rep., 1847, Proceedings of Sections, p. 128.

The stone immediately above the Collyweston slate is often crowded with specimens of Polypodites Lindleyi, *Göpp (Pecopteris polypodioides, Lindl.* and Hutt.), with some other ferns and plant remains.

All the Inferior Oolite beds in the neighbourhood of Collyweston and Easton are traversed by a series of master joints, having a very uniform direction of 40° W. of North (magnetic). Another set of joints cuts across the beds almost at right angles to the master joints. By the jointed condition of these rocks their quarrying is, of course, greatly facilitated.

Although the "slate-beds" at the base of the Lincolnshire Oolite of the Midland district have not yielded any of those beautiful mammalian, reptilian, and insect remains, which have made the Stonesfield slate, constituting the base of the Great Oolite Limestone in the south-west of England, so famous, yet it presents a very similar association of generic forms to those found in the latter beds.   The species in the two sets of strata are, however, for the most part distinct, and we are led to infer that while formed under very similar conditions they are of widely separated age.   In both the Stonesfield and Collyweston slate, remains of fish, especially their palatal teeth, abound ; in both there occur the same genera of Mollusca, *Gervillia, Trigonia, Lucina, Alaria,* &c., being especially abundant, while Brachiopods are rare; and in both, the fucoid markings, worm-tracks, ripple-marked surfaces, and evidently drifted plant remains clearly indicate the shallowness of the sea in which they were formed, and the proximity of the land.

The general nature of the fauna of the Collyweston slates is indicated by the accompanying list of fossils collected by the Geological Survey.

Fossils of the Collyweston Slate.

Pterocera Bentleyi, *Lyc. and Mor.*
Alaria, sp.
Natica Leckhamptonensis, *Lyc.*
———, sp.
Patella rugosa, *Sow.*
——— operculum of ?
Arca cancellata, *Sow.*
Cucullæa cucullata, *Goldf.*
———, sp.
Cardium Buckmani, *Lyc. and Mor.*
——— cognatum, *Phil.*
——— Stricklandi, *Lyc. and Mor.*
Ceromya Bajociana, *d'Orb.*
Homomya crassiuscula, *Lyc. and Mor*
Mytilus Sowerbyanus, *d'Orb.*
Lucina D'Orbignyana, *Lyc. and Mor.*
——— Bellona, *d'Orb.*
——— despecta, *Phil.*
——— Wrightii, *Oppel.*
Astarte elegans, *Sow.*
——— excavata, *Sow.*
Trigonia compta, *Lyc.*
——— hemisphærica, *Lyc.*
——— impressa? (var.) *Sow.*
——— Moretonis? *Lyc. and Mor.*
Myacites Scarburgensis, *Phil.*
——— equatus, *Phil.*
Modiola imbricata, *Sow.*
Pholadomya fidicula, *Sow.*
——— ovalis, *Ag.*
——— Heraulti, *Ag.*
———, sp.
Pinna cuneata, *Beax.*
Pecten demissus, *Phil.*
——— paradoxus, *Münst.*
——— personatus, *Münst.*

Pecten lens, *Sow.*
———— texturatus, *Goldf.*
————, sp.
Avicula, sp.
Pteroperna plana, *Lyc.*
———— costatula, *Desloug.*
Lima interstincta, *Phil.*
———— spec. nov.
———— pectiniformis, *Schloth.*
Inoceramus obliquus, *Lyc.*
Hinnites abjectus, *Phil.*
———— velatus, *Goldf.*
———— tegulatus, *Lyc. and Mor.*
Gervillia acuta, *Sow.*
———— monotis, *Desloug.*
Ostrea, sp.
Anomia, sp.
Tracts of Annelids.
Polypodites Lindleyi, *Göpp.*

Between Easton and Stamford the hard, siliceous rock forming the base of the Lincolnshire Oolite and representing the Collyweston slate is exposed. At several points near the bed of the river Welland at Stamford, it has been observed; and here Mr. Sharp procured his interesting specimen of *Astropecton Cotteswoldiæ*, var. *Stamfordensis*, Wright. A fragment of the same beautiful starfish has recently been found at Collyweston.

In the immediate neighbourhood of Stamford the Lincolnshire Oolite is well exposed in many pits. Here the nature and succession of the rocks have been carefully studied, and their beautiful fossil contents have been assiduously collected by Professor Morris, Mr. Bentley, and Mr. Sharp. In some cases the sections exposed at the time when the district was surveyed were not so clear as in former times, owing to the abandonment or partial filling up of certain of the quarries.

As Mr. Sharp, whose long residence at Stamford and great geological attainments admirably fit him for the task, has recently brought together and discussed the relations of the various beds seen in the several pits in the vicinity of that town, I shall here quote his clear statement of the results at which he has arrived (*vide* Quarterly Journal of the Geological Society, vol. xxix. pp. 252-257) :—

" Returning towards Stamford—below the freestone bed of the ' Lings,' is a very close and brittle marly limestone, in which *Rhynchonella Crossii*, Walker, occurs. Below this are the series of marly and crystalline beds of the Lincolnshire Limestone exposed in Tinkler's and Squires's quarries, having a thickness of about 29 feet; some of them very fossiliferous, and containing zones of coral. A particular bed (containing much coral, many *Nerinæa*, and other fossils), very crystalline, and taking a high polish, was formerly called the ' Stamford Marble,' and was much used for chimney-pieces. The bed is still present in the section, but its mineral conditions are so altered as to unfit it for its former uses. In Squires's quarry (which nearly adjoins Tinkler's) a soft marly bed is thickly developed, and yields a very fine cream-coloured stone, easily worked, and (under the name of the ' Stamford Stone ') much used for chimney-pieces and for the interior carved work of churches. It contains many fossils, often in fine condition; many examples of a large *Natica* and of a very large *Lima*, and a beautifully preserved frond of a cycadaceous plant, have been obtained.

" *Fossils from the Marly Bed of Squires's Quarry.*

Hinnites abjectus, *Phil.* sp.
Lima cardiiformis, *Sow.*
———— Etheridgii, *Wright.*
———— impressa, *Mor. & Lyc.*
———— proboscidea, *Sow.*
———— Pontonis, *Lycett.*

Lima Rodburgensis, *Lycett*, M.S.
——, large sp. (allied to L. grandis, *Römer*).
——, large sp.
Pecten aratus, *Waagen.*
—— arcuatus, *Sow.*
—— clathratus, *Römer.*

Arca, large sp. ?
Astarte elegans, *Sow.*
—— recondita, *Phil.*
Cardium Buckmani, *Mor. & Lyc.*
—— subtrigonum, *Mor. & Lyc.*
Ceromya Bajociana, *d'Orb.*
—— similis, *Lycett.*
Cucullæa elongata, *Sow.*
Cypricardia Bathonica, *d'Orb.*
Cyprina Jurensis, *Goldf.*, sp.
—— Loweana, *Mor. & Lyc.*
Lucina Bellona, *d'Orb.*
—— despecta, *Phil.*
—— Wrightii, *Oppel.*
Macrodon Hirsonensis, *d'Orb.*, sp.
Modiola Sowerbyana, *d'Orb.*
Myacites securiformis, *Phil.* sp.
Mytilus furcatus, *Goldf.*
Pholadomya Dewalquea, *Lycett.*
—— Heraulti, *Ag.*
—— lyrata, *Sow.*
—— ovalis, *Sow.*
—— ovulum, *Ag.*
——, sp. ?
Tancredia axiniformis, *Phil.*

Rhynchonella sub-tetraëdra, *Dav.*
Terebratula perovalis, *Sow.*

Natica Leckhamptonensis, *Lycett.*
—— (like) Michelini, *d'Arch.*
——, sp. ?
Nerinæa cingenda, *Bronn.*
—— Cotteswoldiæ, *Lycett.*
—— Jonesii, *Lycett.*
Trochotoma obtusa, *Mor. & Lyc.*
—— tabulata, *Mor. & Lyc.*
Turbo depauperatus, *Lycett.*

Belemnites acutus, *Miller.*

Clypeus Michelini, *Wright.*
Stomechinus germinans, *Phil.*, large var.

Calamophyllia radiata, *Lamx.*
Latimæandra Flemingi, *Edw. & Haime.*
Thecosmilia gregaria, *M'Coy.*

Hybodus (dorsal spine).
Strophodus magnus, *Ag.* (palates).
—— subreticulatus, *Ag.* (palates).

Frond of cycadaceous plant.
Ferns—
Pecopteris polypodioides, *Lindley.*
Wood.

L 2

"Section in Lincolnshire Limestone, Tinkler's Quarry, Stamford.

	ft. in.	ft. in.
1. Rubbly and broken limestone - - -		4 0
2. Soft concretionary marly limestone, containing Coral zones, with *Perna, Lithodomus inclusus,* &c.		3 6
3. Marly limestone in thin layers, shivered - -		4 0
4. Compact marly limestone, in thin and irregular layers [I counted seven] - - -		3 6
5. Very hard limestone, containing oolitic grains sparsely distributed, occasionally very blue-hearted - - - - -	2 0 to	2 6
6. Earthy shale bed, in very thin *laminæ,* containing numerous *Pectens* and other shells, with tests beautifully preserved, but crushed by compression	1 6 to	2 0
7. ' Stamford Marble'—a very hard limestone, blue-hearted, and containing much *Coral, Nerinæa cingenda, N. triplicata,* numerous other shells, and teeth and palates of *Pycnodus Bucklandi* and *Strophodus magnus* and *S. subreticulatus*—formerly much more crystalline than in the present section, and then, when polished, a favourite material for chimney-pieces, &c., hence its name—in two courses - - -	1 0 to	1 6
8. Very hard limestone, coarsely grained, in two courses - - - - - -	2 6 to	3 0
9. Compact marly stone, rather hard - -		1 6
10. Compact marly stone, softer, and containing *Nerinæ*—in three courses - - -	3 0 to	3 6
11. Rather oolitic limestone, a good building stone -		1 0

" Fossils from Freestone and Shelly Beds near to Tinkler's Quarry.

    Arca pulchra, *Sow.*
    Lima proboscidea, *Sow.* sp.
    Pecten lens, *Sow.*
    Pholadomya fidicula, *Sow.*
    Serpula ?
    Stomechinus germinans, *Phil.*
    Strophodus magnus, *Ag.* (palates).

" Fossils from Tinkler's and neighbouring Quarries.

    Avicula clathrata, *Lycett.*
    ——— echinata, *Sow.*
    Gervillia acuta, *Sow.*
    Lima bellula, *Mor. & Lyc.*
    —— Etheridgii, *Wright.*
    —— Pontonis, *Lycett.*
    —— Rodburgensis, *Lycett,* M.S.
    ———, large sp. (allied to L. grandis, *Römer*) ?
    Ostrea flabelloides, *Lam.*
    ——, large flat species.
    Pecten aratus, *Waagen.*
    ——— arcuatus, *Sow.*
    ——— clathratus, *Römer.*
    ——— demissus, *Phil.*
    ——— lens, *Sow.* (or large new sp. ?)
    ——— personatus, *Münst.*

    Arca Prattii, *Mor. & Lyc.*
    Astarte elegans, *Sow.*
    ——— minima, *Phil.*

Ceromya Bajociana, *d'Orb.*
————— similis, *Mor. & Lyc.*
Cyprina Jurensis, *Goldf.*
————— Loweana, *Mor. & Lyc.*
————— trapeziformis, *Römer.*
Cypricardia Bathonica, *d'Orb.*
————— nuculiformis, *Römer.*
Goniomya V-scripta, *Sow.*
Lithodomus inclusus, *Phil.*
Lucina Bellona, *d'Orb.*
————— Wrightii, *Oppel.*
Modiola Sowerbyana, *d'Orb.*
Myacites calceiformis, *Phil.* sp.
————— decurtata, *Phil.* sp.
————— securiformis, *Phil.* sp.
Pholadomya Dewalquea, *Lycett.*
————— fidicula, *Sow.*
————— Heraulti, *Ag.*
————— ovalis, *Sow.*
—————, sp.?
—————, sp. ?
Tancredia axiniformis, *Phil.*
Trigonia costata, var. pullus, *Sow.*
————— sculpta, *Lycett.*
————— V-costata, *Lycett.*
—————, sp. (new)?
Unicardium, sp. ?

———

Rhynchonella Crossii, *Walker.*
————— sub-decorata, *Dav.*
————— sub-tetraëdra, *Dav.*
Terebratula globata, *Sow.*
————— perovalis, *Sow.*
————— phæroidalis, *Sow.*
————— sub-maxillata, *Sow.*

———

Actæonina, large species ?
Natica (Euspira) canaliculata, *Mor. & Lyc.*
————— formosa, *Mor. & Lyc.*
————— grandis, *Goldf.*
————— Leckhamptonensis, *Lycett.*
Nerinæa gracilis, *Lycett.*
————— cingenda, *Bronn.*
————— Jonesii, *Lycett.*
————— Oppelii, *Lycett.*
————— triplicata, *Bronn.*
Phasianella elegans, *Mor. & Lyc.*
Pterocera, sp. ? (like ignobilis, *Mor. & Lyc.*).

———

Ammonites Murchisonæ, *Sow.**
————— subradiatus, *Sow.*
————— terebratus, *Phil.*
————— (large septa, very like species found in Ferruginous beds at Duston).
Nautilus obesus, *Sow.*
————— polygonalis, *Sow.*
Belemnites Bessinus, *d'Orb.*

———

Serpula convoluta, *Goldf.*

———

* In the Museum of the Stamford Institution.

Galeropygus (Hypoclypus) agariciformis, *Forbes.*
Holectypus hemisphæricus, *Ag.*
Pygaster semisulcatus, *Phil.*
Pentacrinus, sp. ?

Anabacia orbulites, *Edw. & Haime.*
Cladophyllia Babeana, *Edw. & Haime.*
Isastræa limitata, *Edw. & Haime.*
Montlivaltia tenuilamellosa, *Edw. & Haime.*
Thamnastræa, sp. ?
Thecosmilia gregaria, *M'Coy.*

Hybodus (large spine).
Pycnodus Bucklandi, *Ag.* (teeth).

Teleosaurus (tooth).

Pecopteris polypodioides, *Lind. & Hutt.*
Coniferous wood.

" Professor Morris, in his well-known Paper on the Lincolnshire Oolites, published in the Society's Journal for 1853, gives, on page 336, the following as a foot note :—

" ' At Tinkler's quarry and the adjoining lands near Stamford, a typical series of the whole district may be observed. In a higher part of the hill, the stratified and bituminous clays, with the ferruginous band, may be observed overlying the freestones (Ketton and Casterton); the lower parts of the free stones from the top of the quarry; below which—

		ft.	in.
1.	Compact oolitic rock, few shells - - - -	2	0
2.	Concretionary compact marly oolite, full of shells, and zones of corals, the bottom more compact, the upper part marly, and decomposes more rapidly, containing shells in great abundance - - -	4	0
3.	Compact hard shelly oolitic rock, Nerinæa, &c. -	2	6
4.	Compact oolitic rock, somewhat crystalline - -	1	6
5.	Shaly bed, irregular laminated, fragments of plants and many compressed shells, Lucina, Pecten, &c. -	2	0
6.	' Stamford Marble,'—very compact, marly limestone, full of shells and corals, Nerinæa abundant - - -	2	6
7.	Indurated, somewhat marly rock - - -	3	0
8.	Compact rock - - - - - -	1	6
9.	Compact, marly, coarse grained, oolitic rock - -	2	6
10.	Fine-grained, oolitic rock - - - -	1	0
11.	Cream-coloured marly rock*; with Nerinæa abundant, Lima Terebratula, Isocardia (Ceromya), Modiola, Lucina, &c.	1	6
12.	Coarse oolitic rock - - - - - 2 feet to 26		0

" ' Probably resting on the sands with slaty beds, which have been found i sinking lower down the hill, overlying the ferruginous rock, which covers th Upper Lias.'

" This series, thus noted by Professor Morris 20 years ago, may still b considered, so far as it goes, to be ' typical' of the district ; but, as migh be expected, the then section in Tinkler's quarry does not exactly agree wi: that now exposed ; which, of course, is at some distance from the former si'e A comparison will exhibit differences, and yet a remarkable coinciden: Although entirely different sets of figures represent the various thicknesses of the beds of the two sections, these figures, when summed up, give tou thicknesses for the two sections almost identical. Thus, the section recent!: measured by me exposes a thickness of about 29 feet, to which may be adde the further thickness of 20 feet penetrated by the well, giving a total thickne: of 49 feet. Professor Morris's measured and estimated thicknesses amour: together to 50 feet ; the difference being only one foot.

---

* This represents the marly bed, the " Stamford Stone," of Squires's quarry.

"The coincidence seems to me very significant. However variable and discrepant the rate of deposition at the two points during the passage of time represented by the whole thickness of beds, the aggregate amount of deposit at both points only differed in the proportions of 49 to 50.

"The measurements of the beds of the Lincolnshire Limestone exposed at Simpson's quarry, on the 'Lings,' in Tinkler's quarry, and in the well, give 65 feet as the total thickness of the formation here.

"A well at Torkington's brick-pit (half a mile to the east) pierces through a thickness of 74 feet of the same beds; this about tallies with the thickness pierced by a well sunk by Mr. Browning the architect, at a somewhat lower level in North Street, allowing for a diminution of thickness at the top.

"Some excavations were recently made, at a lower level than Tinkler's quarry, near to the Scotgate entrance to Stamford; which exbibited the Slate beds reposing on the Lower Estuarine Sands.

"For the foundations and cellars of the houses of the Rock Terrace, hard by, excavations were made in the Ferruginous beds of the Northampton Sand; so that the surface of the Upper Lias Clay cannot be many feet below the level of the street at this point.

"To the east and north-east of Stamford, the various bed are considerably depressed. On the road to Uffington, immediately north of the bridge which passes over the Stamford and Essendine Railway, and abutting upon the deep cutting here, is Mr. Eldret's quarry; in which is a fine section, exposing a thickness exceeding 30 feet of beds of the Lincolnshire Limestone.

"The floor of this quarry is only a few feet higher than the level of the Welland river at this point, although the base of the limestone has not been reached.

"This is a very good typical section of the middle beds of the formation; which here has thickened considerably. It consists of a series of fifteen distinct beds of limestone, of varying character: some are oolitic (one being a true 'freestone'), and these are in an unusual position, at the bottom of the section, while others, and by far the greater part, are marly, and devoid of oolitic grains; some are soft, like the Squires's-pit 'Stamford Stone,' while others are hard, and sometimes crystalline and blue-hearted; some are very fossiliferous, while others are slightly so, and some apparently bare of fossils. In my detailed notes of this section, I have recorded the peculiar names by which the several beds are identified by the quarrymen.

"*Section at Eldret's Quarry, with Quarrymen's Terms.*

		ft.	in.
1.	'Rammel'—broken stone, about	4	0
2.	'Clinkers'—compact marly whitish stone, very good for lime-burning: has a glistening fracture	2	0
3.	'Pendle'—hard, flaggy limestone, rather oolitic, deeper in colour than the last, in thin layers	2	0
4.	'Shelly Course'—composed wholly of shells with corals, very hard, ('Stamford Marble'?)	2	0
5.	'Bullymong'—soft white marly limestone, containing numerous fossils (like the 'Stamford Stone' of Squires's quarry), more compact and harder towards the bottom	4	0
6.	'Blue Limestone'—hard compact stone, blue-hearted, good rubble walling-stone	4	6
7.	Course of cream-coloured clay	0	2
8.	Hard limestone, with oolitic grains	1	0
9.	'Bastard Freestone'—an oolitic limestone, in two courses	3	0
10.	Hard and compact marly course	0	7
11.	Soft white marly limestone (like the 'Stamford Stone' of Squires's quarry), in four courses of different thickness	5	0
12.	'Caley' oolitic bed (like some of the upper beds at Collyweston)	1	0
13.	'Bastard Freestone,' containing concretionary masses of very hard limestone	1	6
14.	'Freestone'—a good oolitic freestone	1	1
15.	Limestone—thickness not ascertained."		

At Stamford the effects of the great Tinwell and Walton fault
are first encountered, as will be seen by a reference to the map.
Owing to this great dislocation, and the cross faults in connexion
with it, the several strata in the vicinity of the town are found
occupying peculiar, and at first sight apparently anomalous, positions. For an account of the exposures of the beds obtained
during the construction of the railway and other works in the
vicinity of the town, I again quote Mr. Sharp's admirable
Memoir:—

"At Stamford Bridge, the Upper Lias Clay is only just up to the level of
the bed of the river; and in ascending the hill from this point through St.
Martin's, will be passed over in succession—the ferruginous beds of the
Northampton Sand, the Lower Estuarine sands and clays, the Collyweston
Slate and Lincolnshire Limestone beds, and the Upper Estuarine Clays; then
again, in reiterated sequence, a great thickness of Upper Lias Clay, the ferruginous beds (worked for ironstone at the top of the hill), the Lower Estuarine beds, the Collyweston Slate, and further on the rock beds of the Lincolnshire Limestone. So that the Collyweston Slate occurs both at the foot and
at the top of the escarpment, with a difference of level of some 150 feet.

" A cross fault has divided the sunken mass; for, in a section at the back
of the Midland Railway Station (levelled out of the side of the hill), the
Lincolnshire Limestone is seen in lateral juxtaposition with the ferruginous
beds of the Northampton Sand. From an excavation in the station-yard I
obtained, from a calcareous band in the latter, fragments of a zone containing
numerous bivalves, the hollows of which being filled with calcite offer a
sparkling contrast to the ferruginous matrix—an effect exactly paralleled by
the *Astarte-elegans* zone in ironstone quarries at Harlestone, near Northampton.

" The railway passes, by a tunnel under St. Martin's, through the subsided
mass of Lincolnshire Limestone, the beds of which have preserved their horizontal position, with little apparent disturbance. At the east end of the
tunnel, the railway (very little above the level of the river) passes over beds of
the Collyweston Slate; from which, at this point, in 1853, I obtained the
beautiful and unique *Astropecten Cotteswoldiæ*, var. *Stamfordensis*, described,
named, and figured, by Dr. Wright, in his Monograph upon the *Asteroidea*,
published in the volume of the Palæontographical Society for 1862."

" St. Martin's, Stamford.

" On the summit of the hill south of and over-looking Stamford, are the
Marquis of Exeter's excavations for ironstone, just within the Burghley Park
Wall.
"At the top of the section, in patches, answering to the surface contour,
appears the Collyweston Slate, weathered into slate from lying so near the
surface: beneath this are the Lower Estuarine sands and clays, having a
thickness of from 6 to 7 feet, the lowest band containing vertical plant
markings: immediately under these, is the ' Best Black ' ironstone (cellular).
then the ' Second,' together from 4 to 5 feet in thickness: a calcareous band
of 6 inches comes in here; and below it succeed—the ' Bottom ' ironstone (so
called), also cellular, 2 feet; a green ferruginous bed, 1½ foot; and a thin
ferruginous band, 'full of water,' and containing small pebble-like nodules
(as in the same bed in different ironstone quarries about Northampton)
9 inches; and under all the Upper Lias. As far as I have been able to ascer-
tain, no fossils have been found in these beds.

" *Section at Burghley Park Ironstone Quarry.*

ft. in. ft. in.
1. Soil and rubble, with patches of Collyweston Slate
   at bottom -   -   -   -   -   - — 2 6

	ft. in.	ft. in.

2. Lower Estuarine series—
   a. Sand, pale yellow, becoming redder towards the
      bottom - - - - - 5 0
   b. Blue clay, with vertical plant-markings - - 1 6
3. Ferruginous beds—   6 6
   a. 'Best black' ironstone, cellular   - - 2 0
   b. 'Second,' less cellular, and more sandy - 2 0
   c. Calcareous band - - - - 0 6
   d. 'Bottom' ironstone, cellular - - - 2 0
   e. Green ferruginous stone, about - - - 1 6
   f. Thin red ferruginous band, with pebble-like
      nodules (as at Duston and Kingsthorpe) - 0 9
                                    8 9

   (The last two beds were 'full of water ').
4. Upper Lias Clay.

" Within a few hundred yards to the west, are Lumby's Terra-cotta Works. A band in the Lower Estuarine Clays supplies an excellent material (mixed with some other ingredients) for this manufacture, and a very durable cream-coloured *terra-cotta* is produced. Similar clay is found at other places in the same bed, and is largely used in the well-known terra-cotta works of Mr. Blashfield of Stamford.

" At a quarter of a mile further south, on the roadside opposite Whincup's Farm, is the old stone quarry of the abolished Trustees of the Great North Road. The Lincolnshire Limestone is here seen in section to the depth of 18 feet : it is divided into eight distinct beds, varying in mineral condition ; some are marly and others oolitic, those near the bottom having much of the character of Barnack Rag, being coarsely oolitic, and containing numerous small shells.

" *Section in the Lincolnshire Limestone in the Old-Road Pit, near Whincup's Farm.*

	ft.	in.
1. Rubble and broken limestone - - -	1	6
2. Compact cream-coloured marly limestone, in thin layers much broken - - - -	3	0
3. Soft white marly limestone, surfaces and angles rounded by weathering (*Lima bellula*, Mor. and Lyc.)- -	2	6
4. Hard cream-coloured limestone, rather oolitic -	3	0
5. Oolitic limestone, like the 'cale' of Collyweston -	2	0
6. Soft crumbling 'caley' oolite - - -	2	6
7. 'Rag' bed—coarse oolite, containing numerous shells, *Lucina Wrightii*, Oppel, *Opis*, &c. - -	1	6
8. Hard oolitic stone, not bottomed - - -	2	6

" WHITTERING.

" A mile south of Whincup's Farm the road descends a small valley, crosses the White Water brook upon the Upper Lias, and, after passing for a mile over various beds of the Lincolnshire Limestone, traverses the area of the old ' Whittering Pendle' quarries. These were very shallow, and, having fallen into disuse, the old familiar pits have long since been levelled down and ploughed over. The ' Whittering Pendle,' although it has been considered identical with the Collyweston Slate, is very different in its mineral character, being very hard, crystalline, and sometimes almost cherty in texture. It was excavated in large irregular slabs, varying in thickness from one inch to two inches, and was used, without being squared, for the door-slabs and rough floors of cottages, for back-kitchens, &c.

" The fossils gathered from this bed are generally characteristic of the Lincolnshire Limestone ; but I must particularly notice a specimen taken by myself from the section nearly thirty years ago, and labelled as a Coral during all that time, but which last July was identified by Professor Phillips, F.R.S., as the spadix or fruit of *Aroides Stutterdi*, Carruth., an Arum-like plant, only previously known, I believe, as occurring in the Stonesfield Slate, and described by Mr. Carruthers in the ' Geological Magazine ' for April 1867.

" *Fossils from the ' Whittering Pendle.*

Gervillia, sp. ?
Hinnites abjectus, *Phil.*
———— velatus, *Goldf.* sp.
Lima cardiiformis, *Sow.*
—— impressa, *Mor. & Lyc.*
—— Pontonis, *Lycett.*
Pecten aratus (?), *Waagen.*
———— lens (?), *Sow.* (or new sp. ?).
———— personatus, *Goldf.*
Perna quadrata, *Phil.*
—— rugosa, *Goldf.*
Pteroperna, sp. ?

Lucina Bellona, *d'Orb.*
———— Wrightii, *Oppel.*
Macrodon Hirsonensis, *d'Arch.* sp.
Modiola, sp. ?

Belemnites Bessinus, *d'Orb.*

Aroides Stutterdi, *Carruth.* (spadix).

Owing to the series of faults already alluded to, the beds of the Lincolnshire Oolite are found considerably to the eastward of their main line of outcrop, and are exposed in more or less isolated sections at many points along the tributaries of the River Nene. The peculiarities presented by the beds at these their most easternly exposures, and where they are rapidly becoming attenuated preparatory to their final disappearance altogether in this direction, will be described in the sequel.

To the west of Stamford the beds of the Lincolnshire Oolite are seen to be considerably disturbed in the neighbourhood of Wilds' Ford, where, as will be seen by a reference to the map, a fault intersects the strata.

At a stone-pit between this last-mentioned point and Stamford, and at a distance of about one mile west of the latter town, the following species were obtained by the fossil-collector of the Survey :—

Natica Leckhamptonensis, *Lyc.*
Nerinæa pseudo-cylindrica, *d'Orb.*
————, sp.
Astarte, sp.
Ceromya Bajociana, *d'Orb.*
Lucina Bellona, *d'Orb.*
Modiola imbricata.
Macrodon Hirsonensis, *d'Arch.*
Myoconcha crassa, *Sow.*
Mytilus Sowerbyanus.
Pholadomya fidicula, *Sow.*
————, ovalis, *Sow.*
————, Heraulti, *Ag.*
————, reticosta.
Lima cardiiformis, *Lyc. & Mor.*
—— bellula, *Lyc. & Mor.*
—— punctata, *Sow.*
—— pectiniformis, *Schloth.*
—— Pontonis, *Lyc.*
Pecten lens, *Sow.*
Pinna cuneata, *Beau.*
Terebratula sub-maxillata, *Dav.*
Thamnastrea Lyelli, *Edw. & Haine.*

Passing again to the outer escarpment of the main line of outcrop we find many exposures of the beds which we are describing. The effect of the series of north and south faults which intersect the strata between Tickencote and Blatherwycke are sufficiently illustrated by the map, and need not be further alluded to here.   Near these faults the strata are often much disturbed, as may be seen at Ketton Station and in the railway-cutting to the eastward of it.

In a railway-cutting east of Luffenham Station the lowest beds of the Lincolnshire Oolite are exposed. The courses of limestone are here seen to be interstratified with beds of white or yellow sand, such as are so frequently found occurring towards the base of the limestone series. Some of the limestone beds are laminated and pass into coarse slates.

In the churchyard of North Luffenham the graves are opened through a bed of slaty rock into the white sands below.

In the South Luffenham cutting of the London and North-western Railway, the oolitic limestone, the Northampton Sand (ferruginous rock with usual characteristics, but only 3 or 4 feet thick), and the Upper Lias Clay are all seen.

About Edith Weston, and again at Whitwell and Barnsdale, the beds of the Lincolnshire Oolite are exposed at a number of points near the escarpment: the strata are here affected by a number of small faults.   In the stone pits above Whitwell and in those of the lime-kilns at Barnsdale Hill we find the lower beds of the Lincolnshire Oolite, consisting of hard compact beds of oolitic limestone with flaggy beds at their base, underlaid by sand.

A pit formerly existing at this place is thus noticed by Professor Morris and Captain Ibbetson:—" *At Edith-Weston a species of *Lingula*, near to, if not identical with, *L. Beanii* (Phillips), occurs in great abundance, indicating like the recent congeners its gregarious habits, and there mixed up with numerous fragments of the *Pecopteris polypodioides* in fructification."

To the eastward, in the neighbourhood of Normanton, there are many exposures of the Lincolnshire Oolite.   Extensive quarries exist near Normanton Lodge, and in the excavations for a large tank in front of Normanton Hall I saw the freestone beds resting on the representative of the Collyweston Slate, and this in turn on the Northampton Sand.

Over an extensive area stretching to the northern limits of Sheet 64 the Lincolnshire Oolite forms a great plateau capped by numerous outliers of the beds of the Great Oolite.   Quarries in the former beds are numerous in this district, but seldom offer any features of interest.   This district is but little obscured by Boulder Clay.

At Tixover the quarries of oolitic limestone have yielded many fragments of *Trickites*; at Pickworth in the same rock a very large *Pecten* (undescribed), with a diameter of seven inches, was found; and the same beds of the Lincolnshire Oolite at Little Bytham have yielded a fine 'Ammonite (*A. polyacanthus*, Waagen).   The extreme rarity of Ammonites, and indeed of all Cephalopods in the Lincolnshire Oolite, has already been noticed; Stamford and Little Bytham are the only localities within Sheet 64 at which these shells have been detected.

At Clipsham Quarries the beds of the Lincolnshire Oolite are extensively wrought for building purposes.   The stone is quarried from beneath a considerable thickness of the Estuarine Clays forming the base of the Great Oolite series. The sections are similar to those of Ketton and Stamford brickyard (Torkington's pit) but not so complete.   The ironstone junction-bed is present, but does not seem to be so persistent as is usually the case.   The Clipsham sections, are, however, somewhat obscure.

The Clipsham freestone which, like that of Ketton and Weldon, is associated with other beds of more or less coarse shelly rag, is an oolitic limestone similar to that of Ketton, but less even in grain, and with a few shells scattered through its mass.   Its characters more closely resemble those of the extensively worked stone of the same age about Ancaster.

At the cross-roads between Greetham and Thistleton there are extensive quarries, exhibiting the Lincolnshire Oolite as a compact, sub-crystalline limestone presenting many of the shells, &c. characteristic of the coralline facies of the formation.

---

* Rep. Brit. Ass., 1847, Trans. of Sec., p. 131.

168   GEOLOGY OF RUTLAND, &C.

In the neighbourhood of Little Bytham the similar beds ¦of the marly or compact variety of the Lincolnshire Oolite are found in some pits to be almost entirely made up of corals, the interiors of which are nearly always filled with beautifully crystallised calcspar. Near the same place we find the peculiar concretions surrounding and enclosing a number of oolitic grains already alluded to. These concretions might at first sight be mistaken for pebbles, but an examination of their internal structure will soon disabuse the mind of this idea. The pit in which they occur presents the following section :—

Pit between Little Bytham and Witham, half-a-mile from the former place.

(1.) Rubble and soil.
(2.) Beds of oolitic limestone, with usual
  characters   -   -   - 5 feet.
(3.) Beds of oolitic limestone, full of the
  irregular concretions   -   - 5 or 6 feet to bottom of pit.

This pit is clearly near the top of the Lincolnshire Oolite, for the Upper Estuarine Clays are seen let down in pockets at the top of the pit.

From Barnsdale northwards to the extreme limits of the sheet, the beds of the Lincolnshire Oolite Limestone do not extend to the outer escarpment, which is entirely formed of the Northampton Sand. The strata of the first-mentioned formation do not here afford any sections of particular interest to the geologist, and the line of their junction with the underlying rocks is in places concealed by Boulder Clay.

In a pit in the oolitic limestone east of Market Overton the beds exhibit evidences of a disturbance which is probably of an entirely local character, and not in any way due to subterranean movement on the large scale. The appearances presented by this section are represented in the woodcut (Fig. 13). Many of the beds here, as is usual in this rock, exhibit much oblique lamination.

Fig. 13. Section in Lincolnshire Oolite Limestone East of Market Overton.

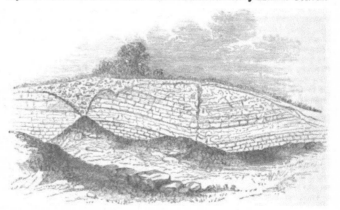

The appearances presented in this section are capable of explanation on the hypothesis that subterranean streams of water, such as certainly occur in the district and notably between Thisleton and South Witham, have dissolved out channels or great subterranean tunnels in the calcareous rock. The formation of such caverns would, in many cases, be followed by subsidences of the super-incumbent strata into them, and thus effects similar to the " creeps " of coal-mining districts might be produced near the surface. The depression is filled with Boulder Clay, which is denuded away from all the area around. This indicates that the subsidence took place before that denudation was complete.

Inliers, &c. of the Lincolnshire Oolite.

Besides the exposures already described along the main line of outcrop, the beds of the Lincolnshire Limestone make their appearance to the eastward, usually in more or less isolated sections, along the lines of the numerous brooks which have cut for themselves valleys through the Boulder Clay and subjacent oolites, and empty themselves into the Nene and Welland. In some cases these patches of Inferior Oolite Limestone are completely isolated, and exist as inliers in the midst of the Boulder Clay or the beds of the Great Oolite series; in other cases their connexion with the main portion of the outcrop of these beds in the district, along the band which we have already described, can be traced. It will be convenient to describe all these more easterly exposures of the formation together, as there are a number of features which are common to them all. Owing to the easternly attenuation of the formation which we have had occasion to notice so frequently, the Lincolnshire Oolite in the localities which we are now about to notice is of far inferior thickness to that which it presents along the line of escarpment to the westward; and in some places we find it with altogether insignificant proportions, and actually see it disappearing altogether, thus permitting the estuarine beds of the Great Oolite to repose directly upon those of the Inferior Oolite. Among the most interesting exhibitions of the easternly part of the Lincolnshire Oolite in this district the following may be noticed. It must be borne in mind that the effect of the faults which traverse the district has been such as to place the beds in a favourable position for their exposure at the surface by denudation.

On the extreme southern limit of Sheet 64 an interesting inlier of the Inferior Oolite (Northampton Sand and Lincolnshire Oolite) occurs, which has been already noticed (see Introductory Essay, pp. 36, 38, and fig. 3). The Inferior Oolite strata show considerable signs of disturbance which appears to have taken place before the deposition upon them of the beds of the Great Oolite series.

Further to the north two other small inliers of the Lincolnshire Oolite similarly occur, in the midst of the same tract of country composed of Great Oolite rocks, and for the most part deeply covered with drift. The small patches of strata exhibit beds greatly disturbed and faulted, and as in the last instance their exhibition at the surface is due to the cutting of a deep valley in the overlying beds by small streams.

Along the valley of the Nene from Aldwinkle to Perio Mill, considerably to the north of Oundle, the limestone of the Lincolnshire Oolite series is altogether absent; the Upper Estuarine series (Great Oolite) resting directly upon the Northampton Sand. It is in the small lateral valley in which the village of Southwick is situated that we first find traces of the great calcareous formation of the district.

At Cross-Way-Hands Lodge, at the bottom of the valley just alluded to, there is a pit in the shelly, oolitic freestone, which is seen to the depth of 12 or 14 feet, with the usual characters and fossils. At the cottages near, a well was sunk to the depth of 30 feet, before water was obtained. The limestone beds can be traced eastwards along the sides of the same valley to Stonepit Field Lodge.

At the last-mentioned locality we find the attenuated representative of the lower part of the Lincolnshire Oolite (Collyweston Slate) on the point of disappearing. The section here exhibits a thickness of 12 to 14 feet of very hard, slaty sandstone, calcareous in places, containing irregular masses of brown oxide of iron, and presenting many mammillated surfaces (" pot-lids," &c.) The fossils in this rock are few and badly preserved; among them occur—

> Gervillia acuta, *Sow.*
> Pecten vagans, *Sow.*
> Pteroperna (plana ?, *Lyc.* and *Mor.*)
> Several bivalves and univalves too imperfect for identification.
> Wood and plant remains.

In the valley in which the villages of King's Cliffe, Apethorpe, and Wood-Newton are situated, we find another series of exposures of the Lincolnshire Oolite Limestone; the beds, as in the previous case, thinning out and disappearing as we follow them to the eastwards.

The slipping of the beds of limestone at King's Cliffe over the subjacent beds has given rise to some picturesque features upon a small scale. A house at King's Cliffe on the left bank of the Willow Brook is built in an old stone-quarry; the face of rock forms the back of the house, and the hard siliceous beds representing the Collyweston slate form its floor. The sands of the Lower Estuarine Series are seen below the rock.

A pit on the left hand side of the road leading from King's Cliffe to Spa Lodge is opened in the oolitic limestone; the rock is here traversed by large fissures (" pipes ") which are filled with the white, marly and sandy clays of the Upper Estuarine Series, here seen covering the oolitic limestone rock. These fissures, which vary from 1 to 5 or 6 feet in width, coincide in direction with the joint planes of the beds, and in all cases show on their sides signs of the solvent action by which they have been formed. In some cases the sides of these fissures are covered with beautiful deposits of stalagmite.

On the side of the hill on the right bank of the Willow Brook and opposite to Cliff, there is a pit showing the lower beds of the limestone resting on the sands below. The basement bed of the Lincolnshire Oolite is a hard, quartzose rock, of more or less laminated structure, with mammillated surfaces beneath, at the junction of the limestone and sand.

On the surfaces of the flags obtained from these pits, which can sometimes be raised of considerable size and are used for rustic bridges, peculiarly shaped concretionary masses are sometimes found. One concretion of this character, found on a slab near King's Cliffe, has attracted much attention in the neighbourhood from the popular belief that it is a "fossil carrot." Small recesses or caverns are sometimes formed by the weathering out of the sands from beneath the hard rock; one of these is known in the district as "the Robber's Cave."

In the very shelly beds of the Lincolnshire Oolite exposed at some points near King's Cliffe many specimens of the drifted fossils, of which they are wholly made up, can be procured. An interesting collection of these shells made by the Rev. Miles J. Berkley, F.R.S., &c., during his residence at this place was obligingly presented by him to the Geological Survey.

Along the line of the Willow Brook, between King's Cliffe and Fotheringhay, a good section of the beds of the district can be made out. Near King's Cliffe the Lincolnshire Oolite consists of hard, compact, marly rock; and on the road from King's Cliffe to Apethorpe this rock is found passing into soft, shelly oolite.

The following fossils were obtained from the Lincolnshire Oolite in the neighbourhood of King's Cliffe:—

> Belemnites acutus, *Mill.*
> Pleurotomaria sulcata, *Sow.*
> ——————, sp.
> Phasianella Pontonis, *Lyc.*
> —————— striata, *Sow.*
> Natica Leckhamptonensis, *Lyc.*
> Trigonia Moretonis, *Mor. and Lyc.*
> ———— - tenuicosta, *Lyc.*
> Pholadomya fidicula, *Sow.*
> —————— - Heraulti, *Ag.*

Myacites Scarburgensis, *Phil.*
———— securiformis, *Phil.*
———— decurtatus, *Phil.*
Mytilus Sowerbyanus, *d'Orb.*
———— lunularis, *Lyc.*
Lucina Bellona, *d'Orb.*
———— Wrightii, *Oppell.*
———— d'Orbignyana, *Mor. and Lyc.*
Cyprina nuciformis, *Lyc.*
Ceromya Bajociana, *d'Orb.*
Cucullæa cucullata, *Goldf.*
Cardium Buckmani, *Lyc. and Mor.*
————, sp.
Arca rugosa, *Lyc. and Mor.*
Hinnites abjectus, *Phil.*
Pteroperna plana, *Lyc.*
Pecten demissus, *Phil.*
———— lens, *Sow.*
———— articulatus, *Sow.*
Gryphæa minima, *Phil.*
Ostrea flabelloides, *Lam.* (O. Marshii, *Sow.*) var.
Lima Pontonis, *Lyc.*
———— bellula, *Lyc. and Mor.*
———— grandis, *Lyc.?*
———— pectiniformis, *Schloth.*
———— punctata, *Sow.*
————, sp.
Terebratula submaxillata, *Mor.*
———————— perovalis, *Sow.*
Rhynchonella varians, *Sow.*
———————— spinosa, *Sow.*, var. Crossi, *Walker.*
Serpula intestinalis, *Phil.*
———— plicatilis, *Goldf.*
————, sp.
Pygaster semisulcatus, *Phil.* sp.
Pseudodiadema depressa, *Ag.* sp.
Galeropygus agariciformis, *Forbes.*
Thamnastræa Lyelli, *Edw. and Haime.*

The Wood-Newton "parish-pit" is opened in the oolitic limestone of the Lincolnshire Oolite, which is here hard and somewhat laminated in structure. In the bed of the stream below white and brownish sands are seen. The strata here exhibit signs of disturbance.

Opposite to Wood-Newton the bed which rests immediately upon the sands of the Lower Estuarine Series is a very hard, fine-grained, calcareous sandstone. This rock contains sufficient carbonate of lime to break along cleavage planes with a brilliant lustre.

In the well at Wood-Newton brickyard the following section was obtained :—

(1.) Clay (Upper Estuarine Series) of white and light-blue
    colour and sandy character, with whitish concre-
    tionary nodules, but no fossils -   -   - 3 to 8 feet.
(2.) Ironstone junction-band.
(3.) Stone, as described above (Lincolnshire Oolite) - 1 ft. 3 in.
(4.) White sands, becoming ferruginous below, and rest-
    ing on rock in which water was obtained (North-
    ampton Sand) -   -   -   -   - 17 feet exposed.

At this point it is evident that the attenuated representative of the Lincolnshire Oolite is on the point of disappearing.

In the cleared space between the Walk of Sulehay, Spires Wood, and Ring Haw, there is a large pit with a limekiln, opened in the beds of the Inferior

Oolite Limestone. The beds are here generally compact, or somewhat sandy, and only occasionally oolitic. The white clays of the Upper Estuarine Series, which rest on the limestones, are well seen in the fields around.

On the road from Ring Haw to Yarwell there is another pit in beds of similar hard, white, sandy, and but rarely oolitic limestone, here dug for road-metal.

To the south-east of the town of Stamford the beds of the Lincolnshire Oolite are well displayed over a very considerable area, owing in part to the great displacement which the beds of the formation have undergone by the faults which traverse the district, and its extensive denudation by the Rivers Welland and Nene (the valleys of which are here closely approximated) and their tributaries. In this area we are able to study the easterly attenuation and disappearance of the formation in the valley of the Nene ; but in that of the Welland the effect of the great fault has been to throw down a higher series of beds along the lower part of the course of that river, before it reaches the fens. Hence the sections presented along these two valleys, which are only a few miles apart, offer many striking points of contrast, as will be seen by an inspection of the map.

In Burleigh Park the Lincolnshire Oolite can be seen both in the low grounds in front of the mansion, where a large excavation, made to receive the drainage, exposed an instructive section, and in the high grounds behind it, where it is found overlying the Northampton Sand, and with that formation constituting the summit of a steep escarpment, the lower slopes of which are formed by the clays of the Upper Lias. Nothing can be more striking than the effects of the Great Tinwell and Walton fault at this point, the fault, as will be seen from the map, passing through the midst of the park.

Over the high ground constituting Wittering Heath the limestone of the Lincolnshire Oolite forms the surface rock. Here the nature of the light, stony soil, of a deep red colour, which these limestones afford is very well illustrated. Some portions of this area have not long been brought under cultivation.

In the neighbourhood of Barnack the very extensive " hills and holes " show what enormous quantities of the celebrated " Barnack-rag " were quarried in former times. Indeed almost all the beautiful ecclesiastical edifices of the Norman, Transition, Early English, Geometric, and Decorated periods in North Northamptonshire and South Lincolnshire, and especially those of the adjoining Fenland, appear to have been constructed of stone derived from these extensive quarries, around which a very considerable population of quarrymen appears in early times to have been established. Far earlier, even in Roman times, the value of this building material seems to have been recognised ; but before the Perpendicular period (15th century) the use of the stone appears to have been abandoned, probably from the exhaustion of the quarries. The excavations of the " hills and holes " of Barnack, now filled up and grass-grown, are continued in Walcot Park, where some of the pits still remain open. Several pits in the Lincolnshire Oolite are still worked near Barnack, but in none of them is a rock of exceptionally fine quality found ; and the general opinion that the Barnack-rag (a freestone of excellent quality almost made up of small shells and other drifted organisms, and containing a few scattered oolitic grains) is now wholly exhausted is probably the correct one. It is only necessary to study some of the beautiful Gothic edifices constructed of this stone to see how freely it was capable of working under the chisel, how suitable it was for buildings with elaborate mouldings and florid decorations, and how its durability so well adapted it for preserving the triumphs of mediæval workmanship, even when exposed in the open air to a rigorous climate.

Of the sections now exposed at Barnack the following may be noticed as typical.

Pit in Lincolnshire Oolite Limestone near Barnack.

(1.) Soil.
(2.) Rubble oolite.
(3.) Rock, made up of small shells and fragments of shells, echinoderms, corals, &c. ; plates and spines of *Cidaris*, with joints of *Pentacrinus*, and many specimens of the minute variety of *Rhynchonella spinosa* (*R. Crossi*, Walker) abound - - - - 4 feet seen.
(4.) Ordinary white, oolitic limestone, not shelly - - 8 feet.
(5.) Beds of yellow and white sand containing hard siliceous concretions - - - - - Base not seen.

The bed (3) is regarded as part of the celebrated bed of the "Barnack-rag," which it greatly resembles. It is here exposed near the surface, and is consequently of little value.

It is not certain whether the bed (5) is to be regarded as representing the higher part of the Northampton Sand, or the base of the Lincolnshire Oolite, *i.e.*, the beds in which, at certain points, the Collyweston Slates make their appearance.

It is interesting to notice that the shelly facies of the Lincolnshire Oolite occurs at Barnack near the base of the series. At many points in this neighbourhood sandy beds occur intercalated in the lower part of the series (Collyweston Slate). At Wittering Heath, as we have already seen, these arenaceous beds are indurated into the beautiful, hard, siliceo-calcareous rock known as "Pendle."

At Southorpe, and along the railway line between Stamford and Wansford, there are a number of exposures of the Lincolnshire Oolite limestone, and of the sands intercalated in the lower part of the series and immediately underlying it.

About Ufford and Helpstone Heath there are many pits in the lower beds of the Lincolnshire Oolite, and nowhere, perhaps, can its relations to the underlying sands of the Lower Estuarine Series be better studied. (*Vide* woodcuts, Figs. 8 and 9, pp. 104, 105.)

About Wansford we find many interesting exposures of the Lincolnshire Oolite, and from this point eastward we can clearly trace the gradual thinning-out and final disappearance of the formation in the vicinity of Water Newton and Castor.

South of the village of Wansford the extensive pits near Wansford Mill afford us a good section of the great limestone series, presenting its ordinary characters.

In the "Wood-pit" at Stibbington the upper surface of the oolitic limestone is seen to be very irregular; but this is, in part at least, due to the percolation of water with carbonic acid which has dissolved the upper portions of the surface of the limestone, and thus let down the superjacent clays, &c. into the holes and pockets ("pipes") thus formed.

The following fossils were collected in this neighbourhood by the late Dr. Porter, of Peterborough, principally from the "Wood-pit" at Stibbington :—

Acteonina glabra, *Phil.*, sp.
Pleurotomaria, sp.
Monodonta lævigata, *Sow.*, sp.
Patella rugosa, *Sow.*
Phasianella, sp.
Trochus Gomondii, *Mor. & Lyc.*
——— spiratus, *d'Arch.*
Turbo Phillipsii, *Mor. & Lyc.*
——— gemmatus, *Lyc.*
———, sp.
Cerithium Beani, *Phil.*
——— cingenda, *Phil.*
Nerinæa Voltzi. *Desh.*
———, sp.
Modiola imbricata, *Sow.*
Mytilus lunularis, *Lyc.*

M

Arca Prattii, *Mor. & Lyc.*
Trigonia formosa, *Lyc.*
Lucina d'Orbignyana, *Lyc. & Mor.*
Astarte elegans, *Sow.*
———— minima, *Phil.*
————, sp.
Opis lunulatus, *Sow.*
—— similis, *Lyc. & Mor.*
Gryphæa, sp.
Ostrea Marshii, *Sow.* (flabelloides, *Lam.*).
—— Sowerby, *Lyc. & Mor.*
——, sp.
Pecten lens, *Sow.*
———— vagans, *Sow.*
Avicula, sp.
Gervillia acuta, *Phil.*
Pteroperna costatula (?), *Desh.*
———— plana, *Mor. & Lyc.*
Lima bellula, *Lyc. & Mor.*
—— duplicata, *Sow.*
Terebratula maxillata, *Sow.*
———— perovalis, *Sow.*
————, sp.
Rhynchonella spinosa, *Schloth.*
————, sp.
Serpula plicatilis, *Goldf.*
Vermicularia nodus, *Phil.*
Acrosalenia hemicidaroides, *Wr.*
———— spinosa, *Ag.*
————, sp.
Holectypus depressus, *Leske.*
Pentacrinus Mülleri, *Aust.*
Pseudodiadema depressa, *Ag.*
Otopteris graphica, *(Bean. MS.) Leckenby.*

Under the sandy, whitish and bluish clays, with irregular plant-beds, we find in this pit the "junction-band," a layer of nodules of more or less compact or earthy brown ironstone. This is underlaid in many places by a bed of white marl, the product of the decomposition of the beds of limestone, and containing apparently waterworn fragments of compact limestone rock, the beds below being very oolitic.

Near the Sibson railway-tunnel there are several very interesting sections exposed in old stone-pits. In the cutting at the west end of the tunnel itself we can trace a most interesting section, exhibiting both the top of the attenuated Lincolnshire Oolite with the overlying beds of the Great Oolite, and also the sandy beds forming the base of the former formation. The top of the oolitic limestone, and its junction with the Upper Estuarine Series, presents us with similar appearances to those which are afforded by the "Wood-pit."

The beds of the Lincolnshire Oolite are again well exposed at the opposite or eastern end of the Sibson tunnel.

In Water-Newton brickyard we find, beneath the sands and clays of the Upper Estuarine Series, 4 feet of beautifully fine-grained oolitic limestone, with the "junction-bed" of nodular ironstone lying on the top of it. Below the limestone bed, which forms two courses, we find other stratified clays and sands, with a plant bed about 6 inches thick in the higher part of the series. At this place it is evident that we have the insignificant representative of the Lincolnshire Oolite separating the two estuarine series, belonging to the Great and Inferior Oolite respectively.

On the opposite side of the river, near Castor, traces of the Lincolnshire Oolite were found; but the country here is greatly obscured by great masses of valley gravel. Further east, as innumerable sections show, the Lincolnshire Oolite is altogether absent, and the Upper Estuarine Series rests directly on the Northampton Sand.

North of Stamford the rivers Glen and Gwash with a number of tributary brooks, have removed over considerable tracts portions of the beds of the Great Oolite Series, and thus exposed the beds of the Lincolnshire Oolite. This district is characterised by the broad flat plateaux constituted by the beds of the great calcareous formation of the district, and everywhere giving rise to a red soil, upon which stand numerous outliers, exhibiting that peculiar tabular outline which the geological student soon learns to associate with the rapidly alternating beds of limestone and clay so abundant in the Oolitic Series. These characteristic features of the scenery of the district are well illustrated in several of the plates.

It was in this district that Professor Morris, taking advantage of the fine sections afforded by the construction of the main line of the Great Northern Railway, carefully studied and described in the year 1853 the interesting succession of strata in this area, and thus called the attention of geologists to the remarkable differences which exist between the sections of the Lower Oolites in the Midland district, and those of the Cotteswold and Yorkshire areas respectively.

By far the best sections in the area just referred to, namely, that lying eastward of the main line of outcrop of the Lincolnshire Oolite, and in the tracts around the scattered outliers of the Great Oolite, are those afforded by the cuttings on the main line of the Great Northern Railway, and in the branch line between Essendine and Stamford.

In the cuttings between Stamford and Essendine, to the northwards of the latter place, and at Carlby, Aunby, Careby, Little Bytham, and Creeton, very beautiful illustrations are afforded of the characters presented by the beds of the Lincolnshire Oolite and of their relations to the overlying beds of the Great Oolite series. These features have been sufficiently described in the country to the southwards, and as these sections are but a repetition of many already given in this Memoir it will not be necessary to notice them in detail, more especially when it is remembered that all their more interesting features were pointed out by Professor Morris so long ago as 1853, when the fresh state of the cuttings offered facilities for their study which do not now exist. Mr. Sharp has also added some interesting notes upon the same district in his recently published memoir.

The following account of such of the fine sections along the main line of the Great Northern Railway as present exposures of the beds of the Lincolnshire Oolite is extracted from Professor Morris' valuable paper (Quart. Journ. Geol. Soc. vol. ix (1853), pp. 328–330).

"The Counthorpe cutting is a continuation of the same series of beds, but increased in thickness and varying in character, in descending order :—

	ft.
Mottled clay with bands of Oysters - - - -	3
Dark bituminous clay - - - - - -	1
Compact, sandy, and occasionally soft shelly rock, with vertical remains of plants; the shells are not numerous, comprising the genera *Natica, Modiola, Trigonia* - -	
Stratified dark green and brown shelly clays -	3
Stratified dark clays with layers of shells, not broken, and indicating the beds to have been deposited under quiet conditions; the shells are *Avicula, Cytherea, Pecten, Lima, Ostrea, Terebratula, Lingula,* and probably *Cyrena*	4
Mottled and dark clays - - - - - -	4
Bituminous band - - - - - -	6
Stiff brown and greyish clays; no shells; numerous vertical plant-markings - - - - - -	0½
	7

M 2

ft.

White and yellow clays - - - - -	3
Ferruginous band - - - - - -	1

Oolite, fine-grained and pinkish, the blocks occasionally
with blue centres*; some of the beds coarser, and containing small shells, as *Cerithium* and *Nerinæa*, from   - 12 to 13

" Two small sections of the oolite occur between this and Creeton cutting,
which latter exhibits the following descending series :—

ft.

Irregular laminated grey and green sands and clays, with layers full of shells in parts - - - -	6
Soft sandy rock full of shells, as *Modiola, Ostrea, Pecten* -	1½
Bituminous and dark green clays, with occasional shelly layers - - - - - - -	5
Greyish clays, in some parts finely bituminous (6 inches), at base - - - - - - -	1½
Greenish sandy rock with vertical plant-markings - -	1½
Various coloured clays, green, grey, brown, without shells	10
Ferruginous band - - - - - -	1

Oolitic rock, thick-bedded and horizontal, with occasional
false-bedding at the upper part; inclination of oblique
laminæ 30° N.

" The Little Bytham cutting presents a similar section, the beds varying somewhat in character (*i.e.* less fossiliferous) and thickness, especially towards the
upper part; the sandy rock with Modiola is wanting, but the clays are full
of small Oysters and much thicker; the total thickness of clays is about
30 feet overlying the oolite†; the latter was quarried to some depth below the
level of the line and presented the following :—

ft.

Pinkish oolitic rock, obliquely laminated (45°), the thicker layers being separated by seams of clay with crystallised gypsum - - - - - - -	1
Oolitic rock - - - - - -	4
Compact oolite with fragments of shells - -	5
Compact marly rock with *Nerinæa* and *Lucina* -	3
Compact oolite rock, about - - - -	8 "

There is one point in connexion with this district which it may
be necessary to call attention to here. The long series of deep
cuttings along these railway lines enable us to perceive that the
whole of the strata are bent into very slight synclinal and anticlinal
folds, which do not however interfere with the general south-
easterly dip of the beds of the district. Although the want of
continuous sections in other parts of the area does not enable us
to recognise so clearly this phenomenon of the incipient folding of
the strata, yet I am convinced, from the manner in which outliers
and inliers of the various strata make their appearance over the
whole district, that the features so clearly traceable in the tract just
described are by no means confined to it, but are equally present
in the whole of the Jurassic formations of the Midland counties.

" * From some recent experiments it would appear that the blue colour of the oolite
may be due to the presence of sulphuret of iron; see a paper by M. Ébelman, Bull.
Géol. Soc. France, 2 ser. tom. ix., p. 221.

† The clays which here cover the oolite (and the observation applies to the whole
district) have materially tended to its preservation as a solid rock, in preventing the
ordinary effects of atmospheric action, which, when the surface is not so covered,
causes it to split up into shivers and renders the upper part comparatively useless as
a building material. This observation may be useful to those who have occasion to
search for or avail themselves of the building-stone of the district."

Mr. Hull arrived at precisely similar conclusions concerning the slight or incipient folding of the Jurassic rocks during his survey of the Cotteswold Hills.[*]

Outliers of the Lincolnshire Oolite.

To the west of the main line of outcrop of the formation there occur a number of outliers of the calcareous rocks of the Inferior Oolite, capping the beds of the Northampton Sand and Upper Lias Clay. The outliers of the limestone beds of the Inferior Oolite are not so numerous as those of the ferruginous and sandy beds which lie below them, for it is evident that in many cases the relics of the former have been removed by denudation, while those of the latter remain. The escape from destruction by denudation of many of the outlying patches of Inferior Oolite strata in the district can, in many cases, be traced to the influence of faults or synclinal flexures in letting down the portions of the strata below the level of the main masses around them.

At Stoke-Albany we find a portion of the Lincolnshire Oolite, which we have represented on the map as doubtfully connected with the masses forming the main outcrop of the beds on the great escarpment. As, however, the relations of this mass of strata are here obscured by the Boulder-Clay, it is possible that it is in reality an outlier.

In the interesting outlier of Inferior Oolite strata at Neville-Holt, the North-ampton Sand already described (pp. 106–107) is capped by beds of the Lincoln-shire Oolite, the whole of the strata evidently owing their preservation to the fault indicated upon the map. The base of the limestone series here is evidently formed by sandy limestones, sometimes exhibiting a fissile character. There is no pit in these beds now open, but they can be traced in the allotment grounds on the western side of the hill. There can be no doubt that these beds really represent the Collyweston Slate. Several pits are seen on the top of Neville-Holt Hill, exhibiting the oolitic limestone with its usual characters. The stone is for the most part of the compact and marly varieties (coralline facies), and at one point, where it is quarried for building purposes, it contains numerous specimens of Brachiopoda. I obtained here—

> Terebratula submaxillata, Mor. (of all ages).
> ————— perovalis, Sow. (adults only).
> Pteroperna costatula ? Mor. and Lyc.

Between Lyddington and Seaton the eminence known as "the Barrows" is capped by beds of limestone, evidently belonging to the Lincolnshire Oolite, and which yielded—

> Ceromya Bajociana, d'Orb.
> Ostrea flabelloides, Lam. (O. Marshii, Sow.) var.
> Avicula, sp.
> Pecten lens, Sow.

The beds were exposed in a drain-cutting, but the masses of drift which overlap them renders it impossible to define on the map the exact limits of this little outlier.

Above the village of Seaton there is an outlier of the Lincolnshire Oolite of very considerable size. Here the beds are well exhibited in a number of large quarries. Near Seaton Church there is a pit exhibiting the basement beds of the formation, consisting of slaty or flaggy calcareous and micaceous sandstone, the equivalent of the Collyweston slate. A little farther to the north we find pits in which the ordinary beds of the Lincolnshire Oolite are dug to the depth of 10 feet without reaching the slaty beds at their base.

At Bisbrook there is a very small outlier of the bottom or slaty beds of the Lincolnshire Oolite. The rock can be traced near the church, and was formerly dug for road-metal, but it is said to have constituted only a band of a few

---

[*] Quart. Journ. Geol. Soc., vol. xi (1855), p. 483.

inches in thickness, with sands above and below it. This band seems to have
been entirely worked out, and now only small quantities of the slaty rock are
collected from the surfaces of the fields for the purpose of mending the roads.
A little to the west of the village the Lincolnshire Limestone with the slaty
beds at its base was exposed in a number of holes opened in different parts of
the fields, but which are now all closed. The slaty beds at the base of the
series were found to rest directly upon white, calcareous sands, and these on the
light-blue, sandy clays of the Lower Estuarine Series.

From the rock forming the small outlier at Bisbrook I collected the following
species of fossils :—

> Gervillia acuta, *Sow.* ⎫
> Pinna cuneata, *Phil.* ⎬ very abundant.
> Numerous small bivalves. ⎭
> Trigonia compta? *Lyc.*
> Pecten paradoxus, *Goldf.*
> Mytilus Sowerbyanus, *d'Orb.*
> Homomya crassiuscula, *Lyc. and Mor.*
> Ceromya Bajociana, *d'Orb.*
> Cardium cognatum, *Phil.*
> Cucullæa cucullata, *Goldf.*

The lower slaty rock here splits up into thin plates after being weathered;
it shows the peculiar siliceous mammillatious appearances with "potlids," &c.,
and has below it the white sands with siliceous concretions. Thus it will be seen
that alike, in its characters and relations, this rock presents a perfect identity
with the Collyweston slate. Some of the slabs of the flaggy rock at Bisbrook
are covered with fucoid? markings and tracks of various kinds. Other slabs
of the stone exhibit great numbers of specimens of Gervillia acuta, *Sow.*

Further north we find two other outliers of the Lincolnshire Oolite, one of
considerable size, on the northern edge of which the village of Pilton is built,
and a much smaller one to the westward on which a part of the village of
Wing stands.

To the west of Pilton there are pits opened in the limestone strata, exhibiting
in their upper parts soft, white, oolitic limestone which is used for lime-burning.
Below this we find hard, slaty, arenaceous limestone, the evident equivalent of
the Collyweston slate, containing many of the usual fossils of that rock,
which is used for building purposes and road-metal.

Between Pilton and Morcott there are other limekilns, the pits in connexion
with which are opened in the white oolitic beds, the slaty beds at the base not
being reached here. At this place I found the largest specimen of *Ceromya
Bajociana*, d'Orb., which has ever come under my notice; it was 6½ inches in
length and 4½ inches in breadth. Among other fossils, were obtained here
the following characteristic forms :—

> Pygaster semisulcatus, *Phil.* sp., abundant.
> Galeropygus agariciformis, *Forbes*, sp., abundant.
> Ceromya Bajociana, *d'Orb.*, very abundant.
> Natica Leckhamptonensis, *Lyc.*
> Pinna cuneata, *Phil.*
> Mytilus Sowerbyanus, *d'Orb.*
> Lima, spec. nov.

On the small outlier at Wing there are traces of old stone-pits, but none
have been opened for the last 30 years. One place retains the name of "Stone-
pit-field garden." The stone dug here is said to have been very hard and
white, and admirably adapted for mending the roads, for which purpose it was
quarried. The pits appear to have been quite exhausted of all the good stone
before they were abandoned; but from fragments lying about, and from the
materials employed in the walls and buildings in the village, I inferred that
the stone dug was, in part at least, the hard and fissile siliceous limestone at
the base of the series, the equivalent of the Collyweston slate.

At Lyndon Park another small outlier of the Lincolnshire Oolite evidently
owes its preservation to the agency of the great fault which bounds it on its
western side. Here a number of old stone-pits enable us to determine that
the rock exposed consisted of the lower hard flaggy-beds at the base of the
limestone series.

To the action of similar faults must be referred the preservation of the outliers at Manton and Martinsthorpe. At the former place, in a pit near the mill occupying one of the highest points in the district, the white limestone was formerly dug under Boulder Clay and was found to rest on beds of white sand. Other old stone-pits occur behind Manton Lodge, but the Boulder Clay which overlaps the whole of this high ground renders the exact limits of this outlier very obscure. To the west of the village of Lyndon a pit shows what may be regarded as a spur stretching from this outlier of the Lincolnshire Oolite, while another spur evidently extended to the high ground above Manton Tunnel.

The evidence of the existence of an outlier of the formation at Martinsthorpe is found in two small pits near the church; but the boundaries assigned to this outlier upon the map are purely conjectural.

The outlier between Hambleton and Normanton, near Armley Wood, could be accurately studied at the time when the survey of the district was made, in consequence of the opening of a large number of field-drains upon the hill which it caps. By the aid of these it became clearly apparent that a small fault has here let down the Lincolnshire Limestone against the Northampton Sand, as is shown on the map, and thus led to the preservation of the small patch of the former.

The most northernly of the outliers of the Lincolnshire Oolite in this district, that above Market Overton, is a small patch of the calcareous strata, separated by denudation from the great mass of the formation which appears a little to the eastwards. Several quarries have been opened in this outlying mass of limestone strata which exhibits considerable signs of disturbance.

Building Stones, &c. of the Lincolnshire Oolite.

At many points within the limits of Sheet 64 the limestones of the Inferior Oolite are dug for lime-burning, the compact marly or sub-crystalline varieties being most highly esteemed for this purpose. The lime procured from this source is largely employed both for agricultural and building purposes.

Where the ironstone of the Northampton Sand is smelted upon the spot, the limestone of the superjacent Lincolnshire Oolite affords a valuable flux for use in the blast furnaces. It is thus employed at Glendon and Holt.

The fine sand which alternates with the limestones at the base of the series, are, like the similar material at the top of the Northampton Sand below it, dug for making mortar. The sand-pits from which such material is obtained are distinguished in the district as " mortar-pits."

But it is for its building stones and fissile rock capable of being employed as roofing material that the Lincolnshire Oolite principally calls for the notice of the economic geologist.

By far the greater part of the quarries in the district meet only a local demand for building materials; from a few, however, the stone is sent to a very considerable distance, while about Ancaster, in the district to the northwards, very large quantities of material are raised in extensive quarries employing a large number of men, and sent to all parts of the country. The most important quarries, which have more than a local interest, within the limits of Sheet 64 are those of Ketton, Barnack, Little Casterton, Stamford, Weldon, and Clipsham.

In the year 1839 a valuable report was presented to Parliament as " the Result of an Inquiry, undertaken under the authority of the Lords Commissioners of Her Majesty's Treasury, by Charles Barry, Esquire, H. T. De la Beche, Esquire, F.R.S. and F.G.S.,

William Smith, Esquire, D.C.L. and F.G.S., and Mr. Charles H
Smith, with reference to the selection of stone for building the
new Houses of Parliament." In this interesting work we find a
number of notices of some of the building stones quarried within
the limits of Sheet 64.

In the introduction to this report it is stated that "many buildings constructed of a material similar to the Oolite of Ancaster,
such as Newark and Grantham churches and other edifices in
various parts of Lincolnshire, have scarcely yielded to the effects of
atmospheric influences." And again "the churches of Stamford,
Ketton, Colleyweston, Kettering, and other places in that part
of the country attest the durability of the Shelly Oolite termed
Barnack Rag, with the exception of those portions of some of them
for which the stone has been ill selected." As further evidence of
the value of the building-stones obtained from the beds of the
Lincolnshire Oolite we may call attention to the especially favourable notice of the Ketton Oolite in this report.

The following are the accounts given of the stone of some of the
principal quarries in the Lincolnshire Limestone within the limits
of Sheet 64 :—

Barnack Mill.—The rock is described as a Shelly Oolite of a
light whitish-brown colour, consisting of carbonate of lime, compact
and oolitic, with shells, often in fragments, the rock being coarsely
laminated in the planes of the beds. The thickness of freestone is
said to be 4 feet, and of common wall-stone 6 feet, and the size
of the blocks procurable to reach 30 feet. The quarry is said to
have been opened four years since (1835) and to be a continuation
of the old quarries in the vicinity, which are very extensive. The
stone from this quarry is reported as being used for troughs and
cisterns which are perfectly impervious.

Among the buildings in which the stone of Barnack is known
or reported to have been employed the following are enumerated:
Burleigh House, Peterborough Cathedral, Croyland Abbey, Boston,
Spalding, Holbeach, and Moulton churches, and the greater proportion of the churches in Lincolnshire and Cambridge.

Ketton.—The stone is stated to be an oolite of a dark cream
colour, consisting of oolitic grains of a moderate size slightly
cemented by carbonate of lime. The workable bed of stone is said
to be 4 feet thick and to form sometimes one and at other times
two courses, and the size of the blocks that can be procured is said
to reach 100 feet. The following general remarks are added on
the Ketton quarries. "The Rag Beds" (lying above the Freestone)
" are of a white tint and the grains are cemented with highly
crystallized carbonate of lime ; the Crash" (above the Rag) "is of
. a dark brown colour, very coarse, full of shells, distinct ova, and
very ferruginous. The ova in the freestone beds are slightly
attached or cemented together, consequently the stone is very
absorbent. Ketton Rag weighs 155 lbs. 10 oz. per cubic foot."
(The weight of the Ketton Freestone is given as only 128 lbs. 5 oz.
per cubic foot.)

"This and the neighbouring quarries, many of which are out of
work, are of great antiquity. Joints 2 to 7 feet apart. Beds dip
slightly."

Of the localities in which the Ketton stone is known or reported to have been employed the following are mentioned: "Cambridge, Bedford, Bury Saint Edmunds, Stamford, London, &c. ; many of the ancient and modern buildings at Cambridge, also in the modern works at Peterborough and Ely Cathedrals; also St. Dunstan's Church, Fleet Street, London."

As illustrating the general chemical composition of the limestones of the Lincolnshire Oolite, we may quote the following analyses by Daniel and Wheatstone from the same report:—

	Oolite of Ancaster.	Oolite Ketton.
Silica	0·0	0·0
Carbonate of lime	93·59	92·17
Carbonate of magnesia	2·90	4·10
Iron, Alumina	0·80	0·90
Water and loss	2·71	2·83
Bitumen	A trace	A trace.

The "crushing weight" for Ketton Rag is stated in this report to be higher than that of any other stone reported upon. For a two inch cube the "crushing weight" required was 321 cwt., and the especial remark is made that "among Oolites the Ketton Rag is greatly distinguished from all the rest by its great cohesive strength and its high specific gravity." For similar cubes of the Ketton, Ancaster, and Barnack freestones the crushing weights were 91, 83, and 65 cwt. respectively.

The following table, extracted from the report, illustrates the density and absorbent powers of several varieties of the limestone of the Lincolnshire Oolite:—

	Specific gravity of the dry specimens.	Specific gravity of the solid particles.	Bulk of water absorbed ; total bulk considered as unity.
Ancaster	2·182	2·687	0·180
Barnack	2·090	2·623	0·204
Ketton Freestone	2·045	2·706	0·244
Ketton Rag	2·490	2·692	0·075
Haydor	2·040	2·691	0·241

In those beds of the Lincolnshire Oolite in which the rock is made up either of shell-detritus or distinct oolitic grains, or of a mixture of these, with only a slight cementing matrix of carbonate of lime, we have useful freestones. Where, on the other hand, the materials of the shelly or oolitic varieties of the rock are cemented by crystallized carbonate of lime, or where the rock itself is compact or sub-crystalline (as in the "coralline facies" of the formation) the material can no longer be dressed for ashlar work, but often constitutes a very valuable "ragstone."

Specimens of the building stones obtained from the most important quarries in the Lincolnshire Oolite are exhibited upon the ground floor of the Museum of Practical Geology, Jermyn Street, London.

As next in importance to the building stones of the Lincolnshire Oolite we must notice the fissile rock (Collyweston slate) which, as we have already seen, is procured from the lowest beds of the formation and has been largely employed as a roofing material.

We have already noticed how the quarrying of this material has declined of late years owing to the comparatively greater lightness, cheapness, durability, and convenience of Welsh slates, now rendered, by the improved railway communication of the district, everywhere available.

The beauty of the Collyweston slate and the manner in which its colour harmonizes with that of the stone employed in the walls of many ecclesiastical edifices, prevents the total abandonment of the industry, and many Gothic architects, and notably Sir Gilbert Scott among others, continue to employ the material in the construction of modern churches. Hence a number of quarries, all in the parish of Collyweston, still remain open. At the period of the Geological Survey of the district, as already mentioned, a little pit was still open between Dene and Rockingham, from which small quantities of slate were raised for local purposes.

The Collyweston Slates have been dug over a considerable area in Sheet 64, old pits being traceable from Wothorp near Stamford to the western side of Collyweston, a distance of more than three miles. At the first of these places they are said, by tradition, to have been met with much nearer the surface than in the present workings, and this statement is confirmed by the geological relations of the beds in this neighbourhood. The valuable fissile character of the beds is merely a local accident; and in some directions the bed of stone has been followed and found to become non-fissile and in consequence worthless for roofing purposes. There is only a single bed of stone (the lowest limestone of the series) which is used for making roofing slates. This varies greatly in thickness, being often not more than 6 inches thick, but sometimes swelling out to 18 inches, and in rare cases to 3 feet; while, not unfrequently, the bed is altogether absent and its place represented by sand. Rounded mammillated surfaces, like the "pot-lids" of Stonesfield, abound in these beds.

The slates are worked either in open quarries or by drifts (locally called "fox-holes") carried for a great distance under ground, in which the men work by the light of candles. The upper beds of rock are removed by means of blasting, but the slate rock itself cannot be thus worked,' for though the blocks of slate rock when so removed appear to be quite uninjured, yet, when weathered, they are found to be completely shivered and consequently rapidly fall into fragments. The slate rock is therefore entirely quarried by means of wedges and picks, which, on account of the confined spaces in which they have to be used, are made single sided. The quarrying of the rock is facilitated by the very marked jointing of the beds, a set of master-joints traversing the rocks with a strike 40° W. of N. (magnetic), while another set of joints, less pronounced, intersect the beds nearly at right angles.

During the spring of the year the water in the pits rises so rapidly that it is impossible to get the slates out.

The slates are usually dug during about six or eight weeks in December and January. The blocks of stone are laid out on the grass, preferably in a horizontal position. It is necessary that the water of the quarry shall not evaporate before the blocks are frosted, and they are constantly kept watered, if necessary, until as late as March. The weather most favourable to the production of the slates is a rapid succession of sharp frosts and thaws. If the blocks are once allowed to become dry they lose their fissile qualities, and are said to be "stocked." Such blocks are broken up for road-metal, for which they afford a very good material. The limestone beds above the slate rock are burnt for lime.

The slates are cleaved at any time after they are frosted. Three kinds of tools are used by the Collyweston slaters. The "cliving hammer," a heavy hammer with broad chisel-edge for splitting up the frosted blocks. The "batting hammer" or "dressing-hammer," a lighter tool for trimming the surfaces of the slates and chipping them to the required form and size. The "bill and helve," the former consisting of an old file sharpened and inserted into the latter in a very primitive manner. This tool is used for making the holes in the slates for the passage of the wooden pegs, by means of which the slates are fastened to the rafters of the roof. These holes are made by resting the slate on the batting hammer and cutting the hole with the bill.

The slates are sold by the "thousand," which is a stack usually containing about 700 slates of various sizes, the larger ones being usually placed on the outside of the stack. The slates when sold on the spot fetch from 23s. to 45s. per thousand. Many of the Collyweston slaters accept contracts for slating, and go to various parts of England for the purpose of executing their contracts.

The land at Collyweston is generally held by slaters by copyhold, the slaters paying 6s. 8d. per "pit" to the lord of the manor (a "pit" is 16 square yards) with an extra charge of 1s. 6d. per pit to the measurer. A few workings are rented of the lord of the manor, the slaters paying 30s. per pit with an additional 1s. 6d. for the measurer. These payments are made every year at the annual "slaters' feast" held in January.

The manner in which the slates are placed on the roof is as follows:—The largest are laid on nearest the wall plate, and the size of the slates is made gradually to diminish in approaching the ridge. The ridge itself is covered by tiles of a yellowish white tint, made at Whittlesea, and harmonising well in colour with the slates themselves. The larger slates are, in the ordinary way, fixed to the rafters of the roof by means of wooden pegs driven through a hole in the upper part of each slate. But roofs are often covered with small slates which are fixed by mortar.

On the ground floor of the Museum of Practical Geology at Jermyn Street, London, specimens of the "slates" made at Collyweston, and of the various tools employed by the workmen are exhibited.

Origin of the Oolitic Structure of the Rocks.

Believing that the time is not yet come for a full discussion of this interesting question, I shall not in this place attempt to do more than to call attention to the facts which, in the district described in this Memoir, appear to throw some light upon the subject. Some valuable remarks upon the subject will be found in the late

Professor Phillips' "Geology of Oxford and the Valley of the Thames," pp. 394–397.

The oolitic structure as is well known is not confined to rocks of any particular age. It is found alike in certain of the beds of the Silurian, the Carboniferous, and the Permian formations, as well as in Tertiary, and even more recent deposits. In England, however, it is so commonly found in limestones of Jurassic age that the structure has come to be regarded as almost characteristic of the rocks of that period. Within the limits of Sheet 64 the oolitic structure is scarcely in a single instance exhibited by any limestone of the Great Oolite period, but it is so constantly presented, in more or less marked degree, by the beds of the Inferior Oolite, that, within the area specified, the structure may be regarded as characteristic of the rocks of the latter age.

In many cases, as is well illustrated by Professor Phillips and other writers on the subject, the concentric coats of which the oolitic grains are made up are seen to be wrapped round some object embedded in the limestone, as a Foraminifer, or a fragment of the test of a mollusc or echinoderm, or a grain of sand. But there are many cases in which the closest microscopical examination fails to detect any distinct object, either organic or inorganic, in the centre of the grains of the oolite.

The size of the oolitic grains varies very greatly in different examples and transitions are found to the coarsest pisolites. Many varieties in the size of the oolitic grains might be instanced from the beds of the Lincolnshire Limestone ; but the rocks of this formation only very rarely assumes the pisolitic character. The interesting features presented by it at Little Bytham have been already noticed.

Sometimes, as in the case of the Ketton Freestone, the rock is almost entirely made up of beautifully globular and uniform grains of oolitic structure. In many other cases we find a compact or sub-crystalline matrix through which oolitic grains are more or less sparsely scattered.

It was suggested by the late Sir Henry De la Beche that grains of sand or fragments of shells or other organisms might, when rolled in water containing much calcareous matter, receive successive coatings of carbonate of lime and thus build up a rock of oolitic structure ; and he adduced some interesting observations of his own made at Jamaica in favour of this suggestion.

That such deposition of carbonate of lime around nuclei constituted by shells, &c. does sometimes take place, all geologists will admit. Indeed, we have some pretty examples of the action in the country described in the foregoing pages; for we have seen that the small organisms constituting the mass of the shelly oolites of the Lincolnshire Limestone are thus often found encrusted. We may even go farther, and admit that this operation may proceed to such an extent as to produce a pisolitic or oolitic structure in the rock built up from such materials.

But it is nevertheless clear, as was suggested by Professor Phillips, that, in the majority of instances, the oolitic structure has been developed in the rock *subsequently* to its deposition. In some cases oolitic grains are found formed in the midst of the substance of shells or other included calcareous organism in the rock ;

and the facts which we have adduced in Chapter VI., concerning the structure of ironstones in this and other districts, show that the oolitic structure is a phenomenon of too wide occurrence, and is exhibited in connexion with too great a variety of conditions of deposition in the rock masses in which it is displayed, to be capable of universal explanation in the way suggested by De la Beche.

That the chemical actions set up in the calcareous mass, saturated as it must be with percolating water, and exposed, by the accumulation of superincumbent strata, to elevated temperature and enormous pressure, may produce the oolitic structure in limestones, and similar forms in dolomitic and other rocks, we can scarcely doubt, when all the facts of the case are taken into account.

In connexion with this subject it may be well to recall attention to the fact that the various tints presented by the several limestones, clays, sandstones, and ironstones of the Jurassic series appear to be entirely due to the effects of weathering. When dug at great depths or otherwise obtained at points where they have not been exposed to atmospheric influences, all these rocks exhibit an almost uniform deep-blue tint, which is apparently communicated to them by a diffusion through their substance of small quantities of sulphide of iron.

CHAPTER VIII.

THE GREAT OOLITE.

The Great Oolite is, in this district, represented by a series of beds of remarkably uniform character, which occupy a very considerable area within it and give rise to some of its most distinctive features. The formation is made up of four members; two of these consist mainly of calcareous materials, and were evidently accumulated under purely marine conditions, while, alternating with them, there occur deposits of argillaceous character, in which we seem to have proofs of a rapid succession of marine, brackish-water, fresh-water, and terrestrial conditions, such as could scarcely occur except within the delta of one or more great rivers.

These four members of the Great Oolite Series are as follows, enumerating them in ascending order:—The "Upper Estuarine Series," consisting of white and variegated clays, with shelly-bands, irregular beds of limestone, "beef" or "bacon" beds, lignite and plant seams, and some sandy and ferruginous strata; the "Great Oolite Limestone," consisting of alternating beds of compact marly limestone and marl or clay, the whole crowded with marine fossils; the "Great Oolite Clays," an argillaceous stratum, frequently variegated, with irregular, sandy, ferruginous, or shelly-bands interspersed through it; and the "Cornbrash" or shelly limestone with some subordinate argillaceous beds included in it.

As explained in the Introductory Essay accompanying this Memoir the formations in the south-west of England, of which these deposits appear to be the equivalents, are the following:—The Upper Estuarine Series is on the same geological horizon as the Stonesfield Slate; the Great Oolite Limestones are merely a continuation of the great calcareous formation which, under the name of the Upper Zone of the Great Oolite, is so familiar to all students of the geology of the south-western districts of England; the Great Oolite Clays may be regarded as representing the Forest Marble and Bradford Clay, while the Cornbrash of the district under description is clearly part of the same remarkably uniform and very distinct stratum, which, throughout nearly the whole of the Jurassic districts of England, maintains such constant and distinctive characters.

Between the district under consideration and Oxfordshire, the members of the Great Oolite Series become more or less attenuated and changeable in character, the argillaceous members, however, suffering much more in this respect than the calcareous. Northwards, in North Lincolnshire, the Great Oolite Series again undergoes much diminution in thickness; but in this case the calcareous beds are those which we find soonest affected. First, the Great Oolite Limestone becomes greatly attenuated, then reduced to one or two inconstant bands, and finally it disappears, allowing the Great Oolite Clays and the Upper Estuarine Series to come into direct apposition. Still farther north the Cornbrash loses its well marked characters, and, no longer presenting its characteristic fauna, but being reduced to a few oyster beds, at last dies out altogether. Finally, in South Yorkshire, all the members of the Great Oolite Series are found to be altogether wanting, and the representative of the Oxfordian rests directly on that of the Inferior Oolite. In North Yorkshire the only representative of the Great Oolite Series appears to be the thin limestone bands with associated clays, known as the "Cornbrash of Scarborough," which must not be confounded with the Cornbrash of the rest of England, with which it happens to present some points of mineralogical resemblance.

It is not easy in every case to distinguish, at first sight, the several divisions of the Great Oolite Series; the two calcareous and the two argillaceous members of the formation being particularly liable to be confounded with one another. It may therefore be well, at the outset, to state the chief points by means of which the discrimination of the limestones may be effected. The argillaceous members can, of course, in all cases be recognised by their relations to the calcareous, when these have been correctly identified.

In the first place it may be well to state that the limestones of the Great Oolite Series are, *within the limits of Sheet* 64, clearly distinguished from those of the Inferior Oolite Series in the same area (the Lincolnshire Oolite) by the almost total absence in them of the Oolitic character. Indeed, only at one or two points near Oundle and Stanion have I found any examples of the Oolitic structure in the limestones of the Great Oolite age. The fossils of the Lincolnshire Oolite, too, are so distinct as a whole from those of the Great Oolite Series, that, although there are a number of species common to both formations, there is rarely the slightest danger of the limestones of the two series being confounded.

With the Cornbrash and the Great Oolite Limestone, however, the case is quite the reverse, and much care is sometimes required, in order to avoid being misled by the mineralogical resemblances and general identity in the fauna of these two sets of calcareous strata.

As a general rule the Cornbrash limestone is distinguished by its finer grain, its reddish-brown colour, and its peculiar wall-like bedding as seen in weathered faces of rock; while the Great Oolite limestone is coarser in grain, of a whitish colour, and weathers out in more solid blocks with broad faces.

The soil formed by the Cornbrash has usually a reddish hue (like that to which the Lincolnshire Oolite gives rise), while that of the Great Oolite limestone has more commonly a black colour. These differences of physical character in the two limestones cannot, however, in every case be relied upon as certain tests; for in some localities the Great Oolite limestone presents the brown colour, the mode of weathering, and the red soil usually characteristic of the Cornbrash; while, on the other hand, the Cornbrash occasionally assumes the characters of the Great Oolite Limestone.

It is to the fossils, then, that we must look for the principal assistance in discriminating these two limestones; and, fortunately, there are certain species eminently characteristic of either of them. The chief of these we now proceed to notice. In both the Cornbrash and the Great Oolite Limestone, beds made up of oysters are by no means uncommon; but, while in the former the species

thus occurring in great aggregations is the massive, strongly plicated
O. Marshii, Sow., in the latter we find, under like circumstances, the
two minute and smooth species *O. Sowerbyi,* Lyc. and Mor., and
O. subrugulosa, Lyc. and Mor. Everywhere, indeed, in this area
the easily recognised *O. Marshii* may be regarded as characteristic
of the Cornbrash, while the equally well marked *O. subrugulosa*
may be regarded as distinctive of the Great Oolite. In the Cornbrash, the Echinoderm *Echinobrissus clunicularis,* Llhwyd, is
abundant, while the *Clypeus Mülleri,* Wright, is rare; in the Great
Oolite, however, the former is rare and the latter very abundant.
Again, in the Cornbrash *Avicula echinata,* Sow., *Gervilia aviculoides.,*
Sow., and *Terebratula obovata,* Sow., are very abundant, while in the
Great Oolite they are rare; and *Terebratula maxillata,* Sow., *Rhynchonella concinna,* Sow., and *Homomya gibbosa,* Sow., which are comparatively rarely seen in the Cornbrash, occur in vast numbers in
the Great Oolite. In the distribution of the Cephalopods we have
another distinguishing feature in the two beds; for, while in the
Great Oolite, *Ammonites* are almost wholly unknown and *Nautili*
tolerably abundant, in the Cornbrash, shells of the latter group
very seldom occur, while *Ammonites macrocephalus,* Schloth, and
A. Herveyi, Sow. abound and *A. discus,* Sow. is also occasionally
found. *Belemnites* are excessively rare in both deposits. There are
a number of species, however, such as *Pholadomya deltoidea,* Sow.,
Myacites decurtatus, Phil., *M. securiformis,* Phil., *Echinobrissus orbicularis,* Phil., *Holectypus depressus,* Leske, &c. which appear to be
equally abundant in both of the limestones. As a general rule it
may be stated that the Cornbrash presents a much greater number
and variety of species than the Great Oolite.

It must be clearly borne in mind, however, that the characters
here enunciated as distinctive of the two limestones of the Great
Oolite Series can only be regarded as such within the limits
described in this Memoir; for as we trace the beds over larger areas
we find them losing their typical character. Thus the Cornbrash
near its northern limits and before its final disappearance, presents
beds of small oysters (*O. Sowerbyi,* Mor. and Lyc.), like the Great
Oolite limestone farther to the south.

These two series of limestones, each resting on a mass of clays,
give rise to the formation, through denudation, of a number of
outliers scattered over the plateau formed by the limestone of the
Lincolnshire Oolite. The tabular and sometimes terraced forms
presented by the hills composed of these Great Oolite strata are
eminently characteristic of the scenery of the district we are
describing, and forcibly recall the forms assumed in the Cotteswold
area by the hills, formed by the hard rocks of the Lower Zone of
the Great Oolite resting on the subjacent softer materials of the
Fuller's Earth.

· We shall now proceed to describe in detail each of the members
of the Great Oolite Series exhibited in Sheet 64.

THE UPPER ESTUARINE SERIES.

This, the lowest division of the Great Oolite, consists of clays,
occasionally very sandy, of various colours, light-blue being the pre-
valent one, but bright tints of green, purple, &c. being not uncommon.

Interstratified with the clays are bands of sandy stone, with vertical plant-markings and layers of shells, sometimes marine, as *Pholadomya, Modiola, Ostrea, Neæra*, &c., at other times fresh-water, as *Cyrena Unio*, &c. Beds full of small calcareous concretions and bands of "beef" or fibrous carbonate of lime also frequently occur, and the sections sometimes closely resemble those of the Purbeck series. In its lower part this series consists usually, but not always, of white clays passing into sands. At the base of these clays there is always found a thin band of nodular ironstone, seldom much more than one foot in thickness; this "ironstone junction-band" is everywhere conspicuous, and marks the limit between the Great and Inferior Oolite Series in the district. There is very decided evidence of a break, accompanied by slight unconformity, between these two series in the Midland area. All the characters presented by the beds of the Upper Estuarine Series point to the conclusion that they were accumulated under an alternation of marine and fresh-water conditions, such as takes place in the estuaries of rivers.

These beds, which probably never exceed 30 feet in thickness and are often much less, were well exposed in the cuttings of the Great Northern Railway described by Prof. Morris in 1853. They are also exhibited at the top of some of the great quarries in the Lincolnshire Oolite, as at Ketton, Clipsham, and Casterton. The clays are admirably adapted for brick-making, for which purpose they are dug at Stamford, Great Oakley, Water Newton, Wood Newton, between Stanion and Brigstock, and between Pilton and Luffenham. In the lower part of the series at Little Bytham, clays are dug from which are made bricks of singular hardness and durability; and at Wakerley, in the same position, a good fire-clay occurs, which is used at Stamford for muffles, and also in the manufacture of terra-cotta.

These beds form a cold, stiff land, which, even when well drained, gives rise to a but very unkindly soil. Consequently, the tracts occupied by these beds are often left waste, and constitute some of the few heaths and commons in this highly cultivated district; among these may be instanced Ailsworth, Helpstone, and Luffenham Heaths.

The clays of the Upper Estuarine Series do not cover any very extensive areas within the limits of Sheet 64. On the contrary, they usually constitute the short and somewhat steep slopes between the tabular masses formed by the limestones of the Great and Inferior Oolite respectively; and in fact, their mode of occurrence is very similar to that of the Fuller's Earth in the Cotteswold Hills. Where, however, these clays do cover any considerable area, they are almost always obscured by drift, while in the steep slopes between the two limestone series clear and valuable sections are often afforded to us. Lying, as they do, upon a great mass of limestones (the Lincolnshire Oolite), the sandy clays of the Upper Estuarine Series are often found let down into "pipes," in consequence of the removal of the calcareous rock by subterranean waters, usually along lines of jointing. Thus, patches of these strata are sometimes seen at considerable distances from their proper lines of outcrop; but such "outliers," are of course, on too small a scale to be represented upon the map.

The outcrop of the Upper Estuarine Series in Sheet 64 may, in the southern part of the area, be followed along the eastern side of the band of calcareous rocks constituted by the Lincolnshire Oolite as already described, and which rises on its western side into the great escarpment. Along the eastern side of the valleys formed by the Harper, and Willow brooks an almost continuous outcrop may be traced in the ridge leading from the plateaux formed by the Great Oolite Limestone to those constituted by the Lincolnshire Oolite Limestone. And on the western side of the same valleys a number of outliers, usually capped by the limestones of the Great Oolite, exhibit the same beds ; these outliers being separated from one another by the denuding action of the numerous small tributary streams which flow into the two brooks we have mentioned.

The valleys formed by the Nene and Welland, with the complicated ramifications formed by their numerous affluents, give rise to very frequent exposures of the beds of the Upper Estuarine Series in the eastern and central parts of the area, as may be seen by a glance at the map.

Lastly, the two branches of the river Glen exhibit, in the sides of their ramifying valleys, an equally complicated series of outcrops in the northern part of the district: and here also, numerous outlying patches of Great Oolite strata diversify the surface of the great plateau of Inferior Oolite Limestone lying to the westward.

Commencing with the southern part of the great line of outcrop, we have several exposures of the basement beds of the Great Oolite Series in the neighbourhood of Geddington. These have, however, been sufficiently illustrated by us in describing the characters and relations of the Lincolnshire Limestone in this locality. (See pp. 145–6.)

In the pits about Pipwell Abbey, Pipwell Lodge, and between Pipwell and Oakley, numerous indications and partial exposures of the beds of the Upper Estuarine Series were detected, some of which have been already referred to. In the abandoned stone-pit at Pipwell Lodge, the light-blue clays were exposed to a depth of 4 feet, and appeared to contain plant remains *in situ.*

At Great Oakley the beds of the Upper Estuarine Series are dug for brickmaking, but, at the time the district was surveyed, there was not, unfortunately, any clear exposure of the strata. The succession of beds here was as follows :—

   (1.) Alternations of fœtid limestone, with *Ostrea* and other marine shells, and bands of clay also full of oysters. (Great Oolite Limestone.)

   (2.) Light-blue, sandy clays, with thin bands of laminated, highly pyritous sandstone of a grey colour, exhibiting plant markings and shells of *Cyrena.* These clays also contain carbonaceous and shelly bands. (Upper Estuarine Series.)

The Inferior Oolite below is not reached here.

By the form of the ground and some small exposures, the same beds can be traced in Great Oakley Park ; while at Little Oakley they suddenly appear at a much higher level, owing to the action of a fault. In the greatly disturbed district between Little Oakley and Stanion, although there is no difficulty in tracing its outcrop, we find no clear sections of the Upper Estuarine Series.

In the brook a little to the east of Little Oakley, the white clays at the base of the Upper Estuarine Series are seen resting on the beds of the shelly facies of the Inferior Oolite, the ironstone junction-band intervening. The upper 5 feet of the Inferior Oolite is reduced to a disintegrated mass by weathering; while the lower 7 or 8 feet consist of hard, shelly rag. The beds dip 3° to the south-east.

At Little Oakley, 20 yards on the east side of the road from Geddington, Harper's Brook, which has been to a great extent flowing underground, reappears at the surface, the shelly Inferior Oolite being seen in the bed of the stream. This marks the junction of the Upper Estuarine Series with the Inferior Oolite.

At Little Oakley stone-pit the beds of the Inferior Oolite (shelly facies) dip 10° to 12° W.N.W. At the north-western part of the pit, 5 or 6 feet of the white clays, with the ferruginous junction-band of the Upper Estuarine Series are seen. The upper part of the stone is much disintegrated, and, where not covered with clay, is worn into large "sand-pipes" which are filled by portions of the Upper Estuarine Series and the Boulder Clay. The higher beds of limestone consist of the soft shelly freestone, and the lower ones of the hard shelly ragstone, but great nodular masses of the latter exist in the midst of blocks of the former.

At the excavations at the brickyard and limekiln at Brigstock Mill between Stanion and Brigstock ("Lord Lyveden's pits") we can trace out the following interesting section. The beds here have evidently undergone considerable disturbance, and the section is not equally clear in every part.

		ft.	in.
(1.)	Soil.		
(2.)	Oyster beds (*A. Sowerbyi*, Lyc. and Mor, &c.)	1	0
(3.)	Blue clay	6	0
(4.)	Ferruginous band	0	6
(5.)	White and mottled, sandy clay	2	0
(6.)	Sandy clays, whitish above and greenish below, full of compressed shells (*Modiola plicata*, Sow. of all ages)	3	6
(7.)	Dark mottled clays full of carbonaceous markings and plant remains - more than	5	0
(8.)	Whitish, mottled, sandy clay	4	6
(9.)	Line of concentric, ferruginous nodules	0	6
(10.)	Irregularly bedded, sandy limestone	2	0?
(11.)	Hard, marly limestone	6	0
	(Coralline facies of the Lincolnshire Oolite.)		
(12.)	Sandy limestone passing downwards into calcareous sand	12 to 14	0
(13.)	Clay	1	6
(14.)	Ironstone rock (Northampton sand).		

The beds (12), (13), and (14) were seen in a well. If, as seems probable, (2) represents the bottom bed of the great Oolite Limestone, then the Upper Estuarine Series here is about 22 feet thick, and the Lincolnshire Limestone, at this point evidently approaching its line of easternly attenuation and disappearance, not much more than 20 feet. The difference in characters presented by the Lincolnshire Limestone at localities within short distances of one another, namely, in the great pits at Stanion and in that at Brigstock Mill, has already been noticed. The section of the Upper Estuarine Series exposed at this point is one of the most complete and interesting in this part of the area.

Between Dene-Thorpe, and Weldon there is an old pit, in which white and blue, clayey and sandy beds are seen, lying upon the shelly oolite of the Lincolnshire Limestone. These beds resemble those described in the last mentioned locality, but there is no clear section.

About one-fourth of a mile south of Dene-Thorpe, and at some height above the stream the light-blue clays of the Upper Estuarine Series are again exposed.

Above Dene and by the side of the road leading to Bulwick we find the limestones of the Great Oolite resting on a series of clays, which in their lower portion are of a whitish or light-blue colour.

In the road-cutting immediately above Bulwick we can trace the following succession of beds.

(1.) Marly limestone.
(2.) Marl beds crowded with *Rhynchonella concinna*, Sow. sp., Ostrea, &c.
(3.) Whitish clays.
(4.) Blue clays.

(1) and (2) evidently constitute the base of the Great Oolite limestone, and (3) and (4) the top of the Upper Estuarine Series. At the bottom of the hill, beds of compact limestone (coralline facies of the Lincolnshire Oolite) appear clearly underlying the clays of the Upper Estuarine beds of the Great Oolite.

In the road between Bulwick and Blatherwycke whitish and bluish clays of the same age are again seen underlying the Great Oolite Limestones.

In the spurs overlooking the valley at Fineshade and Duddington the clays of the Upper Estuarine series give rise to a well marked feature in the contour of the ground, and, at a few points, sections of their peculiar and characteristic beds may be observed.

At the limekiln near the corner of Collyweston and Hornstock Woods there is an exposure, afforded by a clay-pit, of strata which are of considerable interest. (Fig. 14.)

Fig. 14. *Clay-pit at Lime-kiln, corner of Collyweston and Hornstock Woods.*

a. Soil.
b. Upper Estuarine Series (lower part).
c, d, e. Ironstone and Marl (junction-bed).
f. Lincolnshire Oolite Limestone.

The section seen here is as follows :—

	ft.	in.
(1.) Soil		2
(2.) Marly clays, white, light-blue, and mottled, somewhat laminated and "dicey"	about 4	6
(3.) Nodular, ferruginous, sandy bed		
(4.) White marl		
(5.) Nodular, ferruginous, sandy bed	1	6
(6.) Laminated, sandy beds, passing down into sandy, oolitic limestone at the bottom of the pit (Lincolnshire Limestone).		

There are several points of some interest in connexion with this section. In the first place the "ironstone junction-band" at the base is double, this being however merely a local variation. And, secondly, the character of the lower, white, sandy, and argillaceous beds of the Upper Estuarine Series is such, as to forcibly suggest that they may have originated in the denudation of limestone beds like those on which they repose; the soluble calcareous constituents having apparently been removed, and the remaining fine grained materials sorted in moving water. A similar origin has been assigned to other fire-clays of analogous character. The only trace of organism detected in these clays consist of a few fragments of carbonaceous material.

If we now turn our attention to the basin of the Nene, we find in the numerous ramifying valleys connected with that river-basin, a series of sections of the Upper Estuarine Series, along a line parallel to those of the outer escarpment which we have hitherto been describing. Here, however, the Lincolnshire Limestone is absent, at least in the southern part of the basin, having disappeared through its easternly attenuation; and thus we find the Upper Estuarine Series of the Great Oolite resting immediately upon the Lower Estuarine Series of the Inferior Oolite (Northampton Sand) as is the case in the whole of the country to the south-west, namely, in South Northamptonshire and North Oxfordshire. For fuller illustrations of the relations of these beds I must, however, refer to the Introductory Essay to this Memoir and to the sections (Plate II.). In this area it is not always easy to define accurately the limits of the Upper and Lower Estuarine Series.

In the Tichmarsh cutting of the Northampton and Peterborough Railway the base of the Upper Estuarine Series, consisting of a mass of clays about 5 or 6 feet thick, is seen resting directly upon the sandy, and here non-ferruginous beds of the Northampton Sand. This section is, however, just beyond the southern limits of Sheet 64.

South of the village of Wadenhoe, there is a pit exhibiting the following interesting section :—

Ironstone Pit at Wadenhoe.

		ft.	in.
(1.) Soil and rubble of Great Oolite	- - - -	0	0
(2.) White clays	- - - - -	1	0
(3.) Yellow, sandy clay	- - - -	1	0
(4.) Dark, laminated, carbonaceous clay	- -	1	6
(5.) White clays with vertical plant-markings	-	0	9
(6.) Dark, carbonaceous clays -	- - -	0	6
(7.) White clays, with vertical carbonaceous markings and ferruginous stains	- - -	2	0
(8.) Ironstone beds to the bottom	- - -	8	0

A little below the level of this pit the Upper Lias Clay was dug. The Great Oolite and Cornbrash are seen in the high ground above the pit.

If, as seems probable, the beds (2) to (7) inclusive represent the Upper Estuarine Series, this formation has become greatly attenuated and is not more than 8 feet in thickness. The Northampton Sand also is evidently very poorly represented, and we have thus an illustration of the fact, that all the members of the Jurassic series partake in a greater or less degree of that easternly attenuation, which, in the case of the Lincolnshire Oolite, is so marked in degree and so productive of complexity in the relations of the beds.

In the foundations of an engine-house on the south side of the bridge near Lilford Hall the beds of the Upper Estuarine Series were well exposed, and seem to consist of sandy beds at the top, underlaid by about 6 feet of light coloured (bluish and greenish) fresh-water clays.

In the ornamental water near the Lodge of Lilford Park the following succession of beds was seen.

		ft.	in.
(1.) Great Oolite Limestone (with clay partings)	- -	5	0
(2.) Clay	- - - - - -	1	0
(3.) White and light-brown sand passing down into—			
(4.) Light-blue clay, of which the base was not seen.			

The Upper Estuarine Clays of the Great Oolite were exposed in several cuttings on the Northampton and Peterborough Railway, both to the north and south of the town of Oundle.

In the lateral valleys west of Oundle several sections of the same beds are exposed, especially near Oundle Wood and on the road between Oundle and Glapthorne. They can also be traced at several points in the immediate vicinity of the village of Lower Benefield. In this neighbourhood it seems probable that, as at some other points, the nodular ironstone of the "junction-band," at the base of the Great Oolite series, has in former times been dug for the purpose of smelting.

Around the valleys at Glapthorne and Southwick, clays of the Upper Estuarine series can be easily traced; but the only point where they present any feature of marked interest is on the side of the road east of How Wood, north of Southwick, where a plant or "root-bed," is seen, like that described at Danes' Hill, &c. by Professor MORRIS.

Near Cross-Way-Hand Lodge the succession of beds could be clearly traced at the time of the survey in a series of field-drains. Below the Great Oolite Limestone and Clays the fresh-water, sandy clays were well exposed, and only found to be separated by a comparatively thin bed of stone (the Lincolnshire Limestone) from the ferruginous sands of the Lower Estuarine Series (Northampton Sand) which are exposed a little lower down the stream. We are here evidently near the thin end of the wedge constituted by the Lincolnshire Oolite, and as we trace the strata further to the north and west, the thickness of this important series of marine limestones is found continually to increase, and the two estuarine deposits to be separated by greater thicknesses of calcareous rock.

The Upper Estuarine Series, as already noticed, is seen at Wood Newton (p. 171), and also at several points near Apethorpe. And at various pits in the neighbourhood of King's Cliffe the clays of the Upper Estuarine Series with the persistent "ironstone junction-band " at its base is exposed, being often let down into " pipes " or " pockets " in the irregularly eroded surfaces of the Lincolnshire Limestone.

In the woods of the Bedford Purlieus, now to a great extent cleared, the beds of Estuarine Clay can be traced below the Great Oolite. At several of the farm-buildings erected in the area, the same beds were reached in wells.

The strata of the Upper Estuarine Series, on the eastern side of the Nene valley, though exposed at many points, appear to be generally thin and destitute of any features of geological interest till we reach the neighbourhood of Wansford, where we find a number of valuable sections.

In this neighbourhood, as seen at Yarwell and other points, the upper part of the series we are describing often consists of sands instead of clays.

In the "wood-pit " at Stibbington, we have a good section of the fresh-water clays and sands, the shelly oolite beds being quarried beneath them. Here the upper surface of the Oolitic limestone displays great irregularity, but this appearance is, in part at least, due to the percolation of surface waters, which have dissolved the upper surface of the limestone, and let down the superjacent clays into holes and " pockets." Under the sandy, whitish and blueish clays, with irregular plant-beds, we find the "junction-band," a layer of nodules of more or less compact or earthy, brown ironstone. This is underlaid in many places by a bed of white marl probably the product of the decomposition of the limestone and containing apparently waterworn fragments of *compact* limestone, the beds below being *highly oolitic*. This would seem to indicate that a considerable amount of denudation of the Inferior Oolite limestone preceded, at this point, the deposition of the earliest beds of the Great Oolite series.

The strata of the Upper Estuarine Series were well exposed in making the Sibson tunnel on the Northampton and Peterborough Railway, and sections of them may still be traced at either end of it in the deep cuttings. At the western end of the tunnel, near Wansford station, the whole series of beds, from the Great Oolite Limestone (here underlaid by a considerable thickness of freshwater sands and clays, with the ferruginous nodular junction band at their base), down to the thin representative of the Lincolnshire Limestone and Northampton Sand, may be seen.

At the other end of the tunnel the beds of the Upper Estuarine are again seen, but more obscurely. They appear here to present, at their base, features similar to those we have described as occurring in the Stibbington pit.

As already noticed (page 174) the Upper Estuarine Series (its relations to the Inferior Oolite beds below being well illustrated) is exposed in the section at Water Newton brickyard.

The beds we are describing can be traced up the line of the Billing Brook, till we reach the fault shown upon the map, and by means of which the Great Oolite strata are suddenly cut off, and thrown against those of the Oxford Clay.

In the district to the northward, between the valleys of the Nene and the Welland, we find a number of interesting exposures of the strata of this age. They are seen at Bainton Heath surmounted by the Great Oolite Limestone; while at Ufford a well, sunk through the last-mentioned strata, reached beds of green clay crowded with Cyrena and other shells. At Castor Hanglands Wood a considerable thickness of white, sandy clay, forming the base of the Upper Estuarine Series, is seen at the top of the limestone quarries, where the Lincolnshire Limestone has been proved to the thickness of 20 feet. On the top of the hill between Helpstone brickyard and Oxey Wood, we find the following section :—

	ft.	in.
(1.) Light-blue, sandy clay, with some carbonaceous markings	5 to 6	0
(2.) Band of nodular, sandy ironstone, "junction-band" -	1	6
(3.) Hard and compact, argillaceous limestone, of a blue colour, weathering brown, with large smooth joint-planes -	6 to 8	0
(Lincolnshire Oolite.)	to bottom.	

The beds in this pit show great signs of disturbance, being in immediate proximity to the anticlinal roll so well exhibited in Helpstone brickyard, and also to the great Tinwell and Walton fault.

About Milton Park several wells and other sections show that the clays of the Upper Estuarine Series rest immediately upon the sands of Lower Estuarine age, the Lincolnshire Limestone being here altogether absent.

From Stamford northward to the farthest limits of the map, which this Memoir is especially designed to illustrate, as well as beyond that line, the beds at the base of the Great Oolite Series are well exposed in a number of railway-cuttings on the main-line of the Great Northern Railway. It was by the examination of these sections in their fresh state that Professor MORRIS was enabled to give those admirably clear descriptions of these argillaceous strata, which first called the attention of geologists to the fact that we have in the Midland district formations which cannot be exactly identified either with those of the south-west of England or of Yorkshire. These interesting estuarine strata were, however, in the first instance, supposed to be on the horizon of the Forest Marble, and not on that of the Stonesfield Slate, which is now recognised to be their true position.

As the sections on the line of the Great Northern Railway are now for the most part turfed up and rendered much more obscure than they were when studied by Professor MORRIS, I shall quote the excellent observations of that geologist upon the subject.*

" The Careby cutting (denuded in the centre) extends for three-quarters of a mile, and exposes the lower bituminous and brown clays overlying the oolite of 15 feet thickness; it is thick-bedded and blue in its centre, sometimes obliquely laminated and shelly, with zones of marly concretions; the shells are chiefly Lima, Pecten. Ostrea, Terebratula, and a few corals; some of the beds exhibit a bored surface.

* *Quart. Journ. Geol. Soc.*, vol. ix., pp. 330, 331.

" A small section again exposes the lower clays ; and crossing the valley traversed by the river Glen, Danes' Hill cutting (Fig. 15), exhibits a good typical section of the superincumbent clays, viz. :—

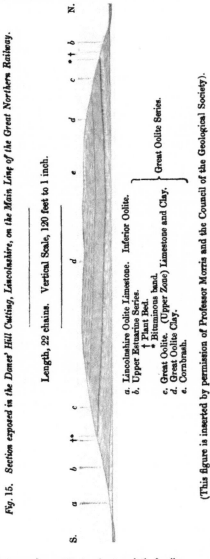

Fig. 15.   *Section exposed in the Danes' Hill Cutting, Lincolnshire, on the Main Line of the Great Northern Railway.*

Length, 22 chains.   Vertical Scale, 120 feet to 1 inch.

a. Lincolnshire Oolite Limestone.   Inferior Oolite.
b. Upper Estuarine Series.
    ↑ Plant Bed.
    * Bituminous band.
c. Great Oolite.   (Upper Zone) Limestone and Clay.   } Great Oolite Series.
d. Great Oolite Clay.
e. Cornbrash.

(This figure is inserted by permission of Professor Morris and the Council of the Geological Society).

		feet.
" Cornbrash in patches, with the characteristic fossils -	-	2 to 3
Compact sandy and marly rock	-	3½
Marly rock, full of shells	-	2

feet.

Oyster-bed, compact at bottom and soft at top, full of oysters flatly arranged, and a few other shells, *Perna*, &c. - -	8
Clay and soft marly rock, very irregular - - -	4
Clay enclosing shelly rock - - - - -	4
Green sandy clay, *Pholadomya*, &c. - - - -	1
Bituminous clay - - - - - -	0¾
Concretionary sand and lime rock - - - -	0¼
Shelly clays, Nœra, &c. - - - - -	0½
Black and green clays (no shells) - - - -	1¼
Shelly and sandy clays, bituminous at base, with fragments of plants horizontally disposed - - - -	1½
Grey sandy and marly rock, upper part (9 inches) less shelly than lower, with vertical plant markings (root or stem-bed) -	2
Shaly clay - - - - - - -	1
Bituminous clay - - - - - -	1¼
Green clays - - - - - - -	3½
Greyish and dark clays, finely laminated - - -	4

" At the southern end these lower clays are about 15 feet thick between the root-bed and the ferruginous band, upon which latter they repose, and below which the oolite extends a few yards only into this cutting. It may be remarked, that the beds exhibit a synclinal dip towards the centre, at the angle of which a small fault is visible, giving to the position of the stem bed in this section an irregularity, and somewhat affecting the parallelism of it in regard to the other sections.

" The Aunby cutting, the contour of which is very irregular, although not exposing so complete a series as the last, still presents some differences, more especially observable in the arrangement of the plant-bed, which in this section exhibits a different mode of accumulation, being here replaced by two distinct bituminous layers, each of which has its accompanying root-bed; the upper bituminous clay attaining a thickness of 2 feet, with lignite and impure coal; the lower is about 3 inches, and, with its accompanying root-bed, thins out towards the north end of the cutting. The following is the series about the middle of the cutting :—

feet.

Grey and whitish clays, with markings of plants at base -	9
Sandy and shelly clays - - - - -	3
Dark clays - - - - - -	5
Green clays, finely laminated - - - -	2
Bituminous clays with lignite and coal - - -	2
Grey sandy clay with vertical plant markings - -	1½
Bituminous clay - - - - - -	0 2 in.
Grey clay with stems - - - - -	2½
White and grey clays - - - - -	7
Ferruginous band - - - - -	1

The oolite extends along the base of the cutting."

Inliers.—The only inlier, of any importance, of the beds of the Upper Estuarine Series is that of the Brigstock Parks, on the extreme southern limit of the area. The interesting relations of the beds here, with the proofs of unconformity exhibited between the Great and Inferior Oolite Series, have been already noticed (page 38). Two sections at this place exhibit clearly the characters of the upper and lower portions respectively of the Upper Estuarine Series.

Section in road-cutting at Stone-pit-Quarter. ft. in.

(1.) Bottom bed of Great Oolite, consisting of hard, white, marly limestone with many shells - - thickness variable.
(2.) Light-coloured stratified clays with Oysters - - 2 0
(3.) Variegated clays, ash coloured, bluish, and greenish - 5 0
(4.) Irregular thin band of marl, with fragments of very thin shells (*Modiola imbricata, &c.*) - - - 0 4
(5.) Lighter coloured marly clays - - - - 0 0
     Connexion with next section not seen.

Pit at the north-east angle of Old Head Wood.

ft. in.

(1.) Soil, Boulder Clay, and Gravel - - - - 2 4
(2.) Dark-coloured, carbonaceous clay - - - - 1 0
(3.) White, sandy clay, with traces of vertical, carbonaceous
markings - - - - - - 7 6
(4.) The nodular ironstone "junction band" well seen here - variable
(5.) Soft, somewhat rubbly oolite, about - - - 1 0
(6.) Hard, compact oolite with Nerinæa and Corals (Lincolnshire Limestone, coralline facies) - - - 5 0
(6.) Brown sand, becoming paler going downwards.

The beds in this pit dip S. 17°.

The difference in level between the bottom of the Great Oolite and the top of the Inferior Oolite is about 30 ft.

There are several small faults in this pit, each of only a few inches throw.

Outliers.—West of the main line of outcrop of the Great Oolite strata a number of outliers occur, for the most part only separated from it by the narrow valleys of the numerous streams, which traverse and furrow the surface of the Great Oolite plateau. It will be only necessary to notice such of these as present sections of some completeness, novelty, or interest. Some of these outliers consist only of the Upper Estuarine Clays, and in such cases are almost always obscured by drift; others are surmounted by higher beds of the Great Oolite series.

The series of outliers, extending from Weldon to Wakerley, are largely concealed by drift, and present no sections of value till we reach the Great Wood south of the latter village. Here the lowest beds of the series, consisting of white fire-clay, have been rather extensively dug and conveyed to Stamford for the purposes of being made into muffles and also for the manufacture, in admixture with other clays, of terra-cotta.

The Wakerley clays are dug immediately below the peaty soil of the wood to the depth of 6 feet being found to rest directly on the oolitic rocks of the Lincolnshire Limestone; and they appear to be here of tolerably uniform character throughout. A pit at a slightly lower level showed only 4 feet of white fire-clay lying upon the limestone.

The large outlier of the Great Oolite east of Luffenham presents us with no good sections of the Upper Estuarine Clays; but their outcrop can be readily traced, and the "cold and hungry" nature of the soil formed from the white clays at the base of the series is very evident at Luffenham Heath.

The next outlier to the north has been encroached upon by the great excavations of the Ketton quarries. Here, above the "Crash-bed" of the Lincolnshire Limestone, we have the "ironstone junction-band" surmounted by a great thickness of clays, the lighter coloured portions of which are seen to be almost wholly made up of *Cyrena* and other shells, while the darker portions abound with carbonaceous matter, and sometimes contain large masses of wood.

North of Stamford we have sections in the Upper Estuarine beds at Little Casterton quarries, and the brickyard near the town, known as Torkington's pit. In the Little Casterton quarries the junction of the clays at the base of the Great Oolite series with the Lincolnshire Limestone is well seen. The surface of the oolitic rock is very irregular; the ironstone junction-band is present, sometimes exhibiting a thickness of several feet, and it is immediately overlaid by the usual white clays. In some of the pits the whole thickness of the Upper Estuarine beds is displayed, but the sections cannot be accurately measured.

Their succession appears to be as follows :—

Section at Little Casterton Quarries.

(1.) Limestone full of shells of *Ostrea subrugulosa*, Lyc. and Mor. (Great Oolite Limestone).
(2.) Light-coloured clays, crowded with shells of *Cyrena*, &c.
(3.) Dark-coloured "bituminous clays," with much wood and many plant remains.

(4.) White, sandy clays.
(5.) Ironstone "junction bed."
(6.) Lincolnshire Limestone, proved to 50 feet in depth.

In the brickyard at Stamford (Torkington's pit) I obtained in 1869 the following section ; the pit is now closed (December 1874).

Section at Torkington's Pit, Stamford.

		ft.	in.
(1.) Soil - - - - - - -		1	6
(2.) Oyster beds of Great Oolite Limestone - - -		3	0
(3.) Dark-coloured, nearly black, carbonaceous and ferruginous clay, without shells - - - -		3	6
(4.) Grey clays, with shells - - - - -		3	0
(5.) Clays of a tea-green colour, sometimes passing to a bright green, and crowded with shells - - - -		5	6
(6.) Black, carbonaceous bed, without shells - -	1 to	2	0
(7.) Green clay (without shells but with masses of jet) -		2	0
(8.) "Skerry," a hard gritty clay used for making fire-bricks. It resembles in texture the "root-beds" but has no vertical plant remains - - - - -		0	8
(9.) Grey clay, blackish in places (but makes fine white bricks and is esteemed the best clay in the pit) - -		4	0
(10.) White clays, very sandy in places - - -		5	0
(11.) Light reddish-brown clay, full of wood - -		1	0
(12.) Ironstone junction-band - - - -		1	0
(13.) Limestone (Lincolnshire Oolite) - - -		74	0
(14.) Sands and ironstone of the Northampton Sand.			

In the "Skerry" (8) and the clays below it iron-pyrites abounds. The total thickness of the Upper Estuarine Series here is 27 feet.

The upper clays burn into a red brick, the "skerry" into a fire-brick, and the grey clays (9) into a fine white brick.

On the small outlier of the Upper Estuarine clays nearly covered by the "spinney" called Tickencote Launde, there is an old stone-pit in the wood, which exhibits oolitic limestone covered by only 5 or 6 feet of whitish clay. There are also in this wood very numerous swallow holes, such as so commonly occur along the line of junction of the Upper Estuarine Clays with the Lincolnshire Limestone.

The other extensive outliers of Great Oolite strata to the northward do not present us with any interesting section of the estuarine beds, constituting the base of the series, till we reach the Clipsham quarries. Here the Oolitic Limestone is quarried under a considerable thickness of the overlying Estuarine clays, the section presented being similar to those of Ketton quarries and the Stamford brick-pit, but not so complete as in the latter. The ironstone junction-band is present, but does not seem to be so constant as is usually the case ; the section is, however, somewhat obscure.

At Little Bytham, at the adamantine clinker works beside the Great Northern Railway, the clays of the Upper Estuarine Series are extensively dug for the purpose of making bricks of peculiarly excellent quality, which, from the ringing sound which they give when struck together, are known as "clinker bricks." We have here a very interesting section exposed.

Section at the "Clinker Works" and Railway Cutting, Little Bytham.

		ft.	in.
(1.) Soil - - - - - -		0	6
(2.) Tea-green clays - - - - -		1	2
(3.) Brown, sandy clay - - - -		1	0
(4.) Greenish clay, full of soft, white, carbonate of lime -		1	0
(5.) Variegated blue and brown, sandy clay - -		1	6
(6.) Blue clay - - - - - -		0	6
(7.) Blue and brown, sandy clay, similar to (5) -		1	6
(8.) Bed of indurated sand with fossils - -		0	6
(9.) Blue clay, slightly mottled - - -		0	4
(10.) Brown and blue mottled, stiff clay, with lumps of soft carbonate of lime - - - - -		0	4

		ft.	in.
(11.)	Tea-green clay, ferruginous at the bottom - -	1	0
(12.)	Dull tea-green clays - - - - -	1	0
(13.)	Lighter-coloured tea-green clays, with seams of comminuted shells and carbonaceous markings - - -	2	0
(14.)	Brown sand, full of shells, and containing carbonaceous markings - - - - - -	0	1
(15.)	Black clay - - - - - -	1	3
(16.)	Lighter-coloured and more compact clay - -	0	7
(17.)	Greenish, compact clay, with ferruginous markings -	1	2
(18.)	Tea-green clays with ferruginous markings - -	0	3
(19.)	Dark-blue, compact clay with ferruginous markings -	1	6
(20.)	Dark-blue, compact clay, becoming ferruginous at the bottom, with vertical plant markings - - -	5	2
(21.)	Brown, ferruginous clay (representative of junction-bed)	1	6
(22.)	Rubbly limestone (Inferior Oolite) - - -	1	0

The following were seen in the Railway Cutting :—

		ft.	in.
(23.)	False-bedded oolitic limestone - - - -	4	0
(24.)	Sandy bed, full of oolitic grains - - - -	0	3
(25.)	Compact, blue-hearted, oolitic limestone, slightly false-bedded - - - - - -	5	6

The interesting appearances presented by this exposure of strata, an unusually fine one for the district, are illustrated in Plate VIII., in which both the section seen in the railway-cutting, and that in the adjoining clay-pits are represented.

It is to Professor MORRIS that geologists are indebted for first pointing out the peculiar estuarine conditions of which the beds we have been describing afford such satisfactory evidence. Having the opportunity of examining the freshly-opened cuttings on the railway, he collected, under the most favourable circumstances, the fresh-water fossils of the beds. These, unfortunately, are usually badly preserved and often so obscure as to be indeterminable. The marine shells of the series appear to be identical with those of the Great Oolite Limestones above, into which formation the beds we are describing insensibly merge. The only fresh-water fossils which have been found capable of identification are *Cyrena Cunninghami*, Forbes, with several species of the same genus, *Unio*, one or more species, and *Paludina*.

As an illustration of the great variability in thickness in the several members of this formation, we quote the following table from Professor MORRIS' Memoir

* " TABLE exhibiting the varying THICKNESS of the CLAYS in the different sections :—

	Essendine.	Aunby.	Danes' Hill.	Little Bytham.	Creeton.	Counthorpe or Swayfield.
	ft.	ft.	ft.	ft.	ft.	ft.
Oyster-bed and marly rock - - -	11	—	16	8	16 {	5
Clays between the above and the stem-bed -	9	20	6	10		4
Stem-bed - -	2½	3	2	⅓	1½	5
Clays below the stem-bed - - -	4	7	15	10¼	10	14
Iron-band - -	—	present	1	1	1	1
Oolitic rock - -	—	—	—	10	8	13 "

SECTION OF THE UPPER ESTUARINE SERIES AND ENGLESKERF SCALE
AT THE RAILWAY CUTTING AND BRICK WORKS AT LITTLE EYTHAM

The beds of the Upper Estuarine Series are not of great economic importance. The clays contain just such a valuable admixture of siliceous matter in a finely divided state as to adapt them for the manufacture, in some cases, of fire-bricks, and in others of tile-ware of peculiar hardness and soundness.

At Wakerley, as we have already noticed, the white clays at the base of this formation are dug rather extensively by the well-known makers of terra-cotta, Messrs. Blashfield of Stamford. It is an excellent fire-clay, and is said often not to contain more than 15 per cent. of alumina ; it is, however, largely made up of finely divided quartz, with a considerable quantity of carbonate of lime, the latter sometimes in small oolitic grains, and at other times even occurring in the forms of lumps of oolitic limestone, which are occasionally of considerable size. The muffle-tiles made of these Wakerley clays are said to withstand the severest heat for a longer time than the celebrated Stourbridge Clay. For pillars of terra-cotta, which are required to sustain a considerable weight, and at the same time to endure a considerable amount of heat (as, for instance, the columns employed in the construction of hospitals and other large buildings, which also serve as flues for conducting hot air), the Wakerley clay forms an excellent "body." For the finer classes of white and ornamental terra-cotta ware the Wakerley clays are of no use, as the roots and vegetable matters which abound in them (the masses being penetrated in every direction by the roots of trees) gives the material made from them, when burnt, an unpleasant yellowish tint.

The red ware at Stamford is usually made of a mixture of clays. These are as follows :—The weathered Upper Lias of the valley of the Welland, which is of a dull brown colour, and full of selenite formed by the decomposition of nodules of iron-pyrites ; the un-weathered clays of the same formation, which are dug at greater depths at Stamford, and the similar Lias Clay from Manton tunnel ; and, lastly, the lighter Oxford Clay from the London Road, Peterborough, which is of a more sandy texture, and is found to prevent the other materials with which it is mixed from shrinking and cracking. These several materials are well crushed and ground together, and for the finer moulded work a proportion of pounded felspar, kaolin, or other ingredients according to circumstances, are added.

For these details concerning the economic characteristics of the several clays of the district I am indebted to Mr. Blashfield of Stamford.

GREAT OOLITE LIMESTONES, &c., UPPER ZONE.

This series of beds, which graduates alike into that which we have just described below it, and into the argillaceous series above, consists of alternate beds of white limestone and marly clay, with seams made up of the shells of small oysters (*O. Sowerbyi*, Mor. & Lyc., and *O. subrugulosa*, Mor. & Lyc.). Sometimes the limestones consist of comminuted shells and then split up into thin flags like the Forest Marble of the South of England, for which they have been mistaken. Beds of this character are seen at Castor, Alwalton, &c. More usually the limestones are soft, white, and marly, abounding in casts of shells, those of the *Myadæ* being especially abundant.

The limestones at the bottom of the series sometimes attain to a
considerable thickness, and very occasionally, as near Brigstock and
Stanion, exhibit traces of oolitic grains ; but, as a general rule,
the Great Oolite of this district is everywhere distinguished from
the Inferior by the total absence of oolitic structure. When dug
under a considerable thickness of clay, all the beds are blue and
of great hardness. Occasionally these beds become somewhat
ferruginous, and are then, in their general aspect, scarcely distin-
guishable from the Cornbrash.

A large proportion of the species of fossils in these beds occur
also in the Cornbrash, but not a few of the species found in the
latter are wanting in the Great Oolite Limestones. A few species
by their great abundance serve everywhere to characterise the
Great Oolite Limestones ; among these we may especially mention
Ostrea Sowerbyi, Mor. & Lyc., *O. subrugulosa*, Mor. & Lyc., *Clypeus
Mülleri*, Wright, and *Homomya gibbosa*, Sow., sp.   In some places,
as at Bottlebridge, near Peterborough, palatal teeth and dorsal
spines of fishes (*Strophodus, Pycnodus, Hybodus, Asteracanthus*, &c.)
occur in considerable abundance with the bones of Saurians, including the gigantic *Cetiosaurus ;* at others the stone contains large
numbers of corals, *Isastræa* being the prevailing genus.

These limestones, marls, and shelly rocks which constitute the
Upper Zone of the Great Oolite, maintain a remarkable uniformity of character over a large part of England ; stretching
southwards as far as Gloucestershire, and northwards from the
district we are describing into Mid-Lincolnshire, where they appear
to thin out and disappear finally.

The beds of limestone are used locally for building purposes
and occasionally for road-metal. The compact, marly beds are
especially valued and everywhere largely dug for lime burning.
Hard, blue, shelly beds of this series were formerly quarried for
ornamental purposes, and were known as "Alwalton Marble." This
material is employed in the Early English portions of Peterborough
Cathedral as a substitute for the celebrated Purbeck Marble in the
small clustered columns which characterise that style.

Except where ferruginous, these beds form a dark coloured soil,
which, from its admixture of clay and limestone, is celebrated for
its fertility.

Extent.—The limestones of the Great Oolite almost always cover
the beds of the Upper Estuarine Series, and in fact the preservation of the soft strata of the latter formation has been evidently
due to the presence of the hard, superincumbent rocks. Consequently the remarks upon the general range and extent of the
beds of the Upper Estuarine Series in this area apply almost
equally well to those of the Great Oolite Limestone. Occupying,
however, generally higher levels, the outcrops of the Great Oolite
Limestone to the westward are more obscured by Boulder Clay and
other drift deposits, than those of the subjacent formation. Hence
it is where the beds of the limestone series are exposed at lower
levels, as along the valleys of the Nene and Welland, that the best
sections are found. It will therefore be well to reverse the order of
description which we adopted in the case of the Upper Estuarine
Series, and to notice, firstly, the numerous clear and unmistakeable
sections exposed along the great lines of the river valleys to the

eastward, and then to turn our attention to the less satisfactory exhibitions of the same strata where exposed at their highest levels towards the great western escarpment of the district.

Although the general uniformity of character in this formation is very marked, not only within the district which we are now describing, but also far to the northwards and southwards, yet there are many local variations in the characters of its beds and in the general assemblage and facies of its fossils, which seem to indicate numerous changes in the depth and other conditions of the seas in which the beds were deposited. The graduation of the strata of the Great Oolite Limestone series downwards into the Upper Estuarine Series, and upwards into the Great Oolite Clays is most perfect. Indeed, as in the south-west of England the three members of the Great Oolite Series, namely, the Lower Zone, the Upper Zone, and the Forest Marble, are connected by the most intimate ties, so the beds, which in the Midland area seem to be their almost exact representatives, are linked together by equally unmistakeable gradations.

Commencing with the valley of the Nene, where the southern limit of Sheet 64 crosses it, we find at Wadenhoe a section of the limestones of the Great Oolite, and are able to trace the relations of the various beds between the Cornbrash above and the Upper Lias Clay below.

At this place the following shells, among others, were obtained from the Great Oolite Limestone.

Arca Pratti, *Lyc. & Mor.*
Lima pectiniformis, *Schloth.*
——— interstincta, *Phil.*
——— duplicata, *Sow.*
Hinnites abjectus, *Phil.*
Pecten demissus, *Phil.*
Pteroperna gibbosa, *Lyc.*
——— plana, *Lyc.*
Ostrea gregaria, *Sow.* var.

Northward, near Pilton Lodge, the limestones of the Great Oolite are dug below the superjacent clays, and, in consequence of being thus protected from atmospheric influences, the rock is of great hardness. There are several sections of the Great Oolite Limestone in Lilford Park, presenting, however, no features of special interest. Near the bridge in this park, the junction of the marine beds of the Great Oolite Limestone with the estuarine strata below was well exposed in an artificial opening. In the ornamental water, near the lodge in this park, the bottom and more solid rocks of the Great Oolite Limestone to the depth of 5 feet, with only some insignificant clay partings, was seen resting directly on the Upper Estuarine Sands and Clays.

As a general rule, the lower beds of the Great Oolite Limestone are more solid and compact, while its upper portion consists of alternations of marls or clays, limestone beds and oyster bands, and it thus graduates upwards into the clays with shelly bands above it.

West of Lilford Lodge, we find a pit of considerable size in the Great Oolite, affording us the following section :—

Section in pit west of Lilford Lodge.

		ft.	in.
(1.)	Soil - - - - - -	1	0
(2.)	Bluish-green and mottled clay - - -	2	0
	(Base of Great Oolite Clays).		
(3.)	Clayey band crowded with oysters - -	1	0
(4.)	Stony band almost made up of oysters, thickness irregular - - - - } from 9 in. to 1		3
(5.)	Bed of compact stone, very hard, and entirely made up of comminuted shells. (This bed greatly resembles the Forest Marble of Dorsetshire) - - - -	1	6

ft. in.

(6.) Soft, white, slightly oolitic rock, becoming marly at its base, and crowded with oysters - - - - 2 0

(7.) Stone, entirely composed of comminuted shells, very irregularly bedded, and with little or no clay in its partings - - - - - - - 6 0

(8.) Somewhat softer, marly bed, full of oysters, &c., irregular in thickness, but averaging - - - - 1 0

(9.) Beds of hard stone, like (7), base not seen—to bottom of pit - - - - - - - 6 0

This pit was formerly dug somewhat lower, but no good stone was found under the bed (9), which rests on a marly band with oysters. It is uncertain whether the clays and sands of the Upper Estuarine Series were reached. The Great Oolite Limestone in this area is probably about 20 feet in thickness.

The Great Oolite Limestone is exposed at several points near Stoke Doyle, and its junction with the clays below is marked by the occurrence of powerful springs.

South of Oundle, the beds of the Great Oolite Limestone are exposed in a number of cuttings on the Northampton and Peterborough Railway. Near Barnwell we obtained the following section :—

Section in railway-cutting, near Barnwell, on the Northampton and Peterborough Railway.

ft. in.

(1.) Great Oolite Clays, blue and mottled, with a thin band of ferruginous nodules at the base. The junction of this bed with the Cornbrash is not seen in this cutting, Thickness seen - - - - - - - 5 9

(2.) Bed of laminated, sandy limestone, with bands of white marl and thin layers of "beef" (fibrous carbonate of lime). There are but few fossils in this bed except the ubiquitous *Modiola imbricata*, Sow., and *Ostrea subrugulosa*, Lyc. and Mor. - - - - - - 1 8

(3.) Beds of hard (" Forest-Marble "-like) limestone, entirely composed of comminuted shells, with a few specimens of *Ostrea subrugulosa*, Lyc. and Mor. - - - 2 0

(4.) White, marly limestone, full of shells, *Modiola imbricata*, Sow., *Ostrea subrugulosa,* Lyc. and Mor., *Pholadomya deltoidea*, Sow., *Pteroperna plana*, Lyc. and Mor., *Myacites decurtatus*, Phil., *Cardium striatulum*, Sow., *Cardium* sp. 1 6

(5.) Beds of hard (" Forest-Marble-like ") stone, composed of comminuted shells, in two courses, with a clay band between them. In other places this clay-band increases to a thick bed of white marl, full of oysters and other shells - - - - - - - 7 0

(6.) Bed of white marl, becoming, in places, hard and nodular, and containing shells - - - - - 3 0

This is the lowest bed exposed in the railway-cuttings.

Near the town of Oundle we find a number of extensive pits in the Great Oolite Limestone, and in one of these, long since closed, was obtained a number of specimens of the beautiful star-fish called *Ophiurella Griesbachii*, Wright. The following species were also obtained here :—

Modiola imbricata, *Sow.*
Lima semicircularis, *Goldf.*
Ostrea subrugulosa, *Lyc. & Mor.*
—— Sowerbyi, *Lyc. & Mor.*

One mile to the westward of the same place the following species were collected by Mr. RICHARD GIBBS :—

Fossils from a pit in the Great Oolite 1 mile west of Oundle.

Nautilus Baberi, *Lyc. & Mor.*
Natica neritoidea, *Lyc. & Mor.*
Nerinæa funiculus, *Desl.*
Anatina undulata, *Sow.*

Corbicella Bathonica, *Lyc. & Mor.*
Cyprina trapeziformis, *Röm.*
Cypricardia Bathonica, *d'Orb.*
————— nuculiformis, *Röm.*
Cyprina Loweana, *Lyc. & Mor.*
Modiola imbricata, *Sow.*
————— furcata, *Goldf.*
Myacites calceiformis, *Phil.*
————— securiformis, *Phil.*
Mytilus sublævis, *Sow.*
Lucina crassa, *Sow.*
————— Bellona, *d'Orb.*
Pholadomya deltoidea, *Sow.*
————— Heraulti, *Ag.*
Trigonia costata, *Park.*
Hinnites abjectus, *Phil.*
Perna quadrata, *Sow.*
Pinna ampla, *Sow.*
Rhynchonella concinna, *Sow.*
————— varians, *Schloth.*
Terebratula globata, *Sow.*
————— maxillata, *Sow.*
Echinobrissus clunicularis, *Llhwyd.*
————— sinuatus, *Leske.*

In a large pit near the town, the limestone of the Great Oolite is thick-bedded and crowded with fossils; at some points the rock exhibits pink and variegated tints. In the great stone-pit at Oundle Union the oyster beds are well seen, lying above the thick-bedded limestones which are quarried for building stone. In the valleys west of Oundle the oyster beds and underlying rag-stone of the Great Oolite Limestones are exposed in a number of pits. The former beds are known locally as "hurr," and are often dug for constructing artificial rock-work. Where covered by the ferruginous gravel of the pre-glacial series (derived from the Northampton Sand, see p. 243), these beds have often acquired, by the percolation of Chalybeate waters, a deep brown colour and great induration.

One of the most interesting pits in which these characters are displayed lies to the north-east of Benefield, where we find the following succession of beds.

Section in stone-pit north-east of Benefield.

(1.) Sandy gravel, containing small, irregular pebbles of brown oxide of iron, derived from the Northampton Sand (pre-glacial beds).
(2.) Breccia of argillaceous limestone and clay, full of Great Oolite fossils.
(3.) "Hurr" beds almost wholly made up of small oyster shells, and in their upper part indurated and stained of a dark brown colour by oxide of iron.
(4.) Bed of blue clay—1 foot thick.
(5.) Beds of good stone to bottom.

Another peculiarity of the Great Oolite Limestone, as seen in the neighbourhood of Oundle, is well displayed in a pit between Upper and Lower Benefield. Here the bottom beds of the series, which can be raised in very large slabs and blocks, exhibit much false-bedding and are crowded with shells; they also contain fragments usually subangular of a compact limestone possibly derived from the Lincolnshire Limestone and indicating the denudation which those beds suffered prior to, and during, the deposition of the Great Oolite.

At a pit in this neighbourhood the following fossils were collected by Mr. RICHARD GIBBS :—

Fossils from Great Oolite at Upper Benefield 4 miles N.W. of Oundle.

Strophodus magnus, *Ag.*
Arca æmula, *Lyc. & Mor.*
Lucina despecta, *Phil.*

O

Modiola imbricata, *Sow.*
Myoconcha crassa, *Sow.*
Trigonia Moretonis, *Lyc. & Mor.*
Tancredia extensa, *Lyc.*
Lima pectiniformis, *Schloth.*
—— duplicata, *Sow.*
Ostrea Sowerbyi, *Lyc. & Mor.*
—— subrugulosa, *Lyc. & Mor.*
Pecten lens, *Sow.*
—— demissus, *Phil.*
—— clathratus, *Röm.*
—— sp.
Anomia, sp.
Acrosalenia hemicidaroides, *Wright.*
Pygaster semisulcatus, *Phil.*

In the road from Glapthorne to Southwick, although the beds of the Great Oolite limestone are themselves concealed, their position is clear, the clays above them and the sandy, estuarine beds below being well exposed : while in the numerous spurs about these villages many small exposures of the Great Oolite Limestone may be detected. In the railway-cuttings north of Oundle, by Cotterstock, Tansor, &c. the beds are so much obscured by the valley gravels that the sections are of little value.

The following fossils were collected in this neighbourhood :—

Fossils from a pit in the Great Oolite 1 mile west of Glapthorn.

Cypricardia rostrata, *Sow.*
Modiola imbricata, *Sow.*
Trigonia costata, *Sow.*
——— Moretonis, *Lyc. & Mor.*
Ostrea Sowerbyi, *Lyc. & Mor.*
Plicatula tuberculosa, *Lyc. & Mor.*
Perna quadrata, *Sow.*

North-west of Cross-Way-Hands Lodge there are two pits in the oyster beds and the white limestone below them belonging to the Great Oolite Limestone. Over the great drift-covered tract, formerly clothed with woods and known as the Walk of Morehay, there are but few exposures until we approach the valley of the Willow Brook. At several points on the edge of Morehay Lawn the limestones and oyster beds of the Great Oolite are seen directly covered by Boulder Clay. But the geological structure of this district is rendered very obscure, by the thickness of the Boulder Clay and through the great tracts of woodland which still remain uncleared.

Descending into the valley of the Willow Brook we find near Apethorpe Lodge several exposures of the beds of the Great Oolite Limestone. A well sunk to the depth of 30 feet passed, in its upper part, through blue clay with stones (Boulder Clay) and reached the thin shelly and stony beds with white marly bands between them, at the top of the Great Oolite. In these water was obtained, and in consequence the well was not carried lower. In the brook below the reservoir we find, beneath the gravel, the bituminous clays *below* the Great Oolite Limestone, while north of the farm-buildings the hard limestones forming the base of the series which we are now describing are seen in the sides of an old stone-quarry at present used as a saw-pit.

West of the same farm-buildings a stone-pit still in use affords the following section :—

		ft.	in.
(1.) Soil - - - - - -	-	1	0
(2.) Irregular stony band full of comminuted shells	-	0	4
(3.) Marly band full of oysters, &c. - -	-	0	6
(4.) Stony and somewhat sandy band - -	-	0	3
(5.) White marl - - - -	-	0	3
(6.) Light-blue, laminated clay - - -	-	0	3
(7.) White marl with oysters, &c. - -	-	1	3
(8.) Beds of hard, white limestone, bottom not seen	-	3	0

Precisely similar sections may be observed in several small stone-pits on the opposite side of the valley to Morehay Lawn.

The "town-pit" of Apethorpe is opened in the lowest hard bed of the white limestone. It is here about 16 inches thick, and is overlaid by hard, cemented, limestone rubble. It is underlaid by a bed of marl, and that in turn rests on a bed of stone 4 inches in thickness. Below this we find a great mass of light-blue clay belonging to the Upper Estuarine Series. Along the line of the valley by King's Cliffe, Apethorpe and Wood Newton to Fotheringhay a number of small pits occur by means of which the general succession of the Great Oolite beds may be traced.

On the north side of the valley of the Willow Brook, we find another extensive tract, like the Walk of Morehay, covered with wood and greatly obscured by drift. This is known as the Westhay Woods, the Bedford Purlieus, and the Walk of Sulehay.

On the slopes leading up to Westhay Lodge, the Great Oolite Limestones (oyster-beds, &c.) are seen directly overlapped by the Boulder Clay. On the Bedford Purlieus the beds of Great Oolite Limestones are exposed in some small openings, and are also reached in two of the wells dug on parts of the old forest-land which, at the time of the survey of the district, were being cleared and laid out in farms in this old forest tract. The same beds were passed through in a well at Cross Leas in the same district.

Returning to the valley of the Nene, we find the Great Oolite Limestones underlying the pre-glacial gravels at Ring Haw Wood. About Elton there are several exposures of the Great Oolite strata, and between that village and Holborn Lodge a well 72 feet deep yielded the following succession of beds :—

<table>
<tr><td>(1.)</td><td>Cornbrash</td><td>-</td><td>-</td><td>-</td><td>-</td><td>- 3 feet seen.</td></tr>
<tr><td>(2.)</td><td>Clays (of Great Oolite)</td><td></td><td>-</td><td>-</td><td>- 14 to 15 ft.</td></tr>
<tr><td>(3.)</td><td>Shaley rock (oyster bands)</td><td colspan="2">{ (Great Oolite Lime-</td><td>5 feet.</td></tr>
<tr><td>(4.)</td><td>Hard rock (limestones)</td><td colspan="2">{   stones.)</td><td>4 to 5 feet.</td></tr>
<tr><td>(5.)</td><td>Indurated sand and clay (Upper Estuarine series) 30 to 40 feet.</td></tr>
<tr><td>(6.)</td><td>Rock (Lincolnshire Limestone.)</td></tr>
</table>

In the last bed water was obtained. What is most remarkable in this section is the thinness of the Great Oolite Limestone, another example of the tendency of its beds to south-easterly attenuation. A somewhat similar section was found in a well nearer to Elton.

At either end of the Sibson tunnel on the Northampton and Peterborough Railway, the whole succession of beds of the Great Oolite is well exposed ; the beds of the Limestone series presenting their usual character and succession.

At Bainton Heath and between this place and Southorpe the strata of the Great Oolite Limestone, and their relations to the clays above, and the estuarine beds below, can be well observed. At Ufford, a well was sunk through the hard limestone rock of the Great Oolite, which required blasting, into the green clays with *Cyrena* (Upper Estuarine Series) below it.

At Helpstone, a number of large pits have been opened in the Great Oolite Limestone, the stone being extensively quarried for road-metal, which is sent to considerable distances in the Fenland. In a large stone-pit, containing a limekiln, above Helpstone, we have the following section :—

<table>
<tr><td></td><td></td><td></td><td></td><td></td><td></td><td>ft.</td><td>in.</td></tr>
<tr><td>(1.)</td><td>Soil, &c.</td><td>-</td><td>-</td><td>-</td><td>-</td><td>- 2</td><td>0</td></tr>
<tr><td>(2.)</td><td>Oyster beds, with bands of clay between them</td><td></td><td></td><td></td><td></td><td>- 3</td><td>0</td></tr>
<tr><td>(3.)</td><td colspan="6">Thick mass of very hard, dark-blue limestone, with</td></tr>
<tr><td></td><td colspan="5">many shells -   -   -   - to bottom of pit.</td></tr>
</table>

A well here, commencing at the top of the oyster beds, and dug to the depth of 12 feet, just reached the top of the clays of the Upper Estuarine Series.

A similar succession of beds is seen in two other large pits at this place. The lowest rock, to the thickness of two feet, is here found to be soft and worthless for road-metal and is not taken out. In the rock here I found—

> Pholadomya deltoidea, *Sow.*
> Trigonia Moretonis, *Mor. & Lyc.*
> Clypeus Mülleri, *Wright,*
> and other fossils.

At Oxey Wood and several other points in the neighbourhood the oyster-beds and limestones of the Great Oolite are exposed.

Above Ailsworth there are good sections in the marly, white limestone of the Great Oolite. The oyster-beds are here seen overlying the limestone, and in the latter fossils are abundant, including—

Pholadomya deltoidea, *Sow.* Very abundant.
Homomya gibbosa, *Ag.* Abundant.
Terebratula maxillata, *Sow.* (Adult forms.)
Rhynchonella concinna, *Sow.*
Clypeus Mülleri, *Wright.*
Holectypus, sp.

At Ailsworth Heath traces of an old pit in the Great Oolite Limestone are seen.

Near this place the following fossils were collected from the Great Oolite Limestone :—

Fossils from stone-pit near Ailsworth.
Strophodus magnus, *Ag.*
Monodonta, sp.
Natica globosa, *Lyc. & Mor.*
Nerinæa funiculus, *Desl.*
————— Voltzii, *Desl.*
Anatina undulata, *Sow.*
Arca Pratii, *Lyc. & Mor.*
Ceromya concentrica, *Sow.*
————— plicata, *Ag.*
Cardium, sp.
Cucullæa Goldfussii, *Röm.*
Cypricardia Bathonica, *d'Orb.*
————— rostrata, *Sow.*
Cyprina nuciformis, *Lyc.*
————— Loweana, *Lyc. & Mor.*
Homomya Vezelayi, *d'Arch.*
Isocardia tenera, *Sow.*
Lucina Bellona, *d'Orb.*
Modiola furcata, *Goldf.*
————— imbricata, *Sow.*
Myacites calceiformis, *Phil.*
————— securiformis, *Phil.*
Pholadomya deltoidea, *Sow.*
————— Heraulti, *Ag.*
Trigonia Moretonis, *Lyc. & Mor.*
Avicula echinata, *Sow.*
Lima duplicata, *Sow.*
Ostrea subrugulosa, *Lyc. & Mor.*
Gervillia aviculoides, *Sow.*
Terebratula maxillata, *Sow.*
————— ornithocephala, *Sow.*
————— submaxillata, *? Mor.*
————— globata, *Sow.*
Rhynchonella concinna, *Sow.*
———— ——— varians, *Schloth.*
Serpula, sp.
Echinobrissus sinuatus, *Leske.*

At Castor the oyster beds of the series are seen, and on Castor Heath the rocks of the Great Oolite Limestone assume the form known as Alwalton Marble, greatly resembling some of the flaggy beds of the Forest Marble of the south of England. The oyster beds and limestones of the Great Oolite can also be traced along the sides of the Billing Brook, till they are cut off by the fault already referred to.

The beds of the Great Oolite Limestone, which are seen at several points about Water Newton, can be traced between that point and Alwalton, at which latter place they are well exposed in the railway-cuttings and old ' marble-pits.'' The steep escarpment of the Alwalton Lynch is formed by the limestones and oyster beds of the Great Oolite, overlying the variegated sandy clays of the Upper Estuarine Series. The beds are well seen in the road leading from the village down to the Nene.

The Alwalton Marble was formerly dug all along the Alwalton Lynch, but the whole of the pits are now closed. The hard, blue, shelly limestone was found to take an excellent polish, but does not appear to have been very durable.

About Milton Park a number of wells showed the beds of the Great Oolite Limestone to vary from 10 to 20 feet in thickness. There is a small pit in the oyster beds in Thorpe Park.

At Orton, near Peterborough, a well gave the following succession of beds:—

(1.) Cornbrash.
(2.) Great Oolite clays   -   -   -   -   13 to 14 feet.
(3.) Great Oolite Limestones -   -   -   -   17 feet.
(4.) Upper and Lower Estuarine Series   -   -   39 feet.
(5.) Ironstone rock (Northampton Sand).

In the admirable exposures of the Great Oolite in the railway-cuttings at Bottlebridge, near Orton, the late Dr. Porter collected large numbers of very interesting fossils.

North of the valley of the Welland the outcrop of the beds of the Great Oolite Limestone can be traced in the district traversed by the line of the main line of the Great Northern Railway, in the cuttings of which, and in those of the Essendine and Stamford Branch Railway, we find some interesting exposures of the beds.

The Belmesthorpe cutting on the last-mentioned railway not only furnishes an excellent section of the beds of the Great Oolite Limestone, but enabled the former collector of the Survey, Mr. RICHARD GIBBS, to obtain an interesting series of its characteristic fossils. North of Essendine, about which place there are numerous exposures of the limestones and oyster beds, we find rocks exposed in this formation which yield a greater variety of fossils than is usually found in the beds of this age. At this point large masses of coral (*Isastræa*) are very abundant in the Great Oolite Limestones.

The fossils collected at Belmesthorpe were as follows:—

Fossils from the Great Oolite in the Railway-cutting at Belmesthorpe.

Nautilus Baberi, *Lyc. & Mor.*
Natica globosa, *Lyc. & Mor.*
Cardium, sp.
Corbicella Bathonica, *Lyc. & Mor.*
Cyprina nuciformis, *Lyc.*
———— Loweana, *Lyc. & Mor.*
Cypricardia rostrata, *Sow.*
———— Bathonica, *d'Orb.*
Isocardia tenera, *Sow.*
Myacites calceiformis, *Phil.*
———— securiformis, *Phil.*
Modiola imbricata, *Sow.*
Pholadomya Heraulti, *Ag.*
Trigonia costata, *Sow.*
———— Moretonis, *Lyc. & Mor.*
Gervillia monotis, *Desl.*
Lima puncturata, *Sow.*
—— cardiiformis, *Lyc. & Mor.*
Ostrea Sowerbyi, *Lyc. & Mor.*
———— subrugulosa, *Lyc. & Mor.*
Pecten demissus, *Phil.*
Perna quadrata, *Sow.*
Pteroperna costatula, *Desl.*
Terebratula perovalis, *Sow.*

On the road from Essendine to Toft there are numerous small pits, exhibiting the oyster-beds and limestones of the Great Oolite with their usual characters.

In the Dane's Hill cutting of the Great Northern Railway the lowest bed of the Great Oolite Limestone presents some interesting characters, which are worthy of remark. It constitutes a mass about 3 feet thick, the upper layer of which contains many long cylindrical spines of echinoderms, especially of *Acrosalenia*. The bed is of a brown colour, and somewhat sandy character. Its analogue does not appear to exist in the Belmesthorpe cutting of the Stamford and Essendine Railway, where we have an equally clear section; but it seems to be represented by a white compact limestone.

At Essendine cutting, on the main line of the Great Northern Railway, a good section was exposed during its construction, which was thus described by Professor MORRIS :—*

"With the Essendine cutting, now to be described, the argillaceous and shelly series terminate, as far at least as the Railway sections are concerned. In descending order, and with a view of rendering the peculiar characters and affinities of these beds more intelligible, the physical features and organic contents will be more fully detailed. Observing the same order of arrangement, we commence with the upper beds (1,) which are full of Oysters, with occasional patches of Serpulæ, 3 to 5 feet; the rock (2) immediately below the oyster-bed is sandy and marly, becoming occasionally very compact, calcareous, and bluish, and sometimes shaly, from 10 to 12 feet,† in the marly portion the fossils are very abundant, as—

> Cardium.
> Modiola imbricata.
> Trigonia Moretonis.
> Cyprina.
> Unicardium varicosum (*Sow.*, sp.)
> Pholadomya lirata.
> Terebratula maxillata.
> Pecten annulatus.
> Lima cardioides.
> —— interstincta.
> Ostrea Bathonica.
> Perna quadrata.
> Natica.
> Turbo tuberculatus.
> Phasianella cincta.
> Nautilus.
> Acrosalema hemicidaroides.

                                                        ft.

3. Green and irregular sandy clays, fossiliferous, with layers of
   Neæra and *Pholadomya*, abundant -   -   -   - 5
4. Marly, sandy and slaty rock, with *Avicula* and other shells - 2
5. Dark green and bituminous, shelly clays, with *Cytherea*
   Neæra, and *Cyrena*   -   -   -   -   - 4
   Bituminous band -   -   -   -   -   - 0½
6. Compact, sandy and marly rock full of *Cardium, Cytherea,*
   Neæra -   -   -   -   -   - 2
     Variegated clays, bituminous, &c.; these beds contain a zone
     of dark clays, with *Cyrena Cunninghami, C.* (sp. ?), and a
     species of *Mactra* -   -   -   -   - 4

>   3. Thracia, abundant.
>   Modiola.
>   Pecten lens, rare.
>   Neæra Ibbetsoni.
>   Pholadomya acuticosta.
>   Lingula.
>   Terebratula obsoleta.
>   Anomia.
>   Gryphæa nana.

---

* *Quart. Journ. Geol. Soc.*, vol. ix. pp. 331, 332.
† " The more solid portions of this bed have been recognised by Mr. PRESTWICH, as being of frequent occurrence in the boulder clay of Norfolk and Suffolk."

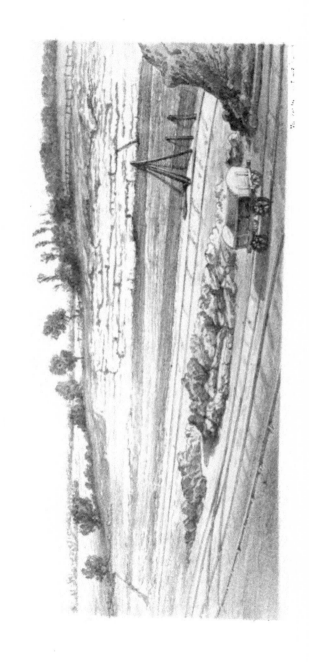

4. Avicula and Modiola, much compressed.
5. Neæra.
   Anomia.
   Mactra.
   Cerithium.
6. Cardium.
   Modiola.
   Neæra.
   Anomia.
   Pinna.
   Ostrea.
   Astarte cuneata.
   Cyprina.

" Some fine saurian remains, obtained from this cutting, were presented by Mr. Reynolds to the Museum of Practical Geology. Among these remains, which have been determined by Professor OWEN, were the tympanic bone of *Cetiosaurus longus*, the metatarsal bone of *Cet. brevis*, a fibula, and a fragment of a large vertebra."

The appearances presented by the Great Oolite Limestone and the underlying clays of the Upper Estuarine Series are represented in Plate IX.

The fossils collected by the officers of the Geological Survey in the Dane's Hill cutting are the following :—

Fossils from the Dane's Hill Cutting.

Arca æmula, *Phil.*
Cardium Stricklandi, *Lyc. & Mor.*
———— subtrigonum, *Lyc. & Mor.*
———— sp.
Ceromya concentrica, *Sow.*
Cucullæa Goldfussii, *Röm.*
Cypricardia Bathonica, *d'Orb.*
———— rostrata, *Sow.*
Cyprina Loweana, *Lyc. & Mor.*
———— nuculiformis, *Röm.*
Isocardia tenera, *Sow.*
Lucina Bellona, *d'Orb.*
Modiola imbricata, *Sow.*
Pholadomya deltoidea, *Sow.*
———— Heraulti, *Ag.*
Macrodon Hirsonensis, *d'Arch.*
Trigonia costata, *Park.*
———— Moretonis, *Lyc. & Mor.*
Anomia, sp.
Gervillia aviculoides, *Sow.*
————, sp.
Ostrea Sowerbyi, *Lyc. & Mor.*
Pecten demissus, *Phil.*
Pteroperna costatula, *Desl.*
————, sp.
Perna quadrata, *Sow.*
Rhynchonella concinna, *Sow.*
Terebratula maxillata, *Sow.*
Serpula, sp.
Cidaris, sp."

Near Careby Mill we have the following section :—

Pit in Great Oolite north-east of Careby Mill.

								ft.	in.
(1.) Soil -	-	-	-	-	-	-	-	1	0
(2.) Clay -	-	-	-	-	-	-	-	2	6
(3.) Oyster beds (*O. subrugulosa*, &c.)	-	-	-	-	2	6
(4.) Hard, compact, blue limestone, in courses	-	-	4	6
(5.) Clay (to the bottom of the pit).									

In the neighbourhood of Witham-on-the-Hill there are many pits exhibiting the beds of the Great Oolite Series, among which we may notice the following as yielding interesting sections :—

Pit between Witham-on-the-Hill and Manthorpe.   Stone dug for road-metal.

		ft.	in.
(1.)	Soil - - - - - - - -	0	9
(2.)	Oyster bed - - - - - -	0	9
(3.)	Dark coloured, stiff clay - - - -	2	0
(4.)	Oyster bed with layers of "Beef" - - -	0	9
(5.)	Marly parting.		
(6.)	Oyster bed with layers of "Beef" - - -	1	0
(7.)	Marly parting.		
(8.)	Oyster bed with "Beef" - - - -	1	6
(9.)	Oyster beds - - - - - -	1	3
(10.)	Marly parting.		
(11.)	Bed of hard, solid, blue-hearted limestone, crowded with shells, especially—		

          Modiola imbricata, *Sow.*
          Perna rugosa, *Sow.*
          Pteroperna plana, *Mor. & Lyc.*
          Lima duplicata, *Sow.*
          Trigonia costata, *Sow.*
          Ostræa subrugulosa, *Mor. & Lyc.*
          Strophodus (tooth).

Pit a little to the north of the former.—

		ft.	in.
(1.)	Soil - - - - - - - -	1	0
(2.)	Oyster bed - - - - - -	0	9
(3.)	Bed of stone - - - - - -	0	4
(4.)	White, marly oyster bed - - - -	1	0
(5.)	Drab, sandy oyster bed - - - -	0	6
(6.)	White, marly stone - - - - -	2	0
(7.)	Sandy oyster bed - - - - -	1	0
(8.)	Hard limestone - - - - -	0	6
(9.)	Mottled clay, containing many vertical plant-markings and some great masses of carbonised wood -	4	0
(10.)	Soft, sandy stone, with many vertical plant-markings	1	6

N.B.—These lower sandy beds exhibit many ripple-marked surfaces. Beds (9) and (10) probably belong to the Upper Estuarine Series.

As already remarked, the beds of the Great Oolite Limestone where they outcrop towards their western limits are much more covered with Boulder Clay, and yield fewer illustrative sections than in the valleys of the Nene and Welland. Numerous outliers of the strata exist here, but, owing to the great prevalence of drift, the beds are seldom well exposed in them.

Immediately south of the limits of Sheet 64 the strata of the Limestone series are well seen about Grafton Underwood, and between that place and Sudborough, exactly on the edge of the area we are describing, there is a pit opened in a bed of white limestone made up of fragments of shells embedded in a marly paste and containing numerous fossils. This is probably the bottom bed of the series.

By the roadside, half a mile east of Sudborough Church, a pit in the Great Oolite Limestone exhibits a thick bed of rock, somewhat oolitic (as in the Duke of Buccleugh's pit at Geddington Chase) and covered by an oyster-bed, with the usual characters, about 1 foot thick. Above the oyster-beds there is a considerable thickness of variegated clays with stony bands, representing the Great Oolite Clays. The beds in this pit, which are just beyond the limits of Sheet 64, appear to be much disturbed.

Some of the beds of limestone in this neighbourhood are coarsely flaggy. They consist of a shelly limestone, like the Forest Marble of the south of England, but have diffused through their masses a few oolitic grains.

The relations of the Great Oolite Limestone to the clays above and to the estuarine strata below it is well seen at many places about here.

At the northern end of Geddington Chase, and not far from the village of Stanion, we find the following very interesting section in the Great Oolite :—

Section in Duke of Buccleugh's pit at Geddington Chase.

		ft.	in.
(1.)	Soil - - - - - - -	0	6
(2.)	Boulder Clay, containing boulders of quartzite, coal measure sandstone, a few flints, but little or no chalk. Near its base traces of a gravel composed of Northampton Sand detritus are seen - -	3	0
(3.)	Variegated (greenish, bluish, and purplish) clay, in some places quite denuded away - - 0 to	1	0
(4.)	Pale greenish white marl, full of irregular, concretionary, hard, sub-crystalline, calcareous nodules, also of a pale greenish-white colour (weathering white; comparable with that at Ailsworth) -	0	6
(5.)	Green and variegated clay with carbonaceous markings - - - - - - -	0	6
(6.)	Grey, fœtid, somewhat sandy, limestone - -	0	4
(7.)	Laminated, marly parting - - - -	0	2
(8.)	Extremely hard, sub-crystalline, drab limestone -	1	6
(9.)	Marly parting - - - - -	0	2
(10.)	Marly bed abounding in " Beef " - -	0	6
(11.)	Variegated, dark, carbonaceous clays, finely stratified	2	0
(12.)	Finely-laminated marl with " Beef " - -	0	3
(13.)	Hard, white, shelly limestone with many shells and an oyster-bed at the bottom, with *O. subrugulosa*, Mor. & Lyc. - - - - -	0	6
(14.)	Marly bed crowded with *O. Sowerbyi*, Mor. & Lyc.	0	2
(15.)	Clay like bed (11) - - - - -	1	0
(16.)	Beds of hard limestone with few traces of marly partings. The limestone is sometimes compact and full of oysters, at others made up of comminuted shells, and becomes in places very oolitic, thus simulating the characters of the Inferior Oolite. Near the bottom there are traces apparently of pebbles of compact oolite (like those seen at Benefield). This limestone contains wood *Ostrœa Sowerbyi*, Mor. & Lyc., *Echinobrissus clunucularis*, Llhwyd, & *E. sp.* - - -	6	0

the bottom
not seen.

The beds in this pit show considerable signs of disturbance and dip S.W. 9°. Beds (2) to (12) probably belong to the Great Oolite Clays, the remainder to the Great Oolite Limestones.

About Brigstock and Stanion both the limestones and oyster-beds of the Great Oolite are exposed at many points. Westward, about Great and Little Oakley and at Pipwell, they are also seen, but do not furnish any very good sections. The best is that afforded by the Great Oakley brickyard, where we have 6 feet of Great Oolite Limestone, consisting of alternate courses, each about 1 foot thick, of Forest Marble-like stone, and marly oyster bands, containing *Ostrea subrugulosa*, Mor. & Lyc., and *O. Sowerbyi*, Mor. & Lyc. Under the rock occur black, carbonaceous clays and, still lower, light, variegated clays, both belonging to the Upper Estuarine Series.

Outliers.—Northwards, both in the outer line of outcrop and in the numerous outliers at Weldon, Dene, Bulwick, Blatherwycke, Laxton, Wakerley, Duddington, Barrowden, Ketton, Stamford, Ryhall, Pickworth, Aunby, Holywell, Clipsham, Little Bytham, &c., we find many exposures presenting repetitions of the characters which we have already so fully illustrated ; but deep or continuous sections seldom occur. We have already remarked upon the general uniformity in character of the beds of this formation over large areas.

The position of the beds of the Great Oolite Limestone, above the clays of the Upper Estuarine Series, causes the spurs and outliers composed of these formations to assume a very marked tabular outline, which is sufficiently pronounced to give a distinctive character to the scenery of this district; as is illustrated in several of the plates in this volume.

The marly limestones of the Great Oolite are highly esteemed for burning into lime, both for building and agricultural purposes, and it is thus very largely employed wherever it occurs. The more solid beds are frequently used locally for building stone, and at a few points, as at Oundle and Geddington Chase, it is susceptible of being wrought as a freestone. As a general rule, however, the limestones of the Great Oolite of this district cannot compete with those of the Inferior Oolite for building and architectural purposes, though they are preferred to the latter as a source for lime.

The beds of the Great Oolite Limestone in this area give rise to the formation of a soil usually of a black colour, but occasionally, from accidental circumstances, of the same red tint as that of the Cornbrash and Lincolnshire Limestone. Owing to the admixture of calcareous and argillaceous materials in them, the soils of this series are considered to be of much higher value than those of either of the other two limestones of the district, which are much lighter in character and in seasons of drought are apt to prove very treacherous to the farmer.

THE GREAT OOLITE CLAYS.

This is a series of variegated, blue, green, yellow, and purplish clays, often containing bands of irregular whitish or pale-green calcareous concretions, and, not unfrequently, ironstone in the form of septaria or in branch-like concretions. These beds are very variable in thickness, attaining a maximum of from 20 to 30 feet. They are usually very barren of fossils, but such as do occur show that their affinities are with the Great Oolite Limestones below. Occasionally thin seams are found almost entirely made up of the shells of a small *Placunopsis* (*P. socialis*, Mor. & Lyc.), and, much more rarely, bands with *Ostrea Sowerbyi*, Mor. & Lyc., and *O. subrugulosa*, Mor. & Lyc. It is not improbable that these beds are, in part at least, of estuarine character. They are now mapped separately for the first time; for though they occur far to the southward of this area, yet they are often reduced to such insignificant proportions that they have not been separated on the Survey Maps from the rest of the Great Oolite.

Occurring, as these clays do, between the hard rocks of the Cornbrash and Great Oolite Limestones, they give rise to a steep slope between two plateaux; in the same manner as is the case with the Upper Estuarine clays lying between the Great and Inferior Oolite Limestones; the constant appearance of this feature is very characteristic of the scenery in a great part of the country included in Sheet 64.

In former times the ironstones of these beds were frequently dug and smelted ; and some years ago a considerable quantity was raised at Bottlebridge, near Overton Longville, on the estate of the Marquis of Huntley ; but the quantity of material requiring to be removed to obtain the ore led to the abandonment of the workings. At New England, near Peterborough, and at Bedford Purlieus, the clays are dug for brick-making.

Extent.—Although this argillaceous formation certainly exists in the country to the southwards, and sometimes indeed presents a considerable thickness of strata united with features of great geological interest, yet it has been found impossible by the officers of the Geological Survey, so inconstant is it in thickness, and so irregular and variable in its mode of occurrence in that district, to map it as a distinct series. Throughout Sheet 64, however, its characters having acquired greater uniformity, and its presence being so persistent, it has been thought advisable to represent its outcrop on the map by a distinct colour. This was felt to be the more necessary, as its mineral characters, so different from those of the Great Oolite Limestones below it, and the Cornbrash above, and the consequent peculiarities of the soil which it produces, taken in connexion with the marked features in the contours of the district which the occurrence of a series of soft clays between the two limestone deposits, have caused us to attach an importance to it beyond what its thickness or palæontological characters would at first sight seem to warrant.

In carrying the geological lines northward from the typical district of the Cotteswold Hills, the surveyors found it impossible to define the limits of the Forest Marble beyond the neighbourhood of Banbury. In the whole of the South Midland district, though the two well-marked and persistent limestone series of the Upper Zone of the Great Oolite and the Cornbrash are often separated by beds, occasionally of some thickness, of clay, sand, or ironstone, yet these are so inconstant in character, and so irregular in thickness, that it has been thought advisable rather to include them with the formation lying below it, than to attempt a separation of them as indicating a strict horizon.

As shown by Professor PHILLIPS, the Forest Marble towards its northern limits occasionally assumes Estuarine characters, containing *Cyrena* and other fresh-water shells. In the Great Oolite Limestone, which may perhaps be regarded as a more northern expansion of the Forest Marble, and certainly occupies the position of that formation relatively to the persistent members of the Great Oolite, the estuarine characters of the strata appear to be even more pronounced.

In the case of the clays of the Great Oolite, the beds of which are seldom of any economic value, it is very seldom that we obtain any clear sections. Sometimes its lower beds are seen at the top of pits opened in the Great Oolite Limestones, and occasionally quarries in the Cornbrash expose its upper members. These, with a few railway-cuttings, occasional field-drains and wells, and one or two pits in which its clays have been dug for brick-making or its ferruginous bands for ironstone, afford almost the only means which we have of studying the characters and succession of the beds which compose this formation. The general line of its outcrop, however, is very clearly defined, owing to its difference of character from the limestone strata which lie respectively above and below it.

At Wadenhoe the position of the clays of the Great Oolite is very clearly defined, though it is evidently quite thin, and throughout the south-eastern part of the area, in the valley of the Nene, so insignificant do these beds here appear to be, that no attempt has been made to represent them, as a distinct formation, on the map. In a pit at Pilton Lodge, however, the clays are well exposed, and are seen lying on the top of the Great Oolite Limestones.

As illustrating the thinness of all the beds of the Great Oolite Series here, I may cite the following estimate of them which I made near this point :—

Cornbrash.

Clays	- - - - - - -	6 feet.
Great Oolite limestone	- - - - -	15 feet.

Clays of Upper Estuarine Series.

The clays of the Great Oolite are seen near Lilford Lodge in Lilford Park, and again near Barnwell Castle, and in the Barnwell railway-cutting (see p. 204). At all these places they appear to consist of dark-bluish and greenish mottled clays, in some places crowded with carbonaceous markings. At some points light-blue, more or less sandy clays, greatly resembling those of the Upper Estuarine Series, appear in their midst.

At Oundle the thick beds of the Great Oolite Limestone are in places seen to be covered with masses of blue clays : and at some points in this neighbourhood nodular bands of ironstone occur in these clays.

In a pit west of Oundle we find the following interesting succession of beds :—

(1.) Cornbrash rubble.
(2.) Beds of very stiff clay, dark-blue, greenish, and mottled, about 12 feet.
(3.) Ferruginous band.
(4.) Clay bed, containing large crystals of selenite.
(5.) Oyster beds.
(6.) Thick beds of hard stone dug to a considerable depth.

The beds (2), (3), and (4) evidently belong to the Great Oolite Clays.

In the valleys leading up from Oundle to Church Field Farm and Benefield, the clays of the Great Oolite can be traced at a number of points; and near Oundle Wood the nodular ironstones which it contains appear to have been worked by the Romans and smelted.

North-east of Benefield the clays of the Great Oolite assume locally a somewhat sandy character; they are stained with oxide of iron, and contain some of the common Cornbrash and Great Oolite fossils in certain marine bands.

In the valley between Upper and Lower Benefield we find a pit affording a very interesting section of the higher beds of the Great Oolite Series, as follows :—

	ft.	in.
(1.) Soil, "loess," and river gravel - - - -	3	0
(2.) Cornbrash rubble - - - - -	2	0
(3.) Variegated clay (with a band of ironstone nodules at its base) - - - - - - -	3	6
(4.) Oyster beds, in places becoming ferruginous -	2	0
(5.) Clay band - - - - - - -	0	10
(6.) Hard and coarse Forest-Marble-like limestone; the lowest bed, which comes out in large slabs, exhibits much false bedding, is crowded with shells, and contains fragments, generally angular, of compact limestone - -	9	0
(7.) Clay.		

The Great Oolite clays are here evidently very thin and insignificant, and hence no attempt has been made to separate them on the map in this part of the district.

On the road between Southwick and Glapthorn the Cornbrash is hidden by drift, but the sandy and ferruginous beds, at its base belonging to the Great Oolite Clays, were well exposed in a deep road-cutting at the time of the survey of the district.

As we go northwards towards the central portion of Sheet 64, the clays of the Great Oolite, though greatly obscured by drift deposits, evidently begin to acquire greater thickness and importance, and it has been found possible to represent their outcrop on the map. Below Calvey Wood, on the Walk of Morehay, the clays are seen below the Cornbrash, and are found to contain numerous branch-like concretions of brown oxide of iron, like those of the equivalent beds at New England, near Peterborough.

On Bedford Purlieus a pit known as "the Duke's brickyard" was opened in the clays of the Great Oolite. They here seem to offer the usual characters, but the state of the pit was such at the time of the survey of the district as to preclude the possibility of my obtaining any clear section of the beds. The presence of the Great Oolite clays was proved in several wells opened on the Bedford Purlieus; and between Elton and Holborn Lodge, on the opposite side of the Nene valley, a well indicated a thickness of 14 to 15 feet for this formation (see *ante*, page 207).

The Great Oolite clays were exposed in the deep railway-cuttings at Wansford tunnel; and a little to the southwards I saw some excellent exposures of them in a number of field-drains. They here consist of a series of very stiff, bluish, and occasionally greenish clays, of varying depth of tint, and containing numerous masses of white, argillaceous, shelly (concretionary?) limestone, which weather to a white colour on their exterior. These yield a few marine fossils of Great Oolite species. Towards their base the beds are almost wholly composed of these shelly and sub-crystalline limestone masses. The shells in them appear to be always fragmentary, and for the most part indeterminable. Above these are beds of clay, crowded with small shells, including *Placunopsis socialis*, Lyc. & Mor. in great abundance, with *Terebratulæ* and *Ostreæ*. The indurated and calcareous condition of the lower beds of the Great Oolite clays may be observed at a number of points in this district.

At the east end of Sutton Wood also, a series of field-drains afforded good exposures of the Great Oolite clays. They were found to consist of light-green and light-blue clays, very tenaceous in character, and containing irregular fragments of compact, argillaceous limestone. These concretions sometimes contain crystalline centres, and exhibit on fracture a pale greenish colour. No fossils were seen in them at this place.

At a well near some new cottages at the western end of the village of Helpstone, I found the following section:—

(1.) "Bearing" of soil and clay.
(2.) Base of Cornbrash.
(3.) Blue clay (Great Oolite Clays), 13 feet.
(4.) Ferruginous rock, yielding an abundance of water, which was, however, unfit for drinking purposes.

The wells sunk at various points round Milton Park show the Great Oolite Clays to have here a thickness of from 15 to 30 feet, and to be very variable in character. The beds were generally light or dark-blue in colour, somewhat sandy, and contained balls of ironstone.

At the railway-cutting near Overton Longville, at a place called Bottlebridge (St. Botolph's Bridge), the clays of the Great Oolite were exposed between the Cornbrash and Great Oolite Limestones. At this place the late Marquis of Huntley commenced digging the ironstone-balls, which form four bands in the midst of the dark-blue clays. The ironstone in the upper bands was soft and of a dark-brown colour, owing to weathering action, but in the lower bands were of a greenish-white colour, and unoxidised, and every gradation between these two varieties occurred. The ironstone is said to have been of good quality, and between 100 and 200 tons of it were sent to Wellingborough to be smelted. Its exploitation was soon abandoned, owing to the quantity of material which had to be removed to obtain the nodules of ironstone.

I was informed by the late Dr. Porter that in an excavation for the New England Gasworks, near Peterborough, the clays of the Great Oolite were found to have a thickness of 22 feet. At New England, near Peterborough, a brickyard has been opened in the clays beneath the Cornbrash. The succession of beds here is as follows:—

(1.) Brick-earth, full of terrestrial and fresh-water shells; very
   variable in thickness - - - - - 1 to 3 ft.
(2.) Gravel - - - - - - - 0 to 4 ft.
(3.) Cornbrash.
(4.) Mottled, greenish, and bluish clays, with bands of ironstone nodules, and thin, stony bands crowded with
   marine shells.

The ironstone nodules in this pit when broken are often found to have their
cavities filled with water.

At Orton, near Peterborough, the thickness of the clays of the Great Oolite
was found, in a well, to be only 13 or 14 feet.

North of the valley of the Welland, the clays of the Great Oolite were exposed in a number of field-drains at Firewards Thorns. Farther north, the
beds may be traced at many places between the limestones of the Cornbrash
and the Great Oolite, everywhere giving rise to a marked feature in the surface
contours, but not presented to study in any open sections.

The only point on the main line of the Great Northern Railway where the
Great Oolite Clays were exposed is the Banthorpe cutting, which is thus
described by Professor MORRIS :—

"The upper part of the Banthorpe cutting (next in order) consists of about
7 to 9 feet of Cornbrash rock, containing the characteristic fossils, and
overlying a dark tenacious clay, sometimes laminated with shelly layers, below
which, and forming the base of the line, is 7 feet of compact shelly bluish
rock, occasionally sandy, and becoming shaly, full of *Ostrea, Gervillia,* and
Avicula."

Along the western line of its outcrop, and in the numerous outliers of the
Great Oolite Series, we find but few interesting exposures of the argillaceous
strata we are describing. At the great pit at Geddington Chase, already fully
described (*vide* page 123), the formation can be admirably studied. It is in
this place seen to consist of variegated and carbonaceous clays, with band of
argillaceous limestone, and fibrous carbonate of lime ("beef"). It here greatly
resembles, as do also the Upper Estuarine beds, the strata of the Purbeck and
Punfield series.

The clays of the Great Oolite Series are not of great importance
in an economic point of view. As we have already seen they are
employed for brickmaking at Bedford Purlieus and at New England
near Peterborough, while at several localities in ancient times, and
at Bottlebridge, near Overton Longville, in recent years, small
quantities of the ironstone bands have been raised for smelting.

The beds of this formation give rise to a cold and wet soil,
very similar in character to that of the lower beds of the Upper
Estuarine Series. Fortunately, however, they do not occupy any
considerable areas in the district, but form only the short slopes
between the Cornbrash and Great Oolite limestones ; and even in
these, the unkindly nature of the soil is usually somewhat tempered
by the downwash from the overlying strata. Some of the tracts
occupied by the beds of this division of the series have only recently
been brought under drainage and cultivation.

THE CORNBRASH.

This, the highest member of the Lower Oolites, presents well
marked characters, which it retains throughout a great part of
England. In the district described in the present Memoir it never
exceeds 15 feet in thickness and is often much less. It consists of
a somewhat ferruginous limestone usually very fossiliferous. When
dug under a considerable thickness of clay this rock is of a blue
colour, exceedingly hard, and can only be quarried by blasting;
but when it has been weathered it breaks up into flat masses of
a light brown colour, each of which is usually coated with stalag-

mite; in this condition the appearance of the rock in section
has been not inaptly compared to that of a loose stone wall or
field-dike. Some of the beds of the Cornbrash are often of a
softer and sandier texture, and from these the fossils are most
readily extracted. At the top of the Cornbrash and at its junction
with the Middle Oolite we usually find an oyster-bed composed
of the great *O. Marshii*, Sow., an oyster which never occurs in the
Great Oolite Limestone below. The various forms of *Ammonites
Herveyi*, Sow., and *A. macrocephalus*, Schloth., are also very abundant
in and characteristic of the Cornbrash; while another Ammonite,
A. discus, Sow., also occurs in it, but is exceedingly rare. Many
species, especially those of the *Myadæ*, abound equally in the
Cornbrash and the Great Oolite, but some forms by their
great abundance serve to characterise the Cornbrash; such are
Echinobrissus clunucularis, Llhwyd sp., *E. orbicularis*, Phil. sp.,
and *Holectypus depressus*, Leske, among Echinoderms; *Terebratula
obovata*, Sow., and *T. lagenalis*, Schloth., among the Brachiopoda;
and *Avicula echinata*, Sow., and *Gervillia aviculoides*, Sow., among
the Conchifera.

The Cornbrash is found cropping out along the sides of many
of the valleys and also as outliers capping certain hills. To the
north and west of Peterborough it covers a considerable area, rising
gradually from the level of the Fen till it forms the high ground
of Castor Heath. At Stilton, on the edge of the Fen, a small patch
of Cornbrash is brought in by a fault, and occurs as an inlier.

The Cornbrash does not yield a good building-stone, but it is occasionally used for rough walling; I have found that in Peterborough
Cathedral all the coarse work, which is out of sight, is constructed
of Cornbrash, on which formation the edifice stands. On account
of its hardness the Cornbrash is everywhere much sought after as
a material for mending the roads, and it is occasionally, though
very rarely, burnt for lime. The rock, from its ferruginous
character, makes a red soil; but in this district it does not enjoy
the reputation among agriculturists which it has in the South of
England, and to which it is indebted for the name it bears. It
seems to be rather to the contrast afforded by the more kindly soil of
the Cornbrash in the south-western parts of England as compared
with the light and treacherous coverings of the other limestone
formations of the Oolitic series, and the cold intractable clays
which alternate with them, that the great agricultural reputation
to which the former stratum owes its designation is due.

Extent.—We have already remarked upon the uniformity of the
characters and fossil contents of the Cornbrash limestone from
Dorsetshire and the Cotteswold Hills, along the whole line of its
strike, till it disappears in North Lincolnshire. We have also seen
that the so-called Cornbrash of Yorkshire is not a stratum continuous with that with which we are dealing, and does not perhaps
represent precisely the same geological horizon.

Owing to the great number, variety, and beauty of their fossils,
the thin limestone beds of the Cornbrash have attracted much
attention from geologists. Lists of the species found in this formation, as developed in the Cotteswold Hills, have been published by
Professor BUCKMAN and Drs. WRIGHT and LYCETT. The fauna of
the same beds in Oxfordshire has been illustrated by Professor

220   GEOLOGY OF RUTLAND, &C.

Phillips, who has also given a catalogue of the species. As a considerable tract of country intervenes between the area to which the list of Professor Phillips refer, and those included in the descriptions of this Memoir, I avail myself of the opportunity of giving a very complete list of the fossils of the Cornbrash as developed in the neighbourhood of Rushden in south Northamptonshire. The rock in the neighbourhood of Rushden is remarkably fossiliferous, and during many years the pits at this place were subject to very diligent search by the Rev. A. W. Griesbach, to whom geologists are indebted for the discovery of a great number of interesting new forms. To Mr. G. Sharman, the present Assistant-palæontologist of the Geological Survey, I am indebted for the following list of species collected at Rushden, and now in his collection, which will be useful for comparison with those of the northern and southern areas respectively.

Fossils from the Cornbrash of Rushden, Northamptonshire.

Anabacia orbulites, *D'Orb.,* E. and H.
Alecto gracilis.
Cellepora, sp.
Diastopora (Berenicea) diluviana, *Milne-Edw.*
Millepora straminea, *Phil.*
Pentacrinus, sp.
Pseudodiadema pentagonum, *McCoy.*
Acrosalenia spinosa, *Agass.*
Stomechinus intermedius, *Agass.*
Pedina rotata, *Wright.*
Holectypus depressus, *Leske.*
Echinobrissus clunicularis, *Llhwyd.*
————— quadratus, *Wright.*
————— orbicularis, *Phil.*
Clypeus Mülleri, *Wright.*
Pygurus Michelini, *Cotteau.*
Goniomya literata, *Sow., Mor. & Lyc.*
Myacites, sp.
————— securiformis, *Phil.*
Gresslya peregrina, *Phil.*
Quenstedtia lævigata, *Phil.*
Unicardium impressum, *Lyc. & Mor.*
Astarte elegans, *Sow.*
Pholadomya Murchisoni, *Sow.*
————— Heraulti, *Ag.*
—————, sp.
Ceromya concentrica, *Sow.*
Isocardia, sp.
Cardium dissimile, *Phil.*
————— citrinoideum, *Phil.*
Trigonia clavellata, *Sow.*
————— costata, *Sow.*
————— pullus, *Sow.*
————— elongata, *Sow.*
————— impressa, *Sow.*
————— tuberculosa, *Lyc.*
Cypricardia Bathonica, *D'Orb.*
Avicula echinata, *Sow.*
————— Münsteri, *Goldf.*
Lucina rotundata, *Römer* (?).
Mytilus cuneatus, *Sow.*
————— imbricatus, *Sow.*
————— Lonsdalii, *Mor.*
————— Sowerbyanus, *D'Orb.*
Gervillia aviculoides, *Sow.*

Lima pectiniformis, *Schloth.*
—— rigidula, *Phil.*
—— ovalis, *Sow.*
—— duplicata, *Sow.*
—— gibbosa, *Sow.*
—— sp.
Hinnites abjectus, *Phil.*
Pecten lens, *Sow.*, *Mor. & Lyc.*
—— arcuatus, *Sow.*, *Mor. & Lyc.*
—— anisopleurus, *Buv.*
—— peregrinus, *Mor.*
Pecten demissus, *Phil.*
—— retiferus, *Mor.*
Ostrea Marshii, *Sow.* (O. flabelloides, *Lam.*).
—— sp.
Chemnitzia vittata, *Phil.*
Natica, sp.
Pleurotomaria granulata, *Sow.*
Serpula, sp.
Terebratula intermedia, *Sow.*
———— ornithocephala, *Sow.*
———— obovata, *Sow.*
———— Bentleyi, *Mor.*
———— cardium, *Lam.*
Rhynchonella morierei, *Dav.*
———— concinna, *Sow.*
Ammonites discus, *Sow.*
———— Herveyi, *Sow.*
———— macrocephalus, *Schloth.*
Nautilus, sp.
Plesiosaurus (paddle bone).
Fish (palatal teeth, several forms).
Astacus rostratus, *Phil.*
Wood.

The Cornbrash, forming as it does the highest portion of the Great Oolite series, follows in its outcrop the same general lines as those of the other members of that formation in the district which we are describing. It is, however, even more obscured by the overlapping masses of Boulder Clay and drift than the subjacent formations. Indeed it may be regarded as certain that the extent of country occupied by the rocks of the Cornbrash is considerably less than that represented on the map as belonging to it. This arises from the fact that, being the last deposited bed before the great mass of argillaceous strata of the Oxford Clay, it is frequently recognised outcropping from below the drifts, in positions where we should be able to detect no traces whatever of softer rocks. Some of the great outliers of Cornbrash are almost certainly capped, to a greater or less extent, by beds of the Oxfordian series, but as no positive evidence of the presence of these, and much less of their extent and boundaries, could be obtained in these drift-buried districts, no attempt has been made to represent them. In one case, however, namely, that of the outlier between Fineshade and Kings Cliffe, recent excavations for a railway have furnished Mr. MONCKTON of Fineshade and Mr. SHARP of Dallington, as the latter gentleman has kindly informed me, with proofs of the undoubted existence of a mass of Oxfordian beds lying upon the Cornbrash.

Excepting near Sudborough, the outer line of the outcrop of the Cornbrash is entirely concealed by an enormous mass of Boulder Clay, in many places probably not less than 200 feet thick. Hence, as indicated by the dotted lines, this part of its range on the map is purely hypothetical. Where, however, the beds appear at a lower level and are exposed along the sides of the valley of the Nene and its tributaries, we have a number of interesting sections, which serve to sufficiently illustrate the characters and fossils of the formation in the district.

Immediately to the south of the limits of Sheet 64, between Thorpe, and Wigsthorpe, the Cornbrash is dug at a place known as " Stone-pit-field." About Achurch and above Wadenhoe the outcrop of the beds can be clearly traced although no good sections of them are exposed.

At a reservoir behind a farm-house at Lilford, the base of the Cornbrash was seen resting on the variegated clays of the Great Oolite.   At Lilford Lodge there is a pit which exposes the rock, with its usual petrological characters and yielding the following fossils :—

Avicula echinata, <i>Sow.</i>

Myacites decurtatus, <i>Phil.</i>

In a pit in the Cornbrash, south of the village of Barnwell All Saints, we find the following section :—

		ft.	in.
(1.)	Soil with pebbles - . - - - -	2	0
(2.)	Fine gravel - - - - -	1 to 2	0
(3.)	Oxford Clay? (very irregular) - -	0 to 1	0
(4.)	Sandy limestone - - - -	1	3
(5.)	Hard compact limestone - - -	1	6

to bottom.

(5.) is a very hard, blue-hearted limestone which contains the usual fossils ; it is seen again in the bed of the stream at this place.

Another pit in the Cornbrash is seen south of Barnwell Station, the rock here contains specimens of <i>Ostrea Marshii</i>, Sow., of great size.

At various points around the town of Oundle, and especially in the sides of the tributary valleys which are connected with that of the Nene, we find a considerable number of exposures of the Cornbrash beds, but nowhere affording sections of sufficient completeness or interest to call for their detailed description in this Memoir.   The following list of the fossils collected at the various pits in this immediate neighbourhood will give a sufficiently clear idea of the general character of the Cornbrash fauna in the southern part of our district.

List of fossils collected from the Cornbrash in the neighbourhood of Oundle.

Ammonites Herveyi, <i>Sow.</i> (small and rare).
Trigonia elongata, <i>Sow.</i> (abundant and characteristic).
————— sp. (casts of a probably new species).
————— Moretonis, <i>Lyc. & Mor.</i> var.
Goniomya literata, <i>Sow.</i> (abundant).
Isocardia tenera, <i>Sow.</i> (abundant).
————— sp.
Pholadomya deltoidea, <i>Sow.</i> (abundant).
————— lyrata, <i>Sow.</i>
Myacites decurtatus, <i>Phil.</i> sp. } very abundant.
————— securiformis, <i>Phil.</i> sp.
Modiola imbricata, <i>Sow.</i>
Lima rigidula, <i>Phil.</i> (abundant).
Pecten lens, <i>Sow.</i>
————— vagans, <i>Sow.</i>
————— inæquicostatus, <i>Phil.</i>
————— Wollastonensis, <i>Lyc.</i>
————— clathratus? <i>Sow.</i>
Avicula echinata, <i>Sow.</i> (very abundant and highly characteristic)
————— Braamburiensis? <i>Sow.</i>
Gryphæa mina, <i>Phil.</i>
Ostrea Marshii, <i>Sow.</i> (O. flabelloides, <i>Lam.</i>) (abundant and characteristic).
————— acuminata, <i>Sow.</i> (rare).
————— Sowerbyi, <i>Mor. & Lyc.</i> (rare).
Terebratula obovata, <i>Sow.</i> (common).
————————— varieties passing into T. digona ? <i>Sow.</i> (very abundant).

Terebratula ornithocephala, *Sow.*, many varieties (very abundant).
——————, maxillata, *Sow.* (rather rare and never large).
—————— Bentleyi, *Dav.* (rare).
Rhynchonella concinna, *Sow.* sp.
Echinobrissus clunicularis, *Llhwyd.*
—————— orbicularis, *Phil.*
Holectypus depressus, *Lam.*

In the valley by Church Field Lodge the beds of the Cornbrash are fairly .well exposed and yielded the following fossils :—

Fossils from the Cornbrash, at Churchfield Lodge near Oundle.

Astarte, sp.
Isocardia tenera, *Sow.*
Lucina, sp.
Modiola imbricata, *Sow.*
Myacites securiformis, *Phil.*
Pholadomya deltoidea, *Sow.*
Myacites decurtatus, *Phil.*
Trigonia elongata, *Sow.*
—————— Moretonis, *Lyc. & Mor.*
——————, sp.
Avicula echinata, *Sow.*
Gervillia aviculoides, *Sow.*
Pecten demissus, *Phil.*
—————— vagans, *Sow.*
Ostrea Marshii, *Sow.* (O. flabelloides, *Lam.*)
Terebratula obovata, *Sow.*
Echinobrissus clunicularis, *Llhwyd.*
Acrosalenia, sp.

Near Polebrook the Cornbrash is dug under the Oxford Clay, and consequently the rock, instead of presenting its usual reddish-brown colour and rubbly character, is very hard and compact, and of a dark-blue colour. Its identity, indeed, might at first sight seem doubtful, but for its geological relations and the following fossils which it yields :—

Trigonia elongata, *Sow.*
Modiola Sowerbyana, *D'Orb.*
Lima rigidula, *Phil.*
Avicula echinata, *Sow.*
Pecten (several species).
Ostrea Marshii, *Sow.* (O. flabelloides, *Lam.*)
Echinobrissus clunicularis, *Llhwyd.*, &c.

Near the same place Mr. RICHARD GIBBS collected the following fossils :—

*Fossils from a pit in the Cornbrash at the Cross-Roads half a mile west of Pole-
brook.*

Chemnitzia, sp.
Gresslya peregrina, *Phil.*
Lithodomus inclusus, *Phil.*
Myacites decurtatus, *Phil.*
—————— securiformis, *Phil.*
Pholadomya deltoidea, *Sow.*
Avicula echinata, *Sow.*
Pecten demissus, *Phil.*
—————— vagans, *Sow.*
Serpula, sp.
Echinobrissus clunicularis, *Llhwyd.*
—————— orbicularis, *Phil.*

On the opposite, or western, side of the Nene valley the Cornbrash is exposed in a number of small pits, &c. about Liveden, being here, however, much obscured by drift.

Between Ashton and Elton the Cornbrash outcrop can be clearly traced at a number of points, but the beds are here much obscured by the valley gravels.

Good stone for road-metal was formerly dug below the gravels at the entrance to the village of Warmington. There were also at one time extensive pits on the south side of the same village, where Cornbrash with its usual characters and fossils was dug under a thickness of 14 or 15 feet of gravel. The stone is still well seen at the side of the road, and at the time of the survey was exposed, together with the clays beneath it, in a number of field-drains. At several other points in the neighbourhood, the Cornbrash has also been quarried under a considerable depth of gravels. There is a pit in the rock opposite to Elton Church.

On the opposite side of the Nene valley the Cornbrash with its usual fossils is well exposed on the south side of Cotterstock Wood. About Glapthorne, Southwick, and Benefield the rock can be traced at many points in the lateral valleys of the district, outcropping from below the drift, but good sections are rare.

The valley of the Billing Brook exposes the Cornbrash and the estuarine (?) sandy clays beneath it at several points : and about Water Newton Lodge the formation is admirably displayed. The rock is here crowded with the usual fossils, and I found in it a specimen of *Ammonites discus*, Sow., which is so rare a species that only one other example of it came under my notice during the survey of the whole district.

Between the valleys of the Nene and Welland, from Wansford to Peterborough, the Cornbrash covers a very considerable area. Indeed, there is perhaps no tract of equal extent occupied by the beds of this formation in the whole country. The general agricultural poverty of the Cornbrash in this area is shown by the fact that this large district occupied by it remained till quite recently in the condition of an open heath, and even now considerable portions of it have not yet been enclosed. Everywhere over the tract the red character of the soil formed by the Cornbrash is very conspicuous and striking. One small outlier of Oxford Clay, greatly obscured by drift, occurs capping the Cornbrash of this extensive tract, which is cut off and, to some extent, bounded on its northern side by the Great Tinwell and Walton Fault. To the eastward, the Cornbrash is found gradually dipping under the clays of the Oxfordian or Middle Oolite Series, which to so great an extent underlie and constitute the foundation of the Fenland.

Between Chesterton and Peterborough, on the south side of the Nene valley, many exposures of the Cornbrash are seen about Alwalton, Overton Waterville, Overton Longville, and Woodstone, the beds here, however, offer no features of interest.

At Ailsworth Heath the Cornbrash rock is seen, crowded with the usual fossils, and among these I found a specimen of the rare *Ammonites discus* of Sowerby, 2½ inches in diameter, and some exceedingly large examples of *Lima pectiniformis*, Schloth. (*L. proboscidea*, Sow.). About Helpstone the Cornbrash is thrown down by the great fault, and in consequence it is found occurring in very unexpected situations, and often exhibiting signs of considerable disturbance. On the west side of Rice Wood there is a pit containing a limekiln ; but though the rock exhibits its usual characters, the fossils were, for the usually prolific Cornbrash, extremely rare. The following species were, however, collected by me :—

> Belemnites, sp.
> Goniomya v- scripta, *Sow.*
> Myacites decurtatus, *Phil.*
> Avicula echinata, *Sow.*
> Ostrea Marshii, *Sow.* (O. flabelloides, *Lam.*)
> Terebratula obovata, *Sow.* (several varieties).

At the western part of Helpstone we find several pits in the Cornbrash, the rocks being covered with clay and consequently very hard and durable. We have here the following section :—

		ft.	in.
(1.)	Clay (drift or reconstructed Oxford Clay)	4	0
(2.)	Soft, sandy layer full of specimens of *Ostrea Marshii*, Sow.		
(3.)	Hard, compact or shelly, blue limestone -	5 or 6	0
(4.)	Soft, sandy bed of limestone, resting on indurated, blue clay.		

The bed (2) seems to be tolerably persistent wherever the top of the Cornbrash is exposed, which is not very frequently the case. The existence of oyster beds with the large plicated oyster, forms, as we have already seen, a striking contrast between the Cornbrash and the Great Oolite Limestone; in which latter, beds of the little *O. Sowerbyi*, Lyc. & Mor., and *O. subrugulosa*, Lyc., abound, while *O. Marshii* is unknown. That these variations in distribution of species are due to differences of condition, rather than to changes of fauna, is shown by the fact that the normal form of *O. Marshii* occurs in the ragstones of the Inferior Oolite, while varieties of it are found in the freestones of the same formation in the Cotteswolds and in those of the Lincolnshire Limestone.

The fossils in these pits about Helpstone are numerous, and include very large specimens of *Ammonites macrocephalus*, Schloth., in which, as is the habit of the species, the exterior ribs and tubercles entirely disappear from the outer whorls in the adult stage, so as to give the shells the appearance of vast *Nautili*, for which they have been frequently mistaken. Some univalves, forms which are usually rather rare in this formation, also occur in the Cornbrash at this place.

In the opening at the side of Hilly Wood, close to the great fault, and where, in consequence, the beds are seen to be greatly disturbed, the bed of *Ostrea Marshii*, before referred to, is well seen lying on the top of the Cornbrash limestone. The beds here generally dip to the north (or away from the upthrow of the great fault), the average amount of their inclination being 15°; this is, however, very variable, and in one place is seen amounting to 65°, while not far off the beds are vertical. The beds of the Cornbrash are also exposed at several other points around Hilly Wood. There is also a good pit in the Cornbrash, here exhibiting its usual characters and fossils, near Lawn Wood.

A pit on the south-west of Helpstone gave the following section :—

							ft.	in.
(1.) Soil and gravel	-	-	-	-	-	-	2	0
(2.) Oxford clay (trace)	-	-	-	-	-	-	0	0 to 9
(3.) Sandy bed, crowded with *Ostrea Marshii*, Sow.								
Variable in thickness, up to	-	-	-	-	-	-	1	0
(4.) Clay parting	-	-	-	-	-	-		
(5.) Stone beds of the Cornbrash	-	-	-	-	3 seen.			

In some of the Cornbrash pits about Helpstone large quantities of fossil wood occur; these are evidently fragments of drift timber, and frequently exhibit serpulæ, and other marine shells attached to them. Here, too, I found a remarkably fine specimen of *Ammonites macrocephalus*, Schloth., having a diameter of 1 foot 6 inches, and a thickness of over 8 inches. The outer surface, as in all adult examples of this species, was quite smooth and destitute of ornamentation, and the masses of oysters and serpula with which it was covered indicated that it had long drifted on the sea-bottom.

South-east of Helpstone the beds of Cornbrash are again brought in by a lateral fracture connected with the Great Tinwell and Walton Fault. Here, however, the beds, which are capped by the Oxfordian clays, are much obscured by Boulder Clay and gravel, and can for the most part be traced only by the aid of field- and other drains. In a field near Woodcroft, however, there is a pit (with a limekiln) opened in the beds of the Cornbrash which here exhibits its usual characters. The wells at Woodcroft obtain their supply of water from the Cornbrash, or, in one case, from the Great Oolite Limestones below. Unfortunately, however, no record of the section observed in this latter case was preserved.

About Walton, and especially in the cuttings of the Great Northern Railway between that place and Peterborough, the Cornbrash limestone is well exposed. In this district, as indeed is almost everywhere the case when exposures of the oolitic beds over a considerable area are seen, we find numerous proofs that the strata are bent into a number of exceedingly gentle synclinal and anticlinal curves, which, though not sufficiently pronounced to interfere with the *general* dip of the strata, have exercised a most important influence in determining the preservation of the several outliers, spurs, and inliers of the various rocks from denudation.

About Peterborough the Cornbrash is exposed at a great number of points, and its fossils have been collected by Mr. Bentley and the late Dr. Porter.

At Dogsthorpe the lowest beds of the Oxford Clay (those representing the Kellaways) are dug for brickmaking, and through the kindness of the owner of the pit, Mr. Thomas Parker, I was enabled to examine the junction of these beds with the Cornbrash. We have here the following section.—

	ft.	in.
(1.) Soil and gravel - - - - -	3	0
(2.) Sandy clay and sandy rock - - - -	8	0
(3.) Hard, blue, "dicey" clay with *Nucula nuda*, Phil. *Corbula*, sp. *Ammonites Herveyi*, Sow., &c. The lowest bed of this clay is crowded with *Rhynchonella* and other fossils - - - -	7	0
(4.) Hard, blue, Cornbrash rock with *Avicula echinata*, Sow., *Ostrea*, sp.		

In the following list I have given the names of the species which have been derived from the very numerous openings in the Cornbrash, in the immediate vicinity of Peterborough.

At the point where the Stamford and Wansford Branch Railway crosses the Syston and Peterborough Branch of the Midland Railway, not far from the Uffington and Helpstone station of the latter, we find a good section of the Cornbrash exposed. The *Ostrea Marshii* bed at its top is here well represented, and this is covered by the light-coloured, sandy clay, representing the Kellaways, which is seen to extend for some distance along the sides of the railway. At this place the Cornbrash is crowded with the usual fossils, including *Ammonites macrocephalus*, Schloth. (in every stage of growth). We also find the following species :—

> Belemnites ?
> Pholadomya deltoidea, *Sow.*
> Goniomya v- scripta, *Sow.*
> Lima pectiniformis, *Schloth.*
> Pecten (several species), &c.

Near Uffington Lodge a pit in the Cornbrash exhibits very numerous specimens of fossils; we here find (often of great size) Ammonites macrocephalus, *Schloth.*

> Homomya gibbosa, *Ag.*
> Trigonia elongata, *Sow.*
> ———-, sp.
> Pinna tetragona, *Phil.*
> Avicula echinata, *Sow.*
> Ostrea Marshii, *Sow.* (O. flabelloides, *Lam.*)
> Terebratula obovata, *Sow.*

and the forms approximating closely to T. digona, *Sow.*

The gregarious habit of *Avicula echinata* is well illustrated at this section.

To the northwards, in the neighbourhood of Belmesthorpe and Uffington Wood, the rock of the Cornbrash forms the surface over a considerable area, and several small pits have been opened in it, the positions of which are shown upon the map. Near Brown's Oak and Banthorpe the cuttings of the main-line of the Great Northern Railway afford some interesting sections of the formation. The latter of these is thus noticed by Professor MORRIS :*—

"In the Casewick cutting the Cornbrash, which is a grey, slightly compact and crystalline, shelly, and thin-bedded rock, occurs throughout the base of the cutting ; its fossil contents are—

> Pholadomya, sp.
> Panopæa calceiformis, *Phil.*, sp.
> Modiola bipartita, *Phil.*
> Gervillia aviculoides, *Sow.*
> Goniomya litterata, *Sow.*, sp.
> Lima rigida, *Sow.*
> Ostrea Marshii, *Sow.* (O. flabelloides, *Lam.*)
> Pecten demissus, *Phil.*
> ———- lens, *Sow.*

---

* *Quart. Journ. Geol. Soc.*, vol. ix. p. 332.

Terebratula Bentleyi, *Mor.*
———— obovata, *Sow.*
Diastopora (Berenicea) diluviana, *Milne.-Edw.*
Serpula, two species.
Portion of a jaw of Chimæra."

Still further north, the Essendine and Bourne branch of the Great Northern Railway crosses the outcrop of the beds of the Cornbrash, but does not expose any particularly good sections. About Wilsthorpe, Braceborough, and Greatford, however, the Cornbrash occupies a considerable area and is exposed in a number of pits. The rock here presents a noteworthy peculiarity; the flat rubbly fragments of which it is made up, being all coated with a deposit of white stalagmitic carbonate of lime, which gives them the appearance, when viewed at a little distance, of having been whitewashed. The fossils found in these pits are those which everywhere characterise the Cornbrash, and the beds here are seen to dip directly under the fens, being overlapped by the deposits of the Fenland gravels.

Above Manthorpe the top of the Cornbrash, with the bed crowded with *Ostrea Marshii*, Sow., is well seen. At Lound a pit occurs which affords the following section :—

Pit in the Cornbrash at Lound dug for road-metal.

	ft.	in.
Boulder Clay - - - - - - -	3	0
Trace of Oxford clay in place (?) - - -	0	0
Bed of laminated stone full of *Ostræa Marshii*, Sow., and other species, and *Ostræa* (large flat species) - -	0	9
Bed of soft, sandy stone - - - - - -	0	6
Bed of hard, whitish stone crowded with fossils (*Lima pectiniformis*, Scholth, *L. punctata*, Sow. &c.) -	0	9
Light-brown, sandy clay - - - - - -	0	6
Hard, blue-hearted stone - - - - -	1	6
Rubbly Cornbrash at bottom.		

Ammonites macrocephalus, *Schloth* (very large specimens).
Ostræa Marshii, *Sow.* (very abundant).
Modiola imbricata, *Sow.*
Gervillia aviculoides, *Sow.*
Lima punctata, *Sow.*
——— pectiniformis, *Schloth.*
Pecten lens, *Sow.*
——— demissus, *Phil.*
Hinnites gradus, *Phil.*
Cypricardia Bathonica, *Mor. & Lyc.*
Pholadomya deltoidea, *Sow.* (abundant).
Goniomya v- scripta, *Sow.*
Myacites securiformis, *Phil.*
Perna rugosa, var quadrata, *Mor. & Lyc.*
Terebratula obovata, *Sow.*
——— maxillata, *Sow.*
Terebratula lagenalis, *Sow.*
Rhynchonella concinna, *Sow.*, sp.
Serpula, sp.

Northwards from this point to Bourn and Edenham, where the Cornbrash is well developed and has yielded some interesting fossils (the original specimen of the *Terebratula Bentleyi*, Mor. was found at Handthorpe near Bourn) we find several interesting exposures of the formation. The interesting sections about Bourn will be described in the explanation of Sheet 70 of the Survey map.

The fossils found in the various Cornbrash pits, in the immediate vicinity of Bourn, were as follows :—

Fossils from Cornbrash of Bourn.

Ichthyosaurus (vertebra).
Nautilus Baberi, *Lyc. & Mor.* (?)

Ammonites Herveyi, *Sow.*
——————— macrocephalus, *Schloth.*
Cardium cognatum, *Phil.*
Goniomya v-scripta, *Sow.*
Gresslya peregrina, *Phil.*
Modiola imbricata, *Sow.*
Myacites decurtatus, *Phil.*
——————— calceiformis, *Phil.*
Pholadomya deltoidea, *Sow.*
Trigonia costata, *Sow.*
Gervillia aviculoides, *Sow.*
Lima pectiniformis, *Schloth.*
—— rigidula, *Phil.*
Ostrea Marshii, *Sow.* (O. flabelloides, *Lam.*).
Pecten demissus, *Phil.*
——————— lens, *Sow.*
——————— sp.
Discina, sp.
Terebratula lagenalis, *Schloth.*
——————— obovata, *Sow.*
Serpula, sp.
Echinobrissus orbicularis, *Phil.*

Outliers.—As already remarked, many of the outliers of the Cornbrash are greatly obscured by the drift deposits which lie upon them, and often overlap their edges. The general position and limits of these outliers being indicated upon the map, it will only be necessary to notice in detail such of them as afford interesting sections.

The outlier shown on the map at Brigstock Parks was proved by some deep wells which, passing through the drift, reached the Oxford Clay, and as this formation is everywhere in the district underlaid by Cornbrash, we have represented it here; but the outlines of the mass are purely hypothetical.

The two outliers of the Walk of Morehay only exhibit the Cornbrash along their eastern margins, where, by the dip, their beds are brought to a lower level. The most southern of these two outliers is capped by a mass of Oxford Clay and Kellaways Sand, the extent of which is doubtful. It is not improbable that the northern outlier is similarly capped, but of this we have no actual proof.

In the case of the outlier between Fineshade and King's Cliffe, however, the recently constructed trial-shafts for a railway have exposed the Oxford Clay and representative of the Kellaways resting upon the Cornbrash (see p. 221). On the eastern side of this outlier the Cornbrash is exposed at Cliffe Parks, where it covers a considerable area. At the upper part of the Cadges Wood its beds are well exposed in a ditch-cutting, and I collected here—

Ostrea Marshii, *Sow.* (O. flabelloides, *Lam.*), large and abundant.
Ammonites Herveyi, *Sow.*
Pholadomya deltoidea, *Sow.*
Myacites decurtatus, *Phil.*
Lima rigidula, *Phil.*
Lucina, sp.
Terebratula maxillata, *Sow.*

The Cornbrash is again seen north of Blatherwycke Mill, and on the western side of the same outlier we can trace the formation capping a number of spurs between Blatherwycke and Duddington. The succession of beds is here clearly seen to be as follows :—

    (1.) " Kale," forming top of spurs (Cornbrash).
    (2.) Stiff, blue clay (clays of Great Oolite).
    (3.) Beds of limestone (Great Oolite).
    (4.) Thick mass of clays in sides of valley (Upper Estuarine Series).
    (5.) Oolitic rock, forming "red land" of the plateau (Lincolnshire Limestone).

In their higher portions these ridges are much obscured by the masses of pre-glacial gravel, which are in turn overlapped by the Boulder Clay. Above Duddington the Cornbrash is seen and at once recognised by its lithological characters, and the presence in it of—

Ostrea Marshii, Sow.
Ammonites Herveyi, Sow.
And the common Cornbrash Echinoderms.

The effect of the great north and south fault upon the Cornbrash in this outlier is very strikingly seen in tracing the outcrop of the beds.

At the outlier of Bedford Purlieus many exposures of the Cornbrash occur, but no good sections. Over a great part of its area the outlier is greatly obscured by drift, and its surface has only been recently cleared of woods.

The outlier of Barrowden Hay and Luffenham Heath, the limits of which can be clearly defined on its eastern side, is also much covered with drift on its western. It does not afford any instructive sections.

North of Stamford a small outlier of Cornbrash occurs on the highest point of the plateau lying north of the town, and known as the "Stamford open field." In the earlier edition of Sheet 64 this outlier was not represented, there being at that time no sufficient evidence of its existence. I am indebted to Mr. Sharp for calling my attention to a number of trial holes for stone, which were opened during the recent enclosure of this tract. From these trial holes, many of which failed in reaching beds of solid stone, it appears that a number of small fragments, vestiges of an outlier of Cornbrash, still exist at the top of this hill. None of these fragments of the cap of Cornbrash exceeded 4 feet in thickness, and so irregular and uncertain is the mode of occurrence of the rock, that its limits can only be represented on the map by a dotted line. It yields, however, Ostrea Marshii, Sow., and several other characteristic Cornbrash fossils, and its identity with that formation is therefore beyond doubt. It is underlaid by a thick mass of clays, with some shelly bands (clays of the Great Oolite). Indeed a very excellent section of the whole of the beds from the Cornbrash to the Upper Lias can be traced at the town of Stamford. This section has been admirably illustrated by Mr. SHARP.

It will not be necessary to describe in detail the various outliers to the northwards, some of which are of quite insignificant proportions, though others cover considerable areas. The small outliers at Firewards Thorns, south-west of Essendine, exhibits only the bottom bed of the Cornbrash, the clays immediately below it being crowded with Ostrea subrugulosa, Lyc. & Mor. In a small outlier to the north, the limestone rock has been wholly removed, and only the clays below it remain; but in one to the west a considerable thickness of the Cornbrash rock is exposed.

A very extensive outlier of the Cornbrash occurs between Careby Lings and Monk's Wood; and numerous smaller ones south of the latter place, at Dogsight, and Holywell Lodge. In the latter of these the Great Oolite Clays below were well exposed in a number of field-drains.

The manner in which slight foldings of the strata have contributed to the preservation of these outlying patches has been already explained, and is well illustrated in the cuttings on the main line of the Great Northern Railway which were so clearly described by Professor MORRIS.

At Clipsham, however, we find an outlier of Cornbrash, considerably to the westward of all those which we have been describing to the north of the Welland, and which evidently owes its preservation to the action of a fault. The rock here presents the usual characters of the Cornbrash and contains Ammonites Herveyi, Sow. and Pholadomya deltoidea, Sow. var.

The great outlier which occupies a great part of Grimsthorpe Park is much obscured by drift, but the beds are exposed in some of the cuttings of the Edenham and Little Bytham Railway.

Inliers.—Several inliers of Cornbrash, seen at the bottom of the valleys cut in the overlying Oxfordian clays, occur within the limits of Sheet 64. The most important of these is the interesting patch of rock near Stilton in Huntingdonshire, where several pits have been opened in it to obtain road-metal. A glance at the map will show at what a considerable distance this exposure of the

Cornbrash rock lies from any other exhibition of the same bed ; and a careful study of the ground indicates that its appearance at this singular and unexpected locality is, in part, due to a considerable fault, which here traverses the beds. The area covered by this inlier is not great, but the patch of rocks is of very great interest indeed, from the number of interesting species of fossils which it has yielded, but still more from the mode in which these are found preserved at this locality. The fossils of the Cornbrash, and especially those with thin and delicate shells, such as the Myadæ, usually occur as internal casts only, but at Stilton these delicate shells, often retaining their pearly nacre, are found very beautifully preserved. At this point Mr. BENTLEY has recently found very beautiful specimens of the rare and interesting Brachiopods *Terebratulæ Bentleyi*, Mor. and *Terebratula coarctata*, Park., the latter species having been formerly supposed to be peculiar to the Bradford Clay of the Bath area. The Cornbrash rock in this inlier is of a paler colour and less ferruginous character than is usually the case with it.

The following fossils have been collected from the rocks of the Cornbrash in this interesting inlier :—

Fossils from the Cornbrash of Stilton, Huntingdonshire.

Ichthyosaurus, sp.
Plesiosaurus, sp.
Teleosaurus, sp.
Strophodus magnus, *Ag.*
————— subreticulatus, *Ag.*
Pycnodus Bucklandi, *Ag.*
Asteracanthus verrucosus, *Ag.*
Ammonites Herveyi, *Sow.*
————— macrocephalus, *Schloth.*
————— modiolaris, *Llhwyd.*
Chemnitzia simplex, *Lyc. & Mor.*
Cardium cognatum, *Phil.*
Cypricardia cordata, *Lyc.*
Goniomya v-scripta, *Sow.*
Homomya crassiuscula, *Lyc. & Mor.*
————— gibbosa, *Sow.*
Isocardia tenera, *Sow.*
Lucina striatula, *Buv.*
Modiola gibbosa, *Sow.*
————— imbricata, *Sow.*
————— Lonsdalei, *Lyc. & Mor.*
————— Sowerbyana, *d'Orb.*
Myacites calceiformis, *Phil.*
————— decurtatus, *Phil.*
————— recurvus, *Phil.*
————— securiformis, *Phil.*
————— sinistra, *Ag.*
Pholadomya acuticosta, *Sow.*
————— deltoidea, *Sow.*
————— lyrata, *Sow.*
————— Phillipsia, *Mor.*
Trigonia Scarburgensis, *Lyc.*
Anomia semistriata, *Bean.*
Avicula echinata, *Sow.*
Lima duplicata, *Sow.*
—— impressa, *Lyc. & Mor.*
—— læviuscula, *Sow.*
—— pectiniformis, *Schloth.*

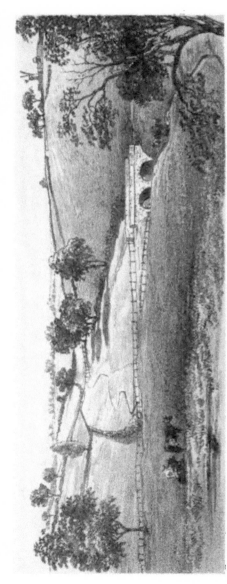

VIEW OF THE EXTRAORDINARY ROCKY PLAIN IN THE GREAT DESERT

Drawn by C. Tilt. Published 1821.

Lima rigida, *Sow.*
—— rigidula, *Phil.*
Pecten anisopleurus, *Buv.*
—— articulatus, *Schloth.*
—— annulatus, *Sow.*
—— demissus, *Phil.*
—— inæquicostatus, *Phil.*
—— lens, *Sow.*
—— Michelensis, *Buv.*
—— vagans, *Sow.*
Rhynchonella concinna, *Sow.*
————— Moorei, *Dav.*
————— obsoleta, *Sow.*
————— varians, *Schloth.*
Terebratula Bentleyi, *Mor.*
————— coarctata, *Park.*
————— intermedia, *Sow.*
————— lagenalis, *Schloth.*
————— sublagenalis, *Dav.*
————— maxillata, *Sow.*
————— obovata, *Sow.*
————— orinthocephala, *Sow.*
Glyphæa rostrata, *Phil.*
Serpula intestinalis, *Phil.*
—— squamosa, *Bean.*
—— tetragona, *Sow.*
Clypeus Mülleri, *Wright.*
Echinobrissus clunicularis, *Llhwyd.*
————— orbicularis, *Phil.*
Holectypus depressus, *Leske.*

At Kate's Bridge the Cornbrash is again exposed as an inlier in the midst of the great spread of Oxford clay. There is, however, no reason for supposing that the exposure of the former beds at this point is contributed to by a fault. The fossils found in the Cornbrash in a well at this place were—

Echinobrissus clunicularis, *Llhwyd.*
Holectypus depressus, *Leske.*
Isocardia tenera, *Sow.*

Where exposed at the surface, the Cornbrash rock of this inlier presents its usual characters.

Near Thurlby Wood a number of extensive pits are opened in the Cornbrash exposed in an inlier contiguous to, and almost continuous with, that of Kate's Bridge. The characters of the rock and the species of fossils here found are those which usually distinguish the Cornbrash.

The Cornbrash is not a rock of any great economic value. Its peculiar bedding renders it quite unfit for a building stone, though it is frequently locally employed in rough constructions and for field-dikes. It is also occasionally quarried for lime-burning in the district, but for this purpose is by no means so highly esteemed as the subjacent Great Oolite. As a road-metal, however, it possesses deservedly a high reputation among limestones; and for this purpose it is very extensively quarried, and occasionally conveyed to considerable distances.

The small esteem in which throughout the Midland district the Cornbrash is held by agriculturists has already been noticed.

The low tabular hills, which characterise the scenery of the districts occupied by the alternations of the clays and limestones constituting the Great Oolite Series are illustrated in Plate X.

CHAPTER IX.
THE MIDDLE OOLITES.

This division of the Jurassic series is only partially exposed within the limits of Sheet 64, being represented by the lower portion of the Oxford Clay with the sandy beds representing the Kellaways Rock at its base. Like the Lias, this formation consists almost wholly of clays, which are usually concealed by a thick covering of glacial clay and gravel. The Oxford Clay was evidently a deep sea deposit and, like the Lias, exhibits evidence that during its formation the fauna gradually underwent very considerable changes, especially in the species of Cephalopoda. We will now describe the succession of its principal beds as represented in this district.

a. Kellaways Sands, Sandstones, and Clays.—These beds, which lie directly upon the Cornbrash, consist of an alternation of clays usually light-coloured, very arenaceous, and sometimes pyritous, with irregular beds of whitish sand. The latter are not unfrequently cemented by calcareous matter into a friable rock, in which case they are usually full of fossils. These fossils belong to the species which characterise the Kellaways rock of Yorkshire and Wilts; *Gryphæa bilobata*, Sow., *Avicula inæquivalvis*, Sow., (*A. expansa*, Phil.), and *Belemnites Oweni*, Pratt, being among the most abundant forms. These beds were first detected in this district by Professor Morris, who saw them exposed in the Casewick cutting of the Great Northern Railway. Although such sandy beds are everywhere in this district found at the base of the Oxfordian, and indeed extend, though perhaps not uninterruptedly, through the country from Yorkshire to Wiltshire, yet they are so variable in thickness and mineral character that it has not been considered advisable to attempt their separation from the Oxford Clay upon the map; the places where they are well seen, however, are indicated by the symbol KEL. The Kellaways beds form a link between the Cornbrash, which was accumulated in rather shallow water, and the Oxford Clay, which was a deep sea deposit; they contain many of the species found in each of these formations, with a few which are peculiar.

The Kellaways beds are dug for brick-making at Oundle, Southwick, Benefield, Dogsthorpe, Uffington, Kate's Bridge, and Warmington; and it is said that the bricks made from them are much superior in quality to those manufactured from the Oxford Clay, especially in respect to the amount of heat which they will bear. The sandy nature of these beds gives a peculiar character to the soil upon them; causing it to exhibit a whitish colour and a dryness very different from that of the Oxford Clay above.

b. Clays with Nucula.—These are laminated, blue shales crowded with compressed *Ammonites* and the little *Nucula nuda*, Phil. They are seen at many points, and are dug for brick-making at Haddon, Eyebury, and Holme.

c. Clays with Belemnites Oweni.—Consisting of dark-blue clays abounding with *Belemnites Oweni*, Pratt, which often attains to a gigantic size. *Gryphæa dilatata*, Sow., appears to commence in these beds, which yield abundantly the bones of saurians and fish, and great masses of wood converted into jet. These beds are exposed in the brickyards at Standground, Fletton, Woodstone, Sudborough, Conington, Luddington, and Great Gidding.

d. Clays with Belemnites hastatus.—These blue clays contain many of the fossils which are found in the last, but are characterised by the appearance, in great numbers, of the little *Belemnites hastatus*, Blain. They are dug at Werrington, Ramsey, and Eyebury.

e. Clays with Ammonites of the group of the Ornati.—These are dark-blue clays containing great flattened nodules of iron-pyrites, with numerous *Ammonites* fossilized by the same mineral. The most abundant species in these beds are *Ammonites ornatus*, Schloth, *Am. Duncani*, Sow., *Am. Bakeriæ*, Sow., *Am. athleta*, Phil., with *Terebratula impressa*, Von Buch. These beds are dug in the brickyards about Whittlesey, and also in those at Thorney, and Eye Green.

f. Clays with Ammonites of the group of the Cordati.—These are exposed only at the Forty-foot-Bridge brickyards, which are just upon the eastern limits of this sheet.

Main Line Outcrop of the Middle Oolites in the District.—In Sheet 64 the Oxfordian strata constitute a band of country, immediately bordering the Fenland, which rises into numerous swelling hills, usually of no great elevation. Throughout this tract the Secondary deposits are greatly obscured by the superincumbent Boulder Clay and gravels; the land formed by the Middle Oolite is in the main devoted to grazing purposes, but some considerable areas of it have been brought under the plough, while others remain as woodland. A few exposures of the Oxfordian strata also occur in the Fenland, to the east of this main line of outcrop; and again in outlying patches capping the Lower Oolites to the west of it.

Immediately to the south of the limits of sheet 64, the beds of the Oxford Clay were well exposed in the Wigsthorpe cutting of the Northampton and Peterborough Railway. This cutting was examined by Professor Morris and Captain Ibbetson at a time when the beds were well exposed, and they described the section in the following terms :—" The Oxford Clay is well seen in the Wigsthorp cutting, near Thorpe Aychurch, and is marked by zones of Septaria, frequently containing fossils. *Am. Konigii*, &c., the lower part of the section being thin slaty clays full of *Ammonites Jason* or *Elizabethæ* much compressed, *Belemnites, Avicula*, and numerous bivalves."*

In a well at the same place, which extended to the depth of 30 feet, I also saw a good section of the same beds consisting of dark blue clays abounding with *Gryphæa dilatata*, Sow., and many *Ammonites* and *Belemnites* which were too imperfect for identification.

At Sudborough brickyard beds near the base of the Oxford Clay are dug. They yield abundantly very large specimens of *Belemnites Puzosianus*, d'Orb; *Ammonites* and saurian remains also occur at this place.

---

* See Morris and Ibbetson, notice of the geology of the neighbourhood of Stamford and Peterborough, Brit. Ass. Rep. for 1847, Trans. of sect., p. 127.

At the reservoir constructed for the supply of Lilford Hall, on the south-west side of the park, the Oxford Clay was just reached in one corner of the excavation under a great mass of boulder clay : the beds exposed here are evidently low down in the Oxfordian series, and consist of dark blue clay full of crushed specimens of *Ammonites*, with many examples of *Nucula nuda*, Phil.

Near Barnwell railway-station, the lower beds of the Oxford Clay were exhibited in a number of drains, at the time of the survey.

At Oundle brickyard the lowest beds of the Middle Oolite, consisting of light-coloured, somewhat sandy clay, with bands of hard, sandy and ferruginous rock, are well seen. The bands of sand-rock which alternate with the clays are seldom more than 7 or 8 inches in thickness, and often thin out altogether within very short distances. They are often so crowded with fossils that the abundance of carbonate of lime does great injury to the bricks during their burning. The clay here is said to form an inferior kind of fire-brick capable of withstanding a considerable degree of heat. On sinking through the clay at this place, it is said that ferruginous beds were found from which strongly chalybeate springs arose. I am uncertain whether these beds are to be regarded as the Cornbrash, or to belong to one of the sandy ferruginous beds of the same kind as those exposed in the pit. It is evident from the fossils which they contain, that the rocks exposed in the Oundle brickyard are the representative of the Kellaways.

At Benefield brickyard the same series of beds is exposed, consisting of light-blue clay with very irregular and inconstant bands of sandy rock, containing *Serpula, Belemnites, Gryphæa, Avicula*, and other shells. They were also exposed in some other artificial openings in the neighbourhood. The rapidity with which the surface water soaks away over the areas, throughout which these sandy beds representing the Kellaways outcrop, causes their soil to present a remarkable contrast with that of the districts occupied by the stiff and impervious clays of the higher portions of the Oxford Clay. The light-coloured sandy soils formed by the former rocks, constituting what is locally known as "drummy land," can easily be traced, over many miles of country in this district, at the limits of the Oxford Clay and Cornbrash formations.

At the brickyard of Ashton, lying on the opposite side of the Nene valley to that of Oundle, Oxfordian strata, probably a little higher in the series than those of Oundle and Benefield, are worked. These consist of dark-blue clays containing *Nucula nuda*, Phil., many fragments of *Belemnites*, crushed *Ammonites* and large quantities of wood converted into jet. These beds are doubtless the same as those exposed at Wigsthorpe and Lilford which we have before noticed.

At the Warmington brickyard no good section was exposed, but the beds worked are evidently of the same sandy character as those which, throughout the district, immediately overlie the Cornbrash, and by their fossil contents are shown to represent the Kellaways. The Cornbrash is reached under the Oxfordian beds by wells sunk at a number of points in the neighbourhood of this pit.

The very considerable tract of Oxfordian strata lying between the Nene valley and the Fenland is almost entirely obscured by the great drift deposits (boulder clay and gravel), which are, indeed, seldom cut through by the valleys so as to expose the subjacent rocks. Consequently, exposures of these latter are exceedingly rare in the district.

At Luddington brickyard we find, under a thickness of 5 or 6 feet of drift, Oxford Clay of a light-blue colour which is dug to the depth of 30 feet. It contains *Gryphæa dilatata*, Sow., *Belemnites Puzosianus*, d'Orb, and, somewhat rarely, *Ammonites*.

At the Great Gidding brickyard, which is just beyond the southern limit of Sheet 64, similar beds of Oxford Clay, of a light colour, are found. Specimens of *Serpulæ* were the only fossils which I detected at this spot.

Along the course of the Billing Brook I found several exposures of light-coloured and sandy clays belonging to the Oxfordian series. These are exposed in consequence of the thick drift deposits of the area being cut through by the deep valley in which this stream flows.

Along the road between Elton and Haddon the Oxford Clay was well seen in some deep drains. It consisted of light-coloured, very tenaceous, clay, in which fossils were only sparingly distributed. Specimens of *Belemnites Puzosianus*, d'Orb, and fragments of wood were, however, not rare.

Near Haddon Church a well sunk at the new parsonage penetrated the Oxford Clay to a depth of more than 30 feet, but no water was obtained. The clay brought np was dark coloured and highly laminated. It contained many fossils, including :

> Belemnites Puzosianus, *d'Orb.*
> Ammonites ornatus, *Schloth.*
>   „   other species (indeterminable).
> Nucula nuda, *Phil.*

The fossils were all crushed and very imperfectly preserved. At Haddon brickyard similar clays with *Nucula nuda* and *Belemnites* were dug. The brickyard at Morborne is now abandoned, and I could obtain no information concerning the beds and fossils formerly exposed in it.

A little to the south of Fletton the Oxford Clay was exhibited in a number of field-drains. The beds here contained great numbers of *Nucula nuda*, Phil., which were however very badly preserved.

In the neighbourhood of Peterborough the various beds forming the lower part of the Oxfordian series are well exposed.

At Dogsthorpe the brick pits exhibit light and dark-blue clays, often mottled, becoming in some places very sandy and passing in others into light-brown sands which are somewhat indurated. The sandy rock here does not appear to form regular beds in the clay, but to constitute nests and irregular lenticular masses. I am indebted to the owner of these pits, Mr. Thomas Parker (who had preserved a considerable number of fossils and rendered me important aid in the examination of the district) for making an experimental sinking through the lower beds in the pits, whereby the following section was exposed :—

						ft.
(1.) Soil and Gravel	-	-	-	-	-	3
(2.) Sandy Clay with stony bands		-	-	-	-	8
(3.) Hard blue " dicey " clay	-	-	-	-	-	7
(4.) Cornbrash limestone.						

In (2) the clays appeared to be totally destitute of fossils, but in the sandy stone, great numbers of specimens of *Gryphæa bilobata*, Sow., and *Belemnites Puzosianus*, d'Orb, including individuals of all ages, occurred.

The clays (3) had at their base a band crowded with fossils including *Ammonites Herveyi*, Sow., *Nucula nuda*, Phil., *Corbula* sp., and *Rhynchonella* sp.

The Cornbrash limestone (4) was identified, both by its petrological characters and by its containing *Avicula echinata*, Sow., and *Ostrea Sowerbyi*, Lyc. and Mor. The bricks made from the sandy clays of Dogsthorpe are said to be capable, like those of Oundle and Benefield, of withstanding a very considerable degree of heat.

At Standground, Fletton, and Woodstone, near Peterborough, dark-blue clays containing large quantities of fossil wood, which, by their fossils, are shown to belong to a rather higher portion of the Oxfordian series than those just described, are dug for brick-making. From these pits the late Dr. Porter, of Peterborough, obtained a number of very interesting fossils. These include :—

> Belemnites Puzosianus, *d'Orb.* (extremely abundant.)
> Ammonites Bakeriæ, *Sow.*
>   „   convolutus ornatus, *Quenst.*
>   „   macrocephalus, *Schloth.*
>   „   heterophyllus ornatus ? *Quenst.*
>   „   hecticus, *Rein.*
>   „   arduenensis, *d'Orb.*
> Rhynchonella varians, *Schloth.*

with very many bones of Saurians, and spines and teeth of fish.

Among these, are especially worthy of notice, large portions of the skeleton of *Steneosaurus*, the teeth of *Strophodus reticulatus*, Ag., and the dorsal spines of *Asteracanthus verrucosus*, Eg. The last-mentioned fossils sometimes attain to very large proportions, specimens 12 inches in length, with a girth in their thickest part of five inches, and a thickness of two inches, having been found. Some fragments have also occurred indicating even greater dimensions than these.

The very large quantities of wood, either converted into jet or mineralized by pyrites, is a specially noteworthy circumstance at these localities near Peterborough. This wood sometimes occurs in masses of great size; it is evidently drift-timber, which, floating in the open sea, became water-logged and sunk to the bottom, there to be buried in the fine clays in association with the numerous marine animals of the Oxfordian period.

By the great Stamford and Helpstone fault the line of outcrop of the Middle Oolites, like that of the Lower Oolites, is subjected to great displacement, and the strata appear far to the westward of the positions at which their occurrence might be anticipated.

Between Marholme and Woodcroft the beds of sandy stone, representing the Kellaways, and the overlying blue clays were exhibited in a number of field drains.

At the westernmost of the two mills at Werrington a brickyard exhibits beds of Oxford Clay, overlaid by thick masses of Boulder Clay with patches of gravel at its base. The Oxford Clay here yielded,—

> Ammonites Duncani, *Sow.*
> Belemnites Puzosianus, *d'Orb.*
> Icthyosaurus sp. (Vertebræ and other bones.)
> Plesiosaurus sp.   (Ditto.)

In the clay-pit at the east end of the village of Werrington the clays yield rather numerous fossils, including, besides some *Ammonites* and vertebrate remains which were not determined,—

> Belemnites hastatus, *Blainv.* (very abundant).
> ,,   Puzosianus, *d'Orb.* (rare).
> Gryphæa dilatata, *Sow.*
> Nucula nuda, *Phil.*
> Serpula vertebralis, *Sow.* (abundant).

Omitting the special mention of many small and obscure sections, we have, in the Casewick cutting of the Great Northern Railway, as described by Professor Morris in 1853, some very interesting and instructive sections of the lowest beds of the Oxfordian series. This interesting section is now, however, almost wholly concealed in consequence of the sides of the cutting being turfed up.

This section (*see* Fig. 18, page 244) is described by Professor Morris, as follows:—

"Resting upon this bed" (the Cornbash) "is the equivalent of the Oxford clay, consisting of 10 feet of dark laminated unctuous clay, with gray-brown sandy ferruginous clay; the dark clay contained *Ammonites Herveyi* abundantly, as well as *Modiola bipartita, Trigonia clavellata, Thracia depressa, Nucula nuda*, Phil., and Saurian bones. The brown sandy clay, which passed into ferruginous rock, contained many well preserved fossils, the most abundant being,—

> Gryphæa bilobata, *Sow.* (in every stage of growth).
> Belemnites Oweni, *Pratt* (Puzosianus ? *d'Orb*).
> Ammonites Calloviensis, *Sow.*
> Nautilus sp.
> Pholadomya acuticosta, *Sow.*
> Panopæa peregrina, *Phil.* sp.
> Lima rigidula, *Phil.*
> Avicula expansa, *Phil.*
> Pecten demissus, *Phil.*
> ,,   lens? *Sow.*

"These fossils would indicate that the ferruginous rock and gray sand were the equivalent of the Kellaways rock, which has not been previously noticed in this district."*

Throughout the remainder of the outcrop of the Oxfordian beds to the northward, within the area now being described, there are few good sections. At all points, however, where the strata are sufficiently free from drift, the outcrop of the sandy

---

* Quart. Journ. Geol. Soc., vol. ix. (1853), p. 333.

beds, representing the Kellaways, can be readily recognised by the distinctive characters of the soil which they form.

At Kate's Bridge four miles south of Bourne there are two pits in the Kellaways strata. In one of these, the thickness of clay overlying the Cornbrash rock is only 6 feet, the beds consisting of light-blue sandy clay containing *Belemnites, Gryphæa, Avicula,* and other shells.

At Bourne we have, in a brickyard, the following section of the same beds:—

	ft.	in.
(1.) Soil	1	6
(2.) Clay becoming sandy and yellow below	1	6
(3.) Light-blue and yellow mottled sand	2	0
(4.) Light-coloured, laminated clay	2	6
(5.) Sandy rock (very irregular)	4	0
(6.) Light-blue clay	8 to 9	0
(7.) Cornbrash?		

The bed (5) contained,—
Belemnites Oweni, *Pratt* (Puzosianus? *d'Orb.*)
Avicula expansa, *Phil.*
Gryphæa bilobata, *Sow.*
Wood.

The Oxford Clay appears to constitute the substratum of that portion of the Fens included within Sheet 64. The process of claying the land (that is, digging deep trenches through the superficial peat and silt into the clay beds below, and spreading portions of these latter over the surface) occasionally affords fair exposures of the strata and fossils of the dark-blue Oxfordian Clays. At a few points, however, the rock, met with under these circumstances, is the Boulder Clay; patches of which appear to have escaped the wide-spread marine denudation, which has produced the plain of the Fenland. Besides these local and temporary exposures of the Middle Oolite strata within the Fenland, we have a few brickyards which afford sections of the same strata within this area.

South of Bury a brickyard in the Oxford Clay exhibits a section of dark-blue clays containing much pyrites, which yield the following fossils:—
Gryphæe dilatata, *Sow.* (abundant).
Belemnites Puzosianus, *d'Orb.* (rare).
" hastatus, *Blainv.*
Ammonites Lambertii, *Sow.*
" cordatus, *Sow.*
With imperfect specimens of both bivalves and univalves, and some bones of Saurians.

At Ramsey, near the railway station, the Oxford Clay was formerly largely dug and burnt as a substitute for gravel, a use to which the clays of this formation are frequently applied.

At Ramsey Heights there are several brickyards still open, the clay used being that of the Middle Oolite (locally termed "Galt"). At one of these, the bricks made are burned with peat. Neither of the clay pits at these brickyards, however, afford any sections of special interest to the geologist.

At Forty-foot-Bridge there are two clay pits opened in the Oxford Clay. In one of these, a band of hard rock, 8 or 10 inches in thickness, is found at a depth of 15 feet. The clays at this place are crowded with *Ammonites Lambertii* Sow. (many varieties): *Belemnites hastatus,* Blainv., is also very abundant, while *Belemnites Puzosianus,* d'Orb, is rare. *Gryphæa dilatata,* Sow., occurs in moderate abundance.

At Conington brickyard blue clays of the Oxfordian series are dug, which yield abundant specimens of *Belemnites Puzosianus,* d'Orb, and, somewhat rarely, examples of *Gryphæa dilatata,* Sow. Similar clays are dug at the Holme brickyard.

32108. Q

A cutting on the main line of the Great Northern Railway, between Farcett and Yaxley, exposes a considerable thickness of light-blue Boulder Clay full of chalk detritus, with some irregular gravelly beds intercalated in it. At the bottom of this drift occur the dark-blue Oxfordian Clays containing very large septaria and yielding many fossils, among which were,—

Belemnites Puzosianus, *d'Orb*.
,, hastatus, *Blainv*.
Ammonites excavatus, *Sow*.
,, athleta, *Phil*.
,, Duncani, *Sow*.
,, cordatus, *Sow*.
Gryphæa dilatata, *Sow*. (very large).
Serpula vertebralis, *Sow*.
,, sp.

And a number of bivalves too imperfectly preserved for identification.

In the neighbourhood of Whittlesea there are several brickyards in which the beds of the Oxford Clay are exposed in good sections.

To the North-west of Whittlesea the clays are dug in a very extensive pit; they are of a deep-blue colour and contain much pyrites and wood. The fossils are often, indeed so thickly encrusted with pyrites that it is impossible to determine their species. Among them are,—

Belemnites Puzosianus, *d'Orb*.
,, hastatus, *Blainv*.
Ammonites athleta, *Phil*.
,, (several other species).
Gryphæa dilatata (very abundant).
Serpula sp.

The large clay-pits at the town of Whittlesea have yielded great numbers of beautiful specimens of *Ammonites*, especially those belonging to the *Ornatus* group, including—

Ammonites Duncani, *Sow*.
,, ,, ,, (variety).
,, Elizabethæ, *Pratt*.
,, Comptoni, *Pratt*.
,, ornatus, *Schloth*.
,, Jason, *Rein*.
,, Bakeriæ, *Sow*.
,, cordatus, *Sow*. (variety).
,, tatricus, *Pusch*. (young).
,, Constantii, *d'Orb*.
,, plicatilis, *Sow*.

Belemnites, bones of Saurians, and specimens of *Gryphæa dilatata*, Sow., also abound in these pits.

At Eastrea brickyard, clays, probably somewhat higher in the Oxfordian series, are exposed; these yield,—

Belemnites Puzosianus, *d'Orb* (very rare).
,, hastatus, *Blainv*.
Ammonites Lambertii, *Sow*.
Rhynchonella varians, *Sow*.
Saurian remains.

At the brickyard at Eyebury a number of interesting vertebrate remains have been collected by Mr. Leeds. Some of these are now in the Oxford Museum. The clays at this place have yielded a considerable number of specimens of *Terebratula impressa*, Von Buch.

Near Eye several pits opened in the Oxfordian strata expose beds of blue clay with *Gryphæa dilatata*, Sow., and numerous *Belemnites* and *Ammonites*.

At Eye Green a thin ferruginous stony seam occurs in the midst of the Oxford Clay. At this place there are found in the clays great numbers of *Ammonites* in all stages of growth, including many varieties of *Ammonites Jason*, Rein., and *A. ornatus*, Schloth : *Belemnites Puzosianus*, d'Orb, is very rare here. while *B. gracilis*, Phill., is abundant. *Terebratula impressa*, Von Buch, also occurs at this locality.

At Thorney there is an excellent section of the Oxford Clay, it being here dug to a considerable depth. *Ammonites* of the *Ornati* and *Armati* groups are abundant, but the specimens are usually encrusted with pyrites. *Gryphæa dilatata*, Sow., occurs in prodigious numbers, but *Belemnites Puzosianus*, d'Orb, is very rare.

Outliers.—The outliers of Oxford Clay are almost always thickly covered with drift. Their boundaries are usually indicated by dotted lines upon the map, and in very few instances have any instructive sections been obtained in them. Under these circumstances it will be unnecessary to notice them in detail; the only sections observed were as follows:—

At Brigstock Parks a deep well, at one of the farmhouses, afforded unmistakeable evidence that, under the thick covering of Boulder Clay, the Oxford Clay occurs *in situ*. The extent and boundaries of this outlying patch are however purely hypothetical.

At Southwick there is a brickyard exhibiting the lowest strata of the Oxfordian series, which here consist of the light-coloured, sandy clays, and stony beds, representing the Kellaways Rock. These contain —

> Belemnites Puzosianus, *d'Orb*.
> Avicula expansa, *Phil*.
> Gryphæa bilobata, *Sow*.

As may be inferred from the account given of the formation in the preceding pages, the various clays of the Oxfordian series are extensively dug, for brick and tile-making, at many points within this area. The materials thus produced vary greatly in quality, at different places, owing to the great range of differences in mineral character which the clays from the several horizons in this formation present when compared with one another. The most conspicuous of these differences, and that which has the greatest effect in determining the characters of the materials manufactured from the clays, consists in the proportion and quality of the sand occurring in admixture with the plastic mass.

As the Oxford Clay is so frequently covered with drift within this area, it exerts but a comparatively small direct influence on the nature of the soils.

CHAPTER X.

THE POST TERTIARY DEPOSITS.

These deposits, as already pointed out, are of far later date than those we have been describing, and lie indifferently and unconformably upon the whole of them. Their classification and nomenclature is in a much more unsettled and unsatisfactory condition than that of the Jurassic rocks. The divisions and terminology employed in this memoir must be regarded as provisional only, as they may be to some extent modified and corrected by future investigations. Nevertheless, though different conclusions may ultimately be arrived at as to the age of certain of these beds of gravel and sand, yet their boundaries as indicated upon the map will not be affected thereby; it should, however, be remembered that these boundaries are themselves usually much less clearly defined than those of the Jurassic rocks, and hence they have been represented only by faint dotted lines.

As the survey of the drifts in the sheets to the south of 64 is not yet completed, and the map of the superficial deposits of the latter as yet unpublished, only a very general sketch of the characters presented by these overlying formations will be included in the present memoir; and in this sketch attention will be principally directed to the illustration of their relation to the older formations, the description of which is the chief object of this memoir. Descriptive memoirs on the drifts of the Midland district and on the geology of the Fenland will be eventually published by the Geological Survey.

The great mass of Boulder Clay, with its associated gravels and sands, which occupies so large an area in this sheet, marks a grand and well defined epoch in the deposition of the Post-Tertiary beds, which is known as the *Glacial-Period*. Hence we have classed all the beds of this age as the Glacial Series. There are certain Post-Tertiary deposits which everywhere underlie these Glacial Beds, and are therefore of older date than them; while others were, as clearly, deposited at periods subsequent to the Glacial epoch, for they are found lying upon the glacial beds, and contain materials derived from them. Hence the Post-Tertiary beds fall naturally into three groups—the Pre-Glacial, the Glacial, and the Post-Glacial. (*See* the Table on page 56.)

In the present state of the inquiry I have not felt myself justified in discussing the relation of the drifts in this area to those of the East Anglian and north-western districts of England. It may be, as suggested by Mr. Searles Wood, Junr., that the Boulder Clay of the district under consideration only represents the younger of two distinct glacial series, and that the deposits which, in this district, are *Pre*-glacial will have to be grouped in a more general classification as *Mid*-glacial.

A. PRE-GLACIAL DEPOSITS.

In this division are included a series of deposits of marine, fluviatile, or estuarine origin, which are found lying directly upon the various Secondary rocks of the district, and are covered by the Boulder Clay or other glacial deposits.

a. Pre-glacial Valley gravels.—These consist of well stratified gravels, composed almost wholly of the detritus of the Jurassic rocks. In this respect they offer a very marked contrast with all the gravels of Post-Glacial age, which usually contain abundance of chalk-flints, and pebbles of rocks foreign to the district, these having been derived from the Boulder Clay. These gravels, which are never of great horizontal extent, are seen either skirting the edges of areas of Boulder Clay or capping hills from which that deposit has evidently been denuded. In certain sections they are seen to lie directly upon, and to fill up hollows in, the Jurassic rocks, and to be covered with Boulder Clay, often of very great thickness. One of the best sections illustrating this fact is that in the gravel pit a little to the north of Upper-Benefield. (*See* woodcut, Fig. 16.)

Fig. 16.   *Section in gravel-pit, near Upper Benefield.*

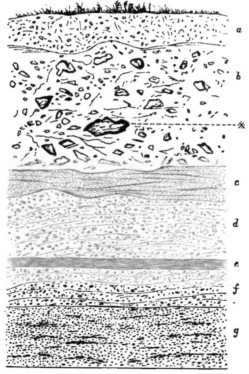

a. Soil - - - - - - 1 to 2 ft.
b. Boulder Clay (*Boulder of Red Chalk) - - 6 ft.
c. Finely-laminated, greenish sand with seams of clay 12 to 20 inches.
d. Irregularly stratified fine gravel - - - 3 ft.
e. Clay-band - - - - 6 inches.
f. Irregularly stratified fine gravel - - - 2 ft.
g. Fine sand, with seams of irregularly stratified gravel, bottom not seen - - - 3 feet.

Pre-Glacial series.

Another interesting exposure of these Pre-glacial gravels is seen near Newell Wood, between Pickworth and Holywell. (Fig. 17.)

Fig. 17. Gravel-pit on South side of Newell Wood.

a. Soil - - - - - - - - - 1 ft.
b. Light-blue clay with a few fragments of chalk and flint
    (Boulder Clay) - - - - - - 1 to 2 ft.
c. Reddish-brown sands with a few pebbles and waterworn
    fragments of ironstone - - - - - 12 to 18 inches.
d. Well stratified gravels, almost wholly made up of pebbles (all well water-
    worn) of the Lincolnshire Oolite Limestone with some of the harder beds
    of the Northampton Sand.

Note.—The upper surface of these gravels is very irregular, the sands and clays above being let down into the hollows of its surface.

Frequently we find at a similar level upon opposite sides of a modern valley, or at two points on the skirts of the same outlier of Boulder Clay, small patches of this gravel, and in some cases evidence has been obtained in wells, of the existence of these gravels at intermediate points under the Boulder Clay. All the characters presented by these point to the conclusion that they occupy the beds of old rivers which drained the country before the deposition of the great marine glacial series. It is even possible, by comparing the positions and levels of these patches of gravel, to arrive at some approximate results as to the courses in which these old pre-glacial rivers flowed. The existence of similar old river channels under the Boulder Clay of Scotland has been described by Messrs. Croll[*] and R. Dick.[†] At Ring Haw Wood, one mile west of Yarwell, we have a section of these beds displaying very interesting features. Lying on the Great Oolite we find beds of white gravel 8 to 12 feet thick, made up of water-worn fragments of the Lincolnshire Oolite limestone. This white gravel gradually passes up into, and is covered by, beds of dark brown gravel, made up almost exclusively of the detritus of the Northampton Sand. Bearing in mind the relative position of these parent rocks, we are at once led to conclude that the river, which formed this gravel, must have flowed from the west, and have cut its valley in the higher part of its course, first through the Lincolnshire Oolite and then down into the Northampton Sand. In some places, as near Holywell Lodge, we find these gravels cemented by calcareous matter into great masses of solid rock.

b. Pre-glacial brick-earths.—There is only one point within the limits of Sheet 64 at which I have found these beds exposed, namely in the brickyards at Melton Mowbray. Similar beds, however, occur at Billesdon, at Moulton, near Northampton, and at a number of points in the district of the Keuper. In all cases they appear to be formed of the detritus of a local rock, rearranged and finely stratified. At Melton this local rock is the clay of the Lower Lias, and the beds might at the first glance be easily mistaken for the undisturbed beds of the Lias, especially as they include numerous derived fossils from that formation. At this place these brick-earths are overlaid by beds of sand, and these by the ordinary Boulder Clay, which near here attains a thickness, as proved by well sections and borings, of not less than 200 feet.

c. Pre-glacial Sands and Gravels.—These beds, which are much more widely distributed than the two former classes, present very variable characters. Sometimes they consist of beds of well stratified sand, with a few well rounded pebbles; but they pass by insensible gradations into gravels, in no respect different from those intercalated in the Boulder Clay, and from which they are only distinguished by their position below that formation. They are probably of marine origin, but as yet, unfortunately, neither bones nor shells have been detected in any of the Pre-glacial beds of this district; and we have no palæontological evidence to assist us in determining their age.

---

* On two river channels buried under drift, belonging to a period when the land stood several hundred feet higher than at present, by James Croll. Trans. Edinb. Geol. Soc., Vol. I. p. 330.

† On the discovery of a " Sand-dyke " or old River Channel running north and south from near Kirk of Shotts to Wishaw, Lanarkshire, by Robert Dick. *Ibid,* p. 345.

d Pre-glacial? Lacustrine deposit.—In the Casewick cutting of the Great Northern Railway a deposit, of small extent, containing plants and shells of freshwater and terrestrial species, was observed and described by Professor Morris.* This deposit occupies a depression in the Kellaways beds, and is covered by gravels, which apparently belong to the glacial series. It seems to have been accumulated in a shallow pond or small lake; but its precise geological age is very doubtful.

Professor MORRIS' description of the section exposed in the Casewick cutting at the time of the construction of the Great Northern Railway is as follows:—

"*Casewick Cutting. Freshwater beds.* The Casewick cutting traverses oolitic rock, which represents the Kellaway, Rock and Oxford Clay. These strata are overlaid by a deposit of gravel 7 or 8 feet thick. Towards the central part of the cutting a freshwater deposit is intercalated between the oolite and gravel, occupying an excavation in the surface of the former. This deposit is about 30 yards in width; and it has an average thickness of about 8 feet, and varies in thickness and character on each side of the cutting. It consists in the upper part of grey sandy clay, 2 feet; brown sandy clay and veins of gravel, 1½ foot; a layer of peaty clay with fragments of plants and shells, 1½ foot; dark sandy clay, with plants and shells, pebbles of chalk and flint, and portions of the northern clay drift in fragments. The base of the deposit is extremely irregular in outline (see Fig. 18 c.), and the surface of the oolitic stratum is slightly disturbed and re-aggregated, as it is throughout the cutting. The following is the list of shells†:—

Bithinia tentaculata and opercula, plentiful.
Valvata piscinalis, plentiful.
———— cristata, rather rare.
Planorbis marginatus, rare.
———— carinatus.
———— imbricatus, only one.
Limneus pereger, rare and immature.
Succinea putris, rare and immature.
Ancylus fluviatilis, rather plentiful.
Veletia lacustris, rather plentiful.
Cyclas cornea, rare : fragments.
Pisidium amnicum, rather rare.
———— pulchellum ⎫
———— pusillum ⎬ mostly immature.
———— obtusale? ⎭
Helix hispida, rare.
———— pulchella, only two.

Fig. 18. Section of the Gravel, Freshwater Bed, and the Oolites of the Casewick cutting. Length, 29 chains. Vertical scale, 120 feet to 1 inch.

a. Gravel and sand in wavy seams.
b. Sand and fine gravel with *Belemnites*, &c.
c. Freshwater deposit.
d. Sandy bed of the Oxford Clay.

e. Sandy rock (Kellaways).
f. Dark laminated Oxford Clay.
g. Cornbrash, along the base of the cutting.

(Inserted by permission of Professor MORRIS and the Council of the Geological Society.)

* *Quart. Journ. Geol. Soc.*, vol. ix. (1853), p. 321, Fig. 2.
† "The above list has been corrected by Mr. PICKERING, who has kindly examined some portions of the clay from this deposit. To Mr. T. R. JONES I am obliged for determining the above mentioned Cyprides."

Helix aculeata (young), only one.
Carychium minimum, only two.
Cypris (small species), one valve.
? Candona lucens (young), one valve.
Candona reptans, three valves.

Spine of Echinus - - -	⎫
Belemnites - - - - -	⎪
Arca - - - - -	These are
Cerithium - - - - -	derived from
Other casts and fragments of marine animals - - - -	the Oxford Clay. ⎬
Seeds and other vegetable remains, as Ceratophyllum, Equisetum, &c. -	⎭

The freshwater deposit on one side of the cutting appeared to be intercalated with the superincumbent gravel, but on the eastern side there appeared a well-defined line between it and the overlying gravel, as if the freshwater deposit had been eroded ; the gravel forming a continuous and uniform covering over this bed and the adjacent sandy and argillaceous strata, in a depression of which the freshwater bed had been previously accumulated. The gravel deposit ' consists, chiefly of rounded and angular flints, rolled quartz pebbles, and a few other rocks, as oolite, &c., and some small sandstone boulders, irregularly stratified with occasional layers of small pebbles, seams of clay and loam, and others much mixed with a chalky paste, the larger pebbles occurring at the base. The gravel overlies 3 feet of greyish brown sandy clay, containing fragments of *Belemnites* and *Gryphœa*, with veins of gravel at the upper part, which is irregular and wavy."

Three miles to the westward, in the valley of the Gwash, another freshwater deposit, about 6 feet thick, intercalated with gravel, has been met with ; it contains land shells, &c., and bones, and may be of slightly later date than the one above described.

B. GLACIAL DEPOSITS.

This division includes a great mass of deposits, which, although they have suffered very extensive denudation, yet are often of great thickness in this district; in places probably not less than 300 feet. They were evidently deposited during a period of intense cold, in which the land had undergone very extensive submergence; that portion of it which remained above the sea appears to have been enveloped with great glaciers, like those which are now only found in the arctic and antarctic regions, while all over the bed of the ocean transported fragments of rock were dropped by floating icebergs.

a. Glacial or Boulder Clay.—No formation occupies so large an area in this sheet as the great mass of clay usually crowded with fragments of all sizes of rocks, for the most part foreign to the district, and which is known as the Glacial or Boulder Clay. This clay where unweathered is usually of a blue colour, and though it occasionally appears to be rudely stratified, yet it is generally characterised by the absence of any regular arrangement in its materials, the confused heaping together of which is a most striking feature. The rock fragments included in it, which often exhibit the polishing, striation, and grooving characteristic of glacier- or iceberg-borne masses, consist of very various materials ; chalk and flint being the most abundant, especially in the eastern part of the area. In places the chalk is so abundant

that the bed is little more than a reconstructed mass of that rock,
and even produces the vegetation which characterises the chalk
soils. Thus the Rev. M. J. Berkeley informs me that he, many
years ago, found growing on a patch of very chalky Boulder Clay
at Benefield specimens of the *Orchis ustulata*, Linn.; a species
which is usually confined to chalk downs and never appears on non-
calcareous soils. It was probably a patch of this kind at Ridlington
in Rutland which led to a notice in the Philosophical Transaction
for 1821 on the discovery of chalk in that county, which has been
referred to both by Mr. Lonsdale and Dr. Fitton.* Next in
abundance to the fragments of chalk and flint, are those of the
Jurassic rocks, which become more numerous in the western part
of the area; then follow blocks of coal-measure sandstone, millstone-grit, and carboniferous limestone, while the older Palæozoic
and granitic rocks are comparatively rarely represented. The
Boulder Clay is found in many places capping the hills composed
of Jurassic rocks; but in other cases it may be seen extending to
the bottom of some of the deepest valleys, and it even underlies a
portion of the Fens. It appears to have been spread like a great
mantle over the surface of the denuded and submerged older
rocks. When a junction is seen, these latter often present the
appearance of having been eroded or reconstructed to the depth
of several feet before the deposition of the Boulder Clay.

The far transported boulders in this district do not generally
attain to any great size, though blocks of coal-measure sandstone
and millstone-grit up to six feet in diameter are occasionally
met with, as at Upton and Hallaton, which have been left on the
surface by the denudation of the enclosing Boulder Clay. But
the transported masses of local rocks are sometimes of enormous
size, especially in the northern portion of this area, and in that to
the north (Sheet 70). The attention of geologists was first directed
to these great transported masses by Professor Morris, who found
that at the south end of the Stoke tunnel on the Great Northern
Railway, an enormous mass of the Lincolnshire Oolite limestone
lay on undoubted Boulder Clay. During the mapping by Messrs.
Holloway, Skertchly, and myself, of the districts which I have indicated, we have found a number of such transported masses, some
of them far exceeding in size that described by Professor Morris,
and composed both of the Inferior Oolite and the Marlstone
Rock-bed. The position of these transported masses is indicated
upon the drift map. They always appear to occur in the lower
part of the Boulder Clay; and by the denudation of the softer
surrounding material often make a distinct boss, rising above the
general surface. Stone pits are often opened in them, and they
sometimes give off springs at their base. The largest of these
transported masses, that capping Beacon Hill in Sheet 70, is
more than 200 yards across and is composed of the Marlstone
Rock-bed. It is noteworthy that these masses always belong to

---

* *Phil. Trans.*, vol. lxxxi. pt. 2, p. 281, referred to by Dr. FITTON in *Trans. Geol.
Soc.*, 2nd ser., vol. iv., p. 308, and notes, p. 388*.

the rocks which form the highest ground, and, which in the glacial submergence would constitute the last points remaining above water. The only agency, it appears to me, by which these enormous masses could have been transported, is that of floating ice. Some of the masses of the Marlstone Rock-bed have been carried across deep valleys, a distance of probably not less than 30 miles.

b. Glacial Gravels.—These consist of an accumulation of fragments of rock, often of considerable size, and, not unfrequently, retaining their glacial markings; they often exhibit the most remarkably contorted stratification. Their materials are almost identical with those of the boulders in the Boulder Clay, consisting of rounded fragments of hard chalk, often in prodigious abundance, angular flints, masses of Oolitic, Liassic, and Carboniferous rocks with some from older formations. Indeed these gravels might aptly be described as Boulder Clay in which, from the action of some local cause, the argillaceous matrix has not been deposited. These gravels are in some places seen to be actually interstratified with the ordinary chalky Boulder Clay, and at times to pass insensibly into it; while they are often found, through denudation, capping hills of Boulder Clay; they are quite as often found underlying a great thickness of that deposit. It is an interesting and significant circumstance, that in the western parts of the district, where the glacial series occupies the highest grounds, these gravels acquire great importance, while in the eastern part of the area they are generally confined to thin seams and patches in the midst of the Boulder Clay. Probably we should be right in regarding the glacial gravels as exhibiting the littoral condition of the Boulder Clay.

Sometimes these beds of gravel are very violently contorted, exhibiting evidences of just such lateral pressure as would be produced by the grounding of icebergs. A good typical section of these greatly contorted glacial gravels is exhibited in the large pit between Whadborough and Ouston. (*See* Fig. 19, p. 248)

As is well known, similarly highly contorted beds are not unfrequently found in the midst of the Glacial Series, as in the cliffs of Norfolk, Suffolk, &c. · These remarkable appearances have been variously interpreted in different cases; by the grounding of icebergs, the thrusting up of ice-floes on a shelving coast during storms, and the melting of great masses of ice, enclosed in the deposits of mud and sand.

Although some geologists have attempted to show that the great glacial formations composed of clay, and sand or gravel, respectively, belong to perfectly distinct periods and mark different climatal and physical conditions in the Midland district of England, and even entire changes in the disposition of the land and sea of the period; yet nothing can be clearer that in the area we are more particularly describing the beds of glacial clay, sand and gravel, replace one another in the most capricious manner, and are evidently dependent on the action of causes of extremely local character.

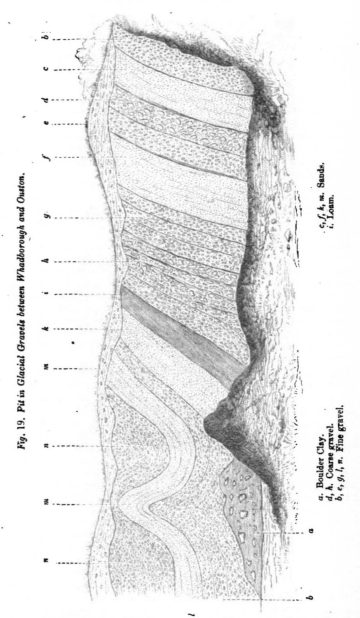

Fig. 19. *Pit in Glacial Gravels between Whadborough and Ouston.*

c, f, k, m. Sands.
i. Loam.

a. Boulder Clay.
d, h. Coarse gravel.
b, e, g, l, n. Fine gravel.

c. Glacial Sands.—These are coarse, siliceous sands usually of
a red colour, and with much false bedding, sometimes, as near

Pickwell, attaining a considerable thickness and being interstratified with the other glacial deposits. Their relations to the Boulder Clay are identical with those of the last described beds, into which, indeed, they sometimes pass by insensible gradations.

C. Post Glacial Deposits.

In this group we include all those masses of material, which, from actual superposition, or from the fact of their containing derived fragments of the glacial beds, are inferred to be of later date than the last mentioned.

a. Cave Deposits.—The facility with which all limestone rocks are hollowed into caverns by the solvent action of subterranean waters is frequently illustrated in this district; but the rapidity with which the Oolitic rocks undergo denudation has probably, in most cases, prevented such caverns from being the means of preserving the exuviæ of extinct animals like the great caves of the Carboniferous and other older and harder limestone rocks. The only point within the limits of Sheet 64 at which a cavern has been found is at Tinkler's Quarry near Stamford. Here, during the quarrying operations about 30 years ago, a small cave was met with, the earth on the floor of which contained the teeth and bones of Carnivora, Ruminants, and Elephants. All traces of this cavern, which was of no great size, have disappeared in consequence of the continued working of the quarry, and the remains found in it appear to have become scattered. Fortunately however some of them have been secured for scientific examination by the zeal of S. Sharp, Esq., formerly a resident at Stamford. These were submitted to Professor Rolleston of Oxford, who pronounced them to be as follows :—

Hyæna. Teeth of two individuals.
Elephas. Portion of a tooth of a small individual.
Cervus megaceros. Tooth.
Cervidæ. Various remains.

The long bones appear to have been in all cases broken for the extraction of the marrow, and in some instances they exhibit indications of having been gnawed.

I was unable to obtain exact information as to the size of this cave: by some, who saw it, it is said to have been from 15 to 20 ft. square, by others, to have resembled only a large fissure. There can be no doubt that this, like the caves of Settle and Kirkdale in Yorkshire, the caves of the Vale of Clwyd in North Wales, the Gower Caves in Glamorganshire, Wookey Hole in Somersetshire, and other similar caverns, was once the den of hyenas, and that the other bones belonged to animals which had been seized and carried, by the carnivores, to their lair to be devoured.

b. Valley Gravels.—These gravels are found occupying the bottoms and sides of the existing river valleys, and in some places extending to elevations of from 40 to 50, or even a great number of feet, above the present levels of the rivers. They are at once distinguished from the pre-glacial valley gravels, before noticed, not only by their relations to the present system of drainage, but by being composed of materials evidently derived from the Boulder Clay of the district, such as chalk flints and fragments of Palæozoic rocks, and mingled with the detritus, derived directly from the beds of the Jurassic series. The pre-glacial valley gravels consist, as we have already seen, of the latter class of materials only. It is along the valleys of the Nene and Welland that we find the largest deposits of these gravels; but along the sides of some of the minor valleys, such as those of the Chater, the Gwash, and the Glen, fringes of similar gravels are also found. At some points, as about Elton, the passage of water through these masses of gravel has, by the solution and re-deposition of calcareous matter, resulted in the formation of indurated masses like those described as occurring in the pre-glacial gravels.

Along some of the larger valleys, these gravels may be classed as belonging to two different series, according to their elevation above the present level of the river; and these are called the high-level and low-level valley gravels.

Occasionally the valley gravels yield shells which are found to be all of a fresh-water character and belong to species still living in the rivers which now occupy the valleys. Such shells are by no means common in the valley gravels of this area, and are very local in their mode of occurrence. It is only where a thin seam of sandy loam occurs interstratified with the gravels that we have usually any chance of detecting such molluscan remains preserved.

Mammalian remains however are much more common in the district, and local collectors might probably, by watching the excavation of some of the large gravel pits of the district, obtain interesting series of such fossils. As is well known the mammalia, represented by the bones, teeth, &c. found in these gravels, include species altogether extinct and others now only found in far distant regions; and these are mingled with remains of forms still living in the area. The tusks and teeth of elephants, with the teeth of the rhinoceros, hippopotamus, hyæna, and horse, and the horns of the red-deer and urus occur in the valley gravels of this district.

These valley gravels have of late years attracted much attention owing to the discovery in them of flint implements, undoubtedly fashioned by human agency and associated with the remains of extinct mammalia. No such discovery of flint implements has as yet, however, been found within the limits of Sheet 64.

At some points, as New England, near Peterborough, the valley gravels are found to be covered by deposits of loam crowded with terrestrial shells of recent species. These loams appear to be analogous in their character, and mode of occurrence, with the continental "Loess."

c. Estuarine Gravels.—The valley gravels afford ample evidence that the existing rivers formerly flowed at much higher elevations than at present. We have also clear proof that, at the periods when these higher level gravels were formed, the whole of the flat lands of the fens were submerged beneath the sea, and the estuaries of the Nene and Welland were at the points now occupied by the towns of Peterborough and Deeping. At some distance above these points the gravels, which form a continuation of the valley gravels just noticed and serve to form a link between them and the marine deposits of the Fenland, were of estuarine character and contain an admixture of fluviatile and marine shells. Such estuarine gravels have been found at Peterborough and at Overton Waterville. At the latter locality they have yielded *Ostræa edulis, Cardium edule, Planorbis carinatus, Ancylus fluviatilis, Bithinia tentaculata, Lymnea glütinosa, Pisidium amnicum,* &c. With these shells were associated the remains of *Elephas primigeneus, Rhinoceros tichorinus, Equus caballus, Canis lupus, Hyæna spelæa, Cervus elaphus, Bos primigenius,* &c.

d. Marine Gravels of the Fenland.—As the ordinary valley gravels graduate into the estuarine gravels, so these last pass insensibly into the marine gravels of the Fenland. In the materials of which they are composed, indeed, these several gravels are quite indistinguishable from one another, and the classification adopted for them is based on their geological relation and the nature of their organic remains. The gravels of the Fenland sometimes contain an abundance of marine shells and some marine mammalia, these being mingled with the bones, teeth, and horns of the same terrestrial species as occur in the estuarine and fluviatile gravels. The marine shells are almost all of existing species, and such as inhabit neighbouring seas; they usually present a marked littoral facies. Among those most commonly found are *Cardium edule, Littorina littorea, Turritella communis, Buccinum undatum, Tellina solidula, Ostrea edulis, Mytilus edulis, Cyprina Islandica,* &c. The only indication of the prevalence of climatal conditions differing from those of the neighbouring shores which I have found in these gravels, is the abundance of *Cyprina Islandica,* a shell which, however, occurs in sufficient abundance on the coast of Yorkshire, only a little distance to the northwards.

These marine gravels evidently formed beaches surrounding the old sea which once covered the Fenland, and they are clearly seen, not only at the boundary between the Fens and the higher land surrounding it, but forming belts round the numerous islands, composed of Oxford Clay or Boulder Clay, which diversify the surface of the former. In some cases the gravels are found extending to considerable distances below the silt and peat of the fens; and such deposits may mark the gradual extension of marine conditions over the area in consequence of subsidence. The marine gravels of the Fenland may therefore be considered as representing the littoral condition of a considerable series of deposits, among which are the silts to be hereafter noticed that were formed while the greater part of the district was covered by the sea : the small eminences which now make such marked features in the Fens, such as those occupied by the towns of

Whittlesea and Crowland, and the villages of Eye, Thorney, &c. then forming islands or shoals.

e. Peat interstratified with Marine silt.—Over the southern part of that area of the Fenland included within the limits of Sheet 64, extensive beds of peat, intercalated with marine silt, occur at the surface, but to the northwards these are covered under a greater or less thickness of the marine warp deposited by tidal waters, which we shall have to further notice hereafter. The former district is distinguished by the prevailing black colour of the soil, while that of the latter exhibits a marked reddish tint : while the former, too, is comparatively infertile and can only be rendered of service to the farmer by extensive operations of trenching and "claying" (that is digging the substratum of Oxford Clay or Boulder Clay and spreading it over the surface); the latter is, as soon as it is drained, remarkable for its great productiveness.

There are usually two, and occasionally more, beds of peat, varying in thickness in different places, and separated by masses of marine silt. The peat, as is well known, is made up of vegetable remains, those of a species of *Sphagnum* constituting a great part of the mass. Trees of large size, including the oak, birch, and other species still growing in the country, are very frequently dug out of the peat. The remains of animals which once roamed through these old forests are also very commonly found. Among the most abundant of these are the wild oxen (*Bos primigenius and B. frontosus*), the Irish elk, the wild boar, the red deer, bear, otter, beaver, wolf, fox, &c.

The marine silt which is interstratified with the peat, and indicates the occasional submergence of the old terrestrial surface beneath the surface of the sea, is generally of a light-blue or grey colour and is locally known as the "buttery clay." Marine shells such as *Ostrea edulis, Cardium edule, Scrobicularia piperata*, are occasionally met with in it, but are by no means common ; many very beautiful species of Foraminifera have, however, been collected from it. The remains of marine mammalia, such as the whale and seal, are by no means uncommon in it.

The substratum of the peat, &c. of the fens is usually the Oxford Clay which is locally known as "galt." In some places, however, the Boulder Clay is found lying immediately below the peat and silt; and sometimes, where the peat is thin, beds of sand and gravel occur.

The removal of the water from the peat, by drainage operations, causes a great contraction in the mass and, in consequence, a subsidence of the surface, which is often of very considerable amount. An interesting example of this may be seen in the main line of the Great Northern Railway where it crosses the Fenland in this area. Although, originally laid quite level, yet, when the eye is placed at the surface of the ground the rails are now seen to form a well marked curve, owing to this subsidence. At St. Mary's Station, in consequence of the shrinkage of the peat, one wall has had to be built on the top of another, which has been swallowed up. Near Holme, an iron column erected upon the foundation of the subjacent Oxford Clay shows that a contraction of the superficial deposits of the fens, in that place, to the extent of seven feet has occurred since 1848.

The peat is extensively dug and used locally for fuel. It is possible that a more extended application of this material, so abundant in the district, may result from some of the important methods of treatment for it which have been invented during the last few years. The marine silt is sometimes dug for brick-making. Some years ago it was worked for this purpose at Crowland, which is within the district described in this Memoir. .

f. Alluvium of the Old Fen Lakes.—Within recent years the old lakes or "meres" of the Fenland have all been drained, and the sites of Wittlesea Mere, Ramsey Mere, Ugg Mere, and others are now only marked by patches of alluvium or freshwater silt. These lacustrine deposits are of a light-gray colour, and often so crowded with shells of *Unio, Anodon, Paludina, Planorbis, Lymnea*, &c., as to constitute a shell marl, which imparts fertility to the land once occupied by the lakes. These lake alluvia are, however, usually of insignificant thickness, and the operations of the farmer are rapidly obliterating even these traces of the once famous Whittlesea Mere and other similar lakes; of which there will soon remain nothing but the name.

g. Alluvium of the present Rivers.—The flat bottoms of the valleys of the existing rivers are covered with a fine black loam or silt which is still in process of formation, a constant accession to, and redistribution of, its material taking place as the result of ordinary river action. This loam is often crowded with the shells of those molluscs which live on terrestrial surfaces or in marshes; and the deposit, which is in course of accumulation, in every respect resembles that found at higher levels in connexion with the old valley gravels, and which, as we have already stated, presents so striking a resemblance to the continental "Loess." The flats formed by these alluvial deposits, which are very extensive in the valleys of the Nene and Welland, are, during the winter season, for the most part under water; they are distinguished for their great fertility and constitute most admirable grazing lands.

h. Marine Alluvium or Warp of the Fenland.—With the recent deposits just noticed as still undergoing accumulation we must notice the marine silts, which by the action of tidal waters are formed in the "washes" of the Fens. Beds of this character are, however, of very limited extent within the limits of Sheet 64, being confined to the Cowbit and Crowland Washes. Except where beds of peat intervene, it is impossible to separate these deposits, which are still being formed, from the old marine silt before noticed as being probably of the same age with the gravels which surround the Fenland.

CHAPTER XI.

POSITION AND DISTURBANCES OF THE STRATA, FAULTS &c.

General Dip.—As already intimated, the whole of the Jurassic Rocks rise steadily towards the N.W. corner of Sheet 64, so that, in that part of the area, beds as low in the series as the Marlstone Rock-bed form very prominent hills, rising to heights of more than 700 feet above the sea level; while the beds of Oxford Clay form the substratum of the Fens in the S.E. corner of the map. A line drawn from the Roman Camp, on Burrow on the Hill, to Peterborough passes in succession over all the Jurassic rocks, from the Marlstone to the Cornbrash inclusive, and is about 27 miles long; while the first-mentioned spot is, however, more than 700 feet above the sea the latter is only between 20 and 30 feet above high-water mark. Knowing the thickness of the different strata of the Upper Lias and Lower Oolites, we have thus the necessary data required for calculating the general dip of the strata between the two localities. This is found to amount to about 1 in 120 or 44 feet per mile.

This area which, as we have shown, is so remarkably interesting from exhibiting an almost totally new succession of beds, as compared with the Oolites of the south of England, the Cotteswolds and Oxfordshire, presents likewise some noteworthy phenomena in the character of the disturbances which its beds have undergone.

Foremost among these we must call attention to the remarkable change which takes place in the direction of the dip and strike of the Jurassic strata. From the Cotteswold Hills to the northern boundary of Northamptonshire, the strike of all the Secondary strata is from N.E. to S.W., and their dip from N.W. to S.E. Throughout Lincolnshire and South Yorkshire, however, the strike is changed to nearly due N. and S., and the dip to E. and W. The line at which this change of direction takes place nearly coincides with that at which the Welland and its tributary streams has made a breach through the scarped table-lands formed by the Middle Lias and the Inferior Oolite beds. It is noteworthy that along this line occur the two greatest faults of the district, namely, that passing by Billesdon and Loddington and that from Tinwell to Walton. Between these occur a number of smaller faults running in the same general W. by N., and E. by S., direction, with others transverse to them. In pointing out this fact, it is of course not sought to be intimated that the existing valley of the Welland has been directly produced by the faults in question; although, by throwing down the softer beds against those less susceptible to denuding forces, by determining the initial course of streams when the land rose at successive periods above the sea-level, and by the influence which they can scarcely have failed to produce on the contours of the surface, they have doubtless directed, controlled, and modified the effects of subaërial forces. The subterranean action to which these faults are due must have acted side by side with the meteoric forces in producing the existing forms of the surface ; and in this manner have contributed to the definition of the position and form of the valley in question.

Through the long line of the Cotteswold Hills and to the southwards, it is noticeable that the strike of the Jurassic rocks again becomes nearly due N. and S., or nearly parallel to that of the strata of Lincolnshire. Where the change of strike takes place we have here again a number of important faults ; namely, those producing, by the downthrow of the Inferior Oolite, the great outlying masses of Bredon, Dumbleton, and Oxenton Hills ; those traversing the great Cotteswold plateau ; and those which, in the country S.W. of Banbury, throw the Northampton Sand and the Marlstone Rock-bed into such frequent close proximity, and have thus been the occasion of difficulty to many early observers who ought to study the order of succession of beds in the area. The direction of these great lines of faults is nearly identical with that of those we have alluded to in Sheet 64. In North Yorkshire the line of strike of the Jurassic beds again changes to N.E. and S.W. At the line along which this change takes place the Jurassic strata are almost wholly concealed by the overlapping of the unconformable Upper Cretaceous rocks. There are indications however, that transverse faults do occur at this line of change of strike and dip, as well as the others already noticed.

Although the general dip is, as we have noticed, of small amount in the area we are describing, the beds are affected by a great number of local dips ; these are like the perturbations which affect a planetary orbit, but do not seriously interfere with the great curves in which the body moves. Such minor curves can only be detected where the geological lines are capable of being exactly followed over considerable areas, though their effects are often manifest in the preservation of small outliers and inliers. When, however, the strata of a district are exposed in a sea-cliff, as on the Yorkshire coast, these long sweeping curves, into which the strata are thrown, are sufficiently obvious, especially when they are seen foreshortened. Occasionally in railway-cuttings the same phenomenon is visible, and this is the case within the district under consideration in several of the very deep sections on the main line of the Great Northern Railway. Thus in the Danes' Hill cutting the strata evidently lie in a long shallow synclinal (see fig. 15, p. 196), and similar evidence of slight foldings of the beds are to be seen in other cuttings on the same line. Sometimes the same phenomenon is manifested when the small local dips are carefully observed. Cases of this kind occur north of Elton and elsewhere, and are recorded on the map. Precisely similar phenomena have been described in the case of the Cotteswold Hills by Professor Hull. (See Quart. Journ. Geol. Soc., vol. xi. (1855), p. 483). At a few points the strata are evidently bent into folds of a much more decided character. Thus at Helpstone brickyard the

Upper Lias Clay is brought up among the Lower Oolites, through the agency of a very sharp fold and the dips here amount to as much as 30°. This fold is situated close to, and is doubtless connected with, the great Tinwell and Walton Fault. The inlier of Upper Lias Clay seen at Thornhaugh is probably exposed in consequence of a similar but much less violent folding of the strata. At Wild's Ford, three miles west of Stamford, there is evidence of another small anticlinal and this is near to, and probably connected with, a small fault. Near Walton station the Cornbrash beds show signs of disturbance, and a small anticlinal can be traced. In the two small inliers of Brigstock Parks and Little Oakley the Inferior Oolites and Upper Lias have been subjected to a number of small rolls and faults, which do not affect the Great Oolite beds lying unconformably above them. One of these anticlinals is admirably exhibited in an old pit in the Northampton Sand opened in a field midway between Sudborough Lodge and the lodges in Brigstock Parks.

By far the largest amount of disturbance in the district is however due to the great faults which traverse it. The principal of these cross the area in a W. by N. and E. by S. direction. They have occasioned downthrows towards the N., some in places amounting to not less than 150 feet.

The Billesdon and Loddington Fault has produced a very marked effect on the geological configuration of the country. The lateral displacement occasioned by it has thrown the outcrop of the Marlstone Rock-bed far from its normal position, and caused it to form the two great spurs culminating in Billesdon Coplow and Burrow Hill respectively. It has also been the cause of the preservation of a large tract occupied by the Upper Lias Clay and of the interesting outliers of Northampton Sand capping Whadborough Hill, Robin-a-Tiptoes, Barrow Hill and another hill behind Loddington. Colborough Hill, too, though now entirely formed of Upper Lias Clay, evidently owes its form and preservation to a cap of the Northampton Sand, which certainly once existed at its summit, but has now been wholly removed by denudation. The actual junctions along this line of fault are often much concealed by great masses of Glacial gravel and Boulder Clay. Where these are cut through by streams, as near Tilton Wood, south of Wildbore's Lodge, and at Loddington some very interesting cases of the juxtaposition of beds of different age may be made out. This fault appears to diminish in amount towards the E. ; but towards the W. it can no longer be traced, as it traverses a district composed of various Lower Lias beds almost wholly of an argillaceous character, which are deeply covered by drift. The portion of this fault which is determinable is about 7 miles long.

The great Tinwell and Walton Fault has a throw, probably of at least equal amount with the last and, traversing, as it does, a number of comparatively thin and well marked strata, its effects are very striking, even to a superficial observer of the structure of the country. The curious manner in which the various beds of the

Lower Oolite and the Upper Lias are thrown together at different points is very interesting ; as can be seen by an inspection of the map; some of these junctions have been described in detail by Mr. Sharp in his valuable memoir. Among the points of special interest along this line, where its effects are strikingly exhibited, we may instance Stamford, where, on one side of the fault, the Inferior Oolite is seen, capping the hill south of the town, while on the other side of the fault it occupies the valley. At Helpstone brickyard, the effects of the fault are very conspicuous, for here, in combination with the anticlinal roll already mentioned, it brings into contact the Cornbrash and the Upper Lias Clay. To the action of this great fault is due the circumstance that, although on the south of the Welland valley at Stamford the plateau is formed of the lower beds of Lincolnshire Oolite, diversified by a number of inliers of Northampton Sand and Upper Lias Clay ; yet northwards of Stamford the plateau is formed of the highest beds of the Lincolnshire Oolite, over which a number of outliers of the various strata of the Great Oolite are scattered. The length of the Tinwell and Walton fault is about fourteen miles ; it appears to diminish in amount and at last to die out both towards the east and west.

At the town of Stamford, as proved by the different levels at which many of the springs arise, the district is complicated by several faults parallel to the great one just described; but the impossibility of obtaining reliable information concerning the wells and other artificial openings, as well as the small scale on which the map is constructed, has prevented their being indicated.

Between the two faults which we have just described, there are a number of smaller ones which have a parallel direction, and, lying in the country between them, may be presumed to belong to the same system of disturbance. These are the small faults at Whitwell, at Hambleton and Normanton, and at Lynton, the effects of which, in the displacement of the strata, will be sufficiently obvious to any one examining the map.

Running transversely to these E. and W. faults are a number of others which appear to be connected with them, but are of less amount and appear to represent cross fractures. They have a general N. and S. direction.

Such small faults are seen between Bainton and Barnack and east of Helpstone, on the downthrow side of the great Tinwell and Walton Fault. At Stamford is another similar fault which is of very great interest in consequence of the manner in which it is exhibited. Its effects, in throwing the Northampton Sand against the Lincolnshire Oolite, are sufficiently obvious in mapping the country; but, fortunately, the line of fault is actually crossed by a cutting at the Midland and North-Western Railway Station at Stamford. This interesting section is represented in Fig. 7, page 103.

Running southwards from Wild's Ford are several faults, one of which can be traced for a distance of eight miles, by Ketton and Duddington. Its effects are well exhibited in the broken strata of the Geeston cutting on the Midland Railway, and still

better by the interesting lateral displacement of the Cornbrash
and Great Oolite strata south of Duddington. This fault appears
to have its greatest throw in the central part of its course, west of
the village of Collyweston, but to gradually diminish in amount
and finally to die away both northwards and southwards. In
the outlier south of Duddington, the throw is probably about
40 or 50 feet. The neighbouring parallel faults do not present
any feature of special interest, and their effects are sufficiently
illustrated by the map.

To the westward we find, running through Pilton and near
Lyndon and Normanton towards Whitwell, a north and south
fault, of about four miles in length, which appears to be connected
with the three east and west faults already noticed. This fault
has been the cause of the preservation of some interesting small
outliers of Inferior Oolite.

Besides the faults already noticed, which appear to have a
connection with one another and to form a system traversing the
central part of the area described in this Memoir, there are a
number of other, generally small, dislocations which affect the
beds in other parts of the area. Some of these have a marked
parallelism with the two great faults described above, others
appear to have an equally marked transverse or north and south
direction, while in a few cases the direction does not enable us to
class them with either.

The interesting fault passing to the north of Elton has a
parallel direction, but an opposite throw, to that of the great Tinwell and Walton fault, from which it is distant six miles; its effects
are, however, much less marked, as the amount of vertical displacement of the beds is probably not more than 30 or 40 feet.
A similar, but shorter fault occurs on the opposite side of the
Welland near Yarwell.

The faults at Neville-Holt, Rockingham, Wilbarston, and
Stoke-Albany run in a nearly N.W. and S.E. direction. They
all appear to be of small vertical amount. The Neville-Holt
fault has produced an interesting result in the letting down, and
consequent preservation, of a mass of Northampton Sand and
Lincolnshire Oolite, now forming a very conspicuous outlier.
The Wilbarston fault is probably continuous with that which
runs through Pipwell, of which the effects are very marked. The
Stanion fault has a nearly parallel direction but an opposite
throw to the last, and consequently to a great extent reverses its
effects.

The N. and S. fault, which, by an upthrow on the W. gives rise
to the appearance of an inlier of Upper Lias and Northampton
Sand, in the course of the Willow Brook at Little Weldon, can
only be traced for a short distance on account of the thick covering
of Boulder Clay which conceals all the higher grounds.

Two other small faults of some interest remain to be noticed.
The first of these is that which passes near Sudborough, in the
sheet to the south of that now described (see Geol. Surv. Quart.
Sheet 52 N.E.), and which is continued in Sheet 64; the second
is the fault running by Stilton and producing great vertical dis-

placement, but of which the length cannot be determined, owing to its passing under the great drift deposits which cover the Oxford Clay country. By this fault a small patch of Cornbrash is thrown down in the midst of the Oxford Clay on the edge of the Fens.

The small faults which cross the inliers of Little Oakley and Brigstock Parks are of very little interest in themselves, but acquire importance from the facts, already sufficiently noticed, of their affecting only the Inferior Oolite and Lias beds, and not the unconformably overlying Great Oolite strata. The same is the case with a small fault shown in Quarter sheet 52 N.W. and just on the border of the district included within Sheet 64.

Illustrations of the manner in which the beds are found to be disturbed as they approach a fault, are seen at many points within the area now being described. One of the most marked examples, among many that might be mentioned, is seen at Hilly Wood, one mile south-west of Helpstone, where, by the Great Tinwell and Walton fault, the Cornbrash is thrown down against the Lincolnshire Oolite; the former is here seen to be bent up violently, in one place at an angle of 65°.

The connection which sometimes exists between faults and the outburst of mineral springs, appears to be illustrated within this area by the Neville-Holt Spa and the Stamford Spa. Possibly some of the other mineral springs to be hereafter mentioned may make their appearance on lines of fault which it has not been possible to detect.

That the faults mapped and described include all which traverse the area is by no means probable. Over considerable areas clays of enormous thickness prevail without any well defined hard beds, and among these it would be impossible to detect dislocations while running the geological lines; other large areas are hopelessly concealed from our observation by thick masses of Boulder Clay and other drifts. Of some of the faults actually detected it is not possible to trace more than a small part of their course, owing to the same causes.

The age of the production of the faults and flexures of the strata in this area cannot generally be fixed within very narrow limits. They have evidently been brought about in the course of some of the great movements which we know to have taken place during that enormous interval which elapsed between the Jurassic period and the deposition of the drifts. An exception must be made in the case of the small foldings and dislocations seen in the inliers at Little Oakley, Stanion, Weekley, &c.; these must, evidently, have been produced in the period which elapsed between the deposition of the lower part of the Inferior Oolite and the Great Oolite; that is, in the period represented by the higher zones of the Inferior Oolite, which in this district was not marked by the deposition of strata, but by a certain amount of upheaval and disturbance, producing unconformity between them and the strata next laid down, namely, those of the Great Oolite.

CHAPTER XII.

MISCELLANEOUS.

Denudation.—Nowhere are the results of denudation more obvious and unmistakeable than among the thin and easily-recognizable beds of the Lower Oolites. That limestones like the Cornbrash and Great Oolite of the district, which everywhere present such uniform characters, both lithological and palæontological, together with the well marked argillaceous strata which alternate with them, once extended completely over the whole district must be plain to every one who has followed the descriptions in this Memoir or traced the beds on the ground. The exact correspondence of the strata on the opposite sides of the valleys is everywhere so striking, that we soon learn in imagination to restore the continuity of the beds.

When, standing in a narrow valley, we note this exact correspondence of the strata which form its opposite sides, the first idea which suggests itself to the mind as the probable cause of the phenomena presented, is that a mass of rock has been rent asunder and that the valley is nothing but a gaping fracture. A little consideration, however, will soon show that this impression is due to the want of correct appreciation by direct vision of the true relations of horizontal and vertical dimensions, and is as truly the result of an optical delusion as the apparent increase in size of the sun or moon when near the horizon. It is only necessary to measure the height of the opposite sides, together with the breadth of the valley, and then to plot the whole on a true scale to be convinced that the hypothesis of fracture is altogether inadequate to explain the phenomena, and that an actual removal of the large masses of rock which once filled the valley has certainly taken place.

This view is confirmed when we come to examine the position of those lines of fracture which, in the preceding pages, we have proved to exist in the area. These seldom bear any direct relation to the contours of the surface of the ground, and in fact the faults as frequently run across to tops of hills as along the lines of valleys. It is abundantly clear, however, as we have already seen, that the faults have very greatly affected the existing contours of the surface of the country by placing beds of different degrees of hardness in new relations.

The truth of these views will be at once manifest to any one who takes the trouble to examine with care the horizontal sections across the area, which are published by the Geological Survey, and are drawn on a uniform horizontal and vertical scale of six inches to the mile.

When we inquire as to the causes which have operated in the removal of these great masses of strata we shall not have far to look. In the stream which flows at the bottom of the valley we

find the instrument, in the peculiar sinuous orms of the valley
we find the characteristic tool marks, and in the patches of gravel
which lie upon its sides we see some of the heaps of chips which
mark different stages of its operation.

This Memoir is not the place to point out the various considerations, such as the forms of the valley, the position and
composition of its gravels, the amount of rock-derived materials
in solution and suspension in the waters of the stream, which
have enabled geologists to demonstrate that the present valleys
have all been excavated by the streams that still flow in them;
and that in a great majority of cases these results have been
produced within periods which, though very great according to
our ordinary methods of computing time, are geologically speaking
of short duration. It is sufficient in this place to remark, that,
to the careful observer, the valleys of the Nene and Welland, and
of the numerous smaller streams which traverse the district,
afford innumerable and very instructive illustrations of the mode of
operation and the results, of the causes referred to.

Along the sides of the valleys and on the slopes of the steep
escarpments the effects of another of the great denuding forces
may be constantly observed. This is the production of landslips
by the slipping of the great masses of solid rock over the clays
on which they so frequently rest. This action is greatly aided
of course by the jointed condition of the limestones, and the
springs which so constantly burst out at their junction with the
clays. Interesting illustrations of these landslips on a considerable
scale are to be observed at the village of Gretton, which is built
on a mass of Inferior Oolite that has slipped for some distance
over the subjacent Upper Lias Clay. That the causes which
have brought about this displacement of the beds have not ceased
to operate, is shown by the fact that cracks appear from time to
time in many of the houses of the village. Similar slipped masses
may be observed at various points along the faces of the two great
escarpments of the district, and indeed their frequency calls for
constant care in mapping the out-crops of the harder beds along
the escarpments; in some places the true position of these out-crops
is so greatly obscured that they have had to be represented by
dotted lines. That evidence exists of similar landslips having
taken place from the great escarpments, which were probably
higher than at present, before the deposition of the Boulder Clay,
has already been shown. The slipping of great masses of limestone rock over the clays along the sides of valleys is well
illustrated on the sides of the Willow Brook, at the village of
King's Cliffe, and at numerous other points which might be
mentioned.

By the agency of the landslips the highest and hardest rocks of
the country are being gradually brought within the influence of
the streams, which in time wear away fragments of the shattered
masses and grind them into pebbles and sand.

The tendency of the effects produced by the erosion of streams
in the lower grounds and the contributory causes of landslips

and atmospheric weathering in the higher and more exposed situations, is to gradually lower the surface of the country and to destroy the prominence of its natural features. Thus it is plain that, in the country under consideration, unless counterbalanced by the action of subterranean causes producing elevation, the valleys are being continually deepened, while the escarpments are gradually receding and so being diminished in height.

In the Fenland we have an illustration of another kind of denuding cause, the mode of operation of which is totally different to those we have been noticing. Between the outcrops of the two great masses of hard rocks constituted by the Chalk and Lower Oolites, there is in the Midland districts a wide extent of country occupied by the soft strata of the Oxford and Kimmeridge clays, which together attain to a thickness of probably not less than from 1,000 to 1,500 feet. The confluence of a number of very considerable rivers, namely, the Witham, Welland, Nene and Great Ouse, which, with their tributaries, drain a very large extent of country, has effected a breach in the great mass of chalk strata and thus the sea has been able to find admission to, and to operate on, the soft clays of the Middle and Upper Oolites. While the hard chalk rocks have been cut back over a breadth of only twenty miles, at the mouth of the Wash, the sea has extended its boundaries through the soft clays over the enormous area known as the Fens or Bedford level. As the erosive action of the ocean is most powerfully displayed at its surface—where it is the constant subject of tides and, at irregular intervals, converted into a most powerful engine of denudation by storms—marine action always tends to produce an extended flat plain. This is the case in the Fenland, where only a few patches, which, on account of the presence of beds of exceptional hardness or from some other accident, rise above the general level and once formed islands or shoals in the Fen Gulf. These and the rest of the old sea margins around the Fenland are frequently fringed with gravels, often full of marine shells, and which are evidently old beaches. The slight changes of level which have certainly taken place in the district, as is evidenced by the raised beaches at many points, on the one hand, and the submerged forests of the Norfolk and Lincolnshire coasts, on the other, can have exercised only a minor and altogether subordinate influence in the production of the features of the Fenland.

In the area included within Sheet 64, it is evident that the present valleys which intersect the great plateau have been mostly, if not wholly, formed since the Glacial epoch. This is shown by the manner in which the beds of Boulder Clay cap the opposite sides of the valleys, across which they were certainly once continuous. I know of no grounds for believing that any of the present valleys, which traverse the plateau, existed during pre-glacial times, were filled with Boulder Clay in the glacial period, and re-excavated since that era. On the contrary, the manner in which the boulder clays are confined to the highest grounds tends to quite the opposite conclusion.

To the west of the great escarpments, however, quite an opposite series of relations prevails. There the glacial clays and gravels are found at every possible elevation, and it is clear that in some cases the present valleys coincide with those of the pre-glacial period.

The present surface of denudation, though the one which can be most easily studied, is not the only one made familiar to us by the observations of the geologist. We have already shown that the valleys in which pre-glacial rivers flowed can be traced by the gravel deposits which occupied them, and by this means the physical geography of the period can to a certain extent be re-constructed. Of that old surface of denudation which marks the newer portion of the Inferior Oolite period, and which lies between the Lincolnshire Oolite and the Upper Estuarine Series, we are able also to obtain fragmentary, but very interesting, information as already noticed.

Scenery.—Although no part of the area described in the present Memoir is remarkable for presenting features of great wildness or grandeur on the one hand, or scenes of striking beauty on the other, yet the charms of a diversified, well cultivated, and richly wooded country belong to it in an eminent degree. The variations of elevation are sufficient to redeem the landscapes from tameness; the constant alternations of field, pasture, and copse, afford pleasing variety to them; and the signs of comfort and productiveness, everywhere apparent, cannot fail to give pleasure to the beholder. The abundance of trees, often evidently of great antiquity, as in the case of the oaks of Morehay Lawn (which are said to date from the reign of King John), gives many parts of the district a remarkably park-like aspect; and perhaps no district of equal area could be pointed out, which exhibits so large a number of stately mansions standing in the midst of spacious demesnes; such are Burleigh, Milton, Exton, Burley, Dene, Apethorpe, Stapleford, Lilford, Farming Woods, Normanton, and others which might be mentioned. Even the almost dead level of the Fenland is not without peculiar charms of its own, as has been so admirably pointed out by Charles Kingsley.

To the eye of the geologist the dependence of the characteristics of the scenery on the nature of the rocks of which the country is composed is everywhere apparent. These rocks, by their position, inclinations, and varying powers of resisting denuding agencies, have determined the situation and nature of the hills and valleys; by their peculiar modes of weathering they have given rise to the varying contours of those features; and, by the soils which they yield, have decided the character of the vegetation by which they are adorned. Further—by the manner in which the outcrops of the various rocks have given rise to the water system of the country, and the sites of its springs and streams, and the way in which they have influenced the nature of the soils and thus also the tillage and other occupations of the inhabitants—the character of the population has been determined, its distribution regulated, and the position of its centres fixed.

As noticed by William Smith the Oolite and Lias districts of Rutland and South Lincolnshire present much bolder features than those of the South Midland area of Oxfordshire and Northampton; and in this respect sometimes even remind us of the Cotteswold Hills. This, as has been already noticed, is due to the great increase of thickness which takes place as we go northwards in the Upper Lias Clay, and the importance which is assumed by the Marlstone Rock-bed. There is one great distinction which must, however, be drawn between the Cotteswold Hills and the North Midland area. In the former there is a single great escarpment formed by all the strata between the Inferior Oolite and the Lower Lias, and this is sometimes more than 1,000 feet in height, the Marlstone forming only a ledge of greater or less breadth along its face. In the latter, on the contrary, the same strata form two distinct escarpments, those of the Inferior Oolite and the Marlstone Rock-bed, usually some miles distant from each other and attaining to nearly the same elevation, which rarely exceeds 700 feet. Some of the most characteristic features of the district are illustrated in the series of plates which accompany this Memoir, prepared from sketches by Mr. Frank Rutley, F.G.S., of the Geological Survey of England and Wales.

The sinuous and branching valleys which diversify the faces of these escarpments often present, in the cliff-like masses of hard rock, rising above the green slopes formed of clay with its covering of talus, features of considerable natural beauty. Among such, we may mention, on the outer or Marlstone escarpment, the valleys below Somerby (*see* woodcut, Fig. 5, p. 53), Pickwell, Burrow-on-the-Hill, and Tilton-on-the-Hill; on the inner or Inferior Oolite escarpment, those about Rockingham Park, Harringworth, Burley-on-the-Hill, and Market Overton; and between the two escarpments, Deepdale, Bushy Dale, and the numerous deep and secluded valleys which intersect the outliers on which Uppingham stands, those near it, and that between Dingley and Brampton.

The outliers of Upper Lias capped by beds of the Inferior Oolite form bold hills, usually of a more or less tabular form, like those of Whadborough, Robin-a-Tiptoes, Barrow Hill, the high grounds about Uppingham, and the Neville-Holt, Slawston, and the Dingley and Brampton outliers.

The great plateau, where it is covered with Boulder Clay, usually shows little diversity in elevation; it slopes gradually towards the S.W. and is in places broken up by long, narrow, winding valleys. This great table land was the site of the great forest of Rockingham, which, though long disafforested and broken up, still presents in places areas only lately enclosed, and others yet covered with extensive woods.

Where the surface of the plateau is not masked by drift, the several hard limestone beds of the Great Oolite, with their intermediate series of clays, give rise to numerous tabular outliers, precisely similar to those formed upon the great Cotteswold plateau by the patches of Great Oolite which rest on the Fuller's earth. The step-like contours presented by the denuded edges of the

VIEW ILLUSTRATING THE TABLAR SCENERY OF THE WEST BANK OF THE JORDAN.

hard strata alternating with series of clays, produce features strikingly characteristic of the oolitic rocks in this country, and by means of which they are almost always easily recognizable even at a distance. Beautiful illustrations of these features are exhibited in the numerous spurs and outliers formed of the various beds of the Great Oolite series which occupy the country to the north of the Welland.

Similar step-like contours, often of very striking characters, are produced along the sides of the Nene and the Welland where they traverse the Great Oolite strata. In these valleys, the windings of the main stream and the falling into it of numerous tributaries, give rise to numerous spurs and occasional outliers, along the sides of which the out-crop of the several harder rocks is often very clearly marked by the outlines which the masses present.

The bottoms of such valleys are covered by the flat plains composed of gravel and alluvium, among which the river winds its devious way, through meadows, which, overwhelmed by constant floods during the winter season, present in the summer plains of unrivalled verdure constituting the richest of pasturages.

The Oxford Clay tract to the east of the Nene is almost everywhere thickly covered with drift, and forms a low undulating country, sometimes well wooded, which slopes gradually towards the Fens.

The Fenland itself does not present such monotonous features as is sometimes supposed. Rising above its generally level surface are a number of tracts composed of the older rocks covered by gravels which were once islands; and these, which constitute the sites of the various towns, villages, and farmhouses, though of but slight elevation, form conspicuous and often striking objects in a peculiar landscape. The extraordinary and unrivalled fertility of some portions of these tracts too, is sufficient to invest them with considerable interest for the traveller during at least some seasons of the year. To those familiar with the scenery of Holland, the resemblances presented by the English Fenland are very striking; and before the introduction of steam engines had swept away the numerous windmills, that were formerly situated at short intervals along the banks of the numerous dykes by which the country is everywhere intersected, the similarity was even still more marked.

Springs.—The frequent alternations, within the district under description, of pervious beds of limestone and sand with impervious clays, gives rise to numerous springs—indeed these are among the three things for which, according to an old adage, the county of Northampton is remarkable. The constant outflow of these along the base of the harder beds, by causing a broken condition of the surface and imparting a freshness to the verdure, sometimes makes the division of the formations very distinct, and enables the eye to trace them even at a considerable distance.

It is interesting to notice the manner in which the presence of springs has determined the sites of the towns, villages, and even isolated habitations of the district. Thus, along the slopes of the two great escarpments we find two series of villages, which obtain their water supplies from the springs arising at the junction of the Inferior Oolite and Upper Lias, and of the Marlstone Rock-bed and Middle Lias Clays, respectively. The presence of such springs would in the first place influence the choice of camping grounds for a nomadic people; and the same localities would for similar reasons be selected, when population first became fixed, as the sites of the rising settlements. Along the sides of the great river valleys of the district, numerous villages have been built, which depend for be their water supply on the springs arising at the out-crops of the various oolitic beds; while other villages have arisen on the sides of the various outliers and inliers, which afford the same advantageous conditions. But over the great intermediate tracts not a single village occurs, and until modern times scarcely a single habitation could be found upon them. In the Fenland, in the eastern part of the area, and the drift-covered Lower Lias clay lands of the western part, the position of the few villages and houses, has been in almost every instance determined by the presence of beds of gravel yielding springs.

The question of the water supply of the area has, in modern times, assumed great importance, and an entirely new aspect. Although springs are so abundant in the district, yet as population has increased it has been found necessary, either for the purpose of supplementing the supply of water or for obtaining it in the most convenient situations, to open numerous wells. These have been for the most part of no great depth, passing merely through the first pervious bed into an impervious one, and thence obtaining, in almost every instance, an abundant supply. But the facility with which the refuse matter of a considerable population can be got rid of, where there is a substratum of porous material, has led to openings in these same rocks of innumerable cesspools and drains. Hence the water supply of the population is often poisoned at its source; wells and cesspools existing in the same rock and at no great distance from one another. Now it has been shown that waters from such a tainted source, though bright and clear to the eye and not unpleasant to the taste, may, nevertheless, be the means of propagating the worst forms of epidemic disease. Fortunately, in the district under notice, there generally exists a remedy, and it is in most cases easy of application; it is in fact only necessary to carry down the wells to the next impervious stratum, and to protect them from infiltration in their upper parts. Thus in the case of a village standing upon the Cornbrash, in which the water-bearing bed has been hopelessly deteriorated by the drainage, it will only be necessary to carry down the new wells through the Great Oolite Clays into the Great Oolite Limestone.

The district being an almost purely agricultural one, the civil engineer is not called upon to make provision for large and closely packed populations, like those which demand such great works for procuring and storage of water supplies in manufacturing districts. In very few cases are the towns of sufficient size probably to need deep artesian wells, such as might be sunk into

the Lincolnshire Oolite Limestone or the Marlstone Rock-bed. At
Bourne, such wells have been sunk to the former stratum and
most abundant supplies of excellent water obtained. In making
similar attempts in other localities, it will be necessary always to
bear in mind that the two rocks thin away towards the south and
east, and that in the case of the former this attenuation takes place
very rapidly. It will be necessary therefore in every instance to
inquire as to the probabilities of the rock, which is to be bored
for, being actually present under the locality at which the trial is
made.

Swallow-holes.—These may be regarded as the complements of
springs, and their abundance in the district is due to the prevalence
of the same set of conditions which produce the latter, namely—
the repeated alternation of rocks of pervious with those of impervious character. When water passing through a pervious bed
reaches a bed of clay or other non-absorbent rock, it flows out at
the surface in the form of a spring. When on the other hand
water flowing over an impervious rock, reaches a pervious stratum,
it is rapidly absorbed, and by its passage downwards gives rise,
either by mechanical or chemical action, to the production of an
underground channel. The openings into such underground
channels are called "swallow-holes." They are very abundant
within the area embraced in Sheet 64; indeed the lines of
junction of rocks like the Upper Estuarine Clays and the Lincolnshire Oolite are often marked by a series of these natural
drains; in many cases a slight depression of the surface level
indicating their position. In some cases the volume of water
carried off by means of a swallow-hole is very great, and the
roar produced by it in descending, is heard at some distance.
In the case of the smaller swallow-holes, they may often be
detected by placing the ear near the surface of the ground.
These swallow-holes are well known to fox hunters, for the long
sinuous fissures worn by the constant passage of water through
the jointed limestone rocks constitute retreats for foxes, from
which it is almost impossible to effect their dislodgement. Doubtless also the caverns so frequently revealed in the midst of limestone
rocks during quarrying operations, owe their formation to the
same agency.

In effecting draining operations, these natural means of carrying
off the surface waters are often imitated, and artificial swallow-
holes constructed. Thus when a tract of Boulder Clay overlapping
limestone is drained, it is only necessary to carry the pipes to the
outcrop of a thick bed of limestone and to allow them to terminate
in an excavation in the latter. Similarly, in draining a bed of
clay overlying a stratum of limestone, an occasional pit sunk
through the former into the latter will serve for the ready removal
even of the largest volumes of surface water. Many examples of
these modes of procedure may be seen in the district described in
this Memoir.

Subterranean Streams.—Frequently when a brook or river,
flowing over an impervious bed, meets suddenly in its course
the out-crop of a stratum of limestone, its volume is greatly

diminished by the escape of part of its waters underground;
these waters are usually thrown out in fresh springs farther down
the valley where the limestone is underlaid by an impervious
rock. Occasionally the whole volume of the stream thus disappears, and for a portion of its course, sometimes several miles
in length, it becomes subterranean. Not a few interesting examples of the disappearance of rivers, which thus leave their beds
for a considerable distance quite dry, occur within Sheet 64. As
especially noteworthy may be mentioned the River Witham, near
Thistleton, the River Glen, between Little Bytham and Careby,
and the brook which flows by the village of Benefield.

Mineral Springs.—The springs of this class found within the
area described in this Memoir are not now of great importance
and do not demand an extended notice at the hands of the geologist.
At an earlier period, and especially in mediæval times, it was otherwise, however, for the wonderful curative powers attributed to
many springs, which are now quite disregarded, led to their being
dedicated to certain saints, and even in some cases to the erection
of hospitals or monasteries in their neighbourhood.   The only
mineral water within the district which has been, during recent
years, resorted to by invalids under medical advice, is that of
Braceborough.   The traditions of the virtues of many of the once
famous springs are still maintained among the peasantry, who
even now make use of them for certain classes of disorders among
themselves and their cattle.

As might be expected in a district which is largely composed
of limestone beds, so called *Petrifying springs* are common. The
water of these contains such an excess of carbonic acid that they
are able to dissolve a large quantity of carbonate of lime; and
this, through the escape of the gas, when the water is exposed to
the atmosphere, is readily deposited in a crust on any object over
which the stream flows. Masses of travertin, or
carbonate of lime deposited under such circumstances, are very
common in many places; good examples may be seen on the side
of the Nene Valley, at Alwalton Lynch near Peterborough. In
some cases tufts of grass, fragments of wood, shells of snails, and
other objects are found encrusted and enclosed in these masses;
while in others only the hollow casts of such bodies are found
traversing the mass in all directions, the objects themselves having
decayed and disappeared. At several localities within the district
are found masses of travertine which enclose numerous encrusted
specimens of plants, in a manner precisely similar to those described by Mr. Sharp, as being found near Old,* which is situated
to the south of the district now being described. In some places,
as at Halstead, the "petrifying springs" have been made use of
like those of Derbyshire, &c., for the purpose of obtaining those
incrustations (erroneously called petrifactions) of objects like
birds' nests, wigs, skeletons, branching twigs, &c. which were at
one time so conspicuous in almost every collection of " curiosities."

The passage of waters of this class through beds of gravel has sometimes effected a cementing of the pebbles into indurated masses, which can sometimes be raised as large blocks of solid stone; these blocks, resisting denudation better than the surrounding unconsolidated portions, sometimes stand in fantastic shapes above the surface of the ground. Examples of this may be seen in the case of the pre-glacial gravels near Clipsham quarries, and in the valley gravels near Elton.

Next in abundance to these springs of hard water, or those containing an excess of carbonate of lime, must be noticed the Chalybeate waters. Some of these contain such a small proportion of iron salt as not to interfere with their use for drinking and ordinary domestic purposes; and such springs only betray their character by the brown crust deposited on the vegetation around, or by the irridescent scum that floats on the pools in which their waters collect. Other springs of the class contain a much larger per-centage of iron in solution, as is manifested by their nauseous, inky taste; and some of these have obtained considerable fame for their curative virtues.

Many of the springs which arise in the ironstone beds of the Northampton Sand, the ferruginous band of the Upper Estuarine Series, or the nodular ironstone bands of the Great Oolite Clay contain a small amount of carbonate of iron in solution. Some of these had sufficiently pronounced chalybeate characters as to enjoy some fame in former times. Such appear to have been the now altogether neglected, if not quite forgotten, Burleigh Park Spa, Wittering Spa, and Tolthorpe Spa, described by Dr. Short in 1734. Waters of this class traversing beds of gravel, sometimes bind the pebbles together with a ferruginous cement into a rock of great hardness; the water which traverses peat bogs, as is well known, readily takes up iron in solution, and frequently the fen-gravels are found, in certain of their beds, cemented into a rock of such extreme hardness that, in order to carry drains through them, blasting has to be resorted to; a good example of this kind of indurated gravel may be seen at Greatford. Occasionally the chalybeate springs traversing certain of the oolite rocks indurate and stain them; such is seen to be the case with the oyster-beds of the Great Oolite between Benefield and Glapthorn, and to the west of Oundle.

Other mineral springs in the district, like those of Kings-Cliffe, Stamford, Neville-Holt, Burton Lazars, Little Dalby, Brentingby, and others, are probably deep seated and owe their existence to the presence of faults in the strata. The proximity of several of these mineral springs to proved lines of dislocation has been already pointed out. Some of these waters are still used by the people dwelling in the neighbourhood, especially for outward application, in cases of cutaneous disorder and diseases of the eyes; but in former times the fame of several of them was very widely spread, and they were resorted to by patients from all parts of the country. The three most noteworthy of these were the mineral waters of Burton Lazars, Neville-Holt, and Braceborough.

Burton Lazars derives its distinctive appellation from the Lazar house, or hospital for lepers, which once existed here. This institution, which was very richly endowed, was devoted to the relief of a class of disease which was extremely common in this country in mediæval times, but which has now, thanks to the existence of better sanitary arrangements, the greater abundance and excellence of food, and the spread of habits of cleanliness among the population, entirely disappeared. In the year 1135 Roger de Mowbray, aided by a general collection throughout England, laid the foundation of an establishment for a master and eight sound brethren of the Order of Saint Augustin, as well as several poor leprous brethren, to whom he gave two carucates of land, at Burton, a house, mill, &c. " The hospital was dedicated to the Blessed Virgin and St. Lazarus, and all the inferior houses in England, were in some measure subject to its master, as was also the master of the Lazars at Jerusalem hospital, belonging to the Knights of St. John of Jerusalem." At its dissolution in 1535 the Burton Lazar hospital had a clear annual revenue of 265l. 10s. 2d., its possessions were granted to the Earl of Warwick and the Duke of Northumberland. The spring at Burton Lazars, beside which this important establishment sprang up, is said to have contained chloride of sodium and a large quantity of sulphuretted hydrogen among its ingredients, and it was resorted to, long after the dissolution of the monastic establishment, by great numbers of persons afflicted with scorbutic disorders; these are said to have obtained great benefit from the use of the waters. As late as the year 1760 a bathing room was built at the spring, but in recent years this has been pulled down; subsequent excavations carried on near the spot have caused this once most famous well to disappear altogether, so that even its very site will soon be known only by tradition.

The Neville-Holt Spa was discovered in 1728, and its composition and medical properties were investigated by Dr. Short (see the list of works at the end of this Memoir, Appendix II.). It appears to have been chalybeate and for a long time its waters were in great request, but they are now almost entirely neglected. The baths erected over this spring still remain.

At Blatherwycke a spring containing sulphuretted hydrogen was discovered through the sinking of a well (see p. 102). Its waters are said to have been analysed, but I have not been able to obtain any record of its composition.

The chalybeate water at Kings-Cliffe Spa at one time acquired some fame; but, as in so many other cases, it has either fallen wholly into disuse or is resorted to only by the peasantry living in the neighbourhood.

The Braceborough Spa does not appear to contain an excessive amount of any particular mineral ingredient, but is remarkable for the quantity of gas (carbonic acid) which rises through it. A bath has been erected over it, and the spring was at one time much resorted to by invalids.

Mineral Resources of the District.—These we have noticed in considerable detail in connexion with each of the formations, and here it is only necessary to remark that, although, with the exception of the iron-ore of the Northampton Sand, the district cannot be regarded as rich in minerals of great economic value, nevertheless to a very large extent, not only the comfort of the population, but the nature of the architecture adopted by them both in their homes and their religious edifices, is due to the excellence of the building materials with which they are so liberally furnished.

Soils.—The principal characteristics of these and their dependence upon the rocks on which they lie have also been noticed in the foregoing pages. Although almost every portion of the area described is now under cultivation, yet such was not always the case. The tracts covered by the richest soils were evidently those which were first cleared and occupied; and the wants of a continually increasing population, combined with the adoption of more settled habits, have occasioned the successive absorption of more and more unpromising areas, till at last waste lands have almost wholly disappeared within the limits of the district.

Conclusion.—No one can have followed the descriptions of the present memoir without reflecting to how large an extent the present characteristics and the past history of the district are dependent on its physical structure. A mere glance at the map, as geologically coloured, will show how the selection of the original sites for those settlements, which have since become villages and towns, must have been, in the first instance, determined by the outcrop of the various water-bearing beds. The features of its surface, the nature of its soils, and the character and abundance of the mineral productions of the district, have evidently been the conditions on which the number and distribution of the population have mainly depended, and the causes to which their industries, their sports, and even their peculiarities, have largely owed their origin.

And the production of the physical features which distinguish the district have been due, as we have seen, to the combined operation of two distinct sets of geological causes. Firstly, the succession of events by which series of rocks of very various characters were deposited within the area; and, secondly, the action upon these of subterranean forces producing upheaval, flexure, and fracture, and acting side by side and in combination with those of subaerial and marine waste; these deep-seated and surface operations working concurrently have gradually moulded and sculptured the surface of the land into the forms which it at present wears.

APPENDIX I.

PALÆONTOLOGICAL TABLES

PREPARED BY

R. ETHERIDGE, F.R.S.,

PALÆONTOLOGIST TO THE GEOLOGICAL SURVEY.

APPENDIX I.

The accompanying tables of fossils have been drawn up expressly to
elucidate the distribution of the Oolitic species through the Lower
Oolites of the counties of Rutland and Northampton, and also to show
their geographical distribution.

Table 1 is devoted to a comparison of the fossils of the Inferior
Oolite of the area above noticed with those of the same formation in the
south-west of England and Yorkshire respectively. This comparison
and correlation is made with the view of ascertaining the relation that
exists between the two distantly separated Faunæ of the same age, or
belonging to the same horizon in time, the physical aspects of which,
however, greatly differing, there being nothing in common litho-
logically between the Oolitic series of Yorkshire, and those of the
Midland district and south-west of England. Yet the species ranging
through the series are identical, and hold the same stratigraphical position, and are of equal value in determining the sequence of the beds
constituting the Oolitic series through the whole of England.

In the column headed " Great Oolite of West of England," are enumerated those species that occur in or are common to both the Great
Oolite of the South, and the Inferior Oolite of one or other of the five
horizons named, viz., the Lincolnshire Limestone, the Collyweston Slates
and Northampton Sand of the Midland district ; also the Inferior Oolite
of the south of England and Yorkshire.

The letters R. C. r. c. denote the rarity or abundance of the species,
the capital R. expressing extreme rarity, and the capital C. extreme
abundance ; the smaller letters their ordinary condition or occurrence.
This must be regarded as only approximative, being really a question of
exhaustive research.

As far as able, I have tabulated every species occurring within the
area described and mapped by Mr. Judd, and embraced in Sheet 64, &c.

Samuel Sharp, Esq., F.G.S., of Dallington Hall, Northampton, who
possesses the finest Collection of Northamptonshire fossils known, submitted the whole series to our examination, and from his materials, with
those collected by the Geological Survey, have been constructed the
tables numbered 1 and 2, the latter being strictly geographical. Mr.
Sharp's two able papers on the Oolites of Northamptonshire[*] contain
every species known to him, arranged both geographically through the
text of the paper, and zoologically tabulated also.

---

[*] On the Oolites of Northamptonshire, by S. Sharp, Esq., F.G.S., *Quart. Journ.
Geol. Soc.*, vol. xxvi. p. 354, and vol. xxix., p. 225.

Table No. 2 illustrates the distribution of the species known in the Great Oolite and Cornbrash of Northamptonshire and Lincolnshire. The Great Oolite of Rutland and the Cornbrash of Stilton (Hunts) arranged in their geological horizons and according to localities.

These two tables thus illustrate the distribution of the fauna of the Lower Oolites of Northamptonshire and Rutlandshire; Table No. 1 being devoted to range and correlation, and in which are tabulated 394 species, whereas Table No. 2 contains 354 known occurrences, through their distribution.

Mr. Judd, in this able memoir, has so completely written the history of the area that no notes of special stratigraphical value can be added to this Appendix, and due attention to the table illustrating the variations of the Lower Oolites of the Midland district at page 6 in the memoir will enable the reader to understand, by comparison with the typical column headed "Geological Horizons," the sequence, distribution, and arrangement of the Rutlandshire and Northamptonshire deposits and fossils.

The recent investigations into the true correlation of the Northern and Southern Oolitic groups, and especially those members of the lower series with the Lincolnshire Oolites and Northampton Sands of the Midland area, has resulted in clearly defining the true stratigraphical place of both horizons. Based upon superposition and on fossil data, both Mr. Sharp, of Northampton, and Mr. Beesley, of Banbury, through independent observations and well directed work over their respective districts, arrived at the same conclusions; and the careful and patient labour of Mr. Judd, as mapped in the field and now detailed in the present memoir, conclusively show, both on stratigraphical and palæontological grounds, the real relation of the Northampton Sands to the underlying Upper Lias Clays and the great Limestone of Lincolnshire above.*

* Professor Morris in 1869 reconsidered his previous views upon the Lincolnshire Limestone, and assigned it to the age of the Inferior Oolite.

TABLE 1.—COMPARISON of the FOSSILS of the Inferior Oolite of the Midland District with those of the same formation in the South of England and Yorkshire respectively.

Class.	Species.	Inferior Oolite of Midland District.			Compared with		
		Lincolnshire Limestone.	Collyweston Slate.	Northampton Sand.	Inferior Oolite of S. of England.	Inferior Oolite of Yorkshire.	Great Oolite of W. of England.
Plantæ	Aroides Stutterdi - Carr.	R					
	Palæozamia pectinata - Brong.	r	.	.	.	+	+
	Pecopteris polypodioides Lind. & Hutt.	r	c	.			
	Polypodites Lindleyi - Gopp.	C	.	.	.	+	+
	Zamites -	r					
	Carpolithes -	.	.	R			
	Coniferous wood -	r					
Cœlenterata	Anabacia orbulites - Lamaroux	c	.	.	+		+
	Eunomia radiata - E. & H.	R	.	.	.	.	+
	Cladophyllia Babeana - D'Orb.	r	.	.	.	.	+
	Isastræa explanulata - M'Coy	c	.	.	+	.	+
	" limitata - Lamaroux	c	.	.	+	.	+
	" Richardsoni - Ed. & H.	c	.	r	+		
	Latomeandra Davidsoni - Ed. & H.	c	.	c	+		
	" Flemingii - Ed. & H.	r	.	.	+		
	Microsolena excelsa ? Ed. & H.	r	.	.	.	?	+
	Montlivaltia De la Bechei Ed. & H.	r	.	.	.	+	
	" lens - Ed. & H.	r	.	.	+		
	" tenuilamellosa Ed. & H.	r	.	.	+		
	" trochoides - Ed. & H.	r	.	R	+		
	" Wrightii - Ed. & H.	r	.	?	+		
	Stylina solida - M'Coy	r	.	.	+	.	+
	Thecosmilia gregaria - M'Coy	C	.	c	+'		
	" Wrightii - Ed. & H.	r	.	.	+		
	Thamnastræa Lyellii - Ed. & H.	c	.	.	.	.	+
	" concinna - Goldf.	c	.	.	+	.	+
	" Defrancii - Mich.	c	.	c	+		
	" Terquimi - Ed. & H.	R	.	R	+		
ANNULOIDA Echinodermata.	Acrosalenia hemicidaroides Wright	r	.	r	+	.	+
	" Lycettii - Wright	r	.	r	+		
	Astropecten Colleswoldiæ var. Stamfordensis Wright	R	R	.	.	.	+
	Cidaris Bouchardii - Wright	r	.	.	+		
	" Fowleri - Wright	r	.	.	+		
	" Wrightii - Desor.	r	.	?	+		
	Clypeus Plottii - Klein.	c	.	r	+	.	+
	" Hughii - Ag.	r	.	.	+		
	" Michelini - Wright	c	.	.	+	+	
	Echinobrissus clunicularis Llhwyd	C	.	c	+	.	+
	Pedina rotata - Ag.	r	.	.	+		
	Galeropygus (Hyboclypus) agariciformis Forbes	C	.	c	+	+	
	Holectypus hemisphæricus Desor.	c	.	.	+		
	Hyboclypus ovalis - Wright	r	.	?	+		
	Pygaster semisulcatus - Phil.	C	.	c	+	+	+
	Pseudodiadema depressa - Ag.	c	.	.	+	+	
	Stomechinus germinans - Phil.	c	.	r	+	+	
	Pentacrinus Milleri - Aust.	R	.	r	+	.	+
	" subsulcatus - Goldf.	R	.	.	.	.	+
	Stellaster Sharpei - Wright, MS.	.	.	R			

Table 1.—Comparison of the Fossils, &c.—*cont.*

Class.	Species.		Inferior Oolite of Midland District.			Compared with		
			Lincolnshire Limestone.	Collyweston Slate.	Northampton Sand.	Inferior Oolite of S. of England.	Inferior Oolite of Yorkshire.	Great Oolite of W. of England.
Annelida	Serpula convoluta	- Goldf. -	r	.	r	+		
	„ intestinalis	- Phil. -	r	.	.	.	+	
	„ plicatilis	- Goldf. -	?	.	?	+	+	
	„ socialis	- Goldf. -	C	.	r	+	+	
	„ sulcata	- Sow. -	r	.	.	+	+	
	Vermicularia compressa	- Y. & B. -	r	.	.	+.	+	
	„ nodus -	- Phil. -	r	.	.	+	+	
	Annelide tubes	-	c	.	.			
Articulata: CRUSTACEA	Remains of -	-	.	.	r			
	Pseudophyllia sp. -	-	R	.				
MOLLUSCOIDA	Spiropora straminæa	- Phil.	.	.	.	+	+	
MOLLUSCA	Lingula Beanii? -	- Lyc.	R	.				
BRACHIOPODA	Rhynchonella angulata	- Sow. -	r	.	r	+		
	„ Crossii	- Dav.	R	.	R			
	„ cynocephala	Rich.	c	.	r	+		
	„ plicatella	- Sow.	C	.	r			
	„ quadriplicata	Ziet.	c	.	c			
	„ Lycettii	- Dav.	r	.	r	+		
	„ spinosa	- Schloth.	C	.	R	+		
	„ sub-decorata	Dav.	r	.	r			
	„ sub-tetra-hedra	Dav. -	c	.	r	+		
	„ tetrahedra	- ? Sow. -	R	.	r			
	„ varians	- Schloth. -	C	.	r	.	.	+
	„ variabilis	- Schloth. -	C	.	c			
	„ var. bidens	Phil. -	c	.	c	+		
	„ var. triplicata	Desh.	r	.	r	+		
	„ concinna	- Sow.	c	.	.	+		+
	Terebratula Buckmani	- Dav.	r	.	r	+		
	„ fimbria -	- Sow.	r	.	r	+		
	„ globata -	- Sow.	c	.	r	+		
	„ impressa	- V. Buch	r	.	?	+		
	„ maxillata	- Sow.	c	.	r	+	+	+
	„ ovoides -	- Sow.	r	.	r	+		
	„ Phillipsi	- Mor.&Dav.	r	.	r	+		
	„ simplex -	- Buckm.	r	.	r	+		
	„ sphæroidalis	- Sow.	c	.	r	+		
	„ sub-maxillata	Mor.	c	c	r	+		
LAMELLIBRANCHIATA (MONOMYARIA).	Avicula Braamburiensis	- Phil.	R	R	R	+	+	
	„ clathrata	- Lycett	.	r				
	„ complicata	- Buckm.	.	.	r	+		
	„ digitata	- Deslong	r	.	r	+		
	„ echinata ?	- Sow.	R	.	.	+	.	+
	„ inæquivalvis	- Sow.	C	.	c	+		
	„ Munsteri	- Goldf.	C	c	c	+	+	
	„ subcostata	- Röm.	r	r				
	Lima bellula -	- L. & M.	c	c	c	+	+	
	„ cardiiformis	- L. & M.	C	c	c	.	.	+
	„ duplicata	- Sow.	C	c	C	+	+	+
	„ Dustonensis, n. sp.	-	c	.	C			
	„ deltoidea, n. sp.	-	.	.	r			
	„ electra -	- D'Orb.	.	.	r	+		
	„ gibbosa	- Sow.	C	c	.	+	.	+

Table 1.—Comparison of the Fossils, &c.—*cont.*

Class.	Species.	Lincolnshire Limestone.	Collyweston Slate.	Northampton Sand.	Inferior Oolite of S. of England.	Inferior Oolite of Yorkshire.	Great Oolite of W. of England.
		Inferior Oolite of Midland District.			Compared with		
Lamellibran-chiata (Mo-nomyaria). —*cont.*	Lima Etheridgii - Wright, MS.	r	.	r	+		
	„ impressa - L. & M. -	C	.	c	+		
	„ interstincta - Phil. -	r	r	r			
	„ ovalis - Sow. -	.	.	.	+	.	+
	„ Luciensis - D'Orb. -	r	.	r			
	„ pectiniformis - Schloth. -	C	c	c	+	+	+
	„ Pontonis - Lycett -	C	.	c	+		
	„ punctata - Sow. -	c	c	.	+		
	„ rigida - Sow. -	C	.	r	+		
	„ Rodburgensis, n. sp. -	C	.	.	+		
	„ rudis - Sow. -	c	.	r			
	„ semicircularis - Goldf. -	r	.	.	+	.	+
	„ Sharpiana, n. sp. -	.	.	R			
	Ostrea acuminata - Sow. -	.	.	R	.	.	+
	„ costata - Sow. -	.	.	r	+	.	+
	„ cristagalli - Quenst. -	.	.	r			
	„ flabelloides - Lam. -	C	.	c	+	+	
	„ gregaria - Sow. -	c	c	c	+		+
	„ sulcifera - Phil. -	r	.	r	+	+	
	Pecten arcnatus - Sow. -	r	.	c	.	+	+
	„ articulatus - Schloth. -	C	c	c			
	„ aratus - Waagen.	r					
	„ clathratus - Röm. -	r	r	r	+	.	+
	„ demissus - Phil. -	c	c	r	+	+	
	and *var.* gingensis Quenst.						
	„ lens - Sow. -	C	c	c	+	.	+
	„ parodoxus - Münst. -	r	r	.	+		
	„ personatus - Münst. -	c	c	R	+	.	+
	„ texturatus - Münst. -	c	r	r	+	.	+
	„ vagans *var.* pere-grinus - } Sow.	c	.	.	+	.	+
	Perna quadrata - Sow. -	r	r	r	+	.	+
	„ rugosa - Goldf. -	r	r	r	+	+	+
	Pinna ampla - Sow. -	.	.	c	+	.	+
	„ cancellata - Bean -	r	c	.	.	+	+
	„ cuneata - Phil. -	c	c	c	+	+	+
	„ Hartmani - Ziet. -	.	.	c	+		
	Placunopsis ornatus - L. & M. -	r	.	.	.	.	+
	„ socialis - L. & M. -	c	r	.	.	.	+
	„ Jurensis - Röm. -	.	.	r			
	Pteroperna costatula - Desl. -	c	r	r	+	.	+
	„ gibbosa - Lycett -	c	.	?	+		
	„ plana - Lycett -	c	r	c	+	+	
	„ pygmæa - Dunker -	r	.	.	.	.	+
	Gervillia acuta - Sow. -	c	c	c	+	. +	
	„ lata - Phil. -	c	.	c	+	+	
	„ ornata ? - Lycett -	r					
	„ pernoides - Deslong -	.	.	r	+		
	„ prelonga ? - Lycett -	.	.	r	+		
	„ (Gastiochæna) tortuosa } Phil. -	.	.	r	+	+	
	„ Hartmannii - Goldf. -	c	.	c	+	+	
	Gryphæa subloba - Desh. -	.	.	r	+		
	Hinnites abjectus - Phil. -	C	c	C	+	+	

Table 1.—Comparison of the Fossils, &c.—*cont.*

Class.	Species.		Inferior Oolite of Midland District.			Compared with		
			Lincolnshire Limestone.	Collyweston Slate.	Northampton Sand.	Inferior Oolite of S. of England.	Inferior Oolite of Yorkshire.	Great Oolite of W. of England.
Lamellibran-chiata (Mo-nomyaria). —cont.	Hinnites tegulatus	- L. & M. -	r	r	.	+	.	+
	„ velatus -	- Goldf. -	c	c	c	+	.	+
	Inoceramus Fittoni ?	- L. & M. -	.	.	?	.	.	+
	„ obliquus	- L. & M. -	R	r	r	.	.	+
	Plicatula tuberculosa	- L. & M. -	c	.	r	.	.	+
	Trichitis nodosus -	- Lycett -	R	.	.	+	.	+
Dimyaria -	Arca æmula *var.* transversa	L. & M. -	r	.	r	.	.	+
	„ cancellata -	- Sow. -	c	.	.	+	.	.
	„ minuta -	- Sow. -	.	.	r	.	.	+
	„ Prattii *var.* rugosa	- L. & M. -	c	.	r	+	.	+
	„ pulchra -	- Sow. -	r	.	r	+	.	+
	Astarte depressa -	- Goldf. -	r	r	r	+	.	+
	„ elegans -	- Sow. -	C	c	C	+	+	+
	„ excavata -	- Sow. -	c	c	c	+	+	+
	„ „ *var.* com-pressiuscula	- L. & M. -	r	r	.	+	.	.
	„ minima -	- Phil. -	c	.	r	+	+	+
	„ Pontonis -	- Mor. -	c	.	.	+	.	.
	„ recondita -	- Phil. -	r	.	.	+	+	.
	„ rhomboidalis	- L. & M. -	c	.	r	+	+	+
	Cardium Buckmani	- L. & M. -	C	c	C	+	.	+
	„ cognatum	- Phil. -	c	.	c	+	+	+
	„ incertum	- Phil. -	r	.	.	.	+	.
	„ semicostatum	- L. & M. -	.	.	?	.	.	+
	„ Stricklandi	- L. & M. -	.	r	.	.	.	+
	„ subtrigonum	- L. & M. -	c	.	.	.	.	.
	Ceromya Bajociana	- D'Orb. -	C	r	c	+	+	.
	„ concentrica	- Sow. -	c	c	c	+	+	+
	„ similis -	- Lycett -	c	.	.	.	.	.
	Corbis (Corbicilla) Batho-nica ? -	- L. & M. -	.	.	r	.	.	+
	Cucullæa cancellata	- Phil. -	c	r	r	+	+	.
	„ cucullata	- Goldf. -	c	c	c	+	.	+
	„ elongata	- Sow. -	r	.	r	+	+	.
	„ Goldfussii	- Röm. -	c	.	.	.	.	+
	„ imperialis	- Phil. -	.	.	r	.	+	.
	„ oblonga	- Sow. -	c	.	c	+	+	.
	„ ornata -	- Buckm. -	.	.	r	+	.	.
	Cypricardia acutangula	- D'Orb. -	c	.	r	+	+	.
	„ Bathonica	- D'Orb. -	c	.	c	+	.	+
	„ nuculiformis	- Röm. -	? c	.	?	.	.	+
	Cyprina Jurensis -	- Goldf. -	r	.	.	.	.	+
	„ Loweana	- L. & M. -	C	.	.	.	.	+
	„ dolabra -	-, Phil. -	r	.	r	.	+	.
	„ nuciformis	- Lycett -	c	.	.	+	.	.
	„ trapeziformis	- Röm. -	r	.	r	+	.	+
	Goniomya angulifera	- Sow. -	.	.	c	+	+	+
	„ literata	- Sow. -	c	c	.	.	+	.
	„ v-scripta	- Sow. -	c	.	.	+	+	.
	Gressalya abducta -	- Phil. -	.	.	r	+	+	.
	„ latirostris	- Ag. -	c	.	r	+	.	.
	„ peregrina	- Phil. -	.	.	c	.	+	+
	„ rostrata -	- Ag. -	.	.	r	.	.	.
	Homomya crassiuscula	- L. & M. -	C	c	.	+	+	.

Table 1.—Comparison of the Fossils, &c.—*cont.*

Class.	Species.		Inferior Oolite of Midland District.			Compared with		
			Lincolnshire Limestone.	Collyweston Slate.	Northampton Sand.	Inferior Oolite of S. of England.	Inferior Oolite of Yorkshire.	Great Oolite of W. of England.
Dimyaria— *cont.*	Homomya (Myacites) uniformis	L. & M.-	c	r	.	.	.	+
	„ Vezelayi	- D'Arch. -	r					
	Isocardia cordata -	- Buckm. -	C	.	c	+	+	
	Lithodomus inclusus	- Phil. -	r	.	r			
	Myopsis rotundata -	- Buckm. -	r					
	Lucina Bellona -	- D'Orb. -	C	r	c	.	.	+
	„ despecta -	- Phil. -	r	r	r	+	+	+
	„ d'Orbigniana -	- D'Arch -	r	c	r	+		
	„ rotundata -	- Röm. -	r	.	r	.	.	+
	„ Wrightii -	- Oppel. -	r	r	r			
	Macrodon Hirsonensis	- D'Arch. -	c	.	c	+	+	+
	Modiola Binfieldi -	- L. & M. -	r	.	r	.	.	+
	„ cuneata -	- Sow. -	c	.	c	+	+	
	„ gibbosa -	- Sow. -	C	c	C	+		
	„ explanata -	- Mor. -	r	.	r			
	„ Leckenbyi -	- L. & M. -	r	.	c	.	+	
	„ Lonsdalei -	- L. & M. -	c	.	r	.	.	+
	„ solenoides -	- L. & M. -	r	.	r	.	.	+
	„ Sowerbyana -	- D'Orb. -	c	c	r	+	+	+
	„ subreniformis -	- L. & M. -	r	.	r	.	.	+
	„ sublævis ? -	- Sow. -	r	.	.	.	.	+
	Myacites æquatus -	- Phil. -	r	r	.	+	+	
	„ Beanii -	- Leck. -	r	.	.	.	+	
	„ compressiusculus	Lycett -	.	.	r			
	„ calceiformis	- Phil. -	c	.	c	+	+	
	„ dilatatus -	- Phil. -	.	.	r	+	.	+
	„ decurtatus -	Phil. -	r	r	r	.	+	
	„ Scarburgensis	- Phil. -	?	.	r			
	„ securiformis	- Phil. -	r	.	r			
	Myoconcha crassa -	- Sow. -	c	.	c	+	.·	+
	„ striatula	- Münst. -	r	.	.	+		
	Mytilus furcatus -	- Goldf. -	r	.	r	+	.	+
	„ imbricatus -	- Sow. -	C	c	c	+	+	+
	„ lunularis -	- Lycett -	r	?	r			
	Opis gibbosus -	- Lycett -	r	.	.	+		
	„ lunulatus -	- Sow. -	r	.	r	+	.	+
	„ similis -	- Desh. -	r	.	.	+	.	+
	Pholadomya acuticosta	- Sow. -	r	.	.	.	.	+
	„ ambigua	- Sow. -	c	.	r			
	„ Dewalquei	- Lycett -	r	.	.	+		
	„ fidicula	- Sow. -	c	r	c	+		
	„ Heraulti	- Ag. -	C	.	r	+	+	+
	„ lyrata -	- Sow. -	c					
	„ ovalis -	- Sow. -	C	r	r			
	„ ovulum	- Ag. -	c	.	r	+	.	+
	„ Zieteni	- Ag. -	r	.	r			
	Pholas oolitica -	- L. & M. -	r	.	r	.	.	+
	Quenstedtia lævigata	- L. & M. -	c	.	c	+	+	+
	„ oblita -	- Phil. -	.	.	c	+	.	+
	Tancredia angulata -	- Lycett -	r	.	r	.	.	+
	„ axiniformis	- Phil. -	r	.	c	+	+	+
	„ donaciformis	- Lycett -	c	.	r	+		
	„ planata -	- L. & M. -	.	.	r	.	.	+

Table 1.—Comparison of the Fossils, &c.—*cont.*

Class.	Species.	Inferior Oolite of Midland District.			Compared with		
		Lincolnshire Limestone.	Collyweston Slate.	Northampton Sand.	Inferior Oolite of S. of England.	Inferior Oolite of Yorkshire.	Great Oolite of W. of England.
Dimyaria— *cont.*	Trigonia Beasleyi - - Lycett -	.	.	R			
	,, compta - - Lycett -	r	r	r			
	,, costata - - Park. -	C	c	c	+	+	+
	,, denticulata - Lycett -	R	.	r	+	+	+
	,, formosa - - Lycett -	r	.	r	+		
	,, Moretonis - - L. & M. -	.	r	.	.	.	+
	,, producta - - Lycett -	.	.	r	+	.	+
	,, hemisphærica - Lycett -	r	r	r			
	,, impressa - - Sow. -	.	c	r			
	,, pullus, *var. of* costata Sow. -	c	.	.	.	+	
	,, Phillipsii - - L. & M. -	r	.	r			
	,, sculpta - - Lycett -	r					
	,, spinulosa - - Y. & B. -	r	r				
	,, signata - - Ag. -	.	.	r	+	+	
	,, subglobosa - L. & M. -	R	.	r	+	.	+
	,, striata - - Sow. -	c	.	c	+		
	,, tenuicosta - Lycett -	R	.	?			
	,, v-costata - - Lycett -	r	.	c	+	+	
	,, Sharpiana - - Lycett -	R	.	R	+	+	
	Unicardium depressum - Phil. -	c	.	r	+	+	
	,, impressum - L. & M. -	c	r	r	.	.	+
	,, parvulum - L. & M. -	r	.	r	.	.	+
	,, gibbosum - L. & M. -	.	.	c	+	+	
GASTEROPODA	Actæon Sedgvici - - Phil. -	.	.	.	+		
	,, pullus - - Koch. -	r					
	Actæonina glabra - - Phil. -	r	.	.	.	+	
	,, parvula - Röm. -	r	.	.	.	.	+
	Alaria armata - - L. & M. -	r	.	r	.	.	+
	,, hamus - - Desh. -	r	.	.	.	.	+
	,, hamulus - - Desh. -	R	.	.	.	.	+
	,, Phillipsii - D'Orb. -	r	r	.	+	+	
	,, sub-punctata - Goldf. -	r					
	,, trifida - - Phil. -	r	.	r	.	.	+
	Ceritella acuta - - L. & M. -	r	.	.	.	.	+
	Cerithium Beanii - - L. & M. -	r	.	.	+	+	
	,, gemmatum - L. & M. -	c	.	r	+		
	,, limæforme - Röm. -	c	.	r	.	.	+
	,, quadricinctum - Goldf. -	c	.	.	+	.	+
	,, (Kilvirtia) strangulatum - D'Arch. -	r	.	.	.	.	+
	Chemnitzia Scarburgensis - L. & M. -	c	.	r	.	+	
	,, vetusta ? - Phil. -	r	.	.	.	+	
	,, Wetherellii? - L. & M. -	r	.	.	.	.	+
	Cirrus nodosus - - Sow. -	.	.	r	+		
	Cylindrites * acutus - Sow. -	r	.	.	.	.	+
	,, cylindricus - L. & M. -	r	.	.	.	.	+
	,, brevis ? - L. & M. -	r	.	.	.	.	+
	,, bullatus? - L. & M. -	r	.	.	.	.	+
	,, gradus - Lycett -	r	.	.	+		
	,, tabulatus ? - Lycett -	r	?	.	+		
	,, turriculatus? Lycett -	r	.	.	.	.	+

* These are all very doubtful species, small and imperfect.

Table 1.—Comparison of the Fossils, &c.—cont.

Class.	Species.		Inferior Oolite of Midland District.			Compared with		
			Lincolnshire Limestone.	Collyweston Slate.	Northampton Sand.	Inferior Oolite of S. of England.	Inferior Oolite of Yorkshire.	Great Oolite of W. of England.
Gasteropoda —cont.	Euspira cincta	- Phil. -	c					
	Delphinula alta	- L. & M. -	R					
	„ Prattii	- L. & M. -	r					
	Natica adducta	- Phil. -	c	.	r	+	+	
	„ (Euspira) canaliculata	- L. & M. -	c	r	c	+	.	+
	„ formosa	- L. & M. -	C	.	.	.	.	+
	„ Leckhamptonensis	Lycett -	C	r	?			
	„ Michelini	- D'Arch -	r	.	.	.	.	+
	„ neritoidea ?	- L. & M. -	r	.	c	.	.	+
	„ punctura	- Bean -	c	.	.	.	+	
	„ Verneuelii	- Arch. -	c	.	c	.	.	+
	Monodonta lævigata	- Sow. -	r	.	+	+		
	„ Lyellii	- D'Arch -	r	.	.	+	.	+
	Nerita costulata	- Desh. -	.	.	r	+		
	„ (Neritoma) hemisphærica	- Röm. -	.	.	r	+	.	+
	Nerinæa cingenda	- Brown -	C	.	r	+	+	
	„ Cotteswoldiæ	- Lycett -	c	.	.	+		
	„ Eudesii	- L. & M. -	c	.	.	.	.	+
	„ gracilis	- Lycett -	c	.	.	+		
	„ Jonesii	- Lycett -	c	.	.	+		
	„ Oppeli	- Lycett -	r	.	.	+		
	„ pseudocylindrica	D'Orb. -	r	.	.	+		
	„ punctata ?	- Voltz. -	?					
	„ triplicata	- Brown -	+	.	.	+		
	„ Voltzii	- Desl. -	c	.	.	+	.	+
	„ Sticklandi ?	- L. & M. -	r	.	.	+	.	+
	Onustus Burtonensis	- Lycett -	?	.	R	.		
	Patella inornata	- L. & M. -	c	.	r	+		
	„ nana	- Sow. -	.	.	r			
	„ rugosa	- Sow. -	c	c	r	+		
	Pleurotomaria aglaia	- D'Orb. -	.	.	r			
	„ armata	- Münst. -	c	.	r	+		
	„ clathrata	- L. & M. -	.	.	r	+		
	„ ornata	- Defr. -	c	.	r	+		
	„ pyramidata	Phil. -	.	.	r			
	„ sulcata	- Sow. -	r	.	.	+		
	Phasianella * acutiuscula	L. & M. -	r	.	.	.	.	+
	„ cincta	- Phil. -	?					
	„ elegans	- L. & M. -	r	.	.	.	?	+
	„ latiuscula	- L. & M. -	r					
	„ parvula	- L. & M. -	r					
	„ Pontonis	- Lycett -	c					
	„ striata	- Sow. -	r	.	.	+	+	
	„ tumidula	- L. & M. -	r					
	Pterocera Bentleyi	- L. & M. -	r	C				
	„ sp.	- -						
	Pileolus plicatus	- Sow. -	r	.	.	+		
	Rimula Blottii	- Desl. -	r	.	r			
	Rissoina obliquata	- Sow. -	r	.	.	+		

* Many of these are very doubtful forms,—small species.

Table 1.—Comparison of the Fossils, &c.—*cont.*

Class.	Species.	Lincolnshire Limestone.	Collyweston Slate.	Northampton Sand.	Inferior Oolite of S. of England.	Inferior Oolite of Yorkshire.	Great Oolite of W. of England.
Gasteropoda —*cont.*	Trochotoma calyx - Phil.	c	.	r	+	+	
	" extensa - L. & M.	r					
	" obtusa - L. & M.	c	.	r			
	" tabulata L. & M.	r	.	r	+		
	Trochus bijugatus ? - Quenst.	r					
	" Dunkeri - L. & M.	r					
	" Ibbetsoni - L. & M.	r					
	" Leckenbyii L. & M.	r	.	.	.	+	
	" Monilitectus - Phil.	.	.	.	+	+	
	" ornatissimus, { D'Orb.	.	.	.	+		
	var. Pontonis { Mor.	c	.	r			
	" spiratus - D'Arch	c					
	" squamiger - L. & M.	c					
	Turbo depauperatus - Lycett	c					
	" gemmatus - Lycett	r					
	" Phillipsii - L. & M.	c	.	.	.	+	
	" sp. -						
Cephalopoda	Ammonites bifrons - Brug.	.	.	R			
	" Blagdeni - Sow.	R	.	.	+	+	
	" garantianus - D'Orb.	.	.	R	+	+	
	" Murchisoniæ - Sow.	c	.	C	+		
	" var. corrugatus - Sow.	.	.	C	+		
	" niortensis - D'Orb.	.	.	r			
	" opalinus - Rein.	.	.	r	+		
	" subradiatus - Sow.	r	.	r	+		
	" Jurensis ? - Ziet.	.	.	r			
	" terebratus - Phil.	r					
	" insignis - Schub.	.	.	r	+		
	Belemnites Aalensis - Ziet.	.	.	c			
	" acutus - Miller	c	.	C			
	" bessinus - D'Orb.	r	.	r			
	" Blainvillii - Voltz.	r	.	c			
	" canaliculatus - Schloth.	r	.	r	+	+	
	" ellipticus - Miller	.	.	r	+		
	" elongatus - Miller	.	.	c			
	" giganteus - Schloth.	.	.	c	+	+	
	Nautilus Baberi - L. & M.	.	.	R			
	" obesus - Sow.	r	.	r	+		
	" polygonalis - Sow.	R	.	?	r		
	" sinuatus ? - Sow.	.	.	r			
Pisces	Strophodus magnus - Ag.	C	.	.	.	.	C
	" subreticulatus - Ag.	C					
	Pycnodus -	R					
Reptilia	Teleosaurus (scale of) -	R	.	R			
	Megalosaurus ? sp., tooth -	.	.	R			

TABLE 2.—Showing the GEOGRAPHICAL DISTRIBUTION of the GREAT OOLITE and CORNBRASH SPECIES, collected and occurring in the area of Sheet 64.

Species.		GREAT OOLITE. Northamptonshire.								
		Wadenhoe.	Oundle.	Glapthorne.	Upper Benefield.	Bulwick.	Ketton.	Wansford.	Allsworth.	Alwalton.
ECHINODERMATA.										
Acrosalenia hemicidaroides	- Wright -	.	.	.	+					
Clypeus Mülleri - -	- - -	.	.	.	+					
Echinobrissus clunicularis	- Llhwyd -	.	+	.	.	.	.	.	.	+
„ Griesbachii	- Wright -	.	.	.	.	.	.	.	.	+
„ sinuatus -	- Leake -	.	+	.	.	.	.	.	+	.
„ Woodwardi	- Wright -	.	.	.	.	.	.	.	.	+
Pygaster semisulcatus -	- Phil. -	.	.	.	+	.	.	.	.	.
ANNELIDA.										
Serpula obliquestriata -	- L. & M.	.	.	.	.	.	.	.	.	+
CRUSTACEA.										
Glyphea rostrata - -	- Phil. -	.	.	.	.	.	.	.	.	+
MOLLUSCA. (Brachiopoda).										
Rhynchonella concinna -	- Sow. -	.	+	.	.	.	.	.	+	+
„ obsoleta -	- Sow. -	.	.	.	.	.	.	.	.	+
„ varians -	- Schloth. -	.	+	.	.	.	.	.	+	.
Terebratula globata -	- Sow. -	.	+	.	.	.	.	.	+	.
„ maxillata -	- Sow. -	.	+	.	+	.	.	.	+	+
„ intermedia -	- Sow. -	.	.	.	+	.	.	.	.	+
„ ornithocephala	Sow. -	.	.	.	.	.	.	.	+	+
„ submaxillata -	- Dav. -	.	.	.	.	.	.	.	+	.
LAMELLIBRANCHIATA. Monomyaria.										
Avicula echinata - -	- Sow. -	.	.	.	.	.	.	.	+	+
„ Munsteri - -	- Goldf. -	.	.	.	.	.	.	.	.	+
Gervillia aviculoides -	- Sow. -	.	.	.	.	.	.	.	+	.
Hinnites abjectus -	- Phil. -	+	+	.	.	.	.	.	.	.
Ostrea gregaria -	- Sow. -	+	.	.	.	.	.	.	.	.
„ Sowerbyi -	- L. & M. -	.	+	+	.	.	.	.	.	+
„ subrugulosa -	- L. & M. -	.	+	+	.	.	.	.	+	+
Perna quadrata -	- Sow. -	.	+	+	.	+	.	.	.	.
Pinna ampla - -	- Sow. -	.	+	.	+	.	.	.	.	.
Plicatula tuberculosa -	- L. & M. -	.	.	+	.	.	.	.	.	.
Pecten annulatus -	- Sow. -	.	.	.	.	.	.	.	.	+
„ demissus -	- Phil. -	+	.	.	+	.	.	.	.	.
„ lens - -	- Sow. -	.	.	.	.	+	.	+	.	.
„ clathratus -	- Röm. -	.	.	.	.	+	.	.	.	.
Pteroperna costatula -	- Deslong -	.	.	.	.	.	.	.	.	+
„ gibbosa -	- Lycett -	+								
„ plana -	- Lycett -	+								
Lima duplicata -	- Sow. -	+	.	.	+	.	.	.	+	.
„ impressa -	- L. & M. -	.	.	.	.	.	.	.	.	.
„ interstincta -	- Phil. -	+	.	.	.	.	.	.	.	.
„ pectiniformis -	- Schloth. -	.	.	.	+	.	.	.	.	.
„ semicircularis -	- Goldf. -	.	+	.	.	.	.	.	.	+

Table 2.—Geographical Distribution of the Great Oolite, &c.—*cont.*

Species.		Wadenhoe.	Oundle.	Glapthorne.	Upper Bene-field.	Bulwick.	Ketton.	Wansford.	Ailsworth.	Alwalton.
		GREAT OOLITE. Northamptonshire.								
Dimyaria.										
Anatina undulata	- Sow.	.	+	.	.	.	.	.	.	.
Arca Prattii	- L. & M.	+	.	.	.	.	.	.	+	.
„ æmula	- Phil.	.	.	.	.	+	.	.	+	.
Cardium Buckmanii	- L. & M.	.	.	.	.	.	.	.	.	+
„ cognatum	- Phil.	.	.	.	.	.	.	.	.	+
Ceromya concentrica	- Sow.	.	.	.	.	.	.	.	+	.
„ plicata	- Ag.	.	.	.	.	.	.	.	+	.
Cypricardia Bathonica	- D'Orb.	.	+	.	.	.	.	.	+	.
„ rostrata	- Sow.	.	.	+	.	.	.	.	+	.
„ nuculiformis	- Röm.	.	.	.	.	.	.	.	+	.
Cyprina Loweana	- L. & M.	.	+	.	.	+	.	.	+	.
„ trapeziformis	- Röm.	.	+	.	.	.	.	.	.	.
Corbicella Bathonica	- L. & M.	.	+	.	.	.	.	.	.	.
Cucullæa Goldfussii	- Röm.	.	.	.	.	.	.	.	+	.
Gresslya peregrina	- Phil.	.	.	.	.	.	.	.	+	.
Isocardia tenera	- Sow.	.	.	.	.	.	.	.	.	+
Homomya crassiuscula	- L. & M.	.	+	.	+	.	.	.	.	.
„ Vezelayi	- D'Arch.	.	.	.	.	.	.	.	.	+
Modiola furcata	- Goldf.	.	+	.	.	.	.	.	.	.
„ imbricata	- Sow.	.	+	.	.	.	.	.	.	.
„ Sowerbyana	- D'Orb.	.	+	+	+	+	+	.	.	+
Lucina despecta	- Phil.	.	.	.	+	.	.	.	.	+
„ Bellona	- D'Orb.	.	+	.	.	.	.	+	.	.
Myacites calceiformis	- Phil.	.	+	.	.	.	.	.	.	.
„ decurtatus	- Phil.	.	.	.	.	.	.	.	.	+
„ securiformis	- Phil.	.	+	.	.	.	.	.	.	.
Neæra Ibbetsoni	- Morris	.	.	.	.	.	+	.	.	.
Nerinæa funiculus	- Desl.	.	.	.	.	.	.	.	.	.
„ Voltzii	- Desl.	.	+	.	.	.	.	.	.	.
Myoconcha crassa	- Sow.	.	.	.	+	.	.	.	.	.
Pholadomya deltoidea	- Sow.	.	+	.	.	.	.	.	.	.
„ Heraulti	- Ag.	.	+	.	.	.	.	.	.	.
„ Lyrata	- Ag.	.	.	.	.	.	.	.	.	+
„ socialis	- L. & M.	.	.	.	.	.	.	.	.	+
Tancredia extensa	- Lycett	.	.	.	+	.	.	.	.	.
Trigonia costata	- Sow.	.	.	+	.	.	.	.	.	.
„ Moretonis	- L. & M.	.	+	+	+	.	.	.	.	+
Gasteropoda.										
Natica globosa	- L. & M.	.	+	.	.	.	.	.	.	.
Nerita minuta	- Sow.	.	.	.	.	.	.	.	.	+
Nerinæa funiculus	- Desl.	.	+	.	.	.	.	.	.	.
„ Voltzii	- Desl.	.	+	.	.	.	.	.	.	.
Cephalopoda.										
Ammonites bullatus	- D'Orb.	.	.	.	.	.	.	.	.	+
Nautilus Baberi	- L. & M.	.	.	.	.	.	.	.	.	+
„ hexagonus	- Sow.	.	.	.	.	.	.	.	.	+
„ subtruncatus	- L. & M.	.	.	.	.	.	.	.	.	+
Pisces.										
Strophodus magnus	- Ag.	.	+	.	+	.	.	.	.	.
Hybodus dorsalis	- Ag.	.	.	.	.	.	.	.	.	+
Pycnodus Bucklandi	- Ag.	.	.	.	.	.	.	.	.	+

Table 2.—Geographical Distribution of the Great Oolite, &c.—*cont.*

Species.		CORNBRASH. Northamptonshire.					
		Oundle.	Churchfield Green.	Benefield.	Polebrook.	Cross Reads W. of Polebrook.	Peterborough.
ECHINODERMATA.							
Acrosalenia	-	+					
Echinobrissus clunicularis	Llhwyd.	+	.	.	.	+	
,, orbicularis	Phil.	.	.	.	.	+	+
Holectypus depressus	Leske	.	.	.	.	.	+
ANNELIDA.							
Serpula intestinalis	Phil.	.	.	.	.	.	+
,, tricarinata	Sow.	.	.	.	.	.	+
Vermicularia nodus	Phil.	.	.	.	.	.	+
MOLLUSCA.							
Brachiopoda.							
Rhynchonella obsoleta	Sow.	.	.	.	.	.	+
,, varians	Schloth.	.	.	.	.	+	+
Terebratula Bentleyi	Morris	.	.	.	.	.	+
,, lagenalis	Schloth.	.	.	.	.	.	+
,, ornithocephala	Sow.	.	.	.	.	.	+
,, obovata	Sow.	+	.	.	.	+	+
,, maxillata	Sow.	.	.	.	.	.	+
LAMELLIBRANCHIATA.							
Avicula echinata	Sow.	+	.	.	.	+	+
,, Munsteri	Goldf.	.	.	.	.	.	+
Gervillia aviculoides	Sow.	+	.	.	.	.	+
Ostrea flabelloides	Lam.	+	.	.	.	.	.
Lima duplicata	Sow.	.	.	.	.	.	+
,, pectiniformis	Schloth.	.	.	.	.	.	+
,, rigida	Sow.	.	.	.	.	.	+
Pecten anisopleurus	Buv.	.	.	.	.	.	+
,, articulatus	Schloth.	.	.	.	.	.	+
,, annulatus	Sow.	.	.	.	.	.	+
,, demissus	Phil.	+	.	.	.	+	
,, vagans	Sow.	+	.	.	.	+	
Isocardia tenera	Sow.	+	.	.	.	.	+
Gresslya peregrina	Phil.	.	.	.	.	+	
Lucina crassa	Sow.	+	.	.	.	.	
Lithodomus inclusus	Phil.	.	.	.	.	+	
Modiola imbricata	Sow.	+	.	.	.	.	+
Myacites decurtatus	Phil.	+	.	.	.	+	
,, securiformis	Phil.	+	.	.	.	+	
Pholadomya deltoidea	Sow.	+	.	.	.	+	
,, ovulum	Ag.	.	.	.	.	.	+
Trigonia elongata ?	Sow.	+					
,, Moretonis	L. & M.	+					
GASTEROPODA.							
Actæonina Scarburgensis	Lycett.	.	.	.	.	.	+
Chemnitzia sp.	-	.	.	.	.	+	
CEPHALOPODA.							
Ammonites maceocephalus	Schloth.	.	.	.	.	.	+

Table 2.—Geographical Distribution of the Great Oolite, &c.—cont.

Species.		CORNBRASH. Northamptonshire.					
		Oundle.	Churchfield Green.	Benefield.	Polebrook.	Cross Roads W. of Polebrook.	Petreborough.
PISCES.							
Pycnodus sp. - - -	-						
Strophodus magnus - - -	Ag. -	.	.	..	.	.	+
„ subreticulatus - -	Ag. -	.	.	.	.	.	+
„ tenuis - - -	Ag. -	.	.	.	.	.	+

Species.		GREAT OOLITE. Lincolnshire.	
		Stamford Open Fields.	Danes Hill.
ECHINODERMATA.			
Acrosalenia hemicidaroides - - -	- Wright -	.	+
Clypeus Mülleri - - -	-	+	+
CRUSTACEA.			
Eryma elegans - - - - -	- Oppel. -	.	+
MOLLUSCA. Brachiopoda.			
Rhynchonella concinna - - -	- Sow.	+	
Terebratula intermedia - - -	- Sow. -	.	+
„ maxillata - - -	- Sow. -	.	+
„ ornithocephala - -	- Sow. -	.	+
„ obovata - -	- Sow. -	.	+
„ sublagenalis - -	- Dav. -	.	+
LAMELLIBRANCHIATA.			
Avicula echinata - - -	- Sow. -	+	
Lima cardiiformis - - -	- L. & M. -	+	
„ duplicata - - -	- Sow. -	+	
Ostrea Sowerbyi - - -	- L. & M. -	+	+
„ subrugulosa - - -	- L. & M. -	+	+
Pecten annulatus - - -	- Sow. -	.	+
Perna rugosa - - -	- Münst. -	.	+
„ quadrata - - -	- Phil. -	.	+
Cyprina Loweana - - -	- L. & M. -	.	+
„ nuciformis - - -	- Lyc. -	.	+
Ceromya concentrica - - -	- Sow. -	+	
„ Symondsii - - -	- L. & M.-	.	+
Cardium cognatum - - -	- Phil. -	.	+
„ Buckmani - - -	- L. & M. -	.	+
„ lingulatum - - -	- L. & M. ?	.	+
„ Stricklandii - - -	- L. & M. -	.	+
„ subtrigonum - - -	- L. & M. -	.	+
Modiola imbricata - - -	- Sow. -	+	+
„ Lonsdalei - - -	- L. & M.	+	+

T 2

Table 2.—Geographical Distribution of the Great Oolite, &c.—*cont.*

Species.					Great Oolite. Lincolnshire.	
					Stamford Open Fields.	Danes Hill.
Myacites securiformis	-	-	-	- Phil. -	.	+
Cypricardia caudata	-	-	-	- Lycett -	.	+
„ nuculiformis	-	-	-	- Röm. -	.	+
Isocardia tenera	-	-	-	- Sow. -	.	+
Pholadomya acuticosta	-	-	-	- Sow. -	+	
„ Phillipsii	-	-	-	- Morris -	.	+
„ lyrata	-	-	-	- Sow. -	.	+
Taneredia angulata	-	-	- ,	- Lycett -	+	
Neæra Ibbetsoni	-	-	-	- Morris -	+	
Trigonia costata	-	-	-	- Sow. -	.	+
„ Moretonis	-	-	-	- L. & M. -	.	+
GASTEROPODA.						
Amberleya nodosa	-	-	-	- Buckm. -	.	+
Natica canaliculata	-	-	-	- L. & M. -	.	+
„ globosa -	-	-	-	- L. & M. -	.	+
„ formosa	-	-	-	- L. & M. -	.	+
„ pyramidata	-	-	-	- L. & M. -	.	+
CEPHALOPODA.						
Ammonites gracilis	-	-	-	- Buckm. -	+	
Nautilus Baberi	-	-	-	- L. & M. -	+	
„ subtruncatus	-	-	-	- L. & M. -	.	+

Species.			Cornbrash. Lincolnshire.			
			Uffington.	Caswick Cutting.	Danes Hill Cutting.	Bourne.
ECHINODERMATA.						
Cidaris Bradfordensis -	-	-	- Wright -	+			
Echinobrissus clunicularis	-	-	- Llhwyd -	+			
„ orbicularis	-	-	- Phil. -	+	.	.	+
„ quadratus	-	-	- Wright -	+			
Holectypus depressus	-	-	- Lam. -	+	.	.	+
ANNELIDA.						
Serpula intestinalis -	-	-	- Phil. -	.	+	.	+
„ tetragona -	-	-	- Sow. -	+			
MOLLUSCA. Brachiopoda.						
Discina -	-	-	- -	.		.	+
Rhynchonella concinna	-	-	- Sow. -	+	+	.	+
„ Morieri	-	-	- Dav. -	.	+		
„ varians	-	-	- Schloth. -	+	.		
Terebratula Bentleyi	-	-	- Morris -	.	+	.	+
„ coarctata	-	-	- Park. -	.	.	.	+
„ intermedia	-	-	- Sow. -	+			

Table 2.—Geographical Distribution of the Great Oolite, &c.—*cont.*

Species.	Uffington.	Caswick Cutting.	Danes Hill Cutting.	Bourne.
		CORNBRASH. Lincolnshire.		
Terebratula lagenalis - - - Schloth. -	+	.	+	+
„ ornithocephala - - - Sow. -	+	.	+	+
„ maxillata - - - Sow. -	.	+	.	+
„ obovata - - - Sow. -	+	.	.	+
„ sublagenalis - - - Dav. -	+	.	+	
LAMELLIBRANCHIATA.				
Avicula echinata - - - - Sow. -	+			
„ Munsteri - - - - Goldf. -	.	.	.	+
Gervillea aviculoides - - - Sow. -	.	.	.	+
Hinnites abjectus - - - - Phil. -	.	.	.	+
Ostrea flabelloides - - - - Lam. -	+	.	.	+
„ Sowerbyi - - - - L. & M. -	.	.	.	+
„ subrugulosa - - - - L. & M. -	.	.	.	+
Lima duplicata - - - - Sow. -	+	.	.	+
„ pectiniformis - - - - Schloth. -	.	+	.	+
„ impressa - - - - L. & M. -	.	+	+	+
„ rigidula - - - - Phil. -	.	+	.	+
„ rigida - - - - Sow. -	.	+	.	
„ puncturata - - - - Sow. -	.	.	.	+
Pecten demissus - - - - Phil. -	.	.	.	+
„ lens - - - - Sow. -	.	.	.	+
„ peregrinus - - - - L. & M. -	.	.	.	+
„ vagans - - - - Sow. -	.	.	.	+
Pinna cuneata - - - - Bean -	.	.	.	+
Cardium cognatum - - - - Phil. -	.	.	.	+
„ subtrigonum - - - - L. & M. -	.	.	.	+
Cyprina Loweana - - - - L. & M. -	.	.	.	+
Goniomya v-scripta - - - - Sow. -	.	+	.	+
Gresslya peregrina - - - - Phil. -	.	.	.	+
Homomya crassiuscula - - - - L. & M. -	.	.	.	+
„ gibbosa - - - - Sow. -	.	.	.	+
Isocardia tenera - - - - Sow. -	.	.	.	+
Lucina Lycettii - - - - Oppel. -	.	.	.	+
Modiola gibbosa - - - - Sow. -	.	.	.	+
„ imbricata - - - - Sow. -	.	.	.	+
Myopsis Jurassi - - - - Brong. -	.	.	.	+
Myacites calceiformis - - - - Phil. -	.	.	.	+
„ decurtatus - - - - Phil. -	.	.	.	+
„ modica - - - - Bean -	.	.	.	+
„ sinistra - - - - Ag. -	.	.	.	+
„ securiformis - - - - Phil. -	.	.	.	+
„ Terquemi - - - - Buv. -	.	.	.	+
Pholadomya deltoidea - - - - Sow. -	.	.	.	+
„ acuticosta - - - - Sow. -	.	+	.	
Trigonia costata - - - - Sow. -	.	.	.	+
„ elongata ? - - - - Sow. -	.	.	.	+
„ cassiope - - - - D'Orb. -	.	.	.	+
„ Moretonis - - - - L. & M. -	.	.	.	+
„ Scarburgensis - - - Lycett -	.	.	.	+
Quenstedtia oblita - - - - Phil. -	.	.	.	+
GASTEROPODA.				
Chemnitzia vittata - - - - Phil. -	+	.		

Table 2.—Geographical Distribution of the Great Oolite, &c.—*cont.*

Species.					Uffington.	Casewick Outting.	Dane Hill Outting.	Bourne.
						CORNBRASH. Lincolnshire.		
CEPHALOPODA.								
Ammonites Herveyi	-	-	-	Sow.	-	.	.	+
„ macrocephalus	-	-	-	Schloth.	-	+	.	+
Nautilus Baberi	-	-	-	L. & M.	-	.	.	+
PISCES.								
Strophodus magnus	-	-	-	Ag.	-	.	+	

Species.					Essendine.	Belmesthorpe.	Ryhall.
						GREAT OOLITE. Rutland.	
CRUSTACEA.							
Eryma, allied to Elegans	-	-	-	-	-	.	+
MOLLUSCA. Brachiopoda.							
Terebratula intermedia	-	-	-	Sow. -	-	.	+
„ perovalis	-	-	-	Sow. -	-	.	.	+
LAMELLIBRANCHIATA.							
Gervillia monotis	-	-	-	Desl. -	-	.	+	+
„ Islipensis	-	-	-	L. & M.	-	+	.	.
Lima cardiiformis	-	-	-	L. & M.	-	.	+	+
„ puncturata	-	-	-	. -	-	.	.	+
Pecten annulatus	-	-	-	Sow. -	-	.	+	
„ demissus	-	-	-	Phil. -	-	.	.	+
„ lens	-	-	-	Sow. -	-	.	+	
Pinna cuneata	-	-	-	Bean -	-	.	+	
Perna quadrata	-	-	-	Sow. -	-	.	+	
Pteroperna costatula	-	-	-	Desl. -	-	.	+	
Ostrea Sowerbyi	-	-	-	L. & M.	-	.	.	+
„ subrugulosa	-	-	-	L. & M.	-	.	+	+
Ceromya Symondsii	-	-	-	L. & M.	-	+	+	
Cardium subtrigonum	-	-	-	L. & M.	-	.	+	
„ Buckmani	-	-	-	L. & M.	-	.	+	
Corbicella Bathonica	-	-	-	L. & M.	-	.	+	
Cyprina depressiuscula	-	-	-	L. & M.	-	.	+	
„ Loweana	-	-	-	L. & M.	-	.	.	+
Cypricardia nuculiformis	-	-	-	L. & M.	-	+	+	+
„ Bathonica	-	-	-	L. & M.	-	.	+	
„ rostrata	-	-	-	Sow. -	-	.	.	+
Gresslya peregrina	-	-	-	Phil. -	-	.	+	
Homomya crassiuscula	-	-	-	L. & M.	-	.	+	
„ Vezelayi	-	-	-	D'Arch.	-	.	+	
Isocardia tenera	-	-	-	Sow. -	-	+	.	+
Myacites calceiformis	-	-	-	Phil. -	-	.	+	+
„ securiformis	-	-	-	Phil. -	-	.	.	+
„ Terquemea	-	-	-	Buv. -	-	.	+	
Modiola imbricata	-	-	-	Sow. -	-	+	.	+

Table 2.—Geographical Description of the Great Oolite, &c.—*cont.*

Species.	Great Oolite, Rutland.		
	Bssendine.	Belmesthorpe.	Byhall.
Macrodon Hirsonensis - - - - D'Arch.	.	+	
Nesæra Ibbetsoni - - - - - Morris	+	.	
Pholadomya deltoidea - - - - Sow. -	.	+	
„ Heraulti - - - - Ag. -	.	+	+
„ oblita - - - - L. & M.	.	+	
„ lyrata - - - - Sow. -	.	+	
„ socialis - - - - L. & M.	+	+	
„ solitaria - - - - L. & M.	.	+	
Tancredia axiniformis - - - Phil. -	+		
Trigonia costata - - - - Sow. -	.	+	+
„ elongata ? - - - - Sow. -	.	+	
„ Moretonis - - - - L. & M.	.	+	
Unicardium varicosum - - - Sow. -	.	+	
GASTEROPODA.			
Natica globosa - - - - - L. & M.	+	.	+
„ grandis - - - - - L. & M.	.	+	
„ formosa - - - - - L. & M.	+	+	
„ intermedia - - - - - L. & M.	.	+	
CEPHALOPODA.			
Nautilus Baberi - - - - L. & M.	.	+	+
„ subtruncatus - - - L. & M.	.	+	
PISCES.			
Hybodus sp. - - - - - -	.	+	
REPTILIA.			
Teleosaurus sp. - - - - - -	.	+	
Pterodactylus sp. - - - - - -	.	+	

CORNBRASH.

STILTON, HUNTINGDONSHIRE.

ECHINODERMATA.

Clypeus Mülleri. Wright.
Echinobrissus clunicularis. Llhwyd.
„ orbicularis. Phil.
Holectypus depressus. Leske.

ANNELIDA.

Serpula intestinalis. Phil.
„ squamosa. Bean.
„ tetragona. Sow.

CRUSTACEA.

Glyphæa rostrata. Phil.

BRACHIOPODA.

Rhynchonella concinna. Sow.
„ Moorei. Daw.
„ obsoleta. Sow.
„ varians. Schloth.

Terebratula Bentleyi. Morris.
„   coarctata. Park.
„   intermedia. Sow.
„   lagenalis. Schloth.
„   sub-lagenalis. Dav.
„   maxillata. Sow.
„   obovata. Sow.
„   ornithocephala. Sow.

LAMELLIBRANCHIATA.

Anomia semistriata. Bean.
Avicula echinata. Sow.
Lima duplicata. Sow.
„   impressa. L. & M.
„   læviuscula. Sow.
„   pectiniformis. Schloth.
„   rigida. Sow.
„   rigidula. Phil.
Pecten anisopleurus. Buv.
„   articulatus. Schloth.
„   annulatus. Sow.
„   demissus. Phil.
„   insæquicostatus. Phil.
„   lens. Sow.
„   Michelensis. Buv.
„   vagans. Sow.
Cardium cognatum. Phil.
Cypricardia caudata. Lycett.
Goniomya v-scripta. Sow.
Homomya crassiuscula. L. & M.
„   gibbosa. Sow.
Isocardia tenera. Sow.
Lucina striatula. Buv.
Modiola gibbosa. Sow.
„   imbricata. Sow.
„   Lonsdalei. L. & M.
„   Sowerbyana. D'Orb.
Myacites calceiformis. Phil.
„   decurtatus. Phil.
„   recurvus. Phil.
„   securiformis. Phil.
„   sinistra. Ag.
Pholadomya acuticosta. Sow.
„   deltoidea. Sow.
„   Lyrata. Sow.
„   Phillipsia. Morris.
Trigonia Scarburgensis. Lycett.

GASTEROPODA.

Chemnitzia simplex. L. & M.
Pleurotomaria granulata. Sow.

CEPHALOPODA.

Ammonites Harveyi. Sow.
          macrocephalus. Schloth.
          modiolaris. Llhwyd.

PISCES.

Strophodus magnus. Ag.
„   subreticulatus. Ag.
Pycnodus Bucklandi. Ag.
Asteracanthus verrucosus. Ag.

REPTILIA.

Ichthyosaurus sp.
Plesiosaurus sp.
Teleosaurus sp.

APPENDIX II.

BIBLIOGRAPHY OF THE DISTRICT.

LIST OF BOOKS, PAPERS, &C., ON THE GEOLOGY, PALÆONTOLOGY, AND MINERALOGY OF THE COUNTY OF RUTLAND, TOGETHER WITH THOSE RELATING TO THE PORTIONS OF LINCOLN, LEICESTER, NORTHAMPTON, HUNTINGDON, AND CAMBRIDGE, INCLUDED WITHIN THE AREA OF SHEET 64.

FROM MATERIALS SUPPLIED BY W. WHITAKER, B.A., F.G.S., &C.

Alphabetical List of Authors, whose writings are cited in this Appendix.

(The numbers refer to the titles as Chronologically arranged.)

Chronological List of the Papers referring to the District.

1671.

1. LISTER, M. A Letter , ... on that of M. Steno concerning Petrify'd Shells. *Phil. Trans., vol. v. (No. 76), p. 2282.*

1712.

2. MORTON, J. Natural History of Northamptonshire, &c. *Fol. Lond.*

1728.

3. LEWIS, REV. —. An Account of the several Strata of Earths and Fossils found in sinking the mineral Wells at Holt.
Phil. Trans., vol. xxxv. (No. 403), p. 489.

1734.

4. SHORT, DR. T. The Natural, Experimental, and Medicinal History of the Mineral Waters of Derbyshire, Lincolnshire, and Yorkshire, Particularly those of Scarborough, ... Together with the Natural History of the Earths, Minerals, and Fossils through which the chief of them pass. *4to. Lond.*

1740.

5. SHORT, DR. T. An essay Towards a Natural, Experimental, and Medicinal History of the Principle Mineral Waters of . . . . . . Northamptonshire, Leicestershire, and Nottinghamshire, Particularly those of Nevile Holt . . . . . . &c. *4to. Sheffield.*

6. ———————— Natural, Experimental, and Medicinal History of the Mineral Waters of England. *4to. Sheffield.*

1765.

7. ANON. [DR. T. SHORT]. A General Treatise on various Cold Mineral Waters in England, but more particularly on those at . . . . . . Neville Holt, &c. *8vo. London.*

1769.

8. EDWARDS, L. Survey of Witham (some geological notes).

1791.

9. BARKER, T. Abstract of a Register of the Barometer, Thermometer, and Rain at Lyndon in Rutland. Note, "Chalk found in a new place." *Phil. Trans., vol. lxxxi., Part 2, p. 281.*

1799.

10. YOUNG, A. Agricultural Report of the County of Lincolnshire, with a Map and Plates. *8vo. London.*

1807.

11. BRITTON, J. A Topographical and Historical Description of Leicestershire. *Beauties of England and Wales, vol. ix., p. 313. 8vo. London.*

12. ———————— A Topographical and Historical Description of Lincolnshire. *Ibid., p. 523.*

1808.

13. BRAYLEY, E. W. A Topographical and Historical Description of Huntingdonshire. *Ibid., vol. vii., p. 325.*

14. BRAYLEY, E. W., and J. BRITTON. A Topographical and Historical Description of Cambridgeshire. *Ibid., vol. ii.*

1809.

15. PITT, W. Agricultural Report of the County of Northamptonshire, drawn up for the Board of Agriculture and Internal Improvement. *8vo. Lond.*

1811.

16. PARKINSON, R. Agricultural Report of the County of Huntingdon, drawn up for the consideration of the Board of Agriculture and Internal Improvement. 8vo. Lond.

1812.

17. TOWNSHEND, REV. J. The Character of Moses established for veracity as an Historian. Recording Events from the Creation to the Deluge; with Plates of Fossils. 4to. Bath and Lond.

1813.

18. BREWER, J. N. A Topographical and Historical Description of the County of Rutland.
Beauties of England and Wales, vol. xii., Part II. 8vo. Lond.

19. PITT, W., and R. PARKINSON. A General View of the Agriculture of the Counties of Leicester and Rutland, drawn up for the consideration of the Board of Agriculture and Internal Improvement, with a Map and Plates. 8vo. Lond.

1816–1818.

20. SOWERBY, J. The Mineral Conchology of Great Britain. Vol. II. 8vo. Lond.

1817.

21. SMITH, W. Stratigraphical System of Organized Fossils with reference to the specimens of the Original Geological Collection in the British Museum. Explaining their state of preservation and their use in identifying the British strata. 4to. Lond.

1818.

22. PHILLIPS, W. A Selection of Facts from the best authorities, arranged so as to form an Outline of the Geology of England and Wales. With a Map and Sections. 12mo. Lond.

1820.

· 23. SMITH, W. A New Geological Map of England and Wales. Lond.

1821.

24. BUCKLAND, REV. DR. W. Notice of the Chalk at Ridlington.
Trans. Geol. Soc., vol. v., p. 539.

25–27. SMITH, W. Geological Maps of Rutlandshire, Leicestershire, and Huntingdonshire. Lond.

1822.

28. CONYBEARE, REV. W. D., and W. PHILLIPS. Outlines of the Geology of England and Wales. 8vo. Lond.

1822–1823.

29. SOWERBY, J. The Mineral Conchology of Great Britain. Vol. IV. 8vo. Lond.

1824–1825.

30. SOWERBY, J. The Mineral Conchology of Great Britain. Vol. V. 8vo. Lond.

1825.

31. SEDGWICK, REV. PROF. A. On the Origin of Alluvial and Diluvial Formations. Ann. of Phil., Ser. 2, vol. ix., p. 241, and vol. x., p. 18.

1826.

32. BATHURST, C. Account of the Geology of the country between Stamford and Bedford. MS.

1826–1829.

33. SOWERBY, J., and J. D. The Mineral Conchology of Great Britain. Vol. VI. 8vo. Lond.

1834.

34. SAUNDERS, J., JUN. History of the County of Lincoln, with a Map and Plates. [Geology, chapter 2, p. 17.] 4to. *London and Lincoln.*

1836.

35. FITTON, DR. W. H. On the strata between the Chalk and the Oxford Oolite in the South-east of England (Chalk at Ridlington). *Trans. Geol. Soc., Ser. 2, vol. iv., p. 308,* and *notes, p. 383*.*

36. LONSDALE, W. Maps of the Oolitic Districts of England. Sheet 64. *MS.*

1838.

37. MITCHELL, DR. J. On the Drift from the Chalk and the Strata below the Chalk in the Counties of Norfolk, Suffolk, Essex, Cambridge, Huntingdon, Bedford, Hertford, and Middlesex. *Proc. Geol. Soc., vol. iii., p. 3.*

1839.

38. DE LA BECHE, H. T., W. SMITH, and C. H. SMITH. The Result of an Inquiry undertaken under the Authority of the Lords Commissioners of Her Majesty's Treasury with reference to the Selection of Stone for building the new Houses of Parliament. *Parliamentary Report.*

1841.

39. OWEN, PROF. R. A description of a portion of the Skeleton of the Cetiosaurus, a gigantic extinct Saurian Reptile occurring in the Oolitic formations of different portions of England. *Proc. Geol. Soc., vol. iii., p. 457.*

1843.

40. PUSEY, P. On the Agricultural Improvements of Lincolnshire. *Journ. Roy Agric. Soc. vol. iv., p. 287.*

41. ROSE, C. B. On the Alluvium of the Bedford Level. *Geologist, p. 73.*

1844.

42. SMITH, W. Memoirs of William Smith by PROF. JOHN PHILLIPS. 8vo. *Lond.*

1845.

43. BRODIE, REV. P. B. A History of the Fossil Insects in the Secondary Rocks of England, accompanied by a particular account of the strata in which they occur, &c. 8vo. *Lond.*

44. SMITH, C. H. Lithology, or Observations on Stone used for Building. 4to. *Lond.*

1846.

45. COLEMAN, REV. W. H. Article on the Geology of the County of Leicester. *W. White's History, Gazetteer, and Directory of Leicester- shire and the small County of Rutland.* With a Map. 12mo. *Sheffield.*

1847.

46. ANDERSON, SIR C. A Short Guide to the County of Lincoln, with notes on the Geology, Botany, &c. 12mo. *Gainsborough.*

1848.

47. IBBETSON, CAPT., LL.B., and [PROF.] J. MORRIS. Notice of the Geology of the neighbourhood of Stamford and Peterborough. *Rep. Brit. Assoc. for 1847, Trans. of Sections, p. 127.*

1850.

48. BRODIE, REV. P. B. Sketch of the Geology of the neighbourhood of Grantham, Lincolnshire; and a comparison of the Stonesfield Slate at Collyweston in Northamptonshire with that in the Cotswold Hills. *Ann. & Mag. Nat. Hist., Ser. 2. vol. vi., p. 256,* and *Proc. Cotteswold Nat. Club, vol. i., p. 52.*

49. MORRIS [PROF.] J., and J. LYCETT. A Monograph of the Mollusca from the Great Oolite. Part I., Univalves [Collyweston, p. 15].
        Palæontograph. Soc. 4to. Lond.

1851.

50. BRODIE, REV. P. B. Remarks on the Stonesfield Slate at Collyweston, near Stamford, and the Great Oolite, Inferior Oolite, and Lias, in the neighbourhood of Grantham [equivalent to No.   , but with slight alterations]. *Rep. Brit. Assoc. for 1850, Trans. of Sections, p. 74.*

51. CLARKE, J. A. Farming of Lincolnshire.
        Journ. Roy. Agric. Soc., vol. xii., p. 259.

52. DAVIDSON, T. A Monograph of British Oolitic and Liassic Brachiopoda. Part II. [Northampton, pp. 10, 40–43, and 58].
        Palæontograph. Soc. 4to. Lond.

1852.

53. BAKER, J. L. An Essay on the Farming of Northamptonshire, with a geological map, &c.   *8vo. Lond.*

54. BEARN, W. On the Farming of Northamptonshire [with description and map of the soils]. *Journ. Roy. Agric. Soc., vol. xiii. p. 44.*

55. DAVIDSON, T. A Monograph of British Oolitic and Liassic Brachiopoda. Part III. [Plates 14–18, and p. 68].
        Palæontograph. Soc. 4to. Lond.

1853.

56. DE LA CONDAMINE, REV. H. M. On a Freshwater Deposit in the " Drift" of Huntingdon. *Quart. Journ. Geol. Soc., vol. ix., p. 271.*

57. MORRIS [PROF.] J. On some Sections in the Oolitic district of Lincolnshire. *Quart. Journ. Geol. Soc., vol. ix., p. 317.*

58. MORRIS, [PROF.] J. and J. LYCETT. A Monograph of the Mollusca from the Great Oolite; chiefly from Minchinhampton and the Coast of Yorkshire. Part II. Bivalves. *Palæontograph. Soc. 4to. Lond.*

59. TRIMMER, J. Notes on the Geology of the Keythorpe Estate, and its relations to the Keythorpe System of Drainage.
        Journ. Roy. Agric. Soc., vol. xiv., p. 96.

60. TRIMMER, J. On some Mammaliferous Deposits in the Valley of the Nene, near Peterborough. *Quart. Journ. Geol. Soc., vol. x., p. 343.*

1854.

61. WRIGHT, DR. T. Contributions to the Palæontology of Gloucestershire. A description, with Figures, of some new Species of Echinodermata, from the Lias and Oolites.
        Ann. and Mag. Nat. Hist. Ser. 2, vol. xiii., pp. 312, 376, and Proc. Cotteswold Nat. Club., vol. ii., p. 17 (1860?).

1855.

62. MORRIS, [PROF.] J., and J. LYCETT. A Monograph of the Mollusca, from the Great Oolite chiefly from Minchinhampton and the Coast of Yorkshire. Part III. Bivalves. *Palæontograph. Soc. 4to. Lond.*

1857.

63. BRODIE, REV. P. B. Remarks on the Inferior Oolite and Lias in parts of Northamptonshire, compared with the same Formations in Gloucestershire.
        Proc. Cotteswold Nat. Club., vol. ii., p. 132, and Ann. and Mag. Nat. Hist., Ser. 2, vol. xix., p. 56.

64. LYCETT, J. The Cotteswold Hills. Hand-Book Introductory to their Geology and Palæontology. *8vo. Lond. and Stroud, p. 131, &c.*

65. WRIGHT, DR. T. A Monograph on the British Fossil Echinodermata of the Oolitic Formations. Part First, containing the Cidaridæ, Hemicidaridæ, and Diademadæ. [Pp. 1–154.]
Palæontograph. Soc. 4to. Lond.

1858.

66. WRIGHT, DR. T. A Monograph on the British Fossil Echinodermata from the Oolitic Formations. Part II., containing the Diademadæ, Echinidæ, Saleniadæ, and Echinoconidæ. [Pp. 155–302.]
Palæontograph. Soc. 4to. Lond.

1859.

67. ANON. [W.] The Deposition of Warp.

68. TROLLOPE, REV. E. On the Alluvial Lands and Submarine Forests of Lincolnshire.
Proc. Geol. and Polytech. Soc.; W. Riding, York, vol. iii., p. 637.

69. WRIGHT, DR. T. A Monograph on the British Fossil Echinodermata from the Oolitic Formations. Part III. containing the Collyritidæ, Echinobrissidæ and Echinolampidæ. [Pp. 303–388.]
Palæontograph. Soc. 4to. Lond.

1860.

70. HULL, E. On the South-easterly Attenuation of the Lower Secondary Formations of England; and the probable Depth of the Coal Measures under Oxfordshire and Northamptonshire.
Quart. Journ. Geol. Soc., vol. xvi., p. 63.

71. WRIGHT, DR. T. A Monograph on the British Fossil Echinodermata from the Oolitic Formations. Part IV. containing the Echinolampidæ. The stratigraphical distribution of the Echinodermata, &c. [Pp. 389–468.]
Palæontograph. Soc. 4to. Lond.

1861.

72. BRODIE, REV. P. B. On the Geology of South Northamptonshire.
Proc. Warwick Nat. and Archæol. Field Club, p. 4.

73. BROWN, —. The Iron Ores of Northamptonshire.
Trans. S. Wales Inst. of Eng., vol. ii., p. 193.
[Discussion, p. 232.]

74. HUNT, R. On the Iron Ore Deposits of Lincolnshire [with analyses and sections].
Proc. Geol. and Polytech. Soc., W. Riding, York, vol. iv., p. 97.

75. PORTER, DR. H. The Geology of Peterborough and its neighbourhood.
8vo. Peterborough.

1862.

76. RILEY, E. On the Manufacture of Iron. [Analyses of Ores and Coals.]
Trans. Soc. Eng. for 1861, p. 59.

77. WRIGHT, DR. T. A Monograph on the British Fossil Echinodermata from the Oolitic Formations, Vol. 2, Part First. On the Asteroidea.
Palæontograph. Soc. 4to. Lond.

1863.

78. LYCETT, DR. J. Supplementary Monograph on the Mollusca from the Stonesfield Slate, Great Oolite, Forest Marble, and Cornbrash.
Palæontograph. Soc. 4to. Lond.

79. PORTER, DR. H. On the Occurrence of ·large Quantities of Fossil Wood in the Oxford Clay, near Peterborough.
Quart. Journ. Geol. Soc., vol. xix., p. 317.

1864.

80. PERCY, DR. J. Metallurgy [Vol. II.], Iron and Steel. [Analysis of Iron Ores, pp. 208, 209, 225, 226.]
8vo. Lond.

1865.

81. WOOD, S. V., JUN. A Map of the Upper Tertiaries in the Counties of
Norfolk, Suffolk, Essex, Middlesex, Hertford, Cambridge, Huntingdon,
and Bedford. (With Remarks and Sections.) *Privately printed.*

1866.

82. ANSTED, PROF. D. T. Physical Geography and Geology of the County
of Leicester. (Natural Hist. of Leicestershire). *4to. Westminster.*

83. HOLDSWORTH, J. On the Extension of the English Coal-fields beneath
the Secondary Formations of the Midland Counties. Also, Does Coal
exist near London? *8vo. Lond.*

84. HULL, E. The new Iron-fields of England.
Quart. Journ. of Sci., vol. iii., p. 323.

85. PHILLIPS, PROF. J. A Monograph of British Belemnitidæ. Part II.,
containing Pp. 29–52, Plates I.–VII. [Liassic.] .
Palæontograph. Soc. 4to. Lond.

86. SEELEY, H. [G.] A Sketch of the Gravels and Drift of the Fenlands.
Quart. Journ. Geol. Soc., vol. xxii., p. 470.

87. —————————— Theoretical Remarks on the Gravel and Drift of the
Fenlands. *Geol. Mag., vol. iii., p. 495.*

1867.

88. WOOD, S. V., JUN. On the Structure of the Post-glacial Deposits of
the South-east of England.
Quart. Journ. Geol. Soc., vol. xxiii., p. 394. Corrections in *Geol.
Mag., vol. v., pp. 43, 534 (1868).*

1868.

89. BRODIE, REV. P. B. A Sketch of the Lias generally in England, and of
the " Insect and Saurian beds," especially in the lower division in the
Counties of Warwick, Worcester, and Gloucester. With a particular
account of the fossils which characterise them.
Proc. Warwick Nat. & Archæol. Field Club, p. 1, with a shorter
title in *Trans. Woolhope Nat. Field Club for 1866, p. 205 (1867),*
and *Trans. Dudley and Midland Geol. and Sci. Soc. (1868).*

90. DUNCAN, [PROF.] P. M. A Monograph of the British Fossil Corals,
Second Series, Part IV., No. 2, pp. 45–73, Plates XII.–XVII. [Liassic].
Palæontograph. Soc. 4to. Lond.

91. MAW, G. On the Disposition of Iron in variegated Strata.
Quart. Journ. Geol. Soc., vol. xxiv., p. 351.

92. MURRAY, G. On the Farming of Huntingdon. (Note on the Geology.)
Journ. Roy. Agric. Soc., Ser. 2, vol. iv., p. 251.

93. WOOD, S. V., JUN., and REV. J. L. ROME. On the Glacial and Post-
glacial Structure of Lincolnshire and South-east Yorkshire.
Quart. Journ. Geol. Soc., vol. xxiv., p. 146.

1869.

94. BRODIE, REV. P. B. Geological Notes on Northamptonshire, &c.
Geol. Mag., vol. vi., p. 236.

95. JECKS, C. On the Ferruginous Sandstone of the neighbourhood of
Northampton.
Geol. and Nat. Hist. Repertory, vol. ii., p. 261; and *Rep. Brit. Assoc.
for 1868, Trans. of Sections, p. 69.*

96. JUDD, J. W. On the Origin of the Northampton Sand. (Abstract.)
Geol. Mag., vol. vi., p. 221.

97. MORRIS, PROF. J. Geological Notes on Parts of Northampton- and
Lincolnshires. *Ibid., p. 99.*

98. OWEN, PROF. R.   Monograph on the British Fossil Reptilia from the
Kimmeridge Clay.   No. III. containing Plesiosaurus grandis, P. tro-
chanterius, and P. Portlandicus.   Pp. 1–12.   Plates I.–IV.
Palæontograph. Soc. 4to. Lond.

99. SHARP, S.   Notes on the Northampton Oolites.
Geol. Mag., vol. vi., p. 446.

1870.

100. PHILLIPS, PROF. J.   A Monograph of British Belemnitidæ.   Part V.
containing pp. 109–128, Plates XXVIII.–XXXVI.   [Oxford Clay and
Kimmeridge Clay.]   *Palæontograph. Soc. 4to. Lond.*

101. SHARP, S.   The Oolites of Northamptonshire.
Quart. Journ. Geol. Soc., vol. xxvi., p. 354.

1871.

102. FAIRLEY, W.   Rambles in Northamptonshire.   (Iron Ores, &c.)
Colliery Guardian, vol. xxi., pp. 362, 472, 533, 577, 662, and *vol. xxii.,
pp.* 7, 60, 83.

103. HERMAN, W. D.   On Allophane and an allied Mineral found at Northampton.   *Quart. Journ. Geol. Soc., vol. xxvii., p. 234.*

104. JUDD, J. W.   On the Anòmalous Mode of Growth of certain Fossil
Oysters.   *Geol. Mag., vol. viii., p. 355.*

105. TOPLEY, W.   On the Comparative Agriculture of England and Wales.
Journ. Roy. Agric. Soc., ser. 2, vol. vii., Part I. p. 268.

1872.

106. BAYNE, A. D.   Royal Illustrated History of Eastern England including
a survey of the Eastern Counties, Physical Features, Geology, &c. of
Cambridgeshire, Essex, Norfolk, and Suffolk.   Vol. I.   8vo.   *Yarmouth.*

107. HULL, E.   A Treatise on the Building and Ornamental Stones of
Great Britain and Foreign Countries.   8vo.   *Lond.*

108. LYCETT, J.   A Monograph of the British Fossil Trigoniæ.   No. I.   Pp.
1–52.   *Palæontograph. Soc. 4to. Lond.*

1873.

109. SHARP, S.   The Oolites of Northamptonshire.   Part II.
Quart. Journ. Geol. Soc., vol. xxix., pp. 225–302.

1874.

110. SHARP, S.   Sketch of the Geology of Northamptonshire.
Proc. Geol. Assoc., vol. iii., No. 6, p. 243.

INDEX.

Barrowden, Lincolnshire Oolite near; 154.
—— Northampton Sand near; 95.
—— Hay, Cornbrash outlier at; 229.
Bath, Fuller's Earth at; 11.
"Bath Oolite," sense in which used; 3.
Bathurst, C., on the country between Stamford and Bedford; 296.
Beacon Hill, mass of Marlstone Rock-bed on; 246.
Bedford Purlieus, formations at; 194.
——, Great Oolite Limestones at; 207.
——, Great Oolite Clays at; 215.
——, Cornbrash at; 229.
——, the Duke's Brickyard on; 217.
Bee Hill, outlier of Northampton Sand; 107.
Beesley, Mr., on age of Oolites near Banbury; 4.
Bain, A. D., geological notes, &c.; 301.
Bearn, W., on farming of Northamptonshire; 298.
Belmesthorpe, Cornbrash near; 226.
—— railway-cutting at; 209.
—— table of Fossils from Great Oolite at; 290.
Belton brickyard, horizon of beds in; 64.
—— list of fossils from; 71.
Bentley, Mr.; 158, 225, 230.
Berkeley, Rev. M. J.; 170, 246.
Benefield, Cornbrash near; 224.
—— —— Table of Fossils from; 286.
—— Kellaways beds at; 232, 234.
—— chalky Boulder Clay at; 246.
—— subterranean stream near; 268.
—— chalybeate spring near; 269.
—— section and list of fossils; 205.
—— Upper and Lower, section in Great Oolite near; 266.
—— Upper, section in gravel-pit near; 241.
—— See also Upper and Lower.
Bibliography of the district; 294.
Billesdon, Brick-earth near; 243.
—— Fault, line of; 254.
—— brickyard, section at; 69.
—— Coplow, boring for coal; 62.
—— and Loddington Fault, effects of the; 71, 256.
Billing Brook, beds along course of the; 195, 208, 224, 234.
Bisbrook, Lincolnshire Oolite at; 177.
—— Northampton Sand at; 109.
Blackingrove, beds and list of fossils at; 27.
Blake, Rev. J., on zone of Ammonites angulatus; 41.
Blashfield, Mr., on clays near Stamford; 201.
Blast furnaces erected in the district; 112.
Blaston, age of beds at; 64.
Blaston, St. Giles, pit in Upper Lias at; 82.
—— St. Michael's section and fossils; 74.
Blatherwycke, chalybeate spring at; 270.
——, inlier of Northampton Sand at; 101.

Blatherwycke, Lincolnshire Oolite at; 149, 153.
——, outlier of Great Oolite; 213.
——, Upper Estuarine Clays at; 192.
—— mill, succession of beds near; 228.
—— Park, Lower Estuarine Series in wells at; 102.
Blisworth, analyses of Iron-ores from; 126, 127.
Boulder Clay, filling sand pipes; 191.
—— and glacial deposits; 240.
—— at Brigstock Parks; 239.
—— at Melton Mowbray, thickness of the; 243.
—— at Werrington Mill; 236.
—— at Yaxley; 238.
——, mode of occurrence; 262.
——, old river channels under the; 243.
—— and pre-glacial gravel; 229.
——, remarkable boulders in the; 246.
——, thickness of the; 141, 221.
—— under the Fenland; 237.
Boring for coal at Billesdon Coplow; 62.
—— at Neville Holt; 107.
—— at Stamford; 85, 104.
Bottlebridge, Ironstone dug at; 215, 217.
—— railway-cuttings at; 209.
Boundary line between the Great and Inferior Oolites in Midland District; 30.
Bourne, fossils from Cornbrash near; 227, 228.
——, section of Kellaways at; 237.
Braceborough, mineral spring at; 268, 269, 270.
Bradford Clay, local character of; 9.
—— represented by Great Oolite Clays; 186.
Brailes Hill beds at; 13, 17.
——, list of fossils from; 18.
——, outlier at; 17.
Brampton and Dingley, outlier of Northampton Sand; 106.
Bramston; Middle Lias at; 76.
Braybrook, Upper Lias at; 81.
Brayley, E. W., on Huntingdonshire and Cambridgeshire; 295.
Breaks in the Lias, probable cause of; 46.
Bredon Hill, fault at; 14, 255.
—— outlier, sections at; 12, 14.
Brentingby mineral spring; 269.
Brewer, J. N., on the county of Rutland; 296.
Brickmaking, Great Oolite Clays for; 189.
Brickyards at Melton Mowbray, beds in; 60.
Brickyard between Whissendine and Pickwell, horizon of; 64.
Brigstock, Upper Estuarine Series near; 189.
——, Great Oolite near; 213.
——, section in Lord Lyveden's pits near; 191.
—— Mill, brickyard and wells at; 101.
—— ——, Lincolnshire Oolite at; 149.
—— Parks, inlier at; 38, 197.
—— ——, outlier at; 228, 239.

C.

Brigstock Parks, disturbances, faults, &c. at ; 38, 256, 259.
—— Inferior Oolite and Northampton Sand at ; 101.
—— sections in inlier at ; 197.
—— Upper Lias Clay at ; 86.
—— well at ; 239.
Brixworth, Northampton sand at ; 30.
Britton, J., on Leicestershire, Lincolnshire, and Cambridgeshire ; 295.
Broadway Hill, Inferior Oolite at ; 12, 14, 15.
Brodie, Rev. P. B., on "Fish and Insect beds ;" 41, 79.
——, Geological papers by, relating to the district ; 297, 298, 299, 800.
—— P. B., on Oolites near Grantham ; 8.
Brook Hall, Rock-bed at ; 76.
Broom Hill Farm, ironstone at ; 20.
Brown, Mr. on the Iron-ores of Northamptonshire ; 299.
Browns Oak, sections near ; 226.
Buckland, Rev. W., on the Chalk at Ridlington ; 236.
"Bucklandi" beds in the Froddingham cutting ; 41, 42.
Buckman, on Cornbrash fossils ; 219.
Building-stones, district celebrated for ; 55.
—— of the Lincolnshire Oolite, durability of the ; 180.
—— for the New Houses of Parliament, report on ; 179.
Bulwick, Great Oolite near ; 191.
—— —— table of fossils from ; 284.
Bulwick, inlier of Northampton Sand at ; 101.
—— Lincolnshire Oolite at ; 149, 153.
—— outlier at ; 213.
Building materials, remarks on ; 176.
Burford, thickness of Jurassic beds at ; 32.
Burghley Park, Ironstone Quarry, section at ; 164.
Burleigh Park, fault at ; 172.
——, iron-ore at ; 104.
——, Northampton Sand at ; 103.
——, sections of Upper Lias in ; 86.
—— spa ; 269.
——, Northampton Sand escarpment at ; 97.
Burley-on-the-Hill, Upper Lias along escarpment to the north of ; 85.
Burrow Hill, Middle Lias at ; 66.
Burrow-on-the-Hill, Middle Lias at ; 66.
—— ; 254.
Burrows, the, outlier of Northampton Sand ; 107.
Burton Latimer, Northampton Sand at; 114.
Burton Lazars, mineral spring at ; 61, 269, 270.
Bury, brickyard with Saurian remains near ; 237.
Bushy Dales, section in Marlstone Rock-bed at ; 72.

Cadges Wood, Cornbrash and fossils near ; 228.
Calcareous beds in Northampton Sand ; 94.
Campden Hill, beds representing zone of *Am. Murchisonae* at ; 15.
Campden, pea grit ; 12.
Carboniferous beds, local character of ; 6.
Carbonate of iron, central nodules of in ironstone ; 133.
Careby, Lincolnshire Oolite at ; 175.
——, railway-cutting, Great Oolite Clays with fossils ; 195.
—— Lings, Cornbrash outlier near ; 229.
—— Mill, pit in Great Oolite N.E. of ; 211.
Carlby, Lincolnshire Oolite at ; 175.
Carruthers, Mr., on plant remains in the Northampton Sand ; 120.
Carruthers, Mr., on plant remains in Whittering "Pendle" ; 165.
Casewick cutting, Lacustrine deposit in the ; 244.
——, Oxfordian series in the ; 282, 236.
——, table of Fossils from Cornbrash at ; 288.
Casterton, building stones at ; 141.
—— Upper Estuarine Clays at ; 189.
Castle Bytham, inlier of Northampton Sand at ; 106.
Castle Bytham, Lincolnshire Oolite (coralline) ; 189.
Castor, disappearance of Lincolnshire Oolite ; 173.
——, Great Oolite at ; 201.
——, Lincolnshire Oolite at ; 143, 173.
——, masses of valley-gravel near ; 174.
——, Oyster beds of Great Oolite at ; 208.
—— Hanglands Wood, Upper Estuarine Series at ; 195.
—— Heath, Cornbrash at ; 219.
—— ——, Alwalton Marble at ; 208.
Catmos, sections in vale of ; 70.
Causes of the decline of early iron manufacture ; 111.
—— —— green colour of some ores ; 127.
—— —— position of towns and villages ; 55.
Cause of uniform character of Oxford Clay ; 51.
Cave deposits ; 249.
Cells, prismatic form of, in the Northampton Iron-ore ; 133.
Cellular structure in iron-ore ; 103, 118.
Chalybeate Waters in the district ; 269.
Changes attendant on the passage of water through the Northamptonshire iron-ore ; 135.
Change from estuarine to marine conditions in the Northampton Sand ; 129.
Chater River, Inliers of Middle Lias in the valley of ; 76.
——, Lincolnshire Oolite along the sides of the valley of ; 153.
——, Northampton Sand in the valley of ; 96.

Counthorpe, railway-cutting and section at; 175.
"Crash-bed," vertical burrows of Lithodomi in upper surface of the; 155.
Creeton, Lincolnshire Oolite near; 175, 176.
Croll, J., on Boulder-clay of Scotland; 243.
Cross, Rev. E., on fauna of zone of *Ammonites semicontatus*; 45, 52.
Cross Leas, Great Oolite at; 207.
Crowland, marine silt of Fenland at; 253.
Cranhoe brickyard, Middle Lias and list of fossils at; 64, 72.
Cross Barrow Hill, Rock-bed at; 72.
Cross-Way-Hands Lodge, Great Oolite near; 206.
——, Upper Estuarine Series at; 194.
——, pit in, Lincolnshire Oolite at; 169.
——, well near; *ib.*
——, thinning out of Lincolnshire Oolite near; 141.
"Curley;" 94.

D.

Dalby, Lower Lias at; 60.
Danes Hill railway-cutting, Great Oolite at; 210.
——, Prof. Morris on section in; 196.
——, synclinal in; 255.
——, table of fossils from, Great Oolite at; 287.
—— ——, cornbrash at; 288.
Darwin, on cause of variations in strata; 50.
Davidson, Mr. T., on Brachiopoda of Oolites and Lias; 298.
Deddington, fault near; 25.
——, outliers and list of fossils near; *ib.*
Deep sea conditions changing to shallow water; 51.
Deepdale, Middle Lias at; 64.
——, Upper Lias near; 84.
Deeping, Estuarine Gravels at; 251.
Dene, Great Oolite outlier at; 213.
——, Lincolnshire Oolite at; 140, 141, 149, 152, 153.
——, Northampton Sand at; 101, 114.
——, slate pits at; 152, 182.
Dene-Thorpe, Upper Estuarine Series; 191.
Denudation; 119, 132, 260.
—— of iron-ore; 119.
Desborough, iron-ore at; 94, 117.
——, section in railway-cutting at; 94.
——, Upper Lias at; 81.
De la Beche, Sir H., on oolitic structure of rocks; 184.
——, report on building stones; 297.
De la Condamine on Drift of Huntingdon; 298
Development and occurrence of subdivisions of the "*Margaritatus*" zone; 64.
Dick, Mr. A. B., analysis of iron-ores; 124.
——, R., on boulder-clay of Scotland; 243.

Difference between oolites of S.W. of England and Yorkshire; 1.
Dingley Lodge, pit in "*Serpentinus*" beds; 75, 81.
Dingley, section in Northampton Sand near; 106.
District formerly celebrated for iron; 55.
Division between Middle and Lower Lias, reasons for, in England; 59.
"Dogger" of Yorkshire; 33, 92.
Dogsight, Cornbrash outlier at; 229.
Dogsthorpe, section in brick-pits at; 226, 232, 235.
Dotted lines on the map, reasons for drawing; 142.
Drainage of the fen-land; 55.
Draughton, Northampton Sand at; 30.
Duddington, Collyweston Slate in, old pits at; 102, 141, 154.
—— cornbrash, outlier section in; 228.
—— fault near; 257.
——, Great Oolite outlier; 213.
——, Upper Estuarine Series; 192.
Dumbleton, fault near; 255.
"Dumbleton Series;" 79.
Duncan, Prof. P. M., on corals; 300.
Duston Slate; 30, 94.

E.

East Carlton, Lower Estuarine Series near 94.
——, Middle Lias near; 75.
East Farndon, Middle Lias at; *ib.*
East Norton, Marlstone at; 72.
——, Upper Lias at; 83
Easton, section of the Northampton Sand at; 103.
——, sections of Collyweston Slate at; 156.
——, structure in iron-ore at; 118.
Eastrea brickyard, Oxford clay with fossils at; 238.
Ebelman, M., on the blue colour of rocks; 127, 176.
Ebrington, outlier of Inferior Oolite; 12, 14, 15, 16.
Echinodermata of oolites near Hotham, and Cave; 4.
Economic uses of the Marlstone Rock-bed; 65.
Edenham, Cornbrash near; 227, 229.
Edith Weston, occurrence of *Lingula* in Inferior Oolite; 167.
——, Northampton Sands at; 96.
Edmondthorpe, sections of Marlstone and list of fossils found near; 64, 71.
——, Upper Lias sections near; 85.
Edwards, L., on river Witham; 295.
Egleton, Middle Lias near; 71.
Eleanor Cross at Geddington, spring at the; 93.
Elton, Cornbrash near; 223.
——, fault at; 258.
——, folding of strata at; 255.
——, indurated gravel at; 250, 269.
——, Oxford clay near; 264.
——, Great Oolite in well near; 207, 217.

LONDON:

Printed by GEORGE E. EYRE and WILLIAM SPOTTISWOODE,
Printers to the Queen's most Excellent Majesty.
For Her Majesty's Stationery Office.
[1125.—525.—4/75.]

Milton Keynes UK
Ingram Content Group UK Ltd.
UKHW042307160224
437951UK00004B/312